A GIFT

OF SANCTUARY

Candace Robb studied for a Ph.D. in Medieval and Anglo-Saxon literature and has continued to read and research medieval history and literature ever since. The Owen Archer series grew out of a fascination with the city of York and the tumultuous 14th century. The first in the series, *The Apothecary Rose*, was published in 1994, at which point she began to write full time. In addition to the UK, Australia, New Zealand, South Africa, Canada and America, her novels are published in France, Germany, Spain and Holland.

She is currently writing the seventh Owen Archer novel, *A Spy for the Redeemer*.

A GIFT OF SANCTUARY

AN OWEN ARCHER MYSTERY

CANDACE ROBB

ARROW

Published in the United Kingdom in 1999
by Arrow Books

1 3 5 7 9 10 8 6 4 2

'The Seagull (Yr wylan deg ar lanw dioer)', by Dafydd ap Gwilym,
translated by Joseph P. Clancy in *Medieval Welsh Lyrics* (Macmillan
and St Martin's Press, 1965), pp 23–4.

First published in the United Kingdom in 1998
by William Heinemann

Arrow Books Ltd
Random House UK Limited
20 Vauxhall Bridge Road, London SW1V 2SA

Random House Australia (Pty) Limited
20 Alfred Street, Milsons Point, Sydney, New South Wales
2061, Australia

Random House New Zealand Limited
18 Poland Road, Glenfield,
Auckland 10, New Zealand

Random House South Africa (Pty) Limited
Endulini, 5A Jubilee Road, Parktown 2193, South Africa

Random House UK Limited Reg. No. 954009

A CIP catalogue record for this book is available from the
British Library

Papers used by Random House UK Limited are natural, recyclable
products made from wood grown in sustainable forests. The
manufacturing processes conform to the environmental regulations of
the country of origin.

Typeset by Palimpsest Book Production Limited,
Polmont, Stirlingshire

Printed and bound in Germany
by Elsnerdruck, Berlin

ISBN 0 7493 2360 4

TABLE OF CONTENTS

For Kate Ross,
Who also enjoyed jousting with poets

ACKNOWLEDGEMENTS

Taking Owen into Wales has been quite a journey for me, but I found some expert guides who were wonderfully generous with their time. I wish to thank in particular Jeff Davies, Fiona Kelleghan, Nona Rees, Compton Reeves, and the staff of the National Library of Wales in Aberystwyth. I also wish to thank my colleagues on the Internet discussion lists Mediev-l, Chaucer, and H-Albion who were ever ready with advice and suggestions.

Heartfelt thanks to Joyce Gibb for sharing the results of her own research, and for taking time out for long conversations and careful readings; to Lynne Drew for making the long journey out to St David's and for an inspired edit; to Evan Marshall for a thoughtful edit; to Christie Andersen for proofreading; and to Charlie Robb for maps, photos, travel arrangements and all the myriad assignments he cheerfully accepts throughout the year.

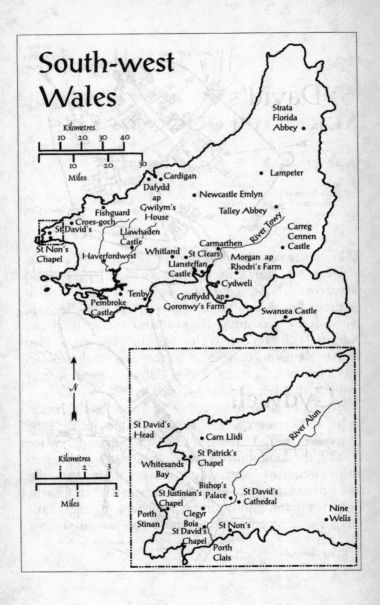

South-west Wales

Kilometres
10 20 30 40

Miles
10 20 30

Strata Florida Abbey •

Lampeter •

• Cardigan
Dafydd ap Gwilym's House

• Newcastle Emlyn

Talley Abbey •

River Towy

Fishguard
• Croes-goch
• St David's

Llawhaden Castle

Carmarthen

Carreg Cennen Castle

St Non's Chapel

Haverfordwest

Whitland

St Clears

Llansteffan Castle

Morgan ap Rhodri's Farm

Cydweli

Tenby •

Gruffydd ap Goronwy's Farm

Pembroke Castle

Swansea Castle

N

Kilometres
1 2 3

Miles
1 2

St David's Head

• Carn Llidi

River Alun

St Patrick's Chapel

Whitesands Bay

Bishop's Palace

St David's Cathedral

St Justinian's Chapel

Porth Stinan

Clegyr Boia
St David's Chapel

St Non's

Nine Wells

Porth Clais

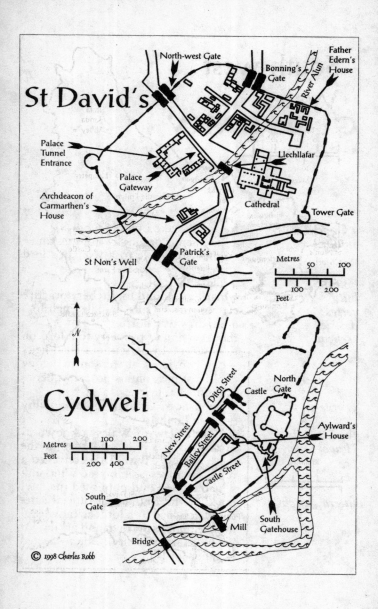

GLOSSARY

a Goddes half	for God's sake (middle English)
amobr	a payment, originally to guarantee virginity, payable to a woman's lord at marriage
bourdon	a pilgrim's staff
butt	a mark or mound for archery practice
certes	certainly, to be sure (middle English)
destrier	a knight's war horse
escheat	the reversion of property to a lord on the owner's dying without legal heirs – one convicted of treason or felony could not pass on his property, hence had no legal heirs.
gentilesse	graciousness, with an air of nobility (middle English)
the Law of Hywel Dda	the native law of Wales is known as Hywel's Law; it is said that in the tenth century Hywel Dda convened a representative assembly at Whitland, which revised and published the law
littera marchi	letter of the March, an official safe-conduct issued by a lord, acknowledging the man as his own and asking for his judicial immunity to be respected in other lordships

:the Marches/	the borders of the kingdom and the lords
Marcher lords	to whom the King granted jurisdiction over them
mazer	a large wooden cup or bowl, often highly decorated
murder hole	an opening in the floor above, from which something such as hot oil can be dropped on intruders
murrain	literally, a parasitic disease among cattle, but often generalised to any widespread disease among livestock
no fors	does not matter (middle English)
receiver	officer who receives money due; treasurer
redemptio vitae	money in exchange for one's life in a criminal case; the amount varies according to the discretion of the lord and the gravity of the offence
scrip	a small bag, wallet, or satchel
solar	private room on upper level of house
spital	early English word for hospital, later 'spitalhouse' and 'hospital'
tourn	a Marcher lord's great court
trencher	a thick slice of brown bread a few days old with a slight hollow in the centre, used as a platter
truck	trade
tun	wooden barrel; bows and arrow sheaves were stowed in wooden tuns for transport
vicar	as a modern vicar is the deputy of the rector, so a vicar choral was a cleric in holy orders acting as the deputy of a canon attached to the cathedral; for a modest annual salary the vicar choral performed his canon's duties, attending the various services of the church and singing the liturgy
vintaine	a company of twenty soldiers

WELSH PRONUNCIATION

Vowels: *a, e, i, o, u, y*, and sometimes *w*. As a vowel, *w* is pronounced like *oo*, either short (look) or long (loon). As a consonant before a *y*, it retains some of its vocalic nature: *wee* or *ooee*.

Consonants: no *j, k* or *z*, nor is there a soft *c* (as in *c*ease).
dd as in tee*the*, not tee*th*
f sounds like a *v*, as in o*f*
ff sounds like an *f*, as in o*ff*
ll sounds like a strongly aspirated *hl*, or even *chl*
rh an aspirated r, or *hr*

PROLOGUE

Pulling the hood of his cloak over his comb- and trinket-twisted hair and fastening it against the wind, the old man rode out on to the sands. He was about to nudge his steed to a gallop when the beast shied. God's grace was upon the man who lay there, that the horse had brought his hoofs down on the bare sand and not on the prostrate form. The old man dismounted to examine this booty of the sea, discovered it was blood, not seaweed that darkened the young man's hair. He glanced round, wary of trespassing on another's battle ground, but the mist and blowing sand prevented him from seeing far. The roar of the breakers muted the sound of any who might share the beach with him.

The old man crouched beside the one sprawled on his back in the sand and studied him. One blood-encrusted hand still held a dagger. Blood darkened the edge of the man's sleeve – another's blood, for the stains higher up were spatters. A deep thrust into the gut or the chest might cause such a flood. The white-haired man guessed that someone had died this day, at this man's hands. It had not been an easy victory; a bruise on this one's throat already darkened and he bled freely from an almost severed ear. It might well be beyond Brother Samson's skill to repair the latter.

But God had crossed their paths today for a reason. The horse was to carry the wounded man to safety. And the dead man? There was no time to look for him. The man here before him might bleed to death while Dafydd or his retainers searched the sands and the caves, or the other's friends might fall upon them. And for all this, he might find no other. No. A search was a waste. Better to attend the living one to whom he had been led.

Grunting as his legs protested straightening, Dafydd whistled for his horse. As the beast crowded near, the white-haired man praised God that his was a short, sturdy Welsh horse and not a destrier. He rearranged the wrapped harp slung beside his saddle, then crouching once more, found the centre of the wounded man's weight and heaved him across his shoulder, eased up, and slid the man across the horse's wide back. Taking the reins in hand, the old man nodded to his horse, and the two figures headed down Whitesands towards St Patrick's Chapel and the track up on to St David's Head. The beast's gait grew jerky as he climbed the rocks above the breakers. The injured man moaned, 'Tangwystl.'

Ah. So they had not fought over smuggled treasures, but the love of a woman. Tangwystl. The white-haired man smiled and softly began to sing:

> 'Go praising a far-famed girl
> To curve of fort and castle.
> Keep a close lookout, seagull,
> For an Eigr on the white fort.
> Speak my neatly woven words:
> Go to her, bid her choose me.
> If she's alone, then greet her;
> Be deft with the dainty girl
> To win her: say I shall die,
> This well-bred lad, without her.'

The wind shivered the gorse and whipped the old man's cloak round him as if it were a fury. Dafydd bent his head into the tempest, his song stilled with the effort to breathe, and he squinted to see the track before him. He heard the horsemen before he saw them. His six men, their heads low against their mounts, eyes half-closed against the wind, came thundering past, down to the beach Dafydd had just deserted. He turned back in wonderment. What did they pursue? He had left them far up at Carn Llidi.

Shielding his eyes, Dafydd made out three, no, four riders beginning the ascent from Whitesands. In pursuit of the wounded man, were they? Did they not see Dafydd's men descending upon them?

With a prayer for the souls of the fools down below, Dafydd continued up the rocky headland, to a cluster of boulders that shielded him and his burden from the wind. He took a linen cloth from his scrip, bound it round the injured man's head to stanch the bleeding. The man moaned, shivered as if a surge of pain followed the binding, then was still. So still Dafydd leaned close to hear his breath.

3

Rasping, difficult, but there. God was not ready to take this man.

It was not long before Dafydd's men reappeared, riding proudly. Madog, the talker, leapt from his steed and hurried forward.

'Master Dafydd, are you injured?'

The wind sucked at Dafydd's breath. He shook his head. 'We must ride quickly.'

Madog lifted the injured man's head, eyes widening as he saw the blood that already soaked half the bandage. 'Who is he?'

Who indeed? What should Dafydd call him, this bleeding soul God had entrusted to him? 'A pilgrim.'

Madog's dark brows came together in doubt, but he did not argue. 'The four we routed,' he said, 'they wore the livery of Lancaster and Cydweli.'

'My pilgrim has powerful enemies.'

'What would you have us do?'

'He has lost much blood. Let us sprout wings to fly him to Brother Samson's healing hands.' Dafydd handed Madog the reins of his burdened horse, slipped his harp from the saddle. 'You ride with the pilgrim. I shall ride your steed.'

One

WEARY PILGRIMS

O wen Archer ached from days of riding. The journey into southern Wales was proving a painful
lesson in how sedentary he had become in York;
though all men said marriage and family softened a
man, as captain of the Archbishop of York's retainers
and one who trained archers, Owen had thought himself an exception. The ride was also a reminder of how
solitary was a winter journey, no matter how large
the company. With head tucked deep inside a hood
that dripped incessantly, a rider limited conversation
to the bare necessities.

Most riders, that is. Two of his companions behaved
otherwise. Even now, as they made their way through
a forest of limbs bent, twisted and snapped by a
relentless gale, where they must guide their horses
and be ready to duck and sidestep trouble, their voices
rose in argument.

'The wind at home is never so fierce,' Sir Robert
D'Arby shouted.

'It is so and more, Sir Robert,' Brother Michaelo retorted. 'You do not enjoy being a wayfaring man, is all. I for one see no difference between this weather and that of the North Country.'

'You dare to speak to me of being a wayfaring man – you, who think silk sheets and down cushions are appropriate for a pilgrim? I have endured years of real pilgrimage.'

'Yes, yes, the Holy Land, Rome, Compostela, I know,' Brother Michaelo said. 'There are worse sins in life than fine bedclothes.' He bowed his head and tugged his hood farther over his face.

'Sybarite,' Sir Robert muttered.

Owen thought his father-in-law and the archbishop's secretary worse than warring children in their ceaseless bickering over trifles. He did his best to ignore them. Geoffrey Chaucer, on the other hand, rode close to them and listened with a smile.

'You find them amusing,' Owen said. 'I would prefer them muzzled.'

Geoffrey laughed. 'Most of their arguments are predictable and repetitive, it is true, but at times they delight with their inventiveness. I wait for such moments. Listen – Sir Robert has changed the subject.'

'Would that we had left earlier so we might reach the shrine of St David on his feast day,' Owen's father-in-law said.

'We would have ridden to our deaths in a winter storm and never reached St David's,' Michaelo said while holding a branch aside for his elderly antagonist.

Geoffrey nodded. 'It is a game to the monk, this argument.'

Owen understood that. And yet not entirely a game. The monk worried that Sir Robert would prevail and have him decked out in the rough robe of a pilgrim, sleeping on the cold, damp, root-infested earth of the forest. Sir Robert wore a long, russet-coloured robe of coarse wool with a cross on the sleeve, and a large round hat with a broad brim turned up at the front to show his pilgrim badges, of which he was justly proud, particularly the scallop shell. Hanging from his neck was a pilgrim's scrip, a large knife, a flask for water and a rosary, and tied across his saddle was a bourdon. Not that he needed the purse of essentials and the walking stick, being well provisioned and on horseback.

'I am caught!' Sir Robert cried suddenly.

Owen hurried forward to retrieve his father-in-law from a thorny branch that had snagged the edge of his hood. 'You will insist on a wide-brimmed hat beneath your hood, that is the problem,' Owen said with little sympathy. 'It makes you a wider target to snag.'

'Mark his words, Sir Robert,' Michaelo chimed in, 'it is as I have been telling you.'

Sir Robert did not even turn in Michaelo's direction. 'I am a pilgrim,' he said to Owen. 'I must wear the garb. It is little enough I do.'

'At your age the journeying itself is enough. Your daughter will have my head if any harm comes to you while in my company.'

'Lucie is more reasonable than that.'

Perhaps. It seemed so long ago that they had said their farewells in York. And it would be so much longer before Owen heard news of his family – his wife and children. Sir Robert did not ease the loneliness; in truth Owen looked forward to seeing his father-in-law and Brother Michaelo safely to St David's and returning with Geoffrey to Cydweli.

But first there was the matter of Carreg Cennen, truly an outpost among the Duke of Lancaster's castles. Here they were to meet John de Reine, one of Lancaster's men from Cydweli.

The purpose of the meeting was to plan their recruiting strategy. Charles of France was reportedly preparing for an invasion of England. John of Gaunt, Duke of Lancaster, planned a counter-attack in summer. To that end, he needed more archers, and hoped to find good recruits in his Marcher lordships. He had requested the assistance of Owen Archer, former captain of archers for the previous Duke of Lancaster; asked Owen to journey to his lordships in southern Wales and select two vintaines of archers. John de Reine would then march the recruits to Plymouth in time for a summer sailing. Geoffrey Chaucer accompanied Owen because he was to observe and report on the garrisoning of the Duke's Welsh castles. The French always looked on the south-western coast of Wales as a good place for spies to slip into the country, and also as a possible landing area for an invasion army. Early in the year, King Edward had ordered that all castles along the coast were to be sufficiently garrisoned to defend themselves in an attack.

Owen and Geoffrey hoped to recruit a few archers from the area round Carreg Cennen and arrange for them to join the others in Cydweli later in the season. It would be good for the recruits to meet Reine, the one who would lead them to Plymouth.

* * *

The forest cover was thick, hiding the castle from view until it seemed suddenly to rear out of the valley of the River Cennen on its limestone crag.

'God meant this site for a fortification,' Sir Robert said, crossing himself. 'But it is no place one wishes to stay long.'

'Where is the village?' Brother Michaelo asked. 'On the far side?'

'There is no village,' Geoffrey said. 'Carreg Cennen is a castle, no more. Only those essential to the garrison and, at present, those working on repairs live within the walls.'

'God have mercy on us,' Michaelo muttered. 'How long do we stay?'

'A day or two,' Geoffrey said. 'I confess it does not look inviting.'

Owen thought otherwise. He had reined in his horse to admire the castle, rising up from the bowl of the valley like a statue in a fountain. The Black Mountains cradled it, and yet the limestone crag with its crowning castle seemed alone, solitary, remote. Something from myth, something one might ride towards forever and never reach. He had forgotten how beautiful his country was, how full of a mystery that seemed the stuff of ballads.

But he did not share such thoughts with his companions. 'How many in this garrison?' he asked.

'Twenty at present,' Geoffrey said. 'A crowd for such a remote place.'

'The Duke believes the French will penetrate so far?'

'It is unlikely, but if they did, they might find many sympathetic to their cause in these mountains.'

'Ah. So Carreg Cennen protects itself against the countryside.'

Geoffrey glanced uneasily at Owen. 'You know, my friend, you must take care else you begin to sound like one of your rebellious countrymen.'

Owen laughed. 'Come. We were expected yesterday. John de Reine will return to Cydweli without us.'

They had been delayed by swollen streams between Monmouth and Carreg Cennen. And Sir Robert's lagging energy. They did not speak of it, but they had slowed their pace as his cough worsened. The River Cennen had given them no trouble, but their climb to the castle was slow, as they followed the narrow track around the valley to the north-east approach, where the steep limestone outcrop gave way to a gentler slope. Such a slow progress gave the guards ample time to make note of a company of fourteen and identify their livery, and by the time they reached the outer gate the doors were opened.

As he dismounted and led his horse through the gateway, Owen paused to admire the design of the barbican. Immediately after entering the outer gate-way the party was forced to turn right, which would give defenders on the north-east tower an excellent target as an intruder halted, confused. And as they turned right, a pivoting drawbridge was lowered by a man up above in a small gate tower.

'They have little need for a garrison,' Geoffrey said. 'This castle defends itself.'

Beyond the small tower lay yet another drawbridge, guarded by an even larger, quite formidable tower. And again, they must turn sharply to enter into the inner ward.

'Twenty men does seem too many,' Owen said. 'A man to control each drawbridge and one for the gate, they have need of few more.'

'What could be so precious here?' Michaelo asked.

'Passage through the valley,' Sir Robert said. 'That is plain.'

'Aye, to one trained in warfare it is plain,' Brother Michaelo muttered. 'I see an inhospitable place.'

'This is naught compared with the mountains of Gwynedd,' Owen said.

'Then I thank God Lancaster has no holdings to the north.'

As the portcullis rose in a wheezy grumble, a large, rough-visaged man stepped through, better dressed than the rest and with an air of authority, though when he spoke he revealed blackened teeth, unusual in Lancaster's captains. 'Will Tyler,' he said with a bob of the head, 'constable of Carreg Cennen. I bid you welcome.' Turning, he led them into the inner courtyard, where he invited Owen, Geoffrey, Sir Robert and Brother Michaelo into a modest room in which burned a most welcome fire. The rest of their company were escorted to the kitchen.

Owen was on his second cup of ale before he spoke, mentioning Lascelles's man, John de Reine.

Tyler gave Owen a look of surprise. 'Your accent. You are a Welshman?'

'I am.'

'Most unusual.'

'Unusual? In what way? Are we not in Wales, where one might expect a multitude of Welshmen?'

'I am not accustomed to dealing with any on – official business.' Tyler shook his head. 'But no matter. As to your question, we have welcomed only you since the workmen arrived from the east. Travellers with English names are ever welcome here, we turn none away.'

'You have had trouble with the Welsh?' Geoffrey asked.

'Not while I have been here, but we are always ready. And we have no Welsh in the garrison. They are a queer race, barefooted and barelegged most of the time, and the shiftiest shave their heads so they may run through the brush more easily, but leave hair on their upper lips to show it is their choice to be thus shorn. A sly, violent people. There is no telling when they will turn – begging your forgiveness, Captain. But you are Lancaster's man or he would not have trusted you here, so I doubt you take it amiss.'

Owen had meant to keep his counsel, but this rotten-toothed man with his foul-smelling breath and rude manner was more than he could bear. 'You look equally unsavoury to my people, Constable. And as you were never invited into our land, I cannot see why you would expect courteous co-operation. But no, I do not take it amiss, for I am sure that rather than thinking for yourself you merely echo the opinion of others.'

The constable nodded towards Geoffrey as if to say, 'You see what I mean about them?'

'My son-in-law is testy after breaking up countless disputes between myself and Brother Michaelo,' Sir Robert said. 'But we cannot deny that we English arrived uninvited and robbed the people of their sovereignty.' Sir Robert raised his hand as the constable opened his mouth to protest. 'I say this not for the sake of argument, but rather to understand. Is that why your numbers here at Carreg Cennen have swelled? Because you expect the Welsh to turn traitor to us if the French get this far?'

Looking slightly frazzled by the shifting mood of the group, Tyler replied to Sir Robert. 'Oh aye. This has ever been a difficult place for us.'

Sir Robert smiled at Owen's puzzled expression and nodded slightly, as if to warn him to desist. Which was good advice, though less satisfying than shocking the constable out of his complacency.

'You have seen nothing of a contingent from Cydweli?' Owen asked Tyler again. 'Nor received a messenger?'

Tyler shook his head. 'Rivers swell this time of year. He may be delayed. But you will be in Cydweli soon, eh? Time enough. I have no spare archers to offer you in any case. Come now. My man will show you where you will rest your heads. And tonight we shall have a merry feast of it. I am eager to hear all the gossip of the realm.' Tyler nodded at Brother Michaelo. 'We would be grateful for a Mass while you are here, Father. It has been some time now since we lost our chaplain. The good bishop has been slow in sending us another.'

Michaelo, who had closed his eyes and tucked his hands up his sleeves as soon as he had quenched his thirst, looking for all the world like a monk lost in prayer (to those who did not know him), frowned now at the constable. 'Lost your chaplain? How?'

'He tumbled down the crag trying to follow his hound.'

Michaelo crossed himself. 'Your chaplain had need of a hound's protection?'

'Nay, Father, he loved the hunt, he did.'

Michaelo glanced at Owen. 'I begin to see your point.' To Tyler, he said, 'Not "Father", but "Brother". I am not a priest.'

Looking more uneasy by the moment about playing host to this party, the constable nodded and said briskly, 'An honest mistake – Brother. God go with you gentlemen. You are most welcome here. My man will show you to your chambers now.'

The travellers rose reluctantly, loath to part with the fire.

'Watch where you step in the ward,' Tyler's man warned as they walked out into drizzle.

It was good advice. The rock on which the castle sat crested here in the inner ward, rising in a shallow, uneven dome. No one apparently saw the need to chip it down and smooth it out. It was a small ward, and in less than a dozen steps they were climbing a stairway to the rooms in the east wall; they were given sleeping chambers on either side of the chapel – narrow, dark, damp and chilled by the wind that rose up the cliff and past the lime kiln, giving the air a chalky scent. But each room had a brazier, already lit, and the pallets were piled with blankets and skins.

'Jumping with fleas, no doubt,' Michaelo said as he lifted one gingerly. 'The constable and his men smell like beasts in a stable.'

'You expected courtiers?' Geoffrey said with an exaggerated bow. 'In an isolated outpost?'

'A Mass. I am surprised they noticed their chaplain's absence.'

'Fighting men are ever concerned about their souls,' Sir Robert said. 'You will not notice their odour when they are saving your neck.'

'You saved our necks with your softening of Owen's tirade,' Michaelo said. 'I am eager to leave this wilderness and continue on to St David's.' The archbishop's secretary was the only one in the group who had but a single purpose, to complete his pilgrimage to St David's in a belated rush of penitence for a past sin. Though Sir Robert seemed the most earnest pilgrim he also hoped to help Owen and Geoffrey with what had been meant to be a secret aspect of their mission, ascertaining where the loyalties of the Welsh lay. Not that Owen had confided in his father-in-law, but Sir Robert was adept at feigning sleep in order to eavesdrop.

'We will wait a few days for Reine,' Owen said. Tyler was right. Just as they had been delayed by the wet weather, so might Reine and his men be delayed in their journey from Cydweli. 'And so that we might enjoy peace in our party, I propose that Geoffrey and Michaelo share a room, and I sleep with Sir Robert,' Owen said.

Geoffrey thought it an excellent suggestion.

Owen and Sir Robert moved on to the room opposite. As soon as the door was closed, Owen expressed his surprise at the last part of Sir Robert's comment to the constable, that there had been some truth in what Owen had said about the English and the Welsh.

As his father-in-law eased down on to the side of the cot closest to the lit brazier, he glanced at Owen with a fierce scowl that was not that of a man who considered himself complimented. 'You have listened too long to my daughter, who believes soldiering robbed me of any ability to contemplate mankind's state.' Sir Robert's voice was a weary whisper, but his expression kept Owen from interrupting to offer him comfort. 'I have noticed much that has dismayed me about the treatment of the folk as we have journeyed into Wales. I do not, however, believe it wise to express one's views too openly. You have come here as Lancaster's man. It is not your place to criticise his actions.'

'You are right.'

'You made us all uneasy.'

'That was not my purpose. I wished only to make Tyler uneasy.'

'Which you did. Is that wise? If there is trouble, we might depend upon him for our safety. I hardly think your people, as you call them, would consider you one of them while wearing the Duke's livery and a Norman beard.'

'I am neither one of them nor one of you, aye. So it will ever be for me.'

Sir Robert looked surprised. 'You are one of us, Owen.'

A few weeks earlier Owen might have agreed. He had truly begun to believe he belonged in York. But this journey was making him feel more and more exiled. 'Come. Let me help you off with your boots so you might rest before we sup.'

'You have come far, my son. Have a care. That is all I ask.'

Owen and Geoffrey sat up in the hall after the others

had retired for the night. Neither was eager to go to his room until his sleeping companion slept peacefully.

Geoffrey sat back, contentedly patting his stomach. 'This may be an isolated pile of rock, but such food! I shall be sad to leave this table.' His legs stuck out comically, the chair oddly constructed, too deep for his short legs.

Will Tyler did manage to feed his men well, stews generously meaty and fatty, breads hearty and fresh, and seemingly unlimited ale. It was a wonder more of the castle's inhabitants had not shared the fate of the chaplain. 'I should think you would find this food simple compared to that at court,' Owen said.

Geoffrey wrinkled his nose. 'I am ever suspicious of a heavily spiced dish – what sins are hidden with such effort, eh? Now your lord, His Grace the archbishop, he knows the value of fresh, simple foods.'

'I would thank you not to call him my lord.'

Geoffrey studied Owen silently for a moment. 'Forgive me. And the constable made you Lancaster's man.'

'Do I look anyone's man but my own?'

'Everyone is someone's,' Geoffrey said, smiling at Owen's growl. 'And you were fortunate enough to have a choice, so they tell me.'

When Henry of Grosmont died, Owen had been given the opportunity of going either into the service of the new Duke, John of Gaunt, or John Thoresby, Archbishop of York and then Lord Chancellor of England.

'Do you regret choosing the archbishop over the Duke so many years ago?'

'I chose the man I thought it would be most honourable to serve. Perhaps I was a fool.' Owen shook his head as Geoffrey opened his mouth to tease. 'And yet I cannot say with any surety that your Duke is worthier.'

'You would do well to court him. You must forge a new alliance. John Thoresby looks pale of late. He behaves as one making his peace with God, preparing for the next world. What will you do when he is gone?'

What indeed? Thoresby was seventy-five – a venerable age, and a vulnerable one. But Owen did not wish to confide his doubts about his future to Geoffrey. He was not yet so good a friend as to be trusted with such knowledge of Owen's insecurities, too in love with his own wit to resist using the information if it would entertain the right people or win him some coveted honour. 'You make too much of his mood. Thoresby is merely in mourning. The Queen's death deprived the archbishop of his closest friend.' It bothered Owen that Geoffrey had noticed Thoresby's failing health. It must be more obvious than he had thought. 'I shall be content to assist Lucie in the shop and the garden when His Grace passes on.' Owen's wife was a Master Apothecary in York, and had trained him to assist her.

Geoffrey made a mocking face. 'Content? I predict that so quiet a life would be such a penance to you it would gain you enough indulgences to wash away all your sins – or it would poison your heart and set you on the path to damnation.'

Another observation too close to the mark, too close to Lucie's prediction. 'It is no fors. Thoresby lives.'

Owen was not deaf to Geoffrey's advice. Lancaster was young, his power growing apace with his ambition. But Owen did not like the thought of such a lord – quick to laughter, quick to take offence. And he did not wish to discuss it tonight. 'I am concerned about John de Reine.'

Geoffrey was suddenly serious. 'Indeed. If someone has learned of his correspondence with the Duke – someone loyal to John Lascelles – he may be in danger.'

When Archbishop Thoresby had told Owen of Lancaster's request, he had alluded to a sensitive issue that would be explained by the Duke himself. He would tell Owen only that it touched on a piece of Charles of France's treachery.

In London, Owen and Geoffrey met with the Duke at his palace of the Savoy. Owen had not seen John of Gaunt since the deaths the year before of both his wife, the beautiful Blanche of Lancaster, and his mother, Queen Phillippa. The Duke was thirty now, and although his fair hair showed no signs of grey and he was yet broad in the shoulders and straight backed, there were shadows beneath his arresting eyes. There was also a wariness about those eyes and a tension in the jaw that the forked beard did not quite hide. The war with France was not going well, and the Duke had been blamed for some of the recent disappointments. Unjustly, according to Geoffrey. For the first time, Owen felt a sympathy for the Duke. He seemed ever to shoulder the blame for the King's mistakes.

But as the Duke began to speak, Owen's momentary sympathy faded. It was with a chilling calm that the Duke described the latest treachery of Charles of France. The French king harboured in his court a Welsh mercenary, Owain Lawgoch, or Owain ap Thomas ap Rhodri ap Gruffudd, sometimes called Owain of the Red Hand, who had an impeccable Welsh pedigree – he was a great-nephew of Llywelyn ap Gruffudd, Llywelyn the Last, who had once united most of Wales, the last of the great kings. Owain Lawgoch was also a soldier of considerable experience, had the confidence of leading French commanders such as Bertrand du Guesclin, and most importantly the support of King Charles. It was said that the French King had loaned Lawgoch some spies to stir up the Welsh and encourage them to betray the English to the French. In exchange, Lawgoch would have a chance to return to Wales as a ruler friendly to his allies across the Channel. King Edward and the Duke of Lancaster wanted Owen and Geoffrey to find out whether Lawgoch was making inroads in Wales. But the Duke had an additional concern.

'It has recently come to my attention that my steward in Wales, John Lascelles, has taken to wife the daughter of a man who fled his home in the March of Pembroke after being accused of harbouring a French spy. It is said that Lascelles offered the fleeing man, one Gruffydd ap Goronwy, sanctuary and land in the March of Cydweli in exchange for his daughter's hand in marriage.

'Traitors both?' the Duke said. 'One traitor and a besotted steward? Or is there no traitor, simply a man unjustly accused and a friend who keeps faith in him?'

John de Reine, the man Owen and Geoffrey were to meet at Carreg Cennen, had been one of the Duke's sources of information on this topic, citing concern for Lascelles's reputation and a strong distrust of Gruffydd ap Goronwy.

'Reine's concern is well motivated,' explained the Duke. 'He is Lascelles's natural son, and owes his position to his father's reputation.'

'Which he impugns by this report,' Geoffrey said.

'It is Lascelles who risks his reputation by this marriage,' the Duke said. 'In his letter, Reine cites concern about his natural father's neglect of his duties beyond Cydweli – he has not been in Carreg Cennen, Monmouth or back in England to see to his estates in nearly two years. Indeed, it is uncharacteristic of Lascelles to behave so.'

Owen had found this reasoning questionable. 'I am with Geoffrey. Reine worries about Lascelles's name and yet suggests to you, Lascelles's lord, that his father is acting in a questionable, perhaps even treasonous manner. I would not call him a fond son.'

'Lascelles need not have used his influence to get his son placed at Cydweli,' the Duke said. 'John de Reine acknowledges this in the letter and says he is grateful.'

'Is he?' Owen had not been convinced.

'You must take the measure of this man I have entrusted with Monmouth, Carreg Cennen, and Cydweli,' the Duke said, rising. 'Reine is to meet you at Carreg Cennen. I hope he will be more at ease discussing his father at a distance from Cydweli – and safer.'

Hence their concern about Reine's absence.

'We know little about the man,' Owen said.

Geoffrey shook his head and blinked, as if Owen's words had pulled him from a reverie. 'The good steward's bastard? Seed sown in youth, reaped in middle age, eh?'

'Here they make little note of whether a child was born within the bonds of marriage and often acknowledge their natural children. Does Sir John practise the Welsh custom to reassure the people he rules?'

'I think not. Reine is reportedly a good soldier, so Sir John can make good use of him. But note he does not carry his father's name. John Lascelles does not formally acknowledge him.'

'Do you think he will come? Has he perhaps changed his mind?'

'His letter to the Duke was that of a man discomfited by circumstances. Puzzled by Lascelles's behaviour. He called him blinded by his wife's beauty and strangeness, led into error by his obsession. Such are not the words of one who will change with the wind.'

Owen was not so sure.

'And you know my suspicion, despite what he wrote in his letter – that the son is in love with the young wife,' Geoffrey said.

Rising to stretch the stiffness out of his back, Owen studied the fire and pondered that possibility. Many a young man grew infatuated with his father's young wife, but it would be a foolish man who involved the Duke in such a rivalry. 'What do you know of John Lascelles?'

'He worked hard for the Duke's previous steward in Wales. He is a recent appointment – his predecessor Banastre died of plague, I believe. Sir John was considered a man worthy of the Duke's trust. Until his marriage the only ill I heard of him was that his arrogant demeanour irritated many.'

Such a description was at war with Owen's picture of Lascelles. He had imagined a man who lived impulsively and by the dictates of his heart. How else explain his welcoming Gruffydd ap Goronwy's family to Cydweli without first consulting his lord Duke? Owen had imagined Sir John's sympathy overriding his good sense when approached by Gruffydd, a man anxious for the family he had left behind in sanctuary in the church at Tenby – a family which included a beautiful daughter. No doubt Sir John might have reasoned that he owed a debt to Gruffydd, who, according to Reine's information, he believed had saved him from drowning in the harbour two years earlier. But, as Reine reported the incident in less dramatic terms, the extent of Lascelles's help begged more motivation than a debt repaid.

'Does Sir John have any Welsh ancestry?'

'No.' Geoffrey watched Owen pace. 'Would that excuse his behaviour? Would you marry the daughter of a traitor?'

Owen dropped back down on to the chair, stretched out his legs. 'I do not think I would grant sanctuary to a traitor in order to gain his daughter's hand in marriage. But you forget that we do not yet know whether Gruffydd ap Goronwy is a traitor. He was accused by the mother of the Lord of Pembroke. Though she married a Hastings, she will ever be a Mortimer, and the Mortimers are fond of accusing their enemies of treason. It is a tidy solution.'

Geoffrey nodded, but his eyes were troubled.

'You do not like my answer.'

'It makes me uneasy. As did your hot temper when Tyler spoke of the Welsh who live in the area.'

'You knew that I was Welsh.'

'Indeed. It is why I wished to have you here.'

'Then what is wrong?'

Geoffrey lowered chin to chest, studied Owen through his eyebrows. 'You itch for an argument? So be it.' He raised his head, looked Owen in the eye. 'You have changed since we crossed the Severn.'

'Changed? It is true that hearing my language spoken all about me has reminded me of much I had forgotten. Do you know how long it has been?'

A roll of the eyes. 'We speak so many languages.'

'*My* people do not. And yours do not speak mine. Ever.'

'Yours. You see?' Geoffrey wagged his finger at Owen. 'What will Lucie think, when you return a Welshman again?'

But Owen was in no mood for teasing. If Geoffrey wanted to know what was on his mind, he would hear it. 'At first I was confused. I could not understand all the words. My own language.'

'You will teach your children?'

'I had already begun. And God grant, I may have new tales of my parents, my brothers and sisters to tell them. They may have cousins.' Geoffrey had that wary look again. 'Would I speak of my children if I meant to desert them? I tell you, I have not changed.'

'Good,' Geoffrey said, but he did not look convinced.

'Enough of this. What of Cydweli's constable? What can you tell me of him?'

'Richard de Burley. A fighting man who sees courtesy as a fault, so I have been told. He is of an old Marcher family . . .'

'. . . which means they are excellent judges of the direction in which the wind blows.'

Geoffrey chuckled, easing the tension between them. 'I have no doubt of that. Lascelles and Burley should make a chilly pair. At such times I regret that my Phillippa cannot accompany me; she is excellent with difficult people.'

'She must have felt the Queen's passing sorely.' The much-loved Queen Phillippa had died the previous summer. Geoffrey's wife, who shared the name Phillippa, had been one of the Queen's ladies-of-the-chamber.

Geoffrey wagged his outstretched hand. 'Phillippa had some money from the Queen, and earned more assisting the Queen's Receiver with the inventory of the household. Now she is busy with our young daughter Elizabeth, and believes she carries another child.'

'God grant her a safe delivery.'

'Phillippa thinks God has little to do with it, I fear. She boasts of her moderate habits and excellent health.' Geoffrey pushed himself from the chair. 'It is time we take ourselves to bed. It has been a long day and tomorrow we shall require our wits.'

Owen drained his cup, pushed back his chair. How cold the room had grown while they talked. He rubbed his hands together, blew on them. 'I would welcome a sunny day.'

Geoffrey had moved towards the door. He turned now, shook his head at Owen. 'You said you were tired.'

'Aye.' Owen joined him.

Geoffrey lifted a torch from a wall sconce, opened

25

the heavy hall door. A draught made the flame dance and smoke. 'Wretched place.'

Owen followed Geoffrey out the door. 'If Reine does not appear, perhaps you should go straight to Cydweli with half our company.'

Geoffrey paused on the steps, turned, held the light up to Owen. 'And you?'

'Our pilgrims still need an escort to St David's.'

'We might find one for them in Cydweli.'

'Sir Robert is already unwell. I cannot in good conscience prolong his journey. And I should wish to see him safely settled.'

For a moment, the wail of the wind through the tower and the hiss of the torch were the only sounds. Then Geoffrey nodded. 'You are right. We shall continue as we planned. Reine knew our itinerary. He would not expect us to go straight to Cydweli.'

Owen put a hand on Geoffrey's shoulder, made him turn. 'You do not trust me.'

Geoffrey laughed. 'You have had too much ale.' His eyes were not merry.

'And too little sleep, aye.'

They climbed the stairs, parted at the landing in silence.

Tired as he was, Owen found it difficult to sleep. Geoffrey had placed a finger squarely on a tender spot, already rubbed raw by Owen's own surprise at his feelings since he crossed the Severn. He should never have come.

Two

TO ST DAVID'S

Dafydd ap Gwilym and his men had ridden hard for two days to reach the bard's home overlooking Cardigan Bay. A difficult journey for the injured pilgrim, and for Dafydd and his men, after a lazy fortnight in the hall of one of the bard's generous patrons. But haste seemed wise. If the four from Cydweli were in pursuit, Dafydd preferred to defend the pilgrim on familiar ground. It was also most convenient that a skilled herbalist from Strata Florida Abbey was assisting him in enlarging his garden. The pilgrim had need of Brother Samson.

Dafydd glanced up from his harp as a servant showed Samson's travelling companion into the room. Dafydd's great, rough-coated hounds rose and padded over to sniff the monk's robe. A pity that Dafydd's moment of pleasure must be disturbed, but the monk was merely answering his summons. Dafydd needed a spy in St David's and a Cistercian would blend in well. Better still, Dyfrig owed him a favour.

'*Benedicte*, Master Dafydd,' the monk bowed, hands up the sleeves of his white robe.

Did they train the monks to that attitude as novices, Dafydd wondered.

'You have need of me?' the monk asked.

'*Benedicte*, Brother Dyfrig. God has granted us sunshine to lift our hearts. It seems we find favour with Him today.' The monk's eyes flickered uneasily towards the tall, shaggy dogs. Dafydd chuckled. 'Be at ease. You should know by now that Nest and Cadwy are gentle creatures to all but the wolves and the deer. They are merely curious about you. You have seen the wounded pilgrim?'

'A pilgrim, is he?'

The monk was bold enough. His doubt did not ring out, but it certainly whispered. 'Why else does one journey to St David's?' Dafydd asked.

'St David's has some commerce, also, Master Dafydd. Both on land and sea.' The ghost of a smile.

'A pilgrim, Brother Dyfrig.'

Another bow. 'You wish me to escort him back?'

'Do you make a joke? Does the man look as if he might ride?'

Another uneasy flicker of the eyes, though the hounds had lost interest and returned to Dafydd. 'No.'

'You will go there with your ears pricked. Discover whether any other gifts from the sea have been found on Whitesands.'

'Whitesands,' the monk repeated. 'You seek the one who severed the pilgrim's ear? I thought that there were four in pursuit.'

'None of them injured. My pilgrim had a blood-soaked sleeve – possibly his own blood, but I think not. His own would not have spattered so.'

The monk crossed himself. 'Yet you call him a pilgrim.'

'The holiest of men may defend themselves when attacked.'

'The four. What if they learn of my mission?'

'Are you such a fool as to announce it? I seek rumours or news, not the man. I doubt the man is of any use to me. Or to anyone in this world. You need not reveal yourself. Merely listen.'

'It will be done, my lord.'

'A name would also please me. A name for our pilgrim.'

'He has said nothing?'

'The name of a woman, that is all, a woman's given name. He lies there mute as to his identity.'

'Perhaps that is as he wishes it, my lord.'

'It is not what I wish.'

'The woman's name might be of help.'

'Tangwystl. It means peace pledge, did you know?'

'Or peace hostage, Master Dafydd.'

What light lit up those dull eyes? The monk was enjoying this. 'Indeed. Go in peace, Brother Dyfrig, you are no hostage here. God speed you on your journey.'

'May God watch over your household. And over me, so it please Him.'

In Carmarthen, Owen's company had word of John de Reine. He had passed through more than a week before, and was travelling alone – odd on both counts.

Odder still, in St Clears they again had news of him.

He was travelling west; he should have headed east from Carmarthen.

'What is he about?' Geoffrey muttered as they mounted the following morning.

'You might have known by now had you gone straight to Cydweli as I suggested,' Owen said.

Geoffrey made a dismissive sound and rode first from the abbey yard.

Sir Robert brought his horse up beside Owen's. 'Have you argued with Master Chaucer?'

'No.' Owen took alarm as a deep, phlegmy coughing fit made Sir Robert curl in on himself, as if he had been punched in the stomach. 'You must look to your health, Father. You should have taken the physick last night. Such a violent spell will bring up blood and weaken you.'

Sir Robert, unable to speak, waved away Owen's concerns.

A chill rain persisted from St Clears to Llawhaden, where they were to spend the night at the bishop's castle. Llawhaden Castle was not so impressive as Carreg Cennen, being more a fortified manor house than a castle, but it was imposing sitting on a rise overlooking the market town and fortified enough that the bishop's prison resided in the base of the chapel tower. The town of Llawhaden was a prosperous borough with a weekly market and twice-yearly fairs; the East Cleddau River provided abundant salmon and sea trout. With the rental of the borough plots, market dues and tolls, and the leasing of the water-mill, fulling mill and fishery in the river, the town was a rich estate for the bishops of St David's. Brother Michaelo thought it an improvement over the isolated Carreg Cennen.

Owen hoped to view the surrounding countryside from the castle towers. But when he mounted to the tower he saw little more than the castle precinct softened by mist. Sir Robert joined him in the cold, windy spot, holding his cloak tightly about his neck.

'You are doing your best to worsen that cough,' Owen grumbled.

'I wished to speak with you away from the others,' Sir Robert said, his voice hoarse.

'You have something to say that they cannot hear?'

'I wish to warn you, my son. Master Chaucer has watched you closely since Carreg Cennen.'

Owen leaned his elbow on the wall, looked out at the misty landscape. This was not something he wished to discuss, and he let his discomfort sharpen his voice as he said, 'Do you think I have not noticed?'

'Do you know why?'

So he was going to play the dog, worry at the bone until it snapped.

'I have a good idea.'

'He wonders where your loyalties lie.'

'He has no need,' Owen said through clenched teeth. If the old man were not so ill, and were not his father-in-law . . .

Sir Robert leaned so close Owen could smell his breath, made sour by his illness. 'You have perhaps been indiscreet.'

'Let us go below, I shall give you a tincture for your stomach and a hot drink for your cough. And tonight I shall—'

Sir Robert caught Owen's hand, pulled it close to force his son-in-law to face him. 'First admit to me that since crossing the Severn you have prickled whenever we speak of the strangeness of this country.'

'You mean I have remembered that I am Welsh.'

Sir Robert studied Owen's face. 'It is more than that. You are questioning all that you have become since you left this place.'

'Not questioning, Sir Robert. Realising what I had forgotten. And wondering what has become of the family I left here.'

'You do not like the way your people are treated.'

'My people?'

Sir Robert's eyes were sad as he dropped his hand. 'Forgive me. I am a meddling old fool who has opened a wound I had not even known was there.'

'Do you fear that I might stay here and desert my family?'

'No. No, my son.' Sir Robert coughed, clutched the wall as if dizzy.

Owen put an arm round Sir Robert to support him, found the old man shivered despite his warm cloak. 'Come. Let me see to that cough and your sour stomach.'

Sir Robert allowed himself to be helped down the steps and into Owen's chamber in the west range. He was unusually silent while Owen worked on him, averting his eyes from his son-in-law as if fearful he might be tempted into a conversation he did not wish to have. What was it he did not want to say? Without his chatter, Owen was keenly aware of the old man's laboured breathing, the unhealthy wheeze and intermittent gurgle as if water collected in his chest.

When Owen could bear the silence no longer he asked, 'What is it? What silenced you up on the tower?'

'I would not speak of it.'

'We have ever been open with each other. I pray you, tell me what lies so heavy on your heart.'

'You brought to mind my wife, Amélie. Once, when I was out of humour with her, I shouted that I would send her home to her people. She said, "My people? You are my people now." Her voice was so sad. I beat her for being ungrateful.' Sir Robert had taken to wife the daughter of a captured Norman noble in lieu of his ransom. 'I believed I had given her a better life than she would have had among the defeated, and she dared to mourn them.' He passed a shaky hand across his eyes. 'I was cruel in my ignorance. What prayer did I neglect in my youth that God allowed me to treat her so, and then, when it was too late, to gain the understanding I had lacked? I do not know.'

Owen knew his father-in-law was not asking now for a comfort he did not believe he deserved. 'I had forgotten my people were defeated,' Owen said. 'Perhaps Amélie had also.' He turned away from the old man's bowed head and put away his medicines.

'The bishop's constable says John de Reine did not come through here,' Sir Robert said hollowly.

'Perhaps he rode through to Haverfordwest. We should reach it tomorrow.' Owen returned to sit beside his father-in-law. 'The bond of blood is strong. Your daughter forgave you all. What breach, what festering sore caused Reine to question his father's loyalty to his lord in such a public, damaging way?'

'He was given a position, not a name?' Sir Robert suggested.

'And so he ruins that name denied him. Perhaps.'

'Do you not think it likely the agent of his failure to meet you at Carreg Cennen was his troubled conscience?'

'He left it too late.'

'As did I.' Sir Robert raised the cup to Owen, drank down the remainder of the tisane for his throat. 'God bless you for this. Already my voice is stronger.'

Owen heard no change.

The rain diminished as they rode on towards Haverfordwest, and gradually a pale sun shone down on the riders. By midday Owen felt the gentle breath of spring in the air, but he found little joy in it for worrying about his father-in-law. Owen and Lucie had argued about the dangers of such a journey for a man of her father's age. Sir Robert was ever vague about his birth date, but Dame Phillippa, his sister, estimated him to be close to fourscore years of age. It was true that when in his prime Sir Robert had been a formidable opponent in battle, but upon the death of Lucie's mother he had gone on a long pilgrimage marked by illness, injury and long fasts. Though Sir Robert had been nursed back to health under his sister's care, one never completely recovered from such a prolonged ordeal.

But Lucie had insisted that Sir Robert so wished for this pilgrimage it would do him harm to be denied it. Owen hoped she thought it worth the loss of him, for he much feared that a wet spring would be more than the old man could survive.

As they rode into Haverfordwest, the river damp aggravated Sir Robert's cough. Owen hurriedly sought directions to St Thomas's Priory, where Sir Robert might warm himself with a cup of mulled wine and a good fire. And tomorrow being Sunday, he would have an extra day of rest.

Three

a spiral dance

H is head wrapped in bandages, the pilgrim reminded Dafydd of an unfortunate doll that had belonged to his favourite niece. She had bitten off the doll's ear in frustration, saying that the doll never listened to her and thus was she punished. Dafydd chuckled at the memory of the incident, and his sister's careful mending, carried out with a delightful solemnity after the child had dissolved in tears of regret.

The monk who watched over the pilgrim frowned his disapproval. 'A Goddes half, you might show more sympathy.'

'I have given him sanctuary, Brother Samson. How might I be more sympathetic?'

'You laugh at his pain.'

'I laugh at a memory of a doll patched in such wise. Laughter as well as prayers are of use in a sickroom. You would do well to learn that.' Dafydd bent down, felt the pilgrim's forehead. Good. Still no fever. 'You have brought him safely through the crisis. For that I

thank you and pray you receive a heavenly reward.'
Still grinning at the monk's discomfiture, Dafydd left
the sick chamber, his hounds following, and collided
with a servant.

'My lord, there are soldiers at the gate.'

Dafydd was delighted. He had anticipated this
moment. 'Find Cadwal. Tell him to meet me there.'

'What shall I tell the soldiers?'

'Nothing. A wait will cool their heads, and their
heels. I shall go to them anon.'

The servant hurried off in search of Cadwal.

Dafydd returned to his chamber, considered his
appearance in a mirror. Acceptably bardic today,
his white hair freshly washed and thus wild, fastened
with silver rings and ornate combs. Ivy and holly inter-
twined in intricate arabesques on his long, flowing
gown, embroidered by a former mistress. He heard a
shout, nodded to his reflection. 'Attend your guests,
Dafydd.'

One hand resting on Cadwy's head and with Nest
on his other side, he walked slowly down the corridor.
He was Dafydd ap Gwilym Gam ap Gwilym ab Einion
Fawr, Chief of Song and Master of the Flowing Verse.
He would not be hurried.

As Dafydd turned into the entry way, the light was
blocked by a huge form.

'Cadwal. We have guests.'

The giant bowed. 'My lord, I am ever ready to dance
at your bidding.'

'Let us see if they are dancing men. Open the door.'
He motioned to the dogs to stay by his side. They were
hosts, not hunters this morning.

In the night a soft rain had blown ashore, swirled

by wild winds. Dafydd waved to the men huddled beneath the oak by the door. 'Come, pilgrims, dry yourselves by the fire within.' But the men hesitated, staring at Cadwal. It was ever so, of course. Cadwal's mother had been frightened by an apparition at a standing stone and the child had grown to resemble one. 'You stand in awe of Cadwal. God blessed this man with the appetite of a destrier, it is true. But never yet has he consumed human flesh. You are quite safe. God watches over all Christians in this house.'

One man stepped forward. 'We need not intrude, my lord. As I told your servant, we seek the body of a thief and murderer who we believe died of his wounds on Whitesands three days hence.'

'In God's name, pilgrim, come within. You may not feel the dampness, but I do. Come within and we may pursue this story in the comfort of a warm fire.'

Cadwal laughed, a sound that came up from deep within his barrel chest and resonated through the courtyard. 'You flatter me with your awe, pilgrims,' he said in hesitant English. 'But Lord Dafydd is master in this house. If he welcomes you, I am bound to welcome you.'

The men at last entered the house, warily. As soon as he closed the door behind them, Cadwal commanded, 'Pilgrims, your weapons have no business with my master. If you would give them to me, I shall keep them safe until you have need of them.'

The spokesman whirled round, sword drawn. 'A trap. I expected as much.'

A growling chord rumbled in the hounds' throats. Dafydd shushed them.

Cadwal stretched out his empty hands, palms up,

raised a craggy eyebrow, looked from side to side, then behind him. 'Where are your attackers?'

The spokesman looked uncertain.

Dafydd spoke. 'What would Lancaster think of your manners, you who wear his livery? And in the lordship of his dear brother, the Prince of Wales. It is simple courtesy to lay down your arms when entering the house of one who means you no harm, who has expressed no enmity towards you.'

The spokesman nodded to his men. They removed their sword belts, their daggers, handed them to Cadwal. He bowed over his burden, withdrew.

'Now. If you will follow me.' Dafydd led the men to the hall.

In the hall, chairs had been drawn up round the fire circle and on a table sat a pitcher of spiced wine and six cups.

'Come. Take some refreshment. Cadwal will join us as soon as he has made safe your weapons.'

The men poured wine. A servant came forth and poured Dafydd's. He took a seat and sipped calmly until the men were settled. Cadwy and Nest lay watchful at Dafydd's feet.

'Now if you would begin again,' said Dafydd. 'You seek a corpse?'

'Perhaps a corpse, perhaps merely an injured man. Three days ago we saw you depart Whitesands with a burden on your horse. Your men prevented us from pursuing you.'

'A burden?'

'We believe it was the body of the man we pursue.'

'Ah. And you have come to claim him?'

'We have.'

'To what end?'

'If he is alive, to take him to Cydweli for trial, my lord. He stands accused of attacking the Receiver of Cydweli and robbing the exchequer. And a member of our guard is missing.'

'And if this man whom you seek is dead?'

'We shall see that his body has a proper burial.'

'What is his name?'

'We believe his name is Rhys ap Llewelyn. Of Pembroke.'

'A Pembroke man stealing from Cydweli, eh? Did the Earl of Pembroke's dam urge him on? Is she to benefit?' John Hastings, Earl of Pembroke, was in France with King Edward's army. His mother, a Mortimer, had wrested control of the lordship while her son was away – it had been a topic of much amusing chatter at his patron's hall. It was the Mortimer way, to steal what they wanted – power, riches – they never won it honestly. Which was how they came to be one of the oldest and most powerful Marcher families. It was said that Pembroke's mother was a Mortimer through and through, devil's spawn, taking offence at everything if only to enjoy destroying the offender – slowly. Had she been a handsome woman Dafydd might have written a poem to her.

'My lord, I know nothing of the man but that he is wanted to answer for his crimes in Cydweli.'

'It is a bold thing, Lancaster's men entering his brother Prince Edward's March and demanding a man who has sought sanctuary here. May I see your letter of protection and your lord's request for my co-operation?'

The spokesman said nothing. But his flushed face made his answer clear enough.

Dafydd set down his cup and rose. 'Your hasty action is commendable, gentlemen. But even if I did have the man under my roof, and even if he was the criminal you call him, I could not in good conscience give him up to you. My lord Duke will understand.'

The spokesman began to rise. Dafydd stayed him with a hand, and a nod to Cadwal, who now stepped forth from the shadows. 'You are welcome to stay by the fire until you are dry,' Dafydd said. 'Then Cadwal will show you out, and at the far gate he will return your weapons. Go in peace, and God speed you on your way.'

Dafydd withdrew, the dogs following. They found Brother Samson standing in the shadows in the corridor. 'How long have you stood there?'

'Is it wise to tease such men, my lord?'

'Wise? Perhaps not. But I feel filled with God's grace. Have I not attacked without violence, without ire?'

'Who is this pilgrim, that you risk so much for him?'

'It was not idle teasing, Samson. I have a name to try on the pilgrim. Shall we call to him, see whether he answers to it?'

'He sleeps at present, Master Dafydd.'

'Good. I shall return to my study. Send for me when he wakes.'

At last the rhyme pleased him. With a contented sigh, Dafydd put aside his harp, then rose and stretched

41

his arms over his head. The only occupation he enjoyed more than wrestling with words was wooing a beautiful woman. The wit required was much the same. A clever, surprising turn of phrase could turn a pretty head. Women liked wit. Men would do well to remember that. Men responded well to a good twist also. Look at those fools today, expecting to bully their way to the pilgrim.

'My lord,' a voice whispered from the doorway.

Dafydd turned. 'He wakes, Samson?'

'He does.'

The bard joined the monk. 'Come. Let us try out a name.'

The young man had been propped up to a half-sitting position, but his eyes were closed when Dafydd and Samson entered the room.

Dafydd was disappointed. 'Did we miss his waking moment?' He bent close to the man, listened to his breath, which was not the slow, deep breath of sleep. 'Do you feign sleep, my pilgrim?'

Slowly the bruised eyes opened. They were sea grey. 'Who are you?' the pilgrim asked in the shaky voice of the weak.

'I am the one who found you wounded on Whitesands. My name is Dafydd.'

With his fingers the pilgrim cautiously explored the extent of the bandages.

'Are you in much pain?' Samson asked. 'How is your throat today?' The bruises were paling to yellow.

The sea-grey eyes focused on the white monk. 'I am in an abbey?'

Samson bent over his patient from the other side.

'This is Master Dafydd's house.' He peered into the young man's eyes. 'Your sight is clear today?' Dafydd wondered at his litany of questions, all ignored by the pilgrim.

'How long have I been here?'

'You do not remember yesterday?' Dafydd asked. 'Or the day before?'

The young man touched Dafydd's embroidered gown. 'I remember this. And even more pain than now.' He looked up into Dafydd's eyes. 'But I do not remember the journey.'

'What do you remember, Rhys?' Dafydd asked.

The eyes warmed. 'Rhys ap Tewdwr, King of Deheubarth.'

'Well, he you certainly are not. But another Rhys?'

A hand went up to the bandaged ear. 'I do not hear from this side, and there is much pain.' His eyes asked the question he could not bring himself to voice.

'You have not lost the ear, my son,' Samson said, gently moving the hand away. 'But it is as Master Dafydd's gown, intricately stitched.'

'Will I be ugly?'

'For Tangwystl?' Dafydd asked.

The eyes filled, and the pilgrim looked away.

'Who is she to you?'

'I do not know.'

Dafydd straightened. 'I shall let you rest now.'

Samson followed him out of the room. 'His answers are not those of one who remembers nothing.'

'You may be right. But why ruin a game of wit?'

'You would be wise to take this more seriously.'

43

'I shall make more headway if I gently tease his story from him, Samson. Why should he trust us?'

'You saved his life.'

'To what end? I do not know. Nor does he. Nor do you. It is in God's hands.'

a BODY at THE GATE

The road from Haverfordwest wound through gently rolling countryside. The scent of early blossoms mingled with salt air. Owen drank it in, feeling as if he imbibed a heady wine. 'In all my travels, no place has ever smelled as sweet to me.' He had forgotten how much he loved this place, riding towards the sea and anticipating the moment at which it spread out beyond the cliffs. He had come here so long ago, from the north that time, proud to be considered man enough to escort his mother and his baby brother on a pilgrimage. His heart had been light, his faith strong. Suddenly the sea appeared, white-capped and unending, just beyond the cliffs.

'Glory be to God the Father,' Sir Robert cried, 'that I have lived to experience this holy place. Michaelo, does this rekindle your ardour?'

Brother Michaelo huddled deeper into his hood. 'I for one do not enjoy a brisk wind from the sea. Water is not the element that kindles the spirit.'

'Be comforted,' Owen said, 'St David's Cathedral and the bishop's palace are in a valley protected from the sea.'

'Praise God,' Michaelo muttered. 'Though I do not much prefer damp.'

Geoffrey wagged a finger at Michaelo. 'You must cease this game of contrariety else God might decide that you are too critical of His creation to deserve indulgence.'

Michaelo sniffed.

Owen reassured them all. 'We shall be in St David's by mid-afternoon, God willing.'

Sir Robert smiled. 'Would that I had the years left to make this journey twice.' It was said that two pilgrimages to the episcopal seat of Menevia, St David's, were equal to one to Rome: *Roma semel quantum bis dat Menevia tantum*. 'But perhaps one is enough to thank God for bringing my family through the pestilence.'

As they approached St David's they joined a crowd of pilgrims coming from Nine Wells and all in the company dismounted, but Sir Robert. When he moved to do the same, Owen forbade it.

'You have been unwell. To ride is more of a penance to you than walking is to many we have passed.'

'Age brings many blessings,' Michaelo said.

'And much humiliation,' Sir Robert retorted.

'It is good for a pilgrim to be humble.'

Owen did not join in their argument, and it soon died.

Geoffrey came alive in the crowd, speaking to as many of the pilgrims as he could, asking whence they came, their purpose in the pilgrimage. He was disappointed that many spoke only Welsh.

Now they saw many Welsh, the women in starched white veils folded up at the front like bonnets, the men in light wool cloaks and long shirts, often bare-legged. All went by foot. Sir Robert towered above the crowd, his face stony.

At last the elderly pilgrim dismounted at the edge of a rough-and-tumble row of houses that led towards Tower Gate, the pilgrims' gateway to the city of St David's. Sir Robert wished to descend on foot to the cathedral. He invited Owen, Geoffrey and Brother Michaelo to accompany him, while the other men took the horses round to Bonning's Gate and through to the stables at the bishop's palace. Owen judged it a reasonable walk for Sir Robert. The city was little more than the cathedral close, comprising the church, the cemetery, the dwellings of those connected to the cathedral either as clerics, administrators or servants, and the hostelries for the pilgrims. The four made their way slowly through a throng of people whispering and jostling one another. There were townspeople as well as pilgrims, judging from their garments.

'Have we forgotten a feast day?' Sir Robert wondered. 'God forgive me if I have.'

Michaelo shook his head. 'St David's Day is past. We are in Lent, but not so far.'

Owen's attention was drawn to a clutch of men who huddled about a point just without the gate. He lingered long enough to hear that at dawn the porter had found a body there. Everyone must now expound their theories and dire predictions.

'It must have been brought here during the night,'

said one man. 'But why did the porter not spy the activity?'

'The man had been gutted, they say,' another whispered.

'There will be war now among the Marcher lords.'

'They say that a shepherd in Ceredigion once ate a box of hosts – the Lord split him open like a gutted pig so that the faithful might witness his sin.'

'What is it?' Sir Robert asked at Owen's side. 'Of what do they speak in such hushed voices?'

Thank God Sir Robert knew no Welsh. 'An argument, is all. It means naught to us.' Owen wanted neither Michaelo nor Sir Robert to learn of the body – one would panic, the other would interfere.

As they passed through the gate, they all paused and exclaimed. Without the gate they could see but the top of the cathedral's central tower. Now, tumbling down the steep hill and spread in the valley below was a small city with cottages and great halls, all clustered within the walls and round two huge and magnificent structures straddling either side of the River Alun, the Cathedral of St David and St Andrew, and the bishop's palace beyond.

Brother Michaelo was most impressed by the palace. 'See the scalloped arcading? That is Bishop Henry Gower's work. Was he not the most ingenious man? Is it not as I described it?'

Geoffrey laughed. 'You mean as Owen described it.' Owen was the only member of the company who had ever been to St David's. 'Though I grant you have often repeated tales of the palace's splendour.'

Years ago, when Owen was thirteen, his mother had brought him here with his baby brother Morgan.

He remembered workmen atop scaffolding, adding clean stone to peeling, mossy walls. His mother had explained how they would then clean the older stone and apply fresh colour. Now Owen saw for the first time the completed result of Gower's work. As he walked down the steep slope along the north side of the cathedral, he admired the sunlight playing on the reds, blues, greens and golds of the palace walls below. He shielded his eye against the brightening sun and gazed in wonder upon the delicate arcading atop the walls, with a chequer-work pattern of alternating small squares of purple and white stone. It was a decorative lace, serving no purpose but beauty – the palace was protected by the wall that enclosed the entire complex, cathedral, palace and additional residences. There was no need for guards to pace the palace roofs.

'It is peaceful here,' Geoffrey said as he paused before the stone bridge over the small, placid River Alun.

'God grant that I find peace here,' said Sir Robert.

Owen observed the unhealthy flush on his father-in-law's cheeks and forehead and prayed that their lodgings at the bishop's palace would be warm and dry. But he said nothing, not wishing to call attention to a weakness that Sir Robert found humiliating. 'Even before St David founded his monastery in this vale, it was a holy place.'

'A heathen holiness,' Michaelo reminded them.

The bridge was a great slab of marble ten foot long, six foot wide, a foot thick. Its surface had been polished by the shuffling feet of hundreds of pilgrims, and was cracked down the middle.

'They might provide a better bridge,' Michaelo muttered.

'You do not replace such a bridge, not until it no longer serves,' Owen said. 'Have you not heard the legends of this bridge?'

'It is but a plain bridge. There is no art to it.'

'This bridge that you so despise is called Llechllafar – the singing stone,' Owen said. 'Once, as a corpse was being carried across it, Llechllafar burst forth with a reprimand so passionate it cracked with the effort. Ever since, it has been forbidden to carry the dead across this stone.'

'A stone cannot speak,' Michaelo protested.

Owen paid him no heed. 'Merlinus predicted that a king of England, upon returning from the conquest of Ireland, would be mortally wounded by a red-handed man as he crossed the stone. Henry Plantagenet crossed it unscathed on his return from his successful campaigns in Ireland; he declared Merlinus a liar.'

'The Lionheart's father was here?' Michaelo said, suddenly more interested.

'Aye, that he was. Come, let us cross over.'

But now Michaelo looked wary as he considered the stone. 'Your people tell tales about everything.'

'Everything has its tale.'

'What happened when the King called Merlinus a liar?' asked Sir Robert.

'Someone in the crowd laughed at the King and said, "Perhaps the prediction spoke of another king, yet to come." It is said that Henry was not pleased, but said no more.'

'Foolish pride,' Geoffrey muttered.

It was a nervous group that crossed the bridge.

The courtyard of the bishop's palace appeared to be a meeting place for pilgrims and the various clerics who lived in the close. From their furtive gestures and excited whispers Owen guessed they, too, discussed the body that had been left at the gate.

But the courtyard in which they stood claimed Michaelo's attention. 'How magnificent,' he said, gazing round.

Sir Robert reluctantly agreed.

Two great porches, approached by broad stone stairways, led to separate wings. Directly in front, the expanse that housed the great hall presented a deep red ochre façade; at a right angle to the left, the wing that held the bishop's private quarters was rendered and whitewashed. Owen and Geoffrey stepped aside to allow Brother Michaelo and Sir Robert to ascend to the porch of the great hall first. They were, after all, the pilgrims.

The porter perked up at Sir Robert's name. 'His Grace left word that you should dine with him this evening, Sir Robert. And this will be Brother Michaelo? Secretary to the Archbishop of York?'

Brother Michaelo bowed low, beaming.

'His Grace requests your presence this evening also. And Master Chaucer.'

Geoffrey started at his name and made a sweeping bow.

But the porter was already looking beyond Geoffrey. 'Captain Archer?'

Owen gave a curt bow.

'My lord Bishop would see you at once, Captain.'

'At once?' Sir Robert said. 'But he has made a long journey—'

Owen shook his head at his father-in-law, silencing him. 'Did His Grace say anything else?' he asked the porter.

'No, Captain.'

A clerk appeared behind the porter and asked Owen to accompany him down into the courtyard to the bishop's wing. Michaelo began to follow.

The porter raised a restraining hand. 'Brother Michaelo, His Grace wishes a private word with the Captain.'

Michaelo turned back, indignation colouring his cheeks. Geoffrey coaxed him back up the stairs to the waiting porter.

Owen followed the clerk down the broad steps and up the matching set to the bishop's porch. An image of St David greeted him as he drew level with the great door that led into the bishop's hall, a painting larger than life. Proud it made Owen, to see the patron saint of his people so honoured. Liveried servants flitted about their duties with curious glances at the two who moved swiftly through the brightly painted hall into a parlour with a window overlooking the gateway of the palace. The voices in the courtyard were muted in here. The figures seemed a dumb show.

'Would you care for wine?' the clerk wheezed, drawing Owen's attention from the window. The man's round face was red with exertion from the short walk. A pampered lot here.

'I would be most grateful. But you must not trouble yourself.' A mere courtesy. Owen knew the poor young man was under orders to give him refreshment.

Alone, Owen went back to his study of the court-yard. But it offered up no explanation for the bishop's summons. Did Thoresby's reach extend so far? Had he found yet another task for Owen?

Bishop Adam de Houghton paused in the doorway as two servants preceded him, carrying wine and goblets. Tall, fair, with aquiline features and a friendly demeanour, Houghton need only stand there smiling to put a stranger at ease. When the servants had ceased their fuss and slipped away, the bishop entered, making the sign of the cross towards Owen. 'God be with you, Captain Archer.' Houghton spoke in Welsh.

Owen was surprised – though Houghton had been born nearby, in Caerforiog in the parish of Whitchurch, he was of old English stock. He was the first Englishman Owen had encountered to extend the courtesy of speaking the native tongue to a Welshman. Owen bowed low and replied in Welsh. His speech was embarrassingly halting. He had become more careful of his words since he left this country, and he must now not only search for phrases in his rusty Welsh but also weigh and consider each word.

The bishop motioned for Owen to be at ease. 'Presently we shall sit and have some refreshment while we talk of your journey and your mission, but first I would explain my purpose in commanding your presence without the courtesy of allowing you to rest from your journey.' His voice, soft and with a raspy character, seemed at odds with his appearance. 'The Duke of Lancaster has spoken highly of your work for him and Archbishop Thoresby. God sent you at a time when I have great need of your talents. We have had a most unfortunate incident today. I do not like to think of it as an omen, but—'

'There was a body.'

Houghton's pleasant countenance darkened. 'Someone told you of it?'

'I heard people discussing it.'

The bishop relaxed. 'Of course. I suppose it is to be expected. Well then, as you may have heard, this morning the porter discovered a body without Tower Gate.'

'A violent death?'

'The sort of wound that – well, you must be accustomed to it. I am sure you have heard many theories about why you lost your eye.'

'My sight, my lord. I still have the eye.' Owen supposed he meant divine retribution for some sin, as with the tale he had heard at the gate.

Houghton squinted at Owen's patch. 'Do you indeed? Well, they would make a moral tale of that, too.' Heavens but the man jabbered. 'My clerk will show you the corpse. You can be the judge of the condition of the body.'

'I—' Owen shook his head. 'Forgive me, Your Grace, but I must disappoint you. I am here—'

'As my guest,' Houghton said in a louder, firmer voice. 'And representing the Duke of Lancaster. I am quite certain he would expect you to assist me in this.'

The sudden assumption of his compliance momentarily robbed Owen of speech. Was this to be his lot in life, ever to drop to his knees and sniff out any pests that discomfited the nobility? A clerk appeared behind the bishop – not the same poor, overheated lump of flesh who had shown him in.

'Ifan, this is Captain Archer, a man who has solved

many problems such as ours for both the Duke of Lancaster and the Archbishop of York. Show him the poor soul below. I shall await you here.'

Owen bowed. 'Your Grace.'

The young clerk bowed to Owen and motioned for him to follow. They crossed the room, slipped behind a hunt tapestry on the east wall, through a door and down a narrow passage into a tower lit by wall sconces, descending stone steps to an undercroft that echoed as a guard moved from the shadows barking a challenge.

'It is Ifan, with an emissary from the Duke of Lancaster,' the clerk announced.

The guard took a good look at Owen, nodded. 'You may pass.'

'You have had no trouble?' Ifan asked.

From whom, Owen wondered, if the victim was dead. Pilgrims staying in the other wing of the palace?

'All is quiet, God help us,' the guard said.

The clerk led Owen into a room lit with many candles.

The warring scents of beeswax, incense, smoke and decaying flesh assailed Owen. 'He has been dead some days.'

'We have done our best to mask the odour.'

'There is nothing hides that stench.' Owen approached the well-lit table on which the corpse lay beneath a loose shroud. He nodded to the clerk to pull the cover aside. An ugly, gaping wound. If it had originally been a simple knife thrust to the belly, then something had been eating at the flesh. 'Have you cleaned the wound?'

'No. We removed the clothes, that is all. The body is very clean, I know.'

The man had lain exposed for some time after being wounded, Owen guessed. One at a time, he lifted the hands, studied the nails and palms. The nails were dark with what might be blood, the palms abraded. Bruises on the face and arms suggested a struggle. The knees, too, were rough with abrasions. The man had been in his prime, muscular, no deformities. His hair, a pale blond, had been neatly trimmed, though now it was wild, stiff with sea water.

'Where are his clothes?'

The clerk stepped back, picked up a basket, which he handed to Owen. Lancaster's livery, with the emblem of Cydweli. Owen poked through the items. 'There was nothing else? No weapon?'

'No.'

Owen lifted the tunic. The tear proved the knife thrust. Whatever had eaten into the wound had no interest in the cloth, which was stiff with blood round the wound, but the remainder of the cloth was rough and brittle, too. Owen lifted the leggings. They also had the feel of having been soaked in brine. The knees were rough. The boots – they were of good quality, sturdy, slightly worn. Owen tilted them. Sand rained down on the stone floor.

'This man lay on the beach. Crawled along the beach, I think. But the tide found him. And he fed the crabs for a time.' Owen stooped, brought a candle close to the pile of sand. He knew of one beach very near with sand of such dazzling colour. 'Whitesands.'

Owen noticed how the clerk peered down, glanced up at him, then quickly away, as if uncertain what to think. That Owen saw too much, even blinded in one eye? Devil take the bishop for putting such thoughts in his head.

Owen straightened. 'Let us ascend to fresh air, Ifan. Warm ourselves with wine.' Though at first it had felt stuffy in the undercroft, that had been the illusion of the smoke of incense and candles. Slowly the underlying chill had seeped through Owen's leather travelling clothes. This valley had once been a marsh. Man's stones and mortar could not keep out the damp chill.

The clerk bent to cover the dead man, then led Owen back whence they had come.

Bishop Adam de Houghton paced as he listened to Owen's assessment. 'He died of the knife wound?'

'I believe he did, though how quickly I cannot say. It may have been a slow death. I believe his wound bled as he lay in the water. The crabs—' He stopped, seeing the bishop blanch. 'Forgive me, my lord bishop.'

'You deserve your reputation, Whitesands.' Houghton was quiet a moment but for the whisper of his costly gown and his velvet shoes on the tiles. 'It is far to carry a body from Whitesands to Tower Gate. Why? Why was he brought to the bell tower?'

Owen neither knew nor cared. 'Your Grace, do I have your permission to join my companions now?'

Houghton looked first surprised, then apologetic. 'Of course. God help me, I am forgetting my duties as a host. You have ridden far, and I have kept you from a well-earned rest. Go in peace, Captain. And tonight, when we dine, we shall not speak of this, eh?'

'Of course not, Your Grace.'

*   *   *

Owen must have slept, for his thoughts as he opened his eyes in drowsy confusion were of York. He had been telling his daughter Gwenllian the tale of the Water Horse of St Bride's Bay, and now she shook him for another story. As he woke he realised it was Sir Robert who gently shook him.

'His Grace sends for you.'

'Again?' Owen groaned, rose slowly, made his way to a table with an ewer and dish for washing.

'I told the servant that you were resting. There is no need to hurry.' Sir Robert sat at the edge of the bed, his eyes worried. 'His Grace wishes a word before we dine tonight. With you and Master Chaucer. What is it about, my son?'

'Houghton mistakenly believes that I care about his problems,' Owen said, splashing water on his face. He departed before Sir Robert had a chance to ask more questions. Geoffrey waited in the main hall, speaking with much gesturing and wagging of the head to a woman who was richly dressed and fair of face. She covered her mouth daintily when she laughed.

'We are summoned,' Owen said to Geoffrey.

The woman's eyes drank Owen in and she smiled brightly, forgetting to cover her bad teeth.

'Mistress Somery of Glamorgan,' said Geoffrey.

'God go with you, Mistress,' said Owen. 'I pray you forgive me, but the bishop is expecting me and Master Chaucer.'

'Captain,' she said with a flirtatious tilt of her head, a flutter of her lashes. 'I look forward to making your acquaintance.'

Geoffrey hurried away with Owen. 'It is not fair how they look on you.'

The man had peculiar priorities. 'Have you any idea why the bishop sends for us?' Owen said.

'Not the least.' With his short legs, Geoffrey had practically to skip to keep up with Owen's long strides, which made him breathless.

Owen relented, slowed down, told him of the body.

Geoffrey was fascinated, but did not see what it had to do with them.

That made a pair of them. 'I cannot but think that the bishop has learned something to link the body with us. What of John de Reine? Do you know anything of his appearance?'

Geoffrey paused, understanding Owen's suspicion. 'I do not like to think—'

'Neither do I. Was he fair?'

'I do not know.'

'Let us hope I am wrong.'

They marched in silence through the corridor leading from the great hall to the bishop's hall.

Bishop Houghton got to the point as soon as he learned Geoffrey knew of the situation. 'How would you proceed in this business, Captain?'

What had transpired since Owen left Houghton? 'Surely you have a coroner, Your Grace. And staff who assist you in keeping the peace?'

Houghton fussed with a sleeve, feigning distraction, as he said, 'He wore Lancaster's livery.'

'I noted that.'

'It is a delicate matter. The Duke of Lancaster and the Duchess Blanche, may God rest her soul, have provided me with the funds to build a college for the vicars. It is much needed. I cannot tell you the trouble the vicars manage to— But that is not the point. The delicacy. You must see, I wish to keep it a secret . . .'

How like Thoresby he sounded. 'It is too late for secrecy – all the city buzzes with the news of the corpse at the gate,' Owen said.

Houghton seemed distracted by the hem of his sleeve. 'I cannot keep the body a secret, of course. But who he was— One of my vicars served as chaplain at Cydweli Castle a year past. He identified the body.'

So that was what had happened while Owen slept. 'Then you have the information you need.'

'His name is John de Reine,' Houghton said, as if he had not heard Owen. 'The man you were to meet at Carreg Cennen.'

'John de Reine,' Geoffrey muttered, as if testing the name against his memory. He stole a glance at Owen.

So he was right. But with the realisation came a twinge of unease. How much did the bishop know? Uncertain how to answer, Owen let the silence lengthen.

Houghton glanced from one to the other with a puzzled frown that suddenly brightened into an embarrassed smile. 'In faith, I leap ahead without explaining,' the bishop said. 'Forgive me. Pray do forgive me. It is a fault with which I continually struggle. I am in the Duke's confidence, gentlemen. You need not worry about what you say to me. The Duke thought it wise that another Marcher lord know of your purpose. Of his concerns about Owain Lawgoch's supporters, whether Lascelles has gone over to their side, what that might mean to Cydweli.'

Looking much relieved, Geoffrey said, 'Would that he had informed us.'

Owen might have used stronger words than Geoffrey's, and his feeling was less relief than irritation.

'What I wish to discover is why John de Reine was in my lordship. He had arranged to meet with you at Carreg Cennen,' Houghton said.

'A sudden urge to go on pilgrimage?' Geoffrey suggested with a grin.

Houghton clenched his teeth and took a deep breath as if to keep himself from saying something he would regret later. 'The man was brutally murdered, Master Chaucer.'

Owen's companion blushed and bowed his head.

'The Duke told you why we were to meet with Reine in particular?' Owen asked carefully.

'He did.' Houghton nodded. 'I confess to being uneasy about the young man's intentions, betraying his father to the Duke.'

He did indeed know the heart of it. 'His was a choice few sons would make out of love,' Owen agreed. 'But Lascelles's choice of a wife seems unwise in these uneasy times.'

'Of course. Still . . .'

'Who was Lascelles's father-in-law accused of harbouring?' Geoffrey asked. 'A known supporter of Lawgoch?'

'One whom the people call merely the Fleming. Amusing, considering how the country round Haverfordwest is overrun by Flemings. As to the man's supporting Lawgoch, he is an opportunist. It was the Earl of Pembroke's mother, a Mortimer, who heeded the rumour, and when Lascelles gave Goronwy sanctuary in the Duke's March, she made haste to inform Lancaster. She knows the Fleming because he has worked for the Mortimers in the past. I do not know what she knows of his present activities.'

'And hence the ambiguity.'

'Indeed. Was Gruffydd ap Goronwy harbouring a real traitor, or had he found himself on the wrong side of the Mortimers?' Houghton rubbed his forehead. 'I did not know it was the son of Cydweli's steward who lay in the undercroft when I sent his fellows away.'

'Whose fellows did you send away?' Owen asked.

'Reine's fellows, Cydweli men.'

'When?'

'This morning. They rode up to Tower Gate and demanded to see the body that had been left there.'

The bishop was full of surprises. 'Cydweli men came here today?'

Houghton nodded. 'Demanding to see the body.'

'What did they say when they saw it?'

'They did not see it. They had no *littera marchi*. I sent them away. They had been sniffing round here earlier – several days ago – though not so boldly.' Houghton paced. 'I assure you, Captain, I am and always shall be the Duke's ally. I would do nothing to impugn him, his authority or his honour. But I am lord here, and I cannot allow the Duke's constable – or his steward – to order his men into my lordship and challenge my authority.'

'I have no quarrel with that.'

'But now it seems I behaved rashly. I had no idea it was John de Reine. He may have known of some danger and sent for the men, who came too late. But they gave me no explanation.'

'Then I very much doubt he had sent for them,' Owen said. 'Yet it is strange, so many from Cydweli in St David's.'

Houghton's pacing became more vigorous. 'Reine took a risk in writing to the Duke of his father's inappropriate marriage. Was he silenced by his own father? Or those loyal to his father?'

'You do not have a high opinion of Lascelles,' Geoffrey remarked.

The bishop stopped. 'You misunderstand me. I have never before had reason to distrust the man. In faith, I know almost nothing of Lascelles. But his natural son has been murdered and left at my doorstep, and I was one of the few people privy to his— Well, you must see that many would consider Reine disloyal to Lascelles.'

'Was the Duke wrong in trusting Reine?' Geoffrey asked.

Houghton paused. 'What?' he asked distractedly. 'Wrong to trust him? No. Not at all. Reine was the personal guard of the Duke's late steward, Banastre, who chose his men with great care.'

'A steward who kept personal guards?' Owen said.

Houghton clasped his hands behind his back, nodded solemnly. 'Banastre considered himself more lord than steward.'

'You have heard nothing more than what the Duke has told you, the general rumour of Gruffydd ap Goronwy and the Fleming?'

'Nothing more.'

'What would you have us do?' Geoffrey asked.

Owen thought that an ill-considered question. What they must do is tell the bishop that this was none of their concern.

'You return to Cydweli soon?' Houghton asked.

'My intent was to depart in a few days,' Owen said.

'I would ask a favour of you.'

'My lord bishop, our duty is—' Geoffrey began, belatedly in Owen's opinion.

'Lawgoch's followers and Lascelles's loyalties,' Houghton said, 'and the more public issue of the garrisons and recruiting archers for the Duke's campaign in France. About the latter I do not agree with the Duke's plan: you take soldiers away from the Marches just as the King orders all to ensure the security of the ports in their lordships. But I honour the Duke's orders and will not detain you. My request should prove a simple matter: I would have you slip away quietly, without any eyes to observe your departure, and bear John de Reine's body back to Cydweli.'

'A simple matter?' Geoffrey muttered.

'You fear the men who came today,' Owen said.

'I am uneasy about them. And about someone's purpose in leaving Reine's corpse at my gate. Caution seems the best approach. I shall provide you with some of my men, armed men, and a priest fittingly to accompany a funeral cortège.'

'A priest?' Owen asked.

'He was lately chaplain of Cydweli – the vicar who identified the body. If Cydweli men meet you on the road they will find no cause to complain about my treatment of their steward's son. In fact, Edern volunteered to escort you when he identified Reine.'

'Why should he care?' Owen asked.

'He is a devoted servant,' Houghton said.

Owen doubted it was that simple. This turn of

events made him uneasy. But it would be difficult to justify denying Houghton's request. The body should return to Cydweli, and they were an armed party headed that way. 'Can this Edern be ready in a day's time?'

'He can be ready in the morning.'

'The morning? What is the haste?' Geoffrey asked.

'Reine has been dead for some days,' Owen said. 'Already the body will be an unpleasant companion. The longer we wait, the worse it will be.'

Geoffrey made a face.

'Where might I find this Edern?' Owen asked. 'I would speak with him before we set off on the road.'

Five

THE VICAR EDERN

'Why should Father Edern wish to accompany us?' Owen muttered as he and Geoffrey departed through the bishop's hall. 'What does he hope to gain?'

Geoffrey paused, turned on Owen. 'You would have us wander in the wilderness with a corpse?'

'Burdened as we shall be, it is the pilgrim road we shall travel, not the wilderness.' But Owen could see by Geoffrey's high colour how much their new mission preyed on his mind. 'We do not need a guide.'

'So the vicar hopes to see a maid he left behind or settle some business – what is the harm? Why must you question everyone's motives?'

'I have found it wise, is all. I pray the vicar proves trustworthy.'

Geoffrey looked as if about to argue, but he walked in silence for a few steps. When he finally spoke, his words surprised Owen. 'The tale you told about the bridge – the red-handed man who was to mortally wound the king – is not Lawgoch also known as Owain of the Red Hand?'

Owen felt a chill on his neck. Could Owain Lawgoch truly be a saviour? But he had heard a different explanation, one not as appealing. 'By "red hand" is meant "Lawgoch", or murderer. His sword-hand is red with blood.'

Still Geoffrey pursued it. 'The Irish consider a red birthmark on the hand the sign of a Messiah.'

Owen waved the subject aside, though he did not feel as indifferent as he hoped he appeared. He left an anxious Geoffrey pacing the great hall of the palace.

Outside, an icy drizzle had emptied the courtyard. Owen paused on the great porch and lifted his face to the sky, finding the soft rain refreshing. He would not find it so for long; soon it would seep through his clothes and chill his joints. He had looked forward to a few days of rest before mounting his horse again. He ached just thinking of resuming his saddle in the morning. He supposed this was what it meant to grow old.

He left the palace gate and stepped out on to the well-worn path to the cathedral. The rain intensified the loamy scent of the soil beneath his feet and the chalky odour of the stones above. He was alone as he crossed Llechllafar and rounded the west end of the cathedral. Here lay the cemetery, in the shadow of the great cathedral and close to the river. The drizzle and the river damp created a charnel fog that appeared to rise from the graves. The soggy ground gave off an odd odour besides loam; bone perhaps, stripped clean by the worms.

Worms that even now worked their way into the corpse in the palace undercroft. Wrapped in several shrouds and enclosed in a good wood coffin, the corpse would still make a grim and unpleasant companion. Such a burden was not new to Owen; in the field, after his blinding, he had devoted himself to the dead and dying. He had foolishly thought that behind him.

He would have his fill of death in the next few days; he hurried across the graves to the lane that led to the houses of the vicars, stone dwellings tucked into the hill that slanted up from the River Alun to the curving close wall. The bishop had described a small house in the far corner, which incorporated the close wall into its fabric. Owen hoped that the vicar was at home and alone.

Here the odours were more domestic, a welcome sign that Owen was back among the living. The sour stench of beer, cooking fires, sweat, urine. A woman stood in a doorway rocking a baby.

Bishop Houghton had felt it necessary to warn Owen that he would see much that was inappropriate in the vicars' close. The Welsh were slow to accept the rule of celibacy in holy orders, and in fact treated many of their vows lightly. Houghton hoped with Lancaster's backing to construct a residential college for the vicars where he might better control their behaviour. Owen had found that amusing; Houghton was naïve if he thought that the collegial setting would wipe out all occasion for sin. The Welsh abbeys were hardly chaste. The most the bishop could hope for was that the vicars would be moved to find separate lodgings for their mistresses and bastards.

The small house built into the wall was easy to find. A man in a dark cleric's gown sat on a wooden bench before the house, back erect, hands tucked in sleeves, eyes closed, moving his lips in prayer. Beside him sat a white-robed Cistercian, head flung back, snoring peacefully.

The dark-robed cleric opened one eye as Owen approached, closed it, bowed his head, crossed himself, then rose to greet his visitor.

'Captain Archer?' he said. He was of average height and average appearance, a man one would not mark in a crowd.

'Father Edern?'

The man bowed slightly. 'If we are to travel together, "Edern" is less cumbersome.'

The white monk woke with a snort.

'Brother Dyfrig, of Strata Florida,' Edern said with a nod towards his companion. 'He is lately arrived and weary from the journey.' The vicar glanced up at the sky. 'The rain begins in earnest. Let us go within.' He opened the door, stepped aside to follow his visitor.

Brother Dyfrig rose. He was a tall, slender young man, narrow faced, with hooded eyes. He nodded to Owen, shuffled into the house.

'I hoped we might privately discuss your proposal to accompany my party to Cydweli,' Owen said.

Edern toyed with a smile, discarded it. 'Dyfrig knows what I know, Captain. I cannot think what we might discuss to which he could not be privy. And I doubt he will pay us much heed. His only concern is that I do indeed make this journey so that he might enjoy the privacy of my home while I am away.'

'A Cistercian who travels alone and stays in a private home?'

'Brother Dyfrig is a singular monk, it is true.'

They moved inside, where the dark, windowless room proved brighter than Owen had expected, with a multitude of candles and oil-lamps.

'Sweet Jesu, I shall pay dearly for this extravagance,' Edern muttered. 'I had lit these to pack. Dyfrig interrupted me.' He moved round the long room, blowing out all the candles. 'Oil is dear enough, but candles . . .' He shook his head. 'You think nothing of such things, I suppose, being Lancaster's man.'

'When not on a mission for the Duke I have my own household in York,' Owen said. 'I know the cost of such forgetfulness.'

Now there were only four oil-lamps and a small fire in the middle of the room. Dyfrig had pulled a stool close to the fire, and sat warming his hands and feet.

Edern motioned Owen to a bench across from the white monk. He filled a wooden bowl from a pitcher, offered it to Owen. 'Welcome to my home, Captain.'

Owen took the bowl, drank. A strong, sour ale.

'You have a wife?' Edern asked as he settled beside Owen. 'And children?'

'I do.'

'It must be difficult to be so far from them.'

'It is. If we arrive quickly and safely in Cydweli I shall be well pleased.'

'The first I can almost promise, God willing and our strength holding. But the latter is partly yours to ensure, Captain. You and your men.'

'I spoke of floods and hobbled horses, not danger from thieves. The roads seemed free of them – or at least of thieves desperate enough to attack armed men.'

'I am glad to hear that,' said Edern.

Enough of this dancing round one another. 'Why did you offer to escort us to Cydweli?'

Dyfrig glanced over, frowning. Edern shook his head as if warning him to be silent. The vicar took his time replying. Hands on thighs, he stared into the fire with a peaceful expression. Then, in an almost sleepy voice, he said, 'For reasons I never knew, I was made to feel unwelcome in Cydweli by most of the men. John de Reine was one of the few who befriended me and attended Mass, sought me out to hear his confessions. I would see him safely delivered to his father, properly buried.'

Brother Dyfrig listened to this explanation with eyes closed, head bowed. When Edern had finished, the monk rocked back and forth slightly, as if nodding his approval.

It was plain to Owen that Edern lied.

'You must excuse me if I find such selfless devotion doubtful under the circumstances,' Owen said. 'It is not pleasant, travelling with a corpse already foul.'

With a sigh, Edern shifted and crooked his left leg on the bench, so facing Owen. 'You are a wary fox, Captain. And I am glad of it, considering our mission. I thought myself clever. I thought I might convince you I was an honourable soul. So be it. My selfless devotion, as you call it, is half the tale. I have a favour to ask the bishop. Undertaking this mission for him should assist my cause.'

'The favour?'

Edern bowed his head, raised his folded hands to his forehead, as if considering the question. 'I have told you what you have a right to know,' he said softly.

'Did you leave Cydweli of your own accord?'

Edern glanced up, puzzled. 'By order of the bishop. I came to take up new duties as vicar choral here at St David's.'

Owen nodded. 'You say you were not welcome at the castle. What about John Lascelles? How did he behave towards you?'

'With courtesy. He is a man who respects a man of God.'

'And the constable?'

A snort. 'Burley respects no one but himself and the man who holds him at knife point, Captain.'

'You never gained his respect?'

'No. More's the pity. I should have liked to draw his blood.'

'I am told that you identified the body left at Tower Gate.'

'I did.'

'John de Reine was to have been at Carreg Cennen, not St David's.'

Dyfrig had begun to snore. Edern shook him.

Owen thought the monk awakened too easily, with too little confusion. 'The warmth in here makes you drowsy after your journey,' Owen said. 'Perhaps you should get some air.'

Smiling slightly, Dyfrig rose, bowed to Owen, wished him a safe journey, and then departed.

Edern had observed the exchange in silence. When

the door closed behind the monk, Edern said, 'You had only to say.'

'I did.'

'So you did. Forgive me. So. Let us continue. Bishop Houghton turned away some armed men in Cydweli livery today, did you know?'

'Aye. Because they had been sent into his jurisdiction without the necessary courtesies,' said Owen.

'Precisely.'

'But what brought them to St David's? Any of them?'

'He did not tell you that? I can see by your look that he did not. Bishop Houghton, for all his chatter, is fond of informing in partial measures. You say Reine was expected at Carreg Cennen. How do you know?'

The time had passed for secrecy. Owen told Edern of his mission, Reine's part in it.

Edern shook his head. 'Rhodri ap Gruffudd ap Llywelyn ab Iorwerth's grandson. Who would have thought Lawgoch would cause such a stir?' There were many Welshmen who laughed at the thought of Rhodri's grandson being the saviour of the Welsh. Rhodri himself had fought in King Edward's army against his brother Llywelyn, and had died in his bed, an English knight, known as Sir Roderick de Tatsfield.

But Owen's purpose was not to discuss Lawgoch's pedigree. 'Now tell me what brought Cydweli men to St David's.'

'They were Constable Burley's men,' Edern said. 'They say the exchequer was robbed. They pursued a man described by Roger Aylward, the receiver who was injured by the thief. When they heard that a body had been found in their livery, they thought perhaps the thief had cleverly stolen livery as well as gold.'

Owen was not pleased to hear of another complication. 'Why would they not guess it was Reine? Or might be?'

'They did not care to say?' Edern suggested, his expression indifferent.

'Was Reine not also Burley's man?'

'I do not know. When last I met Reine, he was the former steward William Banastre's personal guard. But I would be surprised to learn he was Burley's man now. I would guess him Lascelles's man.'

'Trust family before a stranger.'

'Sir John might be wise. Though from what you tell me, the son was not so fond of his father.'

'We may never know what motivated him to write to the Duke. But no matter what is behind Reine's death, it means trouble.'

'Where Richard de Burley is, there is trouble, Captain. He is a man with a flawed soul.'

'What sort of flaw?'

'You will see.'

'You do not care for Burley.'

'I do not care for Englishmen, Captain. Do you?'

'My wife is English.'

A raised eyebrow. 'Then she has taught you tolerance.'

Owen smiled to think how Lucie would respond to that comment. 'She would not say so.'

Edern slapped his thighs. 'Do I pass your inspection, Captain?'

Owen rose. 'You do. I thank you for your hospitality.'

'Until the morning, Captain.'

'God grant you a good night's rest,' Owen said. He ducked through the door and out into steadily falling rain.

He was of two minds about the vicar. Edern still hid something, but he had a confident air about him and knew far more of the situation than Owen had expected. He might prove of more use than a mere clerical escort. Still, Owen would keep him closely watched.

As Owen entered the room he shared with Sir Robert, Michaelo and Geoffrey, the former grasped his son-in-law's arm with surprising strength, then drew back.

'You are wet through. I thought you were with the bishop.'

'I was. And then I took a walk in the close.'

'The bishop has told you about the body left at the gate this morning – that is why he sent for you, is it not?'

Owen hung his wet cloak on a hook, sank down on to the bed he was to share with Geoffrey, pulled the patch off his scarred eye, closed his good one. 'You itch to tell me something of this.'

Sir Robert dragged a stool over, sat down. 'We heard of a young man, a fellow pilgrim, who left the palace abruptly. He has been gone some days – five, they say – but he left his belongings. Folk think it was his body . . .'

They would people the entire courtyard with corpses by tomorrow. Anyone who did not appear at the communal table. 'You may rest easy about your pilgrim.'

'Who was he then?'

Should Owen tell him when the bishop wished to keep his identity a secret? But how futile was that wish? If the man was known to a vicar in this tiny city, he was probably known to others. 'He was from the Cydweli garrison.'

Sir Robert was quiet so long Owen opened his eyes. The old man was praying.

'They say he had been murdered,' Brother Michaelo said. He was perched on the bed opposite.

'Indeed,' Owen muttered.

'Sweet Heaven.' Brother Michaelo drew one of his lavender-scented cloths from his sleeve, pressed it to his temple.

Sir Robert pulled himself from his prayers to look on Michaelo with disgust. 'He took ill at the news, though it has nothing to do with him.'

Michaelo considered himself to have a delicate constitution – cold and dry, melancholic. Indeed, one of Owen's greatest concerns regarding his presence in the company had been the monk's distaste for fresh air and activity. He had expected the man to wrap himself in heavy cloaks and complain about venturing forth in any but the most clement weather. But Michaelo had proved no worse than Sir Robert.

'His head pains are harmless enough,' Owen said.

Sir Robert, the former soldier, sniffed. 'Will you carry the body back to Cydweli?'

'You leave me no news to divulge. Aye, I leave at dawn. A priest accompanies us.'

'So soon?' Sir Robert looked stricken.

'We would have departed in a day or two. Rest easy, the bishop sends some of his own men with us. Armed. And he assures me the priest is trustworthy.'

'May God grant you a safe journey,' Sir Robert whispered. He was very pale.

'In this holy place, prayers go quickly to God. You must remember me in yours.'

Bishop Houghton had been generous in providing accommodations for Sir Robert and Brother Michaelo, a large chamber with a fireplace just beyond the great chapel in the north wing of the palace. The floor was tiled in yellow and black, matching the servants' liveries, and a wall painting depicted King Henry's crossing of Llechllafar. A second bed had been added for Geoffrey and Owen's stay, and in an antechamber eight of their retainers were comfortably bedded for the night – the other two, who would stay behind, were down below with other pilgrims' servants. Owen's only reservation about the arrangements was the necessity to pair Brother Michaelo and Sir Robert – he could not imagine their constant bickering ceasing merely because they had arrived in St David's. But it was rare for any but royal guests to be granted a private room; indeed it was quite an honour for the two to be allowed so much space without sharing.

Owen slept well, despite the upsets of the day and an ache in the back of his left thigh and hip that forced him to sleep on his right side, which he had not done willingly since losing the use of his left eye. His wife Lucie thought it a foolish rule – while he slept, what did it matter whether or not his good eye were pressed into the pillow. But the bedding was soft and clean, the wine had been excellent, and Owen slept as if he had not a care in the world.

Nevertheless, on waking he fell to worrying.

What did John de Reine's death mean for his mission? There were and always had been rumours that French spies prowled the coast of Pembroke and Dyfed. Had one of them heard that Reine was to march archers to Plymouth? He discarded that theory. In that instance Reine's death would resolve nothing, for a new captain would be chosen. No, the man's death most likely had nothing to do with Owen's mission, God be thanked. And yet it would almost certainly complicate his efforts.

Houghton had asked why Reine's body was brought to Tower Gate. Although Owen had chosen to ignore the bishop's question, he thought it one that demanded a response for the residents of this close. What made it important also made it difficult to answer: there was no apparent reason why someone would have brought the body here. If someone had discovered it and worried that they might be accused of murder, they need only walk away. The murderer had presumably managed to commit the deed and disappear; so why would he return and call attention to his crime? Unless he meant it for a warning. A mute warning, which seemed of little use.

Sir Robert stirred on his bed near the fire. Owen propped his head on his hand and looked at his father-in-law. His thin white hair escaped in lank wisps from beneath the cap he wore to keep his head warm at night. One bony, blue-veined hand rested atop the blanket, fingers slightly curled. More claw than hand. Age brought such frailty, even to an old soldier. But until his recent illness, Sir Robert had been hardy. Whenever he stayed in their house in the city he spent most of the day helping with garden chores. The summer before he had fallen into a pond at his manor of Freythorpe Hadden – whilst playing at jousts with Owen's young daughter Gwenllian. A chill had settled on his lungs. Though he had the best care, with his sister Phillippa hovering and Lucie prescribing medicines, it was plain he had suffered some permanent damage. And yet he had insisted on this journey.

The subject of Owen's thoughts suddenly opened his eyes. 'What is wrong?'

'Nothing. Go back to sleep.'

Sir Robert sat up, precipitating a coughing fit. Owen rose and helped his father-in-law to a few mouthfuls of honey water. When the fit eased, Sir Robert closed his eyes for a moment, pressed his palms to his ribs, took several cautious breaths. A grimace, then a nod.

'Better now. You would think I would have the sense to keep a cup beside my bed, eh?' His attempt at a smile was unconvincing.

Owen felt Sir Robert's hands and feet. Cold and dry. That was not helpful to a cough. He pulled the blankets from his own bed, laid them over Sir Robert's feet, though the old man protested.

'I am the most pampered pilgrim.'

'Save your strength for prayer, Sir Robert.'

Geoffrey, bereft of blanket, stirred in his bed, sat up. 'Is it time to rise?'

'Aye. We must ready ourselves,' Owen said.

As Owen dressed, a servant came with bread, cheese

and ale, a most fortifying breakfast. The men in the outer room were likewise fed. Another servant soon arrived to stoke the fire. As the smoke curled round the room before finding the chimney, Brother Michaelo rose, wiping his eyes and complaining.

'You see, Sir Robert, you are not the most pampered pilgrim,' Owen said.

'I would go to the chapel before I break my fast,' Sir Robert said, 'but I fear you might depart before I return.'

'If we are to leave before dawn, we must depart soon, aye.'

Brother Michaelo rose. 'I shall go to the chapel and pray for the Captain and his men, Sir Robert. You take your ease and make your farewells.'

'A pretty courtesy,' said Owen. 'I speak for us both in thanking you.'

Michaelo shook his head. 'Less a pretty courtesy than a selfish plot to avoid listening to your pretty speeches.'

Geoffrey grabbed a hunk of bread and a cup of ale. 'I shall come with you to the chapel for a little while.'

When Geoffrey and Michaelo had departed, Sir Robert and Owen sat down to their meal and spoke of Lucie and the children, wondered how Jasper, their adopted son, was managing as both Lucie's apprentice and the strong back in the garden. Jasper was thirteen years old, tall for his age and strong from his work in the garden and five years of training at the butts with Owen. They passed the time thus pleasantly until they heard a sharp knocking on the outer door and the noise of men gathering their belongings.

Sir Robert leaned across the table, grasped Owen's forearms, looked deeply into his eyes. 'God speed, my son. May He watch over you on the journey to Cydweli, and always.'

'And may you find peace here. Remember to be patient about your return. Wait for a large party in which to travel.'

Sir Robert nodded once, kissed Owen on both cheeks, then released him.

After a second warning knock, Edern entered the room and stood just within the door, a squirrel-lined travelling cloak thrown over one shoulder exposing a sword and dagger. A cap hid his tonsure. In fact nothing suggested he was a cleric except for a small emblem on his gown identifying him as Houghton's man.

The vicar's willing participation still bothered Owen. He had taken the precaution of assigning Iolo, his most trusted man and one familiar with the country-side, to shadow the vicar and ensure his honesty.

Edern nodded to Owen and Geoffrey, who had just returned from the chapel. 'We must make haste. We should use the fog to hide from curious eyes. Though we shall climb out of the vale underground, we must still watch our backs. We would do best to avoid Reine's murderer and whoever left him at the gate.' It was not yet dawn, but the vicar showed no signs of recent awakening, neither in his eyes nor his gestures.

Not so Owen's men, who waited in the outer chamber. Sleep creased their faces, kinked their hair, puffed their eyes, and gave them all an air of con-fusion. Yesterday the men had complained loudly of their paltry rest between journeys, but this morning they were silent. At Owen's command, they stood and followed Edern down into the undercroft. They were joined by four servants who would carry the corpse, now secured in a wooden box, to the cart which awaited them outside the city with two of the bishop's guards. Owen sensed the darkening of his men's already grim moods as Reine joined their procession. Last night they had been made uneasy by a rumour circling the hall, that four soldiers in the livery of Cydweli had been seen combing the beach at Whitesands two days before, heavily armed. Four armed men who had then vanished.

Tom, the youngest of the retainers brought from Kenilworth and the only one who had never set foot in Wales prior to this journey, had been pale with fear when Owen had returned from his meal with the bishop the previous evening. 'Six men have now vanished from this place, Captain. Five of them armed men, one a pilgrim.'

'One of the five lies beneath the bishop's great hall,' Jared had muttered. 'And he wore the same livery as the others.'

'They do say the Old Ones live in this vale,' Tom had continued. 'And that up on St David's Head is a place on which a Christian must not stand, else he will be sucked into the world of the Old Ones.'

'I am not ordering you up on to St David's Head, lad,' Owen said. 'Nor did the men disappear into the world of the Old Ones, as you call them. I would wager that the four were the same who came to the palace yesterday demanding to see the body.'

'Which we shall carry on the morrow,' Jared said.

Sam spat in the corner. 'Why would the guard from Cydweli desert one of their own dead, Captain, eh? Spirited away, they were.'

'And spirited back?' Owen had laughed.

Iolo, the only Welshman among them, grinned and shook his head. 'This is hallowed ground, you fools. Save your fears for a truly bedevilled place.'

'I, for one, pray they are spirits,' said Jared. 'I'd rather spirits lie in wait for us upon the road than well-armed men.'

Sam growled, but said no more.

Iolo's level-headedness reassured Owen that he had chosen the right man to watch Edern.

But this morning, as Edern opened the door to the underground passage through which they would ascend from the vale, even Iolo crossed himself against the yawning darkness.

'What of our horses?' Owen asked.

'They await us on Clegyr Boia, along with the cart.'

'Why should we trust this man, Captain?' Sam asked.

'Because Bishop Houghton trusts him. And what would you have us do? Walk out the gate in plain sight?'

'We have no enemies here.'

'Perhaps not. But the man carried before us may have thought much the same.'

'What is this place to which we climb beneath the ground?' Tom asked.

'The outcrop upon which the Irish chief Boia was converted by St David,' Owen said. There was much more to the legend than that, but all of it far less likely to calm Tom – for it involved human sacrifice and spells that felled cattle and men. He was grateful that Iolo and Edern said nothing. 'Now let us proceed before all the household is awake.'

Six

A GRIM JOURNEY

O wen's company rose from the dark, echoing
tunnel to be enveloped in a fog that clouded
the vale. He thought of St David's ritual fire by
which the saint announced his presence to the Irish
chieftain and druid, Boia. David had lit a huge fire,
letting the smoke collect in the vale and spread to
the surrounding lands, declaring his ascendancy over
all that it touched. Enraged as he looked down from
his fortress on the mound, Boia had sent his warriors
against David. The saint had responded with a spell
that caused Boia's men and his cattle to fall down as
if dead. In awe of David's power, Boia was converted.
But his wife continued to war against David's holy
men – eventually sacrificing her stepdaughter in the
valley. Before that she had warred in subtler ways,
sending her women to bathe naked in the river, hoping
to tempt the monks from their vows. Owen smiled,
imagining them in the River Alun.

'The sun cheers you,' said Geoffrey.

Owen looked round in confusion. Indeed, as they climbed up on to Clegyr Boia they were rising out of the fog that shrouded the vale. 'What is left of Boia's fortress?' Owen asked Iolo.

'Crumbling walls is all.'

Owen was disappointed, but as the magic of his daydream faded he was pleased to find two of the bishop's retainers waiting at the top of the mound, with several grooms, the cart bearing the coffin, and the men's horses.

By the end of the first day, Owen witnessed nothing to criticise in Edern's behaviour. In fact, Edern had made the journey more comfortable than Owen had expected. His knowledge of the countryside was thorough. He had guided them to the pilgrim road, skirting the city to the north and east along farmers' tracks. He knew where to turn off the road to find streams with fresh water, even a farmhouse at which they were offered cider for a good tale at midday. The scowls receded from his men's faces, though young Tom's eyes still anxiously flitted from shadow to shadow.

In the late afternoon sun Owen studied Edern while he asked a passing tinker the conditions of the rivers they must cross in the next few days. The vicar was a nondescript man, pale hair neither red nor blond, grey eyes, freckled complexion, no scars or ticks; the most notable element of his face was his mouth, narrow yet with uncommonly full lips. He was slender, seemingly unmuscular, but he had ridden and walked with undiminished energy throughout the day's journey, and kept his temper, answering all questions patiently and completely enough that no one found cause to

86

complain. Iolo, who tried to stay as close to him as he might, was looking tired.

Or perhaps it was the odour of the corpse affecting Iolo's mood. As the afternoon sun beat down on the pine box, lined though it was, and covered with a heavy canvas cloth, it warmed the decomposing John de Reine, causing all in the company to move as far from the cart as they could while still protecting it.

'An unwelcome reminder of our mortality,' Geoffrey said when Owen wondered aloud whether they would ever wash the odour from their hair and clothes.

Poor Tom had the task of driving the cart for the afternoon.

All were glad to see Haverfordwest rise out of the fields ahead; the priory was just south of the town. They rode in solemn procession along the busy road that led south between the town walls and the Western Cleddau River, past the Dominican friary. Folk covered their faces and stood aside to let the company pass. But despite the grim burden the company was welcomed by the hospitaller at St Thomas's, the Augustinian priory. And so the first day of their journey ended around a table in the guesthouse, the wooden box safely tucked away in a shed built against the far wall of the enclosure. Much to his relief, Owen found that a cup of the canons' strong ale masked the bad taste in his mouth sufficiently to kindle his appetite.

The second morning brought a cool drizzle, which all welcomed. With a good night's sleep and a respite from the stench of their burden, they began the day's journey with more goodwill than the day before. And having found no fault in either Edern's behaviour or that of any of the bishop's men, Owen's men began to relax about the strangers in their company.

The road east from Haverfordwest was empty of pilgrims. In the early morning the company passed farmers approaching the town with carts of produce, and later in the day they met an occasional messenger or small group of weary travellers. The men settled into the slow, steady progress and talked quietly among themselves. They reached their rest at Whitland Abbey without incident, although the abbot told a tale of armed guards from Cydweli who had disturbed the peace of the abbey two nights earlier. He had refused them hospitality until they surrendered their weapons. They told a desperate tale of the theft of the exchequer. The abbot had assured them that there were no thieves in Whitland Abbey, and no weapons. For the sake of a dry bed and plentiful food, the men had at last given up their weapons to the porter.

On the third day Owen's company started out with cautious cheer, hoping that by early evening they should be freed of their burden in Cydweli. Clouds hung low overhead and a cool wind stirred the branches heavy with buds. But by late morning the clouds darkened ominously and the wind whipped their cloaks about them. As the company drew near St Clears, Edern advised a halt at the abbey, perhaps until morning.

'You do not want to ride the Llansteffan ferry during a storm or just afterwards, when the river is swollen. Not with a cart,' he warned.

The men were huddled in their cloaks, fighting

against the wind and yet disappointed about the delay, when Iolo, riding vanguard, cried out that a small armed party approached on horseback, wearing Lancaster's livery. Edern nodded towards a hefty presence on the forward mount. 'Burley himself. We are honoured.' An encounter long anticipated, and dreaded.

Owen called to the company to stop. Burley's company, three men in all, halted a horse's length from Iolo. Owen and Geoffrey rode forward.

The one pointed out by Edern straightened in the saddle and barked, 'Richard de Burley, Constable of Cydweli.' Solidly cast, though Owen guessed he would prove short when dismounted, and the chain-mail he wore no doubt padded him slightly. He had a nose much broken so it lay flat against his face, an upper lip shortened by a tight scar beneath his nose, a strong chin, and glowering eyes under pale brows. He looked the part of a constable.

'Captain Owen Archer and Master Geoffrey Chaucer,' Owen said. The man would know their names.

Burley nodded. 'Some in your party wear the livery of Bishop Houghton.' His men dismounted in response to a slight gesture from the constable. 'Are they also bound for Cydweli?'

'They are.'

Burley's men came forward. Owen nodded, and his men dismounted. Burley's men paused.

'We welcome you to accompany us to St Clears, where we mean to wait out the storm,' Owen said. 'There we shall answer your questions as best we may.'

'What do you carry concealed beneath the canvas?'

Burley demanded, nodding at the cart. Not by the slightest tick did he acknowledge Owen's invitation.

'I wonder you need ask,' Owen said. 'Surely the perfume of decay surrounds our party?'

Burley sniffed, but his expression remained frozen, his eyes unmoving. Owen grudgingly admired the man's discipline. But to what purpose did he make such effort? 'One of your men?' Burley asked.

Owen could see no benefit to answering more questions at the moment. 'As I said, we shall gladly tell you all when we are safely within the abbey.' He motioned his men forward, separating and riding round Burley and his two companions, the cart rattling by with Edern guarding the rear. The constable and the vicar eyed each other with mutual hostility.

'You show poor judgement in your choice of clerics, Captain,' Burley shouted as he turned his men round to follow.

St Clears was a small Cluniac foundation, two monks and a few lay servants – an unexpected company of sixteen would be difficult to accommodate, but Owen preferred talking of John de Reine's mysterious death within the walls of an abbey, where it was hoped Burley would feel constrained by the sanctity of the place. Not that the monks of St Clears often felt so constrained – Edern had entertained Owen and Geoffrey since they decided to stop with tales of the colourful inhabitants and their notoriety since the foundation.

'They will offer good ale and perhaps wine,' Edern had said, 'which will help the men ignore the filthy accommodations.'

It seemed an appropriate place in which to confer with Richard de Burley.

Burley had taken the best chair in the room, the only one with both back and arms, and rested his muddy boots on the edge of the bench on which Geoffrey perched. The constable did not interrupt Geoffrey's statement of the few facts he had concerning the death of John de Reine, and in what wise the corpse had arrived at St David's. When Geoffrey was finished, Burley sat back in his chair, hands gripping the arms, and frowned at the ceiling while moving his head slowly from side to side. 'Reine was to meet you in Carreg Cennen,' he muttered as if to himself. 'He left before the thief struck the exchequer at Cydweli. And yet – had he word on the road that the thief was in flight to St David's? No, no, how could that be? What took him westward?'

'We, too, found it a riddle,' Geoffrey said. 'The constable of Carreg Cennen had received no word of a change of plans.'

They sat in the main room of what was generously called the guesthouse, a farmhouse with a roof much neglected and a mud floor that sucked at their boots. Owen had suggested they talk in this quiet moment while the rest of their parties were busy in the stables with the horses, some frightened by the lightning, and the abbot and one monk in residence had not yet joined them.

Burley gave up his contemplation of the waterfalls between the sagging ceiling timbers and squinted at Geoffrey. 'I wondered at your choice of Reine to head the recruits,' he said. 'I predicted you would wish you had consulted me.'

'Reine was not up to the task?' Geoffrey asked.

'Who recommended him to you?' Burley asked.

Owen sat beneath the one window, using the light to mend a fraying saddle strap. 'The matter was fixed before we were assigned this mission,' he said, not bothering to look up at Burley.

Burley grunted, then grew quiet as a bolt of lightning was followed quickly by a clap of thunder that shook the roof. Men shouted without, geese squawked, a horse neighed in terror. 'Why does Father Edern travel with you?' Burley asked suddenly.

Now Owen glanced up. 'The bishop wished to show his respect by providing an escort befitting the son of Cydweli's steward.'

'Admirable, if true,' Burley said as they were interrupted by the entrance of a train of servants bearing boards and benches.

In the evening, after a filling but peculiar meal of bread pebbly with beans and a root-vegetable stew that tasted much like the bread, Owen sought out a last word with Burley.

'Are we likely to meet more of your men between here and Cydweli? If so, I might ask for the loan of one of your men to assure them we had already explained our mission to you.'

Burley coughed up phlegm and spit just past Owen's boots. 'Would my men and I spend the night in this stinking stable if we did not plan to escort you ourselves?'

That was precisely what Owen had wondered – why they had not had their talk and then parted ways. The storm had eased to a gentle rain. Without a cart they might risk moving on to more comfortable accommodations at Whitland Abbey. 'I do not mean to delay you in your business. The loan of one man . . .'

'I should attend Reine's requiem Mass,' Burley said. 'You are a captain, you understand the importance of showing respect for the fallen. My men will expect it.'

'Aye,' Owen said. 'Then we shall meet in the yard at first light.'

'We shall meet when we wake to piss, Captain. Or did you expect me to sleep with my men and the horses?'

cydwelɪ

They crossed the Towy on the ferry at Llansteffan, where the river widened to join the sea in the shadow of the castle set high on the bluff. It had begun to rain again, no more than a mist, but it made what would normally be a damp crossing even more unpleasant. The current was choppy, the river swollen with the spring rains, and Owen watched in sympathy as Tom, the youngest of his men, tried to hide his sickness from the others.

'Never sailed the sea?' Iolo asked softly as he steadied the young man's horse, frightened by his handler's jerky movements.

Tom shook his head.

'You have done the right thing, letting the sickness come. Best not to fight it. Oft-times a man will discover he is fine once he is empty.'

Edern handed Tom a wineskin. 'Get rid of the taste.' He nodded at the young man's thanks, but did not smile. Still angry about Burley's men taking over the care of the cart, no doubt.

Once across, they had to wait for the second load, which included the cart. Owen lifted his hood as the soft rain quickened. Midday and he already felt a chill in his left shoulder. An old wound. Steel left its mark, caught the cold ever after. His mother had predicted such wounds. On his parting from her many years before, she had given him a jar of mustard, warned him to keep a supply with him always. *Mustard heats the lingering ghost of the sword*. Why his shoulder, but not his eye? It was a dagger that had sliced his eye and blinded him. Why did his eye not ache in the cold damp?

Fragmented childhood memories bedevilled him. The pain when his foot slipped between two frosty rocks as he searched for a lost dog in the mountains, his cries for help echoing loudly in the wintry silence, holding his breath then, terrified that his cries might invite an avalanche of snow. His mother's mash of rosemary and sage to heat the children's blood in winter. Lighting her along a steep track to help with the birth of a neighbour's child. The back-breaking work of reclaiming the kitchen garden in a spring thaw, removing the rocks that had rolled down from the heights in the snow and rain. He had expected his thoughts to turn to Cydweli, but all these were of a far earlier time, in the north, in Gwynedd.

When Owen was fifteen his family lost their sheep to a murrain. Their kin shared what they could, but Owen's father said it was a charity his brothers and cousins could ill afford, as they, too, were struggling. It did not help that Rhodri ap Maredudd, Owen's father, was a proud man. When he heard that in the south Henry of Grosmont, Duke of Lancaster and lord of Cydweli, was allowing families to settle on escheated land if they had a son who would join his army as an archer, Rhodri ap Maredudd saw a way to save his honour and his family. Owen was an excellent archer. And Cydweli was south – the land would be kinder. But Owen's mother had found it difficult enough to leave Clwyd for Gwynedd when she married; to move south – it had sounded like death to her.

It was a measure of Rhodri's desperation that he uprooted the family and took them south before ascertaining the truth of the rumour, for rumour it was; the Duke of Lancaster had made no such offer. But the constable of Cydweli, a man who knew the worth of a good archer, asked to see Owen shoot. Impressed, he had spoken to the steward. Rhodri ap Maredudd was given a small farm north of the town. It was what he had wished for, but it proved a disappointment. The soil was thin, though better than in the north, and their neighbours resented them for taking over the land of a man whose family had lived there for many generations, which he had forfeited for little else than being a Welshman with a careless tongue.

'Are they good memories?' Geoffrey asked, breaking into Owen's reverie.

Owen threw back his hood, let the rain cool him, glanced round. The cart had arrived across the river, and the men were remounting their horses. 'It is a hard thing, returning after all this time.'

It was early afternoon before they crested the hill known as Mons Salomonis that separated Cydweli from the Towy. At last Owen saw before him the white walls of Cydweli Castle.

'You can see why the Duke calls it the pride of his Marcher holdings,' Burley said, joining Owen at the edge of the track.

'The pride? It looks to me as if he finds it wanting.' Stonemasons stood on scaffolding surrounding the south gatehouse, which already looked much larger than Owen remembered.

'All castles in the Marches require improved fortifications with the years else the natives grow too confident.'

Owen felt Burley watching him for a reaction. He did not oblige him, but quietly studied the castle. It was within the magnificent whitewashed walls of the stronghold that his skill at archery had won him a place among Henry of Grosmont's Welsh archers. As Owen watched, a man atop one of the towers turned their way, then ducked down and disappeared. To announce their approach, no doubt.

Geoffrey slipped in between Owen and Burley. 'It is a poor introduction, to come bearing the corpse of one of their own,' he said, nodding towards the castle.

It was true that Lascelles must both wish for and dread their news. And now they would arrive with the worst news a father can hear. Owen had not yet experienced such a dark day, but he well remembered his despair when Jasper, not even yet his adopted son, disappeared and they feared him dead.

'At least we have brought him the body, so that he may know that his son is buried in hallowed ground.'

'A small comfort.' Geoffrey's eyes were dull and sunken. He had found it difficult to sleep since they left St David's.

'We shall walk lighter once we have delivered our burden.'

'True. For that I am deeply grateful.'

In a little while they resumed their slow approach, dipping down into Scholand, the ragtag cluster of tenements that led into Ditch Street and so to the south gate of Cydweli. The cart drew the curious and then sent them scurrying away, full of dread.

At the town's south gate, the gatekeeper walked forth to meet the party. One great hand on the hilt of his sword, the other on his dagger, he rocked towards them in an awkward, bow-legged waddle.

Geoffrey leaned close to Owen and muttered, 'I wonder whether he must needs let go his sword to press back his belly in order to withdraw his dagger.'

Happily unaware of his comical appearance, the gatekeeper demanded to know their business in a swaggering manner and an English so accented that it sounded like Welsh.

'These men are with me,' Burley barked.

The gatekeeper bowed stiffly towards the constable. 'That is as may be, Constable, but my orders are to confront all strangers.'

With a curse, Burley waved his own men past the stubborn gatekeeper. The man in charge of the cart jumped down gladly. 'We shall await you by the castle gatehouse,' Burley shouted to Owen's party.

Geoffrey had dismounted and now solemnly produced his orders from the Duke. The gatekeeper squinted down at the parchment, up at Geoffrey, obviously unable to read. 'You wear the livery of the Duke of Lancaster. So you will be for the castle?'

'My business is with the steward and the Constable of Cydweli, yes,' said Geoffrey.

'This seems to be in order,' the gatekeeper said as he returned the parchment. 'See you make your way direct to the castle, milord.'

'Surely a pause at the tavern . . . ?'

'Not with weapons.'

'There has been some trouble here?' Geoffrey asked.

The gatekeeper hesitated. 'I should not be talking of the castle's troubles.'

Geoffrey began to turn away. 'It is no fors, I shall hear it soon enough.'

The gatekeeper sniffed at that. 'Aye, you will learn far more than I can tell you. It was theft at the castle, you see. Guards have gone forth to catch the thief. That is all we know.'

'*Par Dieu*! A theft at the castle? Now that was a bold thief.'

The gatekeeper warmed to Geoffrey. 'They do say poor Roger Aylward lost a tooth in the attack.'

'And who is this poor man who must eat soft food for some days?'

'The Duke's receiver in Cydweli, and a worthy burgher of this town, milord.'

'Poor man. It is one thing to be injured protecting your own goods, but for the Duke's . . .'

'He will have a good tale to trade, and a gap to show for his honour. It will ease the pain for Master Aylward. But you understand the danger. You see why I count it wise to be wary of strangers bearing blades at such a time.'

'I do indeed. And I shall tell the steward of your wise caution.'

'Er – the cart, milord. What do you carry?'

Geoffrey pulled off his cap, held it to his heart as he bowed his head. 'The body of a noble soldier from the garrison.'

The gatekeeper frowned, took a few rocking steps towards the cart, wrinkled his nose. 'God's blood. It is no wonder the mighty Burley left it to you.'

'And you will equally understand why we wish to deliver our burden as soon as may be.'

The gatekeeper bowed them through the gate. All dismounted and passed through, Edern guiding the donkey and cart.

'That was well done,' Owen said to Geoffrey when they were well within.

Geoffrey bowed slightly and put a finger to his nose. 'I despair of learning your skills, but I have some of my own I thought to put to good use.'

At first Lascelles stared unblinkingly at the vicar, as if still waiting for him to speak. The steward of Lancaster's Marcher lordships was tall and slender, with the pinched lips and stiff shoulders of a man much given to self-discipline. His eyes were pale and cold, his speech and manners those of one brought up to rule with disdain. And yet while Edern had told the tale of the body left at the gate and the bishop's insistence that his own men accompany the corpse, Owen noted a cast to those cold eyes that belied Lascelles's control.

Geoffrey, Edern and Owen had been led into the great hall of the castle and served refreshments.

Lascelles had joined them abruptly, alone, obviously aware that they bore unhappy news.

'I understand that he was your natural son,' Owen said.

Lascelles tilted his head back and drained his cup. A servant came forward, refilled his cup. This, too, he drained in one gulp. The servant filled the cup a third time. Lascelles set it on the table beside him. 'John departed for Carreg Cennen. He had no business in St David's.' He looked oddly pale for the amount of wine he had just consumed, and so quickly. 'But why should that disturb the bishop?'

'We might leave that for later,' Owen said. 'After—'

'Now,' Lascelles said, lifting his cup. 'I shall hear all now.'

'We merely thought business should wait,' Geoffrey said quietly.

'I prefer to hear it now.'

'Very well.' Owen nodded to Edern.

The vicar sat with folded hands and spoke quietly. 'My lord Bishop wants your reassurance that it was not by your orders that Reine and shortly afterwards four other armed men from this garrison came riding into his lordship without first requesting his permission.'

'Is that his concern? That I challenged his authority in his lordship? Well, he may rest assured that I did not. As if I did not know he would run to the Duke—' Suddenly the steward passed a hand across his eyes, shook his head. 'You must forgive me. It is a shock, this news. You are right, Captain. We shall discuss the bishop's concerns at a more appropriate time.' He rose clumsily, gave a curt nod. Sweat glistened on his pale face, his eyes did not focus on his company. 'I forget myself, gentlemen, offering you a paltry cup of wine as comfort upon your arrival. My wife has arranged for warm water to be sent to your rooms so that you might wash the dust from you. And a more substantial refreshment.' He turned and hurried from the hall.

Edern wiped his brow.

Geoffrey slapped the table and rose, tugging up his sagging girdle. 'I have enjoyed warmer welcomes, but in the circumstances he behaved with excellent courtesy.' He glanced round, nodded to the servant hovering in the doorway. 'We would retire to the guest chambers.'

Owen did not share Geoffrey's satisfaction with the steward's welcome. What he had witnessed seemed not the reaction of a man who had just received grievous news, but the behaviour of a man who faced at last what he had long dreaded. For the first time Owen wondered whether Lascelles had a hand in John de Reine's death. Could he have ordered his son silenced?

Edern was to stay with the present chaplain of Cydweli in the chapel tower. Geoffrey and Owen were led across the inner bailey to the guesthouse, where they were to share a room. Servants and soldiers stood about in doorways and corners of the yard, heads together, talking quietly but excitedly. Several glanced up curiously as the two passed. Already the news of Reine's death spread.

Owen dismissed the servant as soon as the young man had helped him off with his boots. The room was large, with a window that looked out towards the great hall and another that faced a small tree valiantly struggling to grow in the shadow of the castle wall. The chamber walls were painted white with yellow and red flowers. It was well furnished, with a brazier in the corner between the two windows, two fair-sized beds, a rack of pegs on which to hang their clothes, a trunk for storage, and a table and two chairs.

'We should be comfortable here,' Owen said. He removed his eye-patch and rubbed the scar beneath.

'Something troubles you,' Geoffrey said.

Owen poured wine from the hospitably large jug on the table and settled down on the bed which smelled of lavender and felt free of lumps. He might sleep well here if he could quiet his mind. 'Sir John did not behave like a grieving father. Or a grieving steward.'

Geoffrey stood looking out the small window that faced on the inner bailey. Without turning, he said, 'He hides his emotions before strangers. A common courtesy.'

'Oh, aye, he would do that. He looks a man who has done everything everyone expected of him, from squire to steward.'

'What of his natural son? There at least was proof of a night of passion.'

'That, too, was expected.'

'You are never satisfied. If he had been Welsh you might have called him perfect.'

'You think I consider my people perfect? If we had been so, we would not be under your thumb.'

Geoffrey sighed, sank down on his bed. 'I consider him a generous host.'

Eight

THE LADY OF CYDWELI

As soon as Owen entered the great hall for the evening meal, he noted John Lascelles, his tall frame draped in a blue silk gown with flowing sleeves, contrasting with the tight gold sleeves of the shift beneath. A richly embroidered gold hat hid his balding head.

Geoffrey, who had arrived earlier and already could put names to many of the faces, joined Owen and nodded towards a man and woman who made their way through the crowd towards Lascelles. 'Mistress Lascelles,' Geoffrey whispered. 'Is she not one of the loveliest women you have ever seen?'

So this was the daughter of Gruffydd ap Goronwy. She had red–gold hair, pulled up in intricate coils exposing a long neck and delicate ears. Her softly rounded form was exquisitely displayed in a low-cut gown in the latest court fashion, made of costly silk and velvet. 'Indeed,' Owen said. 'Who is the man?' He was older than she, though no less handsome.

'I do not know.'

'Gruffydd ap Goronwy?' Owen wondered aloud. The older man was also dressed in elegant clothes, though subtler than the woman's, dark browns and deep blues free of ornament. He had dark hair with a wing of silver over the right temple. Proud of it he must be, for he wore his blue velvet hat tilted to show the silver wing to advantage. His features were regular, perhaps heavy in the brow, his eyes dark as his hair, his expression amiable. His posture emphasised a prosperously wide middle. Owen guessed that the width had been on his shoulder in youth. His left hand was bandaged and he held it as if he still had pain.

'Handsome father, handsome daughter,' Geoffrey said. 'God's blood, you must be right.'

'A chilly welcome,' Owen said as Lascelles caught sight of his wife, stiffened, lifted his chin. As she curtseyed to him, Lascelles appeared to sniff and give a hardly courteous nod.

'How did such an angel alight in this gloomy place?' Geoffrey whispered.

'Let us not forget that she was her father's salvation,' Owen said.

They approached their host, his wife and the stranger.

Mistress Lascelles raised her eyes to the newcomers and smiled. Her eyes were a pale green.

Lascelles was first to speak. 'Master Chaucer, Captain Archer. I do not think I thanked you for escorting my son's body from St David's. You are our most welcome and honoured guests this night. Ask for whatever delicacies you wish after your long and difficult journey.' His voice did not echo the warmth of his words.

'You are most kind,' Geoffrey said, bowing. Owen bowed likewise.

'My wife,' the steward said, inclining his head slightly towards the beauty at his side.

Owen bowed low and greeted her in Welsh, expressing his regret for having brought such sorrow to her family this day. Her smile faded, she bowed her head, and in her own language she said, 'I shall miss John de Reine. He was a kind and gentle man.'

'This is most unfair,' Geoffrey said, 'for I would greet you but have no knowledge of your tongue.'

Mistress Lascelles glanced up. 'Forgive me, Master Chaucer.' Her voice was slightly hesitant in her husband's language. 'May I introduce to you my father, Gruffydd ap Goronwy.'

The handsome man stepped forward. 'Master Chaucer, Captain Archer.' He bowed. 'All of Cydweli is abuzz with your coming. Young men are honing their skills to impress you so that they might join the Duke's forces in the great war.'

Owen happened to glance towards the fair Mistress Lascelles as her father spoke, and was intrigued by the look of surprise on her face. And indeed Gruffydd's voice carried a note that warred with his seemingly genuine smile.

Despite Geoffrey's efforts to keep the conversation light and pleasant, the ensuing meal was an assay of wills: everyone seemed at war – John Lascelles spoke curtly to Burley, who joined them at the table, and seemed irritated by his wife's occasional lapses into Welsh when addressing Owen or her father; Richard de Burley lectured the company at large about the foolishness of the Duke's contradictory orders to reinforce the garrisons while at the same time recruiting archers from their ranks; Mistress Lascelles chided the constable on his poor manners. Gruffydd was the only one in the Cydweli party who seemed determined to enjoy the evening, asking Owen and Geoffrey about their travels and their impressions of Carreg Cennen and St David's. Mistress Lascelles graced her father with an affectionate smile whenever their eyes met.

As it grew late, Owen's mind wandered back to the day's events and he thought of Edern, searched the diners for his face, but saw him not. In Welsh he asked Mistress Lascelles why the priest who had escorted John de Reine's body was not included in their company at the high table.

Mistress Lascelles's white skin flushed as she glanced at her father, then Owen. 'Father Edern of St David's?'

Owen nodded.

'He is here?' she whispered.

'He seemed a suitable choice.'

'No doubt he put himself forward as such,' Gruffydd said. He made no effort to soften the words with a smile.

'I fear my question was clumsy,' Owen said. 'Forgive me, Mistress Lascelles.'

'You were right to ask about your companion,' she said, but she seemed to withdraw into herself. In a little while she rose and begged leave to retire.

Lascelles bowed to her. 'I shall join you later,' he said.

Gruffydd rose to follow his daughter, who already walked away. 'Tangwystl,' he called.

She paused, turned. 'I pray you, stay and entertain our guests in my stead.' She smiled. 'You should enjoy your evenings away from the farm.'

Gruffydd bowed to her and resumed his seat, though he watched her departure with anxious eyes.

Once Mistress Lascelles had departed, Geoffrey complained how weary he was. Soon he and Owen also took their leave of Lascelles. Gruffydd accompanied them to the door of the hall.

'Neither you nor the constable seems fond of Father Edern,' Owen commented. 'He seemed pleasant enough on the journey from St David's.'

'I do not know the constable's mind in this, Captain. My feelings about the man go back many years. They would not interest you.' He stretched, gazed up at the stars. 'The weather has turned in our favour. I bid you good-night, Captain, Master Chaucer. May you sleep well.' He strode away.

'A pleasant man,' Geoffrey said.

'He would certainly have us think so,' Owen said. 'It cannot be an easy thing, to know that all look on him and wonder whether he is a traitor to his king.'

'At least he does not hide.'

'I think his daughter is too fond to allow that. But he dines without his wife. Perhaps she finds it more difficult to face the questions in everyone's eyes.'

'Tangwystl,' Geoffrey said softly. 'A lovely name.'

'Aye, that it is.'

Dafydd ap Gwilym stepped to the edge of the cliff, his robes billowing in the up-draft, and opened his arms to embrace the day. The sea mist kissed his hair, beaded on his lashes, cooled his face. God's morning was magnificent. As he drew his eyes down from the heavens, he saw no break between the grey sky and the grey sea, which this morning appeared to lie placidly in the great arch of Cardigan Bay. A dangerous imagining, a placid sea. Dangerous to one who believed it. The white-tipped waves were merely veiled by the early morning fog, which also muted the sound of the sea crashing against the rocks below with a power mightier than any man might counter.

'I do not think we should take him so near the edge,' Brother Samson said in his low, booming tones. Dafydd had never noted how like the sea breaking on the rocks was Samson's voice.

'It is quite level here.' Dafydd held out his arm to the pilgrim, still unnamed, who limped towards him in the protective shelter of the monk's guiding hands.

The monk spoke softly to the young man, encouraging his efforts, but he glowered at Dafydd. 'You push him too far too quickly.'

Were all healers fretters? Was that what drew them to their calling? The pilgrim walked with a limp, to be sure, and the bandage round his head reminded Dafydd of his terrible injury. He looked weary already, head bowed and shoulders rounded, though he had made a good effort, taken perhaps a hundred steps from the house. Yet his expression, when he lifted his head to Dafydd's, was unchanged – resigned, despairing, ready to give up the effort as soon as permitted.

'Good lad,' Dafydd said. 'You will see, all this effort will prove worthwhile.' To Samson he whispered, 'We agreed that our pilgrim must build his strength for the journey.'

'Build his strength, yes. Such must be done gradually.' Samson, on the other hand, looked overfed and nervous, as if he needed a good month in the fields, preferably behind a plough.

Dafydd wearied of the monk's contrariness. 'You fret that the Duke's men will return, that we must hide our pilgrim, that we must make plans, and yet you wish to take your time readying him? Whence comes this sudden confidence that the Duke's men are not just down the hill?'

The short monk looked up at his charge, steadied him, then moved alone towards Dafydd. 'I am wise enough to know that I cannot change nature. Why do you whisper? Do you fear we will be overheard?'

'It is a morning for secrets and whispers. God sets the tone of the day – listen to the sea, how its voice is hushed by the fog.' Dafydd nodded towards the pilgrim, who had stepped to the edge of the bluff. 'You see? Is it as I said?'

He regretted his words at once as he saw the young man gaze down with such an expression of longing that Dafydd feared he had been unwise in trusting the pilgrim alone so near the edge. Dafydd took a step towards the young man. 'Are you dizzy?'

'I feel I could lean into the wind and go soaring out above the sea like a gull.'

'I do not think that is God's intention,' Samson said, with a nervous gesture as if he might stay the young man with a wave.

'I know I am not a gull.'

'But what are you, then?' Dafydd whispered. 'Are you Rhys?'

The young man turned back to the sea as if he had not heard. Dafydd wished that Dyfrig would return with the gossip from St David's.

Sir Robert had been most grateful to the white monk for his offer to escort him and Brother Michaelo on a circuit of the holy wells in the vicinity. Brother Dyfrig seemed a gentle soul with a ready laugh, and his familiarity with the countryside made him the perfect guide. At St Non's Well, as they awaited their turn at the stone-lined grotto, Dyfrig had mentioned Owen. 'It is a pity your one-eyed companion left in such haste. He might have found solace, perhaps even healing, here. Many eye afflictions have been cured by St Non.'

'He wished to stop here,' Sir Robert had told him. 'But the bishop sped him on his way.' Sir Robert watched as Brother Michaelo knelt on the stones, dipped his fingers in the well and pressed them to his temples. 'My companion hopes to find relief from his head ailment.' Feeling eyes on him, Sir Robert looked up, found a dark-haired man regarding him with a curious expression. He looked vaguely familiar.

'And you, Sir Robert?' Brother Dyfrig was saying. 'You are of a venerable age to undertake such a pilgrimage. From York, you said?'

'It is a long journey for me, but I have been singularly blessed in my old age. God has returned my only child's affections to me. And spared all the family in the last visitation of the pestilence.'

'So your purpose is to give thanks so that you may die in peace?'

'That is my wish.'

'I shall pray for you.' As Michaelo moved away from the well, Dyfrig caught Sir Robert's elbow and helped him drop to his knees on the stones at its edge. Sir Robert dipped his fingers in the well. The water was clear and cool. He crossed himself with his wet fingertips and was filled with a sense of peace. He prayed for Lucie and his grandchildren, and for Owen on his long journey home. When Sir Robert lifted his staff and planted it firmly so that he might use it to help him straighten up, he felt the monk's supporting hand under his elbow. 'You are good to me. God bless you, Brother Dyfrig.' Up higher on the slope, the stranger still regarded them. 'Do you know him?' Sir Robert asked, but by the time Dyfrig glanced up, the man was walking away.

'So many pilgrims. I should not wonder at meeting someone I know.'

They joined Brother Michaelo, who stood at the edge of the gently curving bowl in which sat the well and St Non's Chapel, gazing down at the sea. Sir Robert had not yet been to the cliff's edge. On either side stretched high, rocky cliffs ruffled with inlets, pocked with caves. Directly below them, a rock almost as high as the cliff had separated in some ancient time from the mainland and stood, a sentinel, in the inlet.

'At high tide it is an island,' Dyfrig said.

'That cave on the far side – how comes it to be light within?'

'Daylight from the other side,' Michaelo said. 'I can

see why our King worries about pirates and smugglers along this coast. One would never lack a cave in which to hide.'

'Such villains are rarer here than popular imagination would have it,' Dyfrig said. He turned towards the north-west. 'You should walk along the cliff when the sea is calm and the sky clear. From the north end of this finger of land you can see Ireland, just as Bendigeidfran, son of Llŷr, saw it when Matholwch's thirteen ships came across the sea for Branwen.'

Owen had recently told Sir Robert the story of Branwen, and it had caught his interest. 'Was this Llŷr's kingdom?' Sir Robert asked.

'All this land was his kingdom. But he was not at St Non's Bay when he saw the ships. He sat on a rock in Harddlech, in Ardudwy, at one of his courts.'

'You people speak of the folk in your tales as if they were real,' Brother Michaelo said with a smirk. 'But they are full of too many marvels to be real.'

Brother Dyfrig bowed his head, shook it as if considering something sad. 'What we now call marvels were once ordinary occurrences,' he said softly, as if to himself. 'How our glory has faded.'

Michaelo caught Sir Robert's eye. 'Dreamers,' he muttered. More loudly he said, 'If we are to visit St David's Well before sunset, we must continue.'

Dyfrig glanced out at the westering sun. 'You are right, my friend. Let us proceed.'

As they walked, Dyfrig kept one hand at Sir Robert's elbow, ready to assist him if he stumbled. The paths down to the harbour of Porth Clais were well worn, but muddy with the spring rains, and as they headed down the monk was particularly attentive. While they walked, they talked. 'The palace at St David's – is it comfortable?' Dyfrig asked.

'Certainly we have been provided with everything we could wish for. Bishop Houghton has been most kind,' said Sir Robert.

'There must have been much gossip among the pilgrims concerning the body left at Tower Gate.'

'Oh, indeed. Particularly as a young pilgrim had been missing for several days. Many feared evil had befallen him. They were much relieved to hear that it was not him.'

'The young man returned in good health?'

'Alas, so far he has not returned, nor has anyone come to claim his belongings.' Sir Robert paused at the edge of the sand, bothered by Dyfrig's question. 'But surely you know that Father Edern identified the dead man? I understood you were acquainted with the vicar.'

Brother Dyfrig smiled. 'I did know of it, to be sure. But the dead man also might have been considered a young man. I thought perhaps he had been the young pilgrim of whom you spoke.'

'No. The missing pilgrim was a Welshman. Rhys ap Llywelyn, I was told.'

Brother Michaelo, who had already reached the chapel, retraced his steps to urge them on. 'It grows late,' he whispered.

Sir Robert was embarrassed by his rude companion when Dyfrig had been so kind.

But Dyfrig seemed indifferent. 'Perhaps we should first go to the well, then the chapel if we have time.' He led them towards a small gathering behind the chapel. 'Has the bishop sent anyone out to search for the missing pilgrim?' he asked as they walked through the marshy field.

'I have heard nothing of a search for him,' Sir Robert said.

'But he left his belongings at the palace?'

'Yes.'

'He must be someone of stature to stay at the palace.'

'He had requested an audience with the bishop,' said Michaelo. 'You would do better to ask His Grace about the lad.'

Brother Dyfrig dropped the matter.

For once Sir Robert was grateful for Michaelo's rudeness. He did wish for some quiet in which to pray. The monk's loquacity seemed inappropriate.

Later, as they rested on the climb from Porth Clais to the cathedral close, Sir Robert being short of breath, the monk resumed his chatter, this time asking about Owen Archer and Geoffrey Chaucer. He had been surprised to learn that the former was Sir Robert's son-in-law. 'Then you are privy to his purpose in coming to Wales?'

'No secret has been made of his purpose. Wales is vulnerable to the French at a time when such weakness, both of fortifications and of spirit, is dangerous to the safety of the realm. He is recruiting archers for the Duke while his companion is inspecting the fortifications and the garrisons.'

'Indeed.'

Brother Michaelo had been silent since his outburst at the harbour. But as soon as he and Sir Robert parted from Brother Dyfrig at the palace, Michaelo turned to his companion and hissed, 'You lack all discretion. Do you not see that he is someone's agent? Did you not perceive the thrust of his questions?'

Indeed, as Sir Robert lay in his bed trying to sleep, he thought back on his conversations with the monk with growing unease. In the morning he went in search of Brother Dyfrig. He, too, could ask questions. He would know more of this Father Edern with whom Owen journeyed to Cydweli. But he was told that Brother Dyfrig had departed.

A cloudy, drizzly day in the stone world of a castle seemed greyer to Owen than the same weather in any other place. He had thought to string a bow, work the stiffness out of his arms today. But with the chill damp came the ache in his shoulder. 'I must do it when I dread it most,' he muttered.

'Are you penitential this morning?' Geoffrey's eyes twinkled. 'Did you dream of Mistress Tangwystl?'

Geoffrey plainly thought Tangwystl ferch Gruffydd the paragon of women. Indeed, she exhibited all the standards of beauty – she was slender, pale, graceful in movement, sweet of voice, gentle of smile, all her features fair and even, her hair a lustrous, fiery gold.

'If I do not work the shoulder, the stiffness will worsen.'

Geoffrey's grin broadened. 'I dreamed of her.'

His mood already sour, Owen found Geoffrey's silliness irritating. 'When was the last time you lifted a bow?'

'Me?' Geoffrey raised his short arms, looked at each in turn, then up at Owen with a comical expression. 'Does my body bear witness to such a skill?'

Why did he so enjoy playing the ass? 'You were

raised in a royal household, you would have been drilled at butts.'

A chuckle, a nod. 'And so I was. But it is a few years since I pulled back on a gut.'

'Come, then.'

'Is this my punishment for dreaming of the steward's wife?'

'It is my cure for giddiness.'

Geoffrey laughed at that, picked up his felt hat. 'I accept the challenge.'

As they left the guesthouse, they saw their hosts and Gruffydd ap Goronwy step out from the hall. Gruffydd walked between Lascelles and Tangwystl, slightly hunched forward, beetle-browed, talking excitedly. Lascelles was shaking his head. Tangwystl merely walked and listened. Suddenly all three paused.

'Oh, beauty, that you knew the spell you cast,' Geoffrey murmured.

The steward's lady stood tall, her long neck arched over her low-cut gown. She looked demurely away as one very white hand, her right, was lifted high by her father. He reached for Lascelles's right hand.

'It would seem that father has decreed a reconciliation,' Owen said.

'It is not working,' Geoffrey said as Gruffydd joined their hands. 'Look at their faces.'

Husband and wife both kept their eyes averted, as if disowning the hands Gruffydd held so firmly.

Owen put his hand on Geoffrey's shoulder. 'Come. I doubt they want witnesses.'

But Geoffrey had other plans. 'I would seek out Edern, see how he fares.'

'You are lazy.'

'I would hear what arrangements they have made for John de Reine.'

'As you wish.'

Owen sought out the practice yard. He should see it soon, gauge Burley's progress in gathering the requested archers. He did not expect the recruits to have arrived, but surely he might see a tun of arrow staves and bows for practice, some butts, and where there was a practice yard there would be a hungry soldier who knew his way around the kitchens. Sharing food often made a soldier talkative. Owen might learn more about John de Reine and his aborted journey to Carreg Cennen.

The outer ward of Cydweli Castle was D-shaped, with the straight line along the high bluff over the Gwendraeth, facing south-east. The inner ward was a square with towers at each corner. The main hall stretched along the south-east wall within the inner ward; the guesthouse sat opposite, in the shadow of the north-west wall. Owen guessed that the practice yard would be in the outer ward, which was a bow-shaped area within the arch of the outer walls. Since he had entered by the south gatehouse, he chose the opposite direction, leaving the inner ward by a doorway next to the north-east tower. There he found a north gatehouse, not as impressive as the one on the town side, but well guarded. One of the men directed him round the north-west tower to the practice yard.

It would have been difficult to miss, occupied as it was at the moment by a pair of grunting wrestlers. They were stripped to their leggings and well oiled with sweat, their muscles taut and their expressions fierce. One glanced up at Owen – a momentary shift in his attention that lost him the round as his opponent took advantage of his lapse and pinned him down. Owen nodded to the men and made his way to a wooden tun in a small, open-fronted shed behind them. He was about to lift the lid when a hand clamped firmly down on his forearm.

'A curious stranger is a dead one in such times,' a gruff voice warned in English with a strong Welsh accent. It belonged to the victor in the wrestling match.

'Owen Archer,' Owen said in Welsh. 'Former captain of archers for the old Duke.'

'Owen Archer?' The man stepped back, considered Owen. 'They did say you carried a scar. Welcome to you.' He slipped his hand down to Owen's, clasped it. 'Simwnt is the name. Harold is the one shouting for another match. He cannot speak our language, so we had best continue in English.'

'I was hoping this tun held bows and arrow staves,' Owen said.

'That it does, Captain.' As Simwnt spoke, he pulled on a shirt and then proceeded to use the left sleeve to wipe the sweat from his brow. 'But we have no archers to show you yet.'

'I can wait a while for that. Food is what I need at present.'

A broad grin that showed small, surprisingly perfect teeth. 'We put aside a morsel of bread and sausage – we might truck the food with you for a good tale. A particular tale.'

'And what tale might that be?'

'The death of our friend John. John de Reine, whose requiem Mass we attend this day. They say you found him.'

'No, but I have seen him. And I know something of the circumstance.'

'Aye. That's what we will be wanting. Harold here was his man, you see.'

God smiled on Owen. Simwnt and Harold seemed men with whom he could be easy. 'I will gladly tell you what I know for some food.' Owen eased down on a stone bench built into the wall.

After his carefully selective narrative of events, Owen grew quiet. Soon Harold was talking of Reine, his excellent character, his puzzling change of plans. 'He said he would be gone a week, no more, and I was to be ready to ride with him to Carreg Cennen on his return. I did not like it, him riding off alone, but what could I do?' His voice had grown gruff with emotion.

'He was not ordered elsewhere?' Owen asked.

'Oh no. Burley was that mad when he found Reine gone and me still about. "A week. Where is he off to for a bloody week?" he shouted.'

'St David's,' Owen said.

'Aye,' Harold whispered.

Later, after attending the Mass for John de Reine, Owen strolled over to watch the masons at work on the south gatehouse. Harold and Simwnt had bragged about it, calling it the grandest design, thanks to the good Duke, who saw fit to make his castle of Cydweli as grand as any in England. Owen did not mention how much larger and grander was the Duke's castle of Kenilworth. Grand castles were for living; grand gatehouses were for defence. And as ever in this country the question was whether Lancaster fortified Cydweli against the Welsh or the French. Or both.

'It will be a wonder when completed,' said Gruffydd ap Goronwy, joining him where he stood gazing up the scaffolding. 'Prison to one side, porter's lodge to the other. Not one, but three murder holes.' He chuckled. 'They fear us, these English, eh?'

Had he read Owen's thoughts? 'It is the French that are feared at present,' he said to cover his confusion.

Gruffydd dropped his eyes. 'You have heard of my disgrace.'

It had slipped Owen's mind. 'Forgive me. I meant nothing by it.'

'And why should we not allow the heir to the great Llywelyn to land on these shores? Stay – I know the answer. The French would use Owain ap Thomas ap Rhodri to destroy the Marcher lords and then step over him to claim the victory. I am not such a fool as to think they wish us well.'

'I am glad to hear that. I like to think that my countrymen are not so desperate they will act foolishly.'

Gruffydd turned to Owen, nodded as if approving what he had said. 'Your countrymen. I am glad you still think of this as your country. Which brings me to the matter I wished to discuss. They say you entered the service of Henry of Grosmont from this very castle. Is that true?'

'It is.'

'Are your kin still here?'

'They were here when I departed. My parents and siblings. They had come down from the north. Llŷn.'

'I believe I may know your brother.'

Owen's heart raced. 'My brother Dafydd?'

'No. Morgan. Morgan ap Rhodri ap Maredudd.'

His mother's youngest child, still quite young when Owen left. 'He would not know me.'

'Then you did have a brother by that name. Dark, slight?'

'It was feared he would not survive to manhood. He was a sickly child.' An unpleasant child, difficult to love. What did it mean that he was the one Gruffydd mentioned? Surely the eldest would be most prominent in the area.

Gruffydd was nodding enthusiastically. 'It is him. It must be him. I shall go to him. Invite him to the castle.' Spoken as if he were lord of Cydweli.

'You have heard nothing of Dafydd?'

Gruffydd threw up his hands. 'I did not know to ask. I shall. Who can say what wonders I shall uncover, eh?'

Nine

ANTICIPATION

Gruffydd had marched away with a purposeful
stride. Perhaps he would bring not only Morgan
to the castle but Dafydd, Angie, Gwen, Owen's
parents, Rhodri and Angharad.

As Owen walked back to the guesthouse, he tried
to imagine how it would feel to see his family after all
this time. He doubted he would recognise any of them.
And what would they think of him, scarred and with
an accent that testified to his years in the service of the
English King? Though his parents would remember
that he had saved the family by going into the Duke's
service, would his siblings remember? He feared this
home-coming might prove a bitter draught.

Owen found Geoffrey slumped over a table beneath
the window in their chamber, a cup of wine in one
hand, his other hand stretched out across a parchment, touching a pen but not holding it, though he
stared at it, his face a study in melancholy.

Owen had never seen Geoffrey in such a mood. 'Are you unwell?'

Geoffrey sighed, lifted the pen and set it by his ink pot, pushed back his stool. 'Would that I were, then I might have stayed here this afternoon and avoided humiliation.' He did not look up at Owen, but spoke as if to the wall opposite.

'You went to Edern?'

'I did, but found I must wait until after the Mass to speak with him.'

'And— ?'

'I found—' Geoffrey shook his head.

'He insulted you?'

'No. I was the author of my own shame. Edern is unaware of it.'

'Will you tell me what happened?'

'I found the vicar in the chapel committing— By God! I am well aware such things go on, but never did I think to witness it.'

'Geoffrey.'

'I found him riding Mistress Lascelles's maid. No, in truth she rode him, her breasts slapping against her waist. So huge and heavy they were. And she squealed and giggled as he moaned.' Suddenly, Geoffrey turned to Owen, who had embraced the comical scene conjured by the words as a welcome relief from his thoughts of his family and now could not stop smiling in time. Geoffrey blushed. 'Not that I find large breasts . . . And such enthusiasm . . . Sweet Jesu, in the *chapel*, Owen. After such a solemn Mass.'

'And that is what has brought on this melancholy?'

'Father Francis, the chaplain, found me in the doorway. What must he think?'

Owen fought to regain a solemn expression. 'Unfortunate.'

'Mine was an honest mistake. As I approached, a man hurried from the chapel, muttering to himself – would that I had been closer, perhaps he would have seen me and warned me away.'

'And thus you sit so, unable to write.'

'Worse was to come.'

'Worse? Perhaps I ought to visit the chapel . . .'

'You would not – You make merry of me.'

'In faith, I thought to put you at ease.'

'You choose an odd method of easement.'

'I pray you, tell me what caused your melancholy.'

'The chaplain – what he told me. Gladys – that is Mistress Lascelles's maid – lies with any and all men in the castle, but particularly John Lascelles.' Geoffrey spoke the last four words slowly, watching for a reaction.

Owen thought it a pity that the steward's eye wandered so early in marriage, but such men were sadly common. And yet . . . 'I thought Sir John worshipped his young wife. Else why risk union with the family of a man accused of treason?'

'A woman adored is not always a woman bedded.'

'Aye. And ladies' maids have betrayed their mistresses before.'

'At their mistress's bidding?'

Now he had Owen's full attention. He eased down on to the seat opposite Geoffrey. 'What do you mean?'

'What I said. She has encouraged Gladys and her husband.'

'Should the chaplain have spoken of any of this?'

'It grows complicated.'

'Indeed.'

'He – Father Francis, the chaplain – is certain that Edern has been brought back to resume his duties as chaplain – because Francis – a most pathetic, paunchy, mewling creature – was discovered with Gladys much as I discovered Edern this day. So he wishes me to reveal to Sir John what I witnessed. That Edern is no better than he should be, or at least no better than Francis.'

'But why would he tell you about Sir John and the maid?'

'I protested. I would not disturb Sir John, and through him his lady, for anything. And in any case, Edern was not brought back to resume duties as chaplain.'

'You are a gentle heart, Geoffrey. This chaplain could learn much from you about Christian charity.'

'He did not see it so.'

'Did you agree to speak with Sir John?'

'I muttered a curse in Italian in such a tone he believed me to be promising my help.'

'You made good use of your wit.'

'It is only a halfwit who walks into trouble and then reasons himself out of it.'

Tonight Gruffydd ap Goronwy wore a simple gown befitting a man of his stature, but made of silk, which caught the light and called attention to him. Quite a peacock, Tangwystl's father. Was that why his wife did not accompany him to the castle – because she was busy at home working on his extensive wardrobe?

Gruffydd's dark eyes swept the room. When he

saw Owen, he lifted his chin and eyebrows in a mute greeting and moved towards him through the crowd. As he drew near, Gruffydd grew sombre. Owen guessed he had been wrong about the man he had thought to be his brother Morgan.

'You are looking well this evening,' Owen said.

'God has ever blessed my line with good health, Captain.' Stepping closer, Gruffydd bowed his head slightly and said in a quieter voice, 'I have spoken with your brother.'

Owen's heart gladdened. 'I had thought, when you arrived alone . . .'

A shake of the head. 'He would not come to the castle.'

'Why not?'

'He did not explain. But he invites you, indeed, implores you to come to him.'

'He is unwell? He cannot travel?'

'You will find him well. I shall tell you how to find him.'

Owen could not bring himself to ask about the others.

Dafydd ap Gwilym watched the sunrise, remembering how a spring sunrise long ago caught his love's hair and warmed it slowly from a pale yellow to red–gold, each strand burnished anew as the sun climbed the heavens. She, too, had warmed with the morning, as if kindled by the sun.

Not by his ardour, though he had foolishly thought she loved him. They never loved him well enough to defy their kin and run away with him. A woman loves a poet's praises, the promise of fame and immortality in his songs. But she lusts for a soldier and marries a man of property.

He blinked at the melancholy thoughts. Whence came such shadows on this exquisite morning? Perhaps it was his imminent departure from this beloved place that darkened his mood and his memories. He must shrug off this gloom else he would be no good at convincing the men from Cydweli – whose return was inevitable – that the house had been as empty when last they came as it was now, and that Dafydd had no other goal in the world than his work.

Brother Samson and the pilgrim had departed yesterday for Strata Florida. A good three days' journey on horseback, perhaps four, considering how Samson worried over the young man. Was Samson so old in spirit he had forgotten the resilience of youth? How quickly bones knit, wounds closed, scars faded, muscles eased? Ah, to be young again. It had been nothing for Dafydd to walk over mountains to revisit a lake noted in passing, to refresh his memory as he strove to describe a tree under which he had napped, a glade he had enjoyed with a sweetheart. He would give anything to trade places with the pilgrim.

Enough of that. He would soon prove his mettle when he followed on their trail. But first he would have some sport with the Cydweli men. He awaited their return. Had he gone with Samson and the pilgrim, the men would have found a house empty and would seek the pilgrim's trail. But if they returned to see everything as it had been before – as far as they knew – they might be less diligent about seeking that trail.

Dafydd looked forward to another round with the

men. He had precious few diversions beyond his poetry these days. Each one was to be savoured.

Stretching to his full height, Dafydd took one last look at the sunlit Irish sea and turned towards the house, whistling for his dogs. Nest and Cadwy abandoned their explorations in the gorse and followed. Dafydd walked slowly, making note of the crocuses, the birdsong, the budding trees. When he returned from Strata Florida, where he intended to spend some time in prayer, summer would be full blown – or worse, he might be delayed until the autumn. Who knew what adventures lie ahead?

For he knew not the truth of the pilgrim's story. He knew not whether the armed bullies from Cydweli were right to claim him. He knew not how safe Brother Samson was, travelling with only a young lay brother and the pilgrim.

And it was just that uncertainty that made it worth a temporary absence from this beloved spot. He felt alive, and younger than before he had encountered the pilgrim on Whitesands.

God be praised.

Ten

KIN

Morgan ap Rhodri's house stood on a slope at the narrow end of a valley that rose just beyond to a mountain striped with rushing streams. This was not the homestead of Owen's latter youth; indeed, the setting put him more in mind of Llŷn. How quickly the land changed in just a few hours' ride from Cydweli. The house was long and low, a modest farmhouse, whitewashed and neatly thatched. Chickens pecked in the yard and a nanny goat and her kids gave him a slit-eyed examination from a paddock next to the house.

A woman sat in the doorway mixing something in a large bowl and rocking a cradle with her bare foot. She rose to greet Owen, but as she ceased her rocking the baby cried out in protest. The woman quickly set down the bowl and retrieved the wailing child. By now Owen was close enough to see a pleasant, very young face peering out from the intricately folded wimple. She was quick and compact in movement.

'Owain ap Rhodri?' she asked.

He was glad he had not come here before his ear had readjusted to the language, for her accent was strong. 'Forgive me for coming unannounced,' he said in Welsh, 'I did not wish to wait until a messenger might arrange a meeting.'

'And so you should not, being kin!' She touched her left eye with her free hand. 'So the tales about your eye are true. By a woman's hand, they say. Was it for looking at her?' Her eyes teased.

'She was not a beauty. I had no joy in the struggle.'

'I am sorry for that.' A dimpled smile.

Owen found her charming. 'I do not know your name.'

'I am Elen.'

'When did you hear of my scarred eye?'

'Your arrival at Cydweli has been the talk of the valley for days.'

'Has it indeed! That is a wonder, for I swear I have never set foot in this valley before.'

'We have several youths who hope to be chosen archers for the Duke.'

'Ah. I hope they do not regret their eagerness.'

Elen looked puzzled by his words.

'It is no matter. Why would Morgan not come to see me at Cydweli?'

Elen ducked her head. 'I leave that to my husband to explain. Come. He is near, mending a fallen wall.'

As they began to walk, Owen peered down at the baby, who was preparing to make a fresh clamour. 'And who is this, with a shock of red fuzz to rival my brother Dafydd's?'

'Your youngest nephew, Luc.'

The baby clasped the forefinger Owen offered and held firm, inspiring both adults to laughter.

'He is a strong one,' Owen said.

'Stubborn, is more like.' Elen's giggle was merry and disarming.

They had skirted the paddock and now turned towards the mountain. A low wall encircled an orchard that held perhaps threescore trees of varying age.

'The orchard was wild when Morgan came here,' Elen said. 'My father thought an orchard a gentleman's endeavour, not worth a farmer's time. But Morgan loves the trees and the fruit.'

He took after their mother in that. 'So this is your family's farm?'

'Aye.'

'It is beautiful.'

'It was not always so.' Elen stopped, pointed to a figure in the distance, at the far end of the orchard, crouching by the wall. 'There he is. Go, then. He will be glad to see you.'

A breeze with a touch of ice in it swept down from the mountain, making the orchard cool even in the sunlight. Owen's boots made sucking noises in the grass. Boggy for an orchard. But it looked healthy. Owen's mother had once told him that no matter how experienced and hard-working the farmer, if he did not believe in the earth he tilled he would reap poor harvests.

In his infancy Morgan had suffered from a stomach flux and recurrent rashes. It had stunted his growth, his mother believed. She had coaxed Rhodri into allowing her to take the boy to St David's and the holy wells surrounding it, hoping that the healing waters might cure him. Owen, thirteen years old, had accompanied her to the far west. Morgan had suffered much of the way with a terrible rash. He would wake in the morning bloody from scratching in his sleep. At one point Owen's mother hesitated, wondering whether it was safe to take the boy farther, but a dream convinced her that her son would be cured by the waters. At St Non's Well, they dipped bandages into the water and wrapped Morgan's raw forearms, one thigh that was seeping. Then they continued on to the cathedral city, where Owen's mother prostrated herself in the central aisle of the nave after praying before the shrine of her eldest son's patron saint.

In the morning, Morgan's rash was gone. Within three days, his stomach quieted. By summer's end he had grown three fingers taller.

Such a cure would make a man staunch in his faith. For certain that faith was at work in this orchard.

Now he was close, Owen wondered yet again what he should say to this brother he hardly knew. Begin with an apology for his years away? Explain why he was there? But Gruffydd had likely told him that. Compliment him on his lovely wife? She seemed young, but then Morgan was twelve years younger than Owen; he might be ten years older than his wife. Had he married late? Many men did if they could not afford their own land. Had he married Elen for this farm? It was an unusual thing for a Welsh family, to give such a farm to a daughter and her husband.

Morgan's head jerked up. He had at last noticed that he was not alone in the orchard. He lowered the stone he had been fitting into the crumbling wall, rose slowly, brushed off his hands on his tunic. Unlike many of his countrymen, he wore leggings, though like Elen his feet were bare. He did not look much taller than his wife, and was slender as a boy, with hair as dark as Owen's. He shaded his eyes and stared at Owen, then began to nod.

'You look like the Devil himself, brother.'

Morgan had blue eyes so pale some folk at the wells had thought him blind, skin so pale it showed every welt, every emotion. All still the same. But there were deep ridges in his face from nose to chin, and his voice had a huskiness to it that did not sound healthy.

'I *should* look like the Devil,' Owen said. 'It has been a long journey to this day.'

Morgan stepped forward, held out his hand. 'That it has.'

They clasped hands, then embraced. Morgan was even thinner than he looked. He stepped back first, gazed up into Owen's face.

'You have not had an easy time of it, then.'

'It is not for that a man goes soldiering.'

'You have the Duke of Lancaster's trust. You have done well.'

'It is my wife and children who make me proud.'

'She is English?'

'She is.'

'Is that why you wear that beard?'

Owen touched his chin. 'She has never seen me without it.'

'Then it would be best not to shave it off and frighten the children.'

Owen grinned, thinking Morgan made a joke. But

his brother was not smiling. 'Elen tells me that you have transformed this orchard.'

Morgan gazed at him quietly for a moment, then shook his head as if just noticing Owen had spoken. 'Her father did not think an orchard a fitting thing for this valley. God felt otherwise.'

Owen had never known how to respond to such comments from anyone. Could a mortal be so sure of God's purpose? Owen considered the mountain above with its rushing streams, the boggy soil. He could understand why someone might abandon an orchard in this place. And yet some of the trees were quite old, which proved survival was possible here. Perhaps that was what his brother meant, that the trees were a sign that God had blessed this improbable place.

'God has been good to you.'

Morgan nodded.

Owen grew uncomfortable under his brother's intense gaze. 'Why did you not come to the castle with Gruffydd ap Goronwy?'

'I must think of my family. Our honour.'

'It would be dishonourable to dine with me at the castle?'

'With him. Gruffydd. He is a traitor.' The blue eyes burned into Owen.

'To the English King, perhaps. But our countrymen might think otherwise.'

'A traitor is a traitor, no matter whose side he betrays.'

'Ah.' So Morgan was quite the moralist. 'And those in power might remember that you had accompanied him.'

'Why have you befriended him?'

'I do not know that I have. But I thought that he might know our family, who were also settled on escheated land. I see that you have risen above that trouble.'

'I was fortunate in my first wife. The youngest daughter of an old family much respected.'

'First wife? Then Elen is—'

'My second wife. My first died giving birth to our third child. But I forget my manners. Come to the house. You must try Elen's cider.'

They walked slowly through the orchard as Morgan talked about the trees, pointing out the heavy bearers, telling their ages. He sounded a happy man despite his frailty.

'What of the others? Our parents? Angie and Gwen? Dafydd?'

Morgan paused, scratched his head. 'You have heard nothing?'

'You are the first one I have seen.'

'And I shall be the last. You should have come sooner if you hoped for more.'

It was a cool way to impart such terrible news to kin. Granted, it was something Owen had feared, but had it been his ill fortune to give Morgan such news he would have found a way to soften the blow. 'God grant them peace.'

'Gwen still lives,' Morgan said as he resumed his slow pace. 'In a convent in Usk.'

'Gwen? A nun?' Owen's voice cracked with relief and a sudden, nervous inclination to laugh.

Morgan sniffed. 'You should be proud.'

'I am. Proud and full of gladness to hear she is alive.'

And wishing he were in Usk now, not walking beside this cold brother.

'The others are all gone. I shall do my best to answer your questions in the house.'

Elen had moved the cradle inside and greeted them at the door with foaming cups of cider. As she handed Owen a cup she searched his eye, touched his shoulder. 'I see that my husband has rushed ahead with all the sad news you must have dreaded to hear.'

'You would be wrong in that, wife,' Morgan said. 'I have not told him the tale of our father's passing.'

They had but sat down on facing benches placed near the sole window when Morgan said, 'You should know that our father was struck by lightning while working in the fields.'

'God's blood.' Did his brother enjoy imparting bad news with such a blunt thrust?

'Aye, it was a sudden bolt, no warning. No storm approached, nor did one all that day. All of Cydweli talked about it for years – I am surprised no one told you of this. I think that is what softened their hearts towards us, our father's terrible death.'

'How long ago did this happen?'

'The year of the great mortality. His death was an omen.'

So his father had lived only a few years after Owen's departure. He had guessed his father would go before his mother – Rhodri had little patience with Angharad's efforts to fortify the family against illnesses, and had a quick temper. But so long ago. And in such a strange accident. 'I have heard of such things happening, but to our father. Sweet Jesu.'

Morgan's posture was oddly rigid, his back straight,

his hands on his knees. 'I do not like to think for what terrible sin he was so punished.' He pressed his lips together in disapproval.

'Morgan!' Elen hissed.

Owen looked from Elen's eyes, dark with distress, to his brother's pinched expression. 'Our father was a good man.'

'A good man does not die by fire.'

'I watched many good men die by fire and worse, Morgan.'

'We all have hidden sins.'

Owen fought down angry words. 'What of the others?'

'Our mother saw my first two children. The second coming of the pestilence took her. Our brother Dafydd died of a fever. He had lost a leg – his wagon had fallen on him as he changed a wheel. Many said that had our mother been alive he might yet live. The barber hurried through his work and took no care with his patients. But God chooses our coming and our going.' Morgan closed his eyes a moment.

Who was left? 'Angie?'

Morgan looked straight into Owen's eye, still showing no emotion. 'Sweet Angie. She died giving birth to a stillborn child.' The pale eyes blinked once. 'I am sorry to give you so much sadness, but I do not think it is kinder in the end to tell the tale more slowly.'

Owen turned to stare out the window at the gentle rise that led to the house. 'How long ago did Dafydd and Angie die?' he whispered.

'Dafydd a few years ago. Angie died six years ago.'

At least his mother had not outlived her children,

which was said to be a mother's curse. It gave Owen little comfort. Had he returned but three years ago he might have seen Dafydd, told him how often he thought of him. One thing was certain, Dafydd would have had little patience with Morgan.

As soon as courtesy allowed, Owen took his leave of his brother and Elen and rode back to Cydweli. Apprehensive he had been on his riding out; now he saw that his dread had not been inappropriate. What cruel gift was this to reunite him with the one member of his family he found it difficult to love, impossible to like? God tested him harshly. To hear of one death would have been difficult enough, but four, and one of them so terrible as his father's. Owen's stomach churned as he remembered Morgan's suspicion, *for what terrible sin*. God help him, but he did not see how he could ever forgive his brother for those words.

Weary and heavy-hearted, Owen wished a good day to the guard at the south gate of the castle. He was rewarded with the news that Burley awaited him in the guesthouse hall. He knew better than to ask the constable's purpose. Burley gave orders; he did not explain.

Geoffrey already sat with the constable, and from the droop of his eyelids and the ruddiness of his nose Owen guessed they had sat so for quite a while, shared several cups of wine or ale.

Burley rose at Owen's approach and was surprisingly courteous, offering wine, asking after his brother, apologising for taking his time. His rough voice and abrupt phrases made it plain he found the courtesy unfamiliar and difficult. Owen wondered at his game. But he responded in kind, settled down on a chair and stretched his legs out to the fire burning smokily in the middle of the room, told them of his brother's fine orchard, lovely wife, son who had Dafydd's magnificent hair.

'But you have not come to while away the time talking of my family,' Owen said when he had told them all he cared to. 'Are you here to talk of archers? The garrison?'

Burley wagged his head from side to side. 'My plan was to recruit archers after you arrived. I can tell you that word has already spread among the young men in the March of Cydweli, and they are eager. We shall have no difficulty providing you with the number you require.'

'I am glad of it.'

'As for the garrison, I have encouraged Master Chaucer to move freely among the men, ask what he will, observe them at their stations. I have already provided him with numbers and watches.'

Geoffrey nodded, tapped a parchment beneath his elbow.

'Of course you are also free to move among them,' Burley added.

'I thank you, Constable.' Owen glanced from Geoffrey to Burley, felt a tension between them that had yet to be explained. 'Well, then, you have completed your work without me,' he said, pretending to rise.

'Stay a moment,' said Burley. 'If you would,' he added more softly. 'There is one more item.'

'Is there?' Owen eased back in his chair, propped his feet on the bench opposite.

'The death of John de Reine. What more can you tell me of the event? You say he was left at a gate to the cathedral close in St David's. Did anyone see who left him? Where had he been? How had he died?'

'No one had come forward to say they had seen him left there,' Owen said. 'There was a quantity of sand in Reine's clothes. White sand. But when he had been on the beach, why, how he died, other than the knife wound in his gut—' Owen shook his head. 'I can tell you no more.'

'Why was he in St David's?'

'We do not know. Nor did Bishop Houghton, so I would doubt he had yet been in the city.'

'If not St David's, where?'

'I do not know. Perhaps in the hospice at Llandruidion if he went there as a pilgrim.'

'He was to meet you in Carreg Cennen,' Burley said. 'Why should he suddenly embark on a pilgrimage instead?'

'I did not know him,' Owen said. 'I had hoped you might know his heart.'

'I was his commander, not his confessor,' Burley said. He dropped his gaze to the table, shook his head, and said nothing for a while. Then with a sigh and another shake of the head he looked at Geoffrey, then Owen, and asked, 'Was Whitesands his goal? Or Porth Clais? He did not take his man with him. Had he something to hide, did he await a ship?'

Owen wondered whether the constable's purpose was to sow seeds of doubt about Reine, or whether he asked the question in innocence. 'You suggest he was one of Owain Lawgoch's supporters?'

'It is possible, is it not?'

'Being an Englishman, he is not likely to have supported Lawgoch,' Geoffrey said. 'What say you, Owen?'

'I doubt it. What would be his purpose?'

Burley took a deep breath, nodded as if satisfied. 'I am glad to think well of him. You can tell me nothing else?'

'I can think of nothing,' Owen said.

'Indeed,' Geoffrey said, 'Father Edern was commissioned by Bishop Houghton to learn why Reine and four more of your men were in the bishop's March without permission.'

Owen and Geoffrey exchanged glances as Burley dipped his head and cleared his throat. They had agreed, with Edern's blessing, that they would wait until Burley was alone to confront him about the men. As Lascelles did not seem to interfere in Burley's command they assumed the constable was the one who had sent them.

'How did you hear of them?' Burley fought hard to control his voice, but a vein pulsed in his temple, revealing his agitation.

'They pounded on the bishop's door and demanded to see the body delivered up to him,' Geoffrey said. 'One might say they rudely announced themselves.'

'Ah.' Burley's hands clenched the edge of the table. 'And they were permitted to see him?'

'No,' Geoffrey said. 'They had no letters of safe conduct. An unfortunate omission.'

Burley made a dismissive gesture. 'I saw no need for such letters. My men were told to move discreetly along the trail of the thief.'

'Doing what, Constable?' Owen asked. 'Pounding

on the bishop's door was hardly a discreet move. What is the vicar to tell the bishop?'

Burley had managed to compose himself. His hands relaxed, the pulse quieted. 'That my men were after the thief of the exchequer.'

'In St David's?' Owen asked.

'They followed the trail of a man heard boasting in a Cydweli tavern that he would soon embarrass the entire garrison, and sweeten the victory with a fistful of gold.'

Interesting. The bishop had been told that the injured receiver had identified his attacker. 'Who was this man?' Owen asked.

'A stranger. A Welshman.'

'Might Edern speak with the man who reported this?' Geoffrey asked.

Burley rose. 'I am sorry to say he is one of the men who so disturbed the bishop. They have not yet returned. I thank you for taking the time to talk of this. I shall seek out the vicar and assure him that my men meant no disrespect.'

'That will mean little to the bishop,' Geoffrey said. 'You sent men into his lordship without his permission to remove a felon. You have no such authority.'

Owen was puzzled by Geoffrey's uncharacteristically sharp tone.

'How could I know the trail would lead to St David's? I shall express my deepest apologies,' Burley snarled, and strode from the room.

'Arrogant knave!' Geoffrey hissed as the door closed behind Burley.

Owen found the parting more reassuring than Burley's sincere guise. 'I wonder what version of the story the constable provided for the steward?' Owen said.

Geoffrey warmed his hands before the dying fire. 'I wondered, too.' He turned round, lifted the back of his gown to warm his ankles and calves. 'I asked after the receiver – did I tell you? "He is still abed, his wits addled by the attack," Burley said. More than a fortnight to recover, and yet he was able to identify his attacker at the time.'

'What did Burley say to that?'

Geoffrey made a face. 'I had not the courage to ask.'

'His story is not very convincing. I should like to know more about the receiver.'

Geoffrey hopped up on to the edge of the table by Owen. 'I was able to discover that he lives in the town, and that he was alone in the exchequer and thus the only witness, but no more. He is Welsh, though you would not guess it from his name – Roger Aylward. I thought you might have more luck with him than I would.'

'Why so curious about all this? We should see to our business with the steward and the constable, then depart.'

'How do we know none of this has to do with Owain Lawgoch? Or whatever Gruffydd ap Goronwy did that turned Pembroke's mother against him.'

True enough. 'The receiver lives in the town, does he? I like to hear that, but I wonder what it means?'

'Means? It is not proper for the receiver to live in the town?'

'There was a time when the Welsh were banned from the town. No doubt that is still the law, but it has become inconvenient. Still, I should think the Welsh who are accepted within the walls have proven themselves loyal to Lancaster.'

'And thus a fitting choice for receiver.'

'Or he has bought his way in, won the support of the steward or the constable . . .'

Geoffrey closed his eyes, nodded vigorously. 'Of course. Well. You shall take the measure of the man when you attend his sickbed, eh?'

But Owen's thoughts had turned to the strained relationship between Lascelles and the constable. 'What of Burley's comment that he had not known the thief's trail would lead to St David's? Is it possible that Burley's men followed Reine's trail? By design or by accident?'

Geoffrey jumped down from the table. 'Enough of this. How did you find your brother?'

'Ask me tomorrow,' Owen said. 'I have much to think about. And some mourning.'

Owen thought to excuse himself from supper, but he and Geoffrey were invited to dine with Lascelles in his chamber. Geoffrey considered it an honour; Owen dreaded it. What further unpleasantness was in store for him this day?

The steward's quarters were not above the dais end of the hall as Owen would have expected, but rather above the south end, adjacent to the chapel tower. Two large rooms, one glimpsed through an inner door, with a huge, tapestry-hung bed and a high window that looked on the river, and the anteroom, in which they stood, with an ornate table and throne-like chairs.

'Magnificent,' Geoffrey said, running his hand along the back of a chair, feeling the intricate carving.

'My parents thought to offer some civilised comforts to my new bride,' Lascelles said as Owen and Geoffrey took their seats.

'I am most grateful to them,' Geoffrey said as he wiggled into a comfortable position. He was in remarkably good humour for a man who had spent the better part of the afternoon with Burley. The knack of a professional diplomat, Owen guessed.

Owen, on the other hand, found Lascelles a puzzle he could not resist. 'You have been long in Cydweli,' Owen said. 'You must be anxious to return to England and present Mistress Lascelles to your family. Or did they journey to Cydweli for the wedding?'

Lascelles's laugh was surprisingly bitter. 'The table and chairs, the bed, those gestures might be made quietly, without being noted by gossips. I have not married well in their eyes – in anyone's eyes.'

'They will think differently when they meet her,' Owen said, feeling guilty for having broached a painful subject.

'Will Mistress Lascelles be joining us?' Geoffrey asked.

Lascelles made a noise deep in his throat and motioned to a servant to pour the wine. 'My wife took it into her head to pay a visit to her mother today. She will be gone the night.'

'Is her mother unwell?' Geoffrey asked.

'Slow of wit is more like. Mistress Goronwy—' As Lascelles's tongue twisted on the name, Owen realised the man had already imbibed a goodly amount of wine. The steward shook his head as if to clear it. 'My wife's mother behaves as if I had not put all right with her good husband. She mourns her home in Tenby and complains that all her neighbours shun her. And yet she refuses our hospitality. Gruffydd must come without her to see his daughter. Thus I am denied my wife tonight so that she may stay in a common farmhouse and coddle her addlebrained dam.'

Owen found Tangwystl's absence an odd thing for Lascelles to complain about after what he had heard from Geoffrey regarding the maid Gladys. Weary of courtesies, Owen asked, 'Does her maid attend her?'

Geoffrey nudged Owen under the table and looked about to choke on a mouthful of wine.

Lascelles snorted. 'Why? You have a taste for Gladys tonight? She is yours for the asking, Captain. She is any man's for the asking, truth be told. They tell me even the one-legged beggar in the market square has tasted of her. No, she is not abroad with my wife. She has fallen out of favour with Mistress Lascelles since—' He passed a hand over his eyes. 'Forgive me. I invited you here to enjoy a quiet supper in thanks for your respect for John de Reine. Forgive me.'

'Father Edern is as worthy of thanks as we are,' Geoffrey said.

Lascelles adjusted his chair slightly, studied Geoffrey for a moment. 'You offer him up as if the bishop honoured me with his presence. Yet just last night Father Francis told me of something you witnessed that should give you pause in praising the man.'

Geoffrey coloured. 'In faith your chaplain is a

meddlesome creature. I saw no purpose in telling you of the incident. But it seems Father Francis fears Edern has been sent to replace him. I am sure he wished you to know that Edern was no better than he. A sorry lot, these clerics.'

'Which is why I never invite them to dine in my rooms,' Lascelles said. 'But you remind me of my duties. I shall send for him to join us afterwards for some brandywine.' He called over the servant, explained the errand.

As the fish course was served, Owen thought to turn the conversation to something other than Gladys and Edern. 'Gruffydd ap Goronwy was kind to seek out my brother and arrange our meeting,' he said.

Lascelles nodded enthusiastically as he scooped up several cockles and popped them into his mouth. 'He is a good man, Gruffydd.' He wiped his mouth and took a long draught of wine. 'A victim of panic, poor Gruffydd. Pembroke's mother heard that Owain Lawgoch's fleet was out in the Channel and she blamed the first man she saw. They were bound for Anglesey, for pity's sake. That is where Lawgoch's supporters lurk. Not Tenby.' He shook his head. 'Would an invader look so close to Pembroke Castle? Pah.' He dipped into the seafood pastry.

'Had you met Mistress Lascelles before this trouble?' Geoffrey asked.

Slowly the man raised his head with a dangerous look in his eyes. 'Why do you ask?'

As if oblivious to the threat in that look, Geoffrey said pleasantly, 'I am curious whether the tale I have spun in my head is close to the truth.'

'If you imagined me making a fool of myself over a

beautiful young woman, you would be right,' Lascelles grumbled. 'I learned of her family's trouble, thought to save them and find my happiness all in one noble gesture.'

'You are a fortunate man,' Geoffrey said.

A joyless laugh escaped their host. 'It is the way of enchantments, that the wish one is granted turns against him. I have known little happiness since our wedding night.'

Lascelles sank into a quiet study while the servant moved the fish pastry to one side and filled the table with venison and a pottage of early greens.

Owen toasted Geoffrey silently and turned his attention to the tantalising dishes before him.

Slowly Lascelles woke to his guests and tasted the venison. 'From the Duke's wood,' he said. 'I enjoy a hunt when my spirit is restless.'

'It is a good way to exorcise demons,' Geoffrey agreed. 'A boar hunt even better.'

They fell to talking of hunting. Owen had nothing to contribute. He had been born to a life in which a felled animal was a blessing, not a sport, and used wisely to get all God's grace from it. He spent the time studying Lascelles, a haunted man, far more intriguing than he had thought at first.

It was almost a pleasant end to a troubling day. But the day had been marked from the start. As a servant brought forth the brandywine another in the livery rushed in, white faced, and fell to his knees beside Lascelles's chair. Lascelles leaned toward him, listening with a deepening frown, whispered something, shook his head, and rose, while telling the servant to stay in the room and await his return

– in silence. 'Captain, Master Chaucer, I should be grateful if you would accompany me.' Lascelles strode from the room.

Whatever the news, it had rapidly sobered him.

Eleven

TƆE VICAR'S
CLOAK

As they moved into the corridor without, Lascelles lifted a torch from a sconce. 'A few more torches would be of use,' he called over his shoulder. Owen and Geoffrey availed themselves of others in the corridor.

'What do you suppose happened?' Geoffrey whispered.

'Something he would keep from the other servants, which means trouble to someone,' Owen said.

Geoffrey nodded as if satisfied and hurried after Lascelles, whose light was disappearing down the tower steps. Owen followed with less enthusiasm. He wanted to back away, march straight to the guesthouse, lie down and end this miserable day.

Geoffrey paused on the verge of disappearing round the curved stairway. 'Owen? Are you coming?'

Of course, cursed as he was with the most damnable sense of responsibility.

They continued to descend until they reached the buttery, then immediately turned to a door beside the one they had just exited. It led into the undercroft of the chapel tower. The small room beneath the sacristy was the chaplain's chamber, which he presently shared with Edern. The door stood ajar. Lascelles held the torch before him, illuminating the room. It was so small as to be crowded with two pallets, a table, two chairs and a chest. And someone lying in a heap beneath the high window, one hand stretched towards the wall.

Owen recognised the squirrel lining on the wool cloak. 'Father Edern.'

Lascelles glanced back at Owen. 'How do you know?'

'The cloak.'

'God is merciful,' Lascelles whispered.

'I see nothing for which to be grateful,' Owen muttered.

Lascelles stepped to one side of the doorway and nodded at Owen. 'You have spoken of working with the Duke's surgeons in the field, Captain. Perhaps you should examine the body.'

'You are certain he is dead?'

'That is what the servant reported.'

'Young fools often fright at a person in a faint.' Reluctantly, Owen knelt beside the body. The cloak had fallen over Edern's head. He might have fainted, passed out after a long day of drinking – all was yet possible. But the lack of a snore, a moan, a movement of any kind since they shined the torch on him, and the stench of blood – Owen hesitated. Once the hood was drawn back, the worst would be known. He might be accustomed to death, but one death did not make the next encounter easier. Death dragged one's soul towards despair. Owen said a prayer for Edern, a man he had come to like, then drew back the hood.

'What is this?'

Lascelles came closer. 'What?'

'Perhaps you will not think God so merciful after all. This is Father Francis, not Edern.'

'In Edern's cloak?'

Which was one of those seeming coincidences that Owen ever distrusted. He handed his torch to Lascelles, who dropped it into the sconce by the door, then returned to hold his own over the body. Owen bent to Francis, felt his neck, the wrist of the hand flung out towards the wall, found no pulse.

'He is dead?' Lascelles asked.

'Aye.'

'How long?'

'He is cold, but his fingers have not yet stiffened. Not long. A matter of a few hours. Help me turn him over.'

Geoffrey took Lascelles's torch. The steward crouched on the side of the body opposite Owen, and at the signal began to tilt the body in Owen's direction. Owen caught Francis and lay him on the floor, face up. There was so much blood on the man's face and neck it masked the source.

On the table beside the body were the remnants of a meal soaked in wine from an overturned cup. A candle had followed the cup – it was fortunate for the castle that the flame had been extinguished in the sodden mess. Owen pulled a blanket off the bed, dipped the corner in the wine. 'Bring the torch closer.'

Geoffrey stepped closer.

Owen gently cleaned some of the blood from the priest's face.

'Jesu,' said Geoffrey.

'Aye. Not a pretty sight.' The priest's nose had been broken, one eye had swelled almost shut, and there was a deep gash in his forehead.

'Might he have fallen?' suggested Geoffrey. 'And hit his head on the table or the chest as he fell?'

'A fall would not do so much damage.' Lascelles's voice sounded almost timorous.

Owen glanced at Lascelles, wondering at his swiftly changing moods. 'No.' He examined the priest's hands. One palm was grazed, probably in the fall, but neither showed the bruising or the abrasions of someone who had fought to protect himself from such an attack as this must have been. 'Father Francis was beaten. And then he fell, or was thrown down. What passion provoked such a violent attack?'

Geoffrey stared down at the dead priest. 'Why was he wearing Edern's cloak?'

'Why indeed,' Owen said. 'Who was the intended victim?'

'We must search the castle for Edern,' Lascelles said.

Owen had bent to the table. There was a pool of sealing-wax – crimson, not the pale wax of the overturned candle. A pen and ink-well had been pushed to one side.

'Could Father Francis write?' he asked.

'Of course he could,' Lascelles said with impatience. 'I would not have tolerated an ignorant priest.'

Owen pushed past his hovering companions and

knelt beside the corpse, examined his clerical gown. The priest must have fallen shortly after his nose had begun to bleed, for there was little blood on the gown below the chest. Farther down Owen spied a dried bit of the crimson wax. 'He had sealed a document at this table,' Owen said. 'He spilled a bit of the wax on himself and on the table.' He eased himself up, suddenly aware of his exhaustion. Such a long, joyless day. How fitting for it to close with a death. 'I trust you do not need me to search the castle. I am to bed.'

A banging shutter woke Dafydd from a sweet dream of spring. Shutters were a luxury when properly latched; when left to bang they were cursed nuisances. He lay there, holding his breath so he might guess which shutter to attack. And then the hounds began to bark.

Rising slowly so he might not be heard, Dafydd felt for the stool at the foot of his bed. It was the only item close at hand that he might use as a weapon. A footstep in the corridor located the intruders – his servants went barefoot indoors. A thud made him jump. It also made his intruders pause. Thud thud. The shutter. Not so cursed after all. A shout. Ah. They had encountered the giant in the corridor – Cadwal slept across Dafydd's door at night. Hence the lack of weapons in his room.

For Dafydd had known the men would return, and this time would avoid the front gate. Discourteous but shrewd of them.

Now the thuds and shouts came close together. Dafydd cursed himself for leaving Nest and Cadwy shut in the kitchen. He prayed some of the other men would free the dogs and join Cadwal.

Whilst he stood like a timid old man clutching a stool. Was he a man? Well, he was not as young as he had once been. And he had never been skilled at arms – women's arms, yes; weapons had never interested him. He must think. What might he do to give Cadwal even more advantage than his size? Light. Indeed. For it was certain the intruders had not walked in boldly bearing torches. Dafydd reached for the shuttered lantern beside his bed, halted with his empty hand in the air. No. A light would be the very worst thing he could bring to the fray. Cadwal's advantage was knowing the corridor so well, even in the dark. The intruders would not know where to step, where to duck, what doors opened inward. Ah.

Dafydd took the stool firmly in one hand and with a roar to boost his courage, raced to the door, yanking it open with as much speed as he could manage. Someone fell in, praise God, making far too timid a thud to be Cadwal. Dafydd swung the chair, made contact with something soft. With an oath the man on the floor grabbed for the stool. Dafydd yanked it away, swung it again. With little effect this time, for the man was struggling to his knees.

'Stand aside,' Madog shouted in Welsh, 'I am for him!' The tall man seemed to fly through the doorway, landing at just the right angle and force to knock the rising intruder to the floor. The intruder's head hit with an unpleasant sound – slate floors were much harder on bones than either wood or packed earth.

Out in the corridor Dafydd heard the dogs barking, and oaths and cries in Welsh, Irish, English and

French. The Welsh and Irish oaths were louder, and the Welsh were shouted in more voices. God be praised, the dogs and all Dafydd's men had come to Cadwal's aid, and it sounded as if they were winning.

In a short while things had quieted enough for Dafydd to consider it safe to reach for the lantern and open the shutters wide. 'By my mother's mother's bones,' Dafydd muttered as he viewed the carnage. 'I thought these men were from a garrison.'

'So they are,' Madog said, standing over the man who lay suspiciously still in Dafydd's doorway as Nest pushed forward and sniffed him, 'but they let down their guard, thinking you an old, helpless man.'

'I had introduced them to Cadwal on their last visit, as well as Nest and Cadwy.'

'One giant and a brace of dogs – they thought themselves ready for them, I suppose. But not for five more men. What English bard has a personal guard to protect him from angry cuckolds?'

Cadwal, bloody mouthed and with a swollen eye, nodded happily. 'Will there be more?'

Dafydd came forward, counted four men lying on the floor. 'I think not. Have you not had enough excitement for one night?'

Patrick sat athwart the largest of the men, wiping clean the blade of his knife. 'I was beginning to think this poor blade would never feel living flesh again,' he said. 'God has been merciful.'

'Six against four,' Madog said. 'It was never a challenge.'

The servants now crept from hiding and wandered wide eyed among the bodies. The hounds sat proudly in their midst, tongues lolling in smiles.

Mair dropped down by the man in Dafydd's doorway, crossed herself. 'He is dead?' she whispered. Already her eyes glistened with tears.

'Dead? Not unless the dead wheeze,' Madog said. 'He might pray to die when he wakes and feels his head. And his groin – our master has a terrifying aim.' He grinned at Dafydd.

'You talk too much,' Dafydd muttered. 'Gather them up, take them into the hall and clean their wounds, make them comfortable. We shall play Samaritans now we have made safe our home.'

Dafydd knelt beside Mair and said quietly, 'Use the sheets stained by the pilgrim's blood to wrap them. Then if one should manage a search, he will see nothing to suggest we had an earlier bloodied visitor.'

Mair smiled. 'He is safely at the abbey by now?'

Dafydd had noticed her affection for the handsome young pilgrim. 'Not yet, but very soon. And this night my men have guaranteed his safe passage.'

'I am glad of that, Master Dafydd.' She rose and followed the others.

Dafydd sat on the floor thinking of the light in Mair's eyes. Oh to be young again and inspire such desire.

Twelve

INTERRUPTED SLUMBER

'How can you sleep at such a time?' Geoffrey said as he dropped his second boot to the floor with an even greater clatter than the first.

He had wakened Owen with the door banging against the wall, prior to his loud mutterings and the clattering boots. Owen hoped the man would give up and allow him to sink back into sweet slumber. A foolish hope; he knew Geoffrey well enough by now to know how persistent he could be.

'Edern cannot be found. They have searched the entire castle and found no trace of him.' Geoffrey paused.

Owen could feel the man's eyes on him. He fought to keep his breathing steady, deep.

'The porter remembers Father Francis departing with Mistress Lascelles. He says that even had he not recognised the priest's cloak he would have known it to be the chaplain because Mistress Lascelles called him by name, saying her mother was ill and Father Francis would be a comfort to her. As you will recall, when I asked after Tangwystl's mother's health Sir John said she was not ill.'

Owen did indeed remember. And he found Geoffrey's chatter intriguing. But now he had begun the cat-and-mouse game he was loath to give it up. And at this rate he would know all the news without bothering to sit up and open his eyes.

The priests had exchanged cloaks. So that Edern might pass through the gates? Why could he not pass through in his own cloak? Who had cause to stop him? Had he beaten Father Francis? But why? And where had he gone with Tangwystl? Owen fought a quickening of breath.

'You cannot fool me, Owen. I know the difference between the breathing of a sleeper and the breathing of one pretending sleep.' Geoffrey was moving about the room, disrobing, no doubt. 'Poor Francis. The priesthood is a dangerous undertaking in your country.'

With a groan, Owen sat up, propping himself on his elbow. 'Why do you say that?'

'I *knew* you were awake.' Geoffrey sat at the edge of his bed grinning and dangling his stockinged feet in the air. At such a moment, he seemed oddly childlike to Owen, despite the neat beard he had grown during the journey. Geoffrey had thrown one of the sheepskins over his shoulders, covering his fine linen shift – he must intend to keep up the chatter for quite a while. 'I knew you would come to the defence of your people. But you will have difficulty defending their treatment of their priests.'

Had he news of Edern? 'What do you mean?'

'Remember the priest at Carreg Cennen?'

'There was none.'

'Precisely. Fell down a cliff. Remember?'

'Are you proposing that the deaths of the two priests are connected?'

'No.'

'Then save your energy for useful musings.'

'You begin to sound like my wife.'

'I begin to pity her.'

'Perhaps I do suggest a connection.'

'I think it unlikely.'

'What about the obvious connection?'

Owen frowned.

'John de Reine.'

'He is dead.'

'He failed to appear at Carreg Cennen.'

'And he failed to appear here alive? You see a pattern in that? Stop bobbing your feet!'

Geoffrey obeyed with an insulted grimace. 'I merely suggest,' he said quietly, 'that John de Reine is the key to all that has happened. You remember that Edern came forth with the offer to escort John de Reine's body to Cydweli, do you not?'

'I do.'

'And now he has slyly pretended to be Father Francis for the day, the very day on which Father Francis meets his death.'

'Go on.'

Geoffrey wrung his hands. 'That is it. I know it does not tell us where Edern has gone. Nor what part the lovely Tangwystl plays in all this.'

'Perhaps we should wait till they return in the

morning and ask them. Or have you forgotten that it is still possible they did go to see Tangwystl's mother?'

Geoffrey seemed saddened by the possibility. With a great sigh he swung his feet up on to the bed, shuttered the lantern that hung on a hook beside him, and lay back. 'For a moment I forgot myself,' he said to the dark.

Repenting his anger, Owen said, 'Best to sleep now. The morrow may bring more questions than answers.'

He turned on to his left side, discovered that his shoulder still ached, and rolled over on to his right. He thought of Lucie, wondered whether she still kept their one-year-old son beside her in his cradle or whether Hugh now shared a pallet in the corner with his sister Gwenllian. It was a large bedchamber, and when Owen was away Lucie said she liked Gwenllian's company. Gwenllian enjoyed it, too, though as a pragmatic three-and-a-half-year-old, she worried that Jasper was lonely all alone in the chamber next to them. Gwenllian could not know that at thirteen Jasper likely felt relieved to have the children out of his chamber for a while.

With those domestic thoughts, Owen gradually sank into a drowse that signalled sleep.

But a soft knock on the door woke him at once.

Geoffrey, too, sprung up at the noise. 'Who is it?' he whispered.

'I doubt they can hear you.'

'I might not wish them to hear me.'

A louder knock.

'An attacker would not announce himself so,' Owen

muttered as he rose to go to the door, pulling a blanket round him for warmth. 'Could you rouse yourself enough to open a shutter on your lantern?'

Geoffrey did as requested.

Owen opened the door. A cloaked figure rushed into the room.

'Close the door!' It was a woman's voice, breathless, the language Welsh.

Owen closed the door, walked over to the woman, who had perched on the edge of his bed. He pushed back the hood that hid her face. 'Gladys.' Her eyes were swollen and her nose red, apparently from weeping.

'Sweet Jesu,' Geoffrey muttered, pulling up his legs as if cringing from the presence of the woman who had so embarrassed him two days earlier.

'You must protect me,' Gladys whimpered. 'As the Duke's men you must protect me.'

'What is she saying?' Geoffrey asked.

'She is asking for protection.'

'I would not have thought her one who felt the need for protection,' Geoffrey said.

Owen knelt by the woman, studied her face. She was far younger than he had realised. 'Such eyes. You have cried for a long while.'

She nodded.

He took her hands in his. They were ice cold despite the heavy cloak she had wrapped round her. 'You are very frightened.'

The sympathy begat tears.

'Can you speak English? Or French?' Owen asked.

'A little,' she said in English. 'But you speak my tongue.'

'Master Chaucer does not. If you are asking for his protection as well as mine, he must understand you. But from whom are we to protect you?'

Gladys wiped her nose on her cloak, looked round to Geoffrey. 'They say you are the King's man as well as the Duke's.'

'I am,' he said with a hesitance more appropriate to a less certain response.

She hiccuped.

Geoffrey rose, checked the flagon on the table, found a bit of wine left in it, poured it into a cup, brought it to her. She blessed him and sipped daintily. He backed out of her reach.

'Father Francis is dead, did you know?' she said. 'And *she* is gone. With the Welsh priest.'

'Mistress Lascelles?' Owen asked.

'Yes.'

'What has frightened you?' Owen asked. 'The chaplain's death?'

Gladys's bottom lip began to tremble, her eyes filled. 'She pushed me into my master's bed. She made Father Francis watch us. And now he is dead.'

'So Father Francis told the truth,' Geoffrey whispered.

Gladys looked at Geoffrey in alarm. 'Why did he tell you? Did he know of the danger?'

'What danger?' Owen asked.

'I did what she asked me to do,' she sobbed. 'She frightens me. The moment I saw her ride through the castle gate I feared for my master. She has the look of a demon, she does. I told the master I was no good as a lady's maid, I would knot her hair and stain her dresses with my clumsiness. But he said she liked me, she chose me, and then she made me lie with him. Before it was different, but now he was married, and I was his lady's maid. It was not right.'

'What happened today, Gladys?' Owen asked.

Gladys's eyes filled again. She clutched the cup to her bosom. 'She told me to meet her in the chaplain's cell, told me that I was to be a witness. Was someone to be wed, I asked her, and she laughed, and when she laughs, she does so with her mouth and her voice but not her eyes, have you seen? It is like she is two people.' She hiccuped again. Owen gently took the empty cup from her hands. She blotted her eyes with a corner of the cloak. 'I went to the chaplain's cell. I knew something was wrong and I thought it was the vicar crouching there, his back to me, like he had lost something on the floor. I called his name, but it was Father Francis's voice that answered. His voice was so weak, I knelt beside him, tried to help him up, but he shook his head.' She shook her head once, again. 'And all that blood! I thought he had fallen. So I said I would get help, and then she was calling for me.'

'Mistress Lascelles?' Owen asked.

Gladys nodded. 'And Father Edern, too. "Run, my child," Father Francis told me. His eyes were so sad, he was dying, he used his last breath to warn me. "Run," he told me. "Save yourself." ' She began to sob again.

'Save yourself from whom? Mistress Lascelles?' Geoffrey asked, his tone sceptical.

'I know not,' she sobbed.

Her tears did not stop Geoffrey. 'And why did you not get help for Father Francis?'

'I was afraid!'

'Of whom?'

But the tears were flowing freely now. They learned little more. It had been mid-afternoon when she had gone to the chaplain's room. Since then she had hidden in the undercroft. She did not know how long Tangwystl and Father Edern had spent searching for her.

When Gladys was at last asleep in Owen's bed, the two men crowded into Geoffrey's bed. But sleep was gone for Owen. Scattered strands were joining in his mind. The unhappy marriage. The maid sent to the husband's bed. *She made Father Francis watch us.* Owen had asked how many times the chaplain had observed. Gladys did not know. Thrice, he guessed. There was an old Welsh law, a way for Tangwystl to dispose of an unfaithful husband. Is that what Father Francis was to do? Write a letter stating what he had seen? But what would that do to Tangwystl's family, who were here by the grace of her unwanted husband? And how could an old Welsh law bind John Lascelles, the Duke's man? Why would Father Francis die for it? No. Owen grew confused. Father Edern had been the intended victim, not Francis. Which made even less sense.

Gladys began to snore. God's blood, what were they to do with her?

In the morning, Gladys hid beneath one of the beds while the servant lit the brazier and set their morning ale, bread and cheese on the table. Geoffrey insisted on such luxuries when on official business. Today Owen was glad of it. The ale helped clear his mind. Gladys looked better for a bit of sleep; though the swelling around her eyes had gone down just slightly, she seemed calmer, not so close to tears, and she had a hearty appetite.

'We cannot continue to hide her here,' Geoffrey said.

'You have a knack for stating the obvious,' Owen said. He watched Gladys attack a small loaf of bread, devour it in three bites, then wash it down with mouthfuls of ale.

'Gladys, why did your mistress ask you to lie with her husband? And I would be grateful if you would speak so that Master Chaucer might understand.'

Gladys put down her cup, wiped her mouth with her sleeve. 'To prove to him she had not put a curse on his manhood.'

'Why would he believe such a thing?'

'Because he could not lie with her as he does with me. He never could. He says she put hawthorn leaves in the bed.'

'Hawthorn is used in weddings to bring fertility,' Geoffrey said.

'It is,' said Owen, 'but the leaves are also used just in that way to safeguard a young maid's virtue when temptation is near.'

'I forget you have apprenticed in an apothecary.'

'My wife would say such things are not the business of an apothecary, but folk will ask. And they pay good coin for the leaves.' Yet Owen could not imagine Lascelles pulling up his mattress, much less recognising hawthorn leaves that had been crushed beneath it. He needed to drop back further. Why was the marriage so unhappy? He had a thought. 'Is your mistress in love with another man?'

Gladys dropped her eyes to her hands. 'I do not know.'

'Why else would she continue to push her husband to your bed?' Owen asked.

Gladys did not lift her head. 'It is not my place to wonder such things.'

Owen shook his head as if to a child who had told an obvious, though harmless, lie. 'You could not help but wonder, surely.'

Gladys silently examined her toes.

Geoffrey looked from one to the other, exasperated. 'More to the point, considering he has been murdered, why did your mistress make Father Francis spy on you with Sir John?' Owen had not told him his theory; he doubted Geoffrey would have credited it till now.

'She called him her witness.'

'Witness for whom?'

Gladys looked up, her bottom lip trembling. 'I do not know such things, Master Chaucer. I am but a servant!'

Geoffrey threw up his hands. 'None of this makes any sense, and none of it is benefiting the garrison.' He rose. 'The porter offered to show me round the south gatehouse this morning.'

Owen thought Geoffrey had chosen an odd time to remember his official business.

Owen was of two minds. He was here on the Duke's business; the discord in Lascelles's household was not part of that business. On the other hand, he could not swear that none of the trouble involved the mysterious Lawgoch, nor could Geoffrey be assured of the castle's readiness if Lawgoch had supporters here. Indeed, even if the troubles had nothing to do with the Welshman, chaos in the castle jeopardised its military readiness.

And though Geoffrey could not support his suspicion that all the troubles were connected, he might very well be right.

Promising Gladys that he would consider what must be done, Owen took his leave of her and walked out into the courtyard of the inner ward. He was just in time to see two Benedictine monks enter the ward, led by a servant. Heads bowed, they moved without curiosity through the ward to the hall and disappeared through the door. So Father Francis's requiem Mass was to be said this morning. Owen guessed that it also meant Father Edern had not returned.

Owen fought to order his thoughts. Tangwystl and Edern. How might they have bonded together? He remembered his puzzlement when Tangwystl neglected to include the priest at their table. 'Father Edern of St David's?' she had asked. She knew him. So did her father. It had been clear that Gruffydd disliked Edern; but Owen had been unable to judge his daughter's feelings.

And what of Edern? As Geoffrey had pointed out, Edern had come forward to offer himself as John de Reine's escort. What was their connection?

The time had come to put the skills to work that Owen had learned in Thoresby's service. Nothing would be accomplished while the castle was in chaos. But first he must do something about Gladys.

Thirteen

AN ARGUMENT OVERHEARD

O wen's pacing took him through the inner ward and towards the practice yard. Divine inspiration it must have been, for Harold and Simwnt were loading several empty barrels into a cart cushioned with a good mound of hay.

'Are you going far?' Owen asked, interrupting an argument about whose clumsiness had caused a barrel to drop out of the cart on to Harold's foot.

Simwnt turned round at the sound of Owen's voice, his face brightening. 'Captain Archer! God go with you, Captain. We are on a mission for *you*, truth be told.'

Harold made a great show of leaning against the cart, yanking off his left boot, and rubbing his foot. 'I will not hold *you* responsible, Captain,' he muttered.

Owen laughed, recognising a friendly quarrel. 'I am glad of that, for I know nothing of your mission.'

'No?' Harold eased his boot back on. 'We are after the bows for your recruits.'

'Aye,' Simwnt agreed. 'The constable is in a foul mood about the bowyer who is late with the bows we ordered. Turns out the bows are ready but the bowyer's cart is missing a wheel. He will not be paid if he is much later, and being kin, I thought to give him a hand. He is a good man and a fine bowyer.'

'And you enjoy riding out into the countryside,' Owen added.

'It is not such a pleasure as you may think,' Harold said. 'But with matters as they are here—' He dropped his voice, shook his head. 'The castle is a place to be clear of.'

'There is a search?'

'Aye,' said Simwnt. 'They have searched for the vicar, now the maid Gladys. No one saw her leave the castle, you see.'

'She being one the porter would remember seeing,' Harold said with a wink.

Owen was pleased to find them playing into his hands. 'Would you welcome a companion on your journey?' he asked.

'You feel the gloom as well,' Harold said.

'I would not call it gloom.' Owen motioned for both to step round to the far side of the cart. 'Would two companions burden you? Myself riding alongside the cart and one snug in the hay?'

Simwnt frowned down at the ground. 'You are proposing trouble, Captain.'

Owen could not deny that. 'I am wrong to ask such a thing of you.' He began to walk away.

'Stay a moment,' Simwnt said. 'Would the other companion be the fair Gladys?'

Owen slowed, turned. 'It might.'

'She is one enjoys a nice bit of hay,' Harold said, nudging Simwnt.

'I wish to take her to safety,' Owen said, 'not toss her into your lustful arms.'

'Why would you be sneaking her out?' Simwnt asked. 'You are not of the mind she was the murderer? It took strength to do so much damage.'

'It is for her protection. More than that I cannot say.'

Simwnt and Harold exchanged glances. 'How far would you be going?' Harold asked.

'Not far.' Owen described the valley in which his brother lived.

Simwnt nodded. 'We shall bring the cart round to the guesthouse shortly.'

Gladys threw her arms round Owen. She smelled of sweat and the morning's ale. 'I shall work hard for them, make them glad they have taken me in.'

Owen winced. Now that the first flush of a brilliant idea had faded, he was feeling less optimistic about her welcome in Morgan's home. While not in her presence he was able to imagine it, but now, watching her suggestive movements, her pouting expressions, the flutter of her lashes. Sweet Jesu, how could he fool his brother? 'We do not know that my brother will agree to this. If you are right about your danger, my brother may think it is too much of a risk to ask of him. His first duty is to his family.'

Head tilted, hip thrust to the side – in another

woman such gestures suggested far less – Gladys pouted, then quickly smiled. 'How could your brother be less Christian than you? Did you not suckle at the same breast?'

Owen felt his face grow hot at the last word. 'Morgan goes his own way, Gladys. I do warn you of that.'

'I have been warned. And I trust that God will continue to watch over me.'

As a man, no doubt the Lord would watch over her. But there were things Owen might suggest. 'My brother is a very devout man, Gladys. You must not – flaunt yourself so with him.' He felt his face redden. He was glad Geoffrey was still out.

But Gladys took his hand, pressed it firmly. 'I swear to you that I shall be to him a chaste virgin with no thought of men, Captain.' Her lashes fluttered.

He must be blunt. 'You must meekly bow your head and keep your hands and body as still as possible.'

Gladys immediately took the stance.

'Your gown. Do you have a scarf?'

Gladys surprised him by blushing as she raised her hands to cover her cleavage. 'I have one, but I dare not return to my mistress's apartment for it.'

They improvised with one of the squares of cloth with which Geoffrey cleaned his hands of ink.

Harold and Simwnt had been disappointed when Owen warned them that any conversation with Gladys might jeopardise her safety, and thus she must stay hidden in the hay throughout the journey. But Harold cheered himself and Simwnt with the observation that Gladys would be forever grateful to them.

Sitting high on the seat of the cart, their horses tethered behind, Harold and Simwnt whiled away the time with gossip of the garrison. Owen, riding close beside them, found one item of particular interest.

'Bad luck if that priest has fled,' Harold said. 'We will lose our wager.'

'Aye. I should know by now clerics are a sly lot,' said Simwnt.

It seemed they had both expected the constable to attack Edern on his return, for the priest had persuaded Burley's mistress to return to her husband a few years earlier.

'He cannot forget her, you see,' Simwnt explained. 'Beautiful and spirited was Mererid. He says he has not seen her like since.'

Owen found it an odd thing for Edern to have done.

'He won his comfortable post as a vicar in St David's by the good deed,' Harold said. 'Mererid's husband is brother to a white monk who has the ear of many of the archdeacons of St David's.'

Owen remembered the white monk who had pretended sleep at the vicar's house in the close. Had Edern now come on another mission for Brother Dyfrig?

When they arrived at the farm, Elen was puzzled by Owen's request to take the cart into the barn.

'You fear a thief might drive it away while we are within?' She smiled. 'I heard it long before I saw it.' But at his insistence she tucked the baby Luc on to her hip and led them to the barn.

Once within, Owen called to Gladys to sit up. It took a bit of poking to find her, then some shaking to waken her. As she sat up and got her bearings, Owen explained her presence to a mystified Elen.

'From the castle?' Elen shook her head. 'Morgan will not like this. He has little respect for the steward since he took to wife a traitor's daughter.'

Owen had forgotten that in his concern about Gladys's behaviour. Sweet Jesus, he had been a fool to begin this.

Gladys looked from Owen to Elen with a frightened expression. 'I pray you, good lady, I cannot go back. It is the steward I fear, and his wife.'

Was she at last telling the truth, Owen wondered, or was she just a skilled manipulator?

Elen looked on Gladys with sympathy. 'I shall try to convince my husband. Come within and have some refreshment.'

'It is best that she stay in the barn until the three of us leave with the cart,' Owen said. 'And that Harold and Simwnt watch the barn while I talk to Morgan.'

It was a difficult meeting, to be sure.

As soon as Owen mentioned Gladys's name and position at the castle, Morgan muttered a curse and Elen's free hand went out to catch her husband's arm and muffle the violence with which he brought his fist to the table. She told the older children to go outside.

'You would ask us to harbour that Magdalen?' Two red spots burned on Morgan's pale cheeks.

'Magdalen?' Owen repeated, attempting innocence.

'What do you know of this woman, husband?' Elen asked.

'Send her to the Devil,' Morgan said.

'Husband!'

'What *do* you know of her?' Owen asked.

'I go to the Cydweli market, brother.' Morgan hissed the last word as if it were a curse. His eyes were fixed on Owen's good eye with frightening intensity, as if any moment now he would go into a fit. 'She is known to all in the town as the castle whore.'

'Holy Mary,' Elen whispered. 'Is this true, Owen?'

How could he deny it? 'Elen, forgive me. I had hoped—'

'To fool us, farmers that we are,' Morgan said.

'It is a rumour,' Owen said. 'I have seen no proof of such behaviour.' It was no lie – Geoffrey had witnessed it, but not Owen. 'I had hoped that you would remember Christ's championing of Mary Magdalen.'

Morgan muttered to himself, but his stance had subtly softened.

'What would happen to her if they found her?' Elen asked.

'She fears that whoever murdered the chaplain will also wish to murder her. I do not know who committed the deed, so how can I know to whom I might entrust her? It will be on my conscience if anything happens to her.'

'Why?' Elen asked. 'What have you to do with it?'

'She asked for my protection. I am duty bound to do what I can.' Was he a fool? She had also begged Geoffrey's protection – he had not felt so bound.

Morgan sniffed. 'You express fine feelings for such a woman.'

'I would welcome some help,' Elen said softly.

'You would accept such a woman in our house?' Morgan asked.

'What if we judge her unjustly, Morgan? Then she is

twice injured, by those who spread lies and by us, who believe them without allowing her to defend herself.'

'Gossip. Aye.' Morgan stared down at his hands.

Miraculously, Morgan was softening. Owen could see that Elen's gifts of persuasion were his best hope. 'I shall step without and allow you privacy in which to discuss this.'

Owen did not go far. He crouched down just without the shuttered windows to play with an obligingly friendly cat. He had to stay close to the window to hear the conversation over the shouts of the three children at play in the yard.

'If the rumours are true, Gladys is no worse than her mistress,' Elen was saying to Morgan. 'And yet you do not condemn Tangwystl ferch Gruffydd.'

'Bringing a child to her marriage is not the same as being the castle whore,' Morgan said. 'They say Gladys even lies with the priests.'

A brief silence, then Elen spoke again. 'We might be the agents of her redemption. With whom can she sin in our house?'

'I do not like it.'

'If we send her back and she dies . . . Oh, Morgan, you could not bear to have her death on your conscience. I know you could not.'

'How is it my conscience now, wife? I did nothing. I did not ask my brother to bring her here. It is on his conscience.'

Slowly, patiently, Elen managed to wear Morgan down. Young she might be, but Elen had a clear head and stood her ground. Owen thought Lucie would like her.

At last Morgan stepped out into the yard. 'Come,

brother. Let us go to the barn. I shall relieve you of your burden.'

As he rode away, Owen said a prayer for Elen, the peacemaker. He asked God for a small favour – that for Elen's sake Gladys did nothing to offend Morgan.

Harold hummed a melancholy tune as he drove the cart, his hood up against the rain that had begun abruptly as they reached the track beyond the farm.

Simwnt rode beside Owen. 'You and your brother are good men to help Gladys. I have never known her so fearful. She is not a woman who takes fright easily.'

Owen was only half-listening, his thoughts on the conversation he had overheard. Tangwystl had a child. He had not heard of it at the castle. Did that mean the child was elsewhere? It was common enough, to send a child to foster parents. Is that where she had gone with the priest? He opened his mouth to ask Simwnt what he knew of it, but changed his mind. Poor Simwnt and Harold had already been burdened with what might be dangerous knowledge. He would involve him no further. But there was a place he might learn more.

'Do you know where Gruffydd ap Goronwy lives?' Owen asked, interrupting an inventory of Gladys's physical virtues. He had intended to ask his brother, but had thought better of it.

'What? Gruffydd? Oh, aye. The steward gave his wife's family a comfortable farm. It lies south of the castle, on a bluff above the marsh.'

'Could I reach it by midday?'

'Riding hard, aye.' Simwnt turned in the saddle,

gave Owen an appraising look. 'Milady does not need your escort, Captain. The steward sent a messenger there early this morning. If he found her, she will be on her way home already, I should think.'

'If someone is following us, I thought I might confuse him,' Owen said. 'Force him to choose between you and me.'

Simwnt glanced behind him. 'You have noticed something?'

'No. But if he is good, I would not, would I?'

'Oh, aye.' Simwnt gave Owen careful directions to Gruffydd's farm.

Fourteen

DYFRIG SOWS
SEEDS OF DOUBT

A sullen rain kept Dafydd indoors with the injured intruders. Had it been a real storm – sooty clouds, howling wind, driving rain – Dafydd would have ventured forth to join in the drama, to absorb the energy, to revel in the *presence* of the Almighty. But a half-hearted rain merely dampened him both in body and spirit.

Dafydd withdrew to his writing chamber, where Nest and Cadwy noisily chewed on some bones, drowning out the dull patter of the rain on the thatch. Chin resting on hand, Dafydd grew melancholy as he listened to a memory – the drumming of the rain on the tiled roof of a wealthy patron, a house in which he had been exquisitely happy tutoring a lovely young woman, a woman who had loved him, thought him the fount of all knowledge, the champion of all beauty.

'Master Dafydd,' Mair softly called behind him, 'forgive me for disturbing your work but the one you have awaited is come, the white monk Dyfrig.'

Dafydd rose quickly, turned to find the monk already standing behind him, a tall, narrow, solemn sentinel. Hooded head, hooded eyes. Dafydd wondered why he trusted Brother Dyfrig. Was it his silence that inspired confidence and confidences? It must be a strong impression to override those hooded eyes. The monk's habit steamed as he stood near the brazier. It was not so white after travelling to St David's and back. Nest had lifted her head from her bone to sniff him as he entered the room, but had not bothered to get up and greet him.

Dafydd remembered himself. 'Mair, bring us some refreshment. Brother Dyfrig has had a long, damp journey.'

Mair bobbed a curtsey and slipped away.

'*Benedicte*, Master Dafydd,' Dyfrig bowed. 'I see your hall has become a spital. Had you intended that?'

'Criticism, Dyfrig? From a monk who breaks more vows than he keeps?'

'I meant no criticism, Master Dafydd.'

Then he had not the wit to know when to flaunt his opinion, for he was right in criticising. 'I confess that I had not considered the inconvenience. But then I did not expect such slaughter – how useless is the human carcass. It nourishes no one.'

Dafydd had hoped for an expression of disgust from the monk, but Dyfrig merely said, 'Mother Earth is nourished by us, Master Dafydd.'

'Ah. Then perhaps I should bury them in the garden.'

'I was not aware that any were dead.'

So devoid of expression. Did they teach them that in the monastery? No, the monk had learned it elsewhere, for his fellow Cistercian had not that demeanour. Even the slightest impressions flickered across Brother Samson's florid countenance for all to see.

'All four are alive and look to fully recover, more's the pity. But enough of my woes, let us sit and refresh ourselves while you tell me of your journey.'

Mair had returned with a tray laden with bowls, a jug of cider, cheese and bread. The two men settled at Dafydd's table.

When Mair shut the door behind her, Dafydd said to Dyfrig, 'Eat and then tell me what you learned about gifts from the sea.'

After thirstily downing two bowls of cider and devouring the better part of the cheese, Dyfrig leaned back in his chair, satisfied, and began his tale. And a troubling tale it was. Dafydd had known of John de Reine's death, for the intruders had spoken of it. But somehow he had missed the fact that the man had been murdered on the beach at Whitesands. He rose from his chair, took his uneasiness to the window. The rain continued. 'I had not heard about the sand in his clothes.'

'Few have. From all accounts it is likely he was on the beach about the same time you found the pilgrim,' Dyfrig said to Dafydd's back. 'I also learned of a young pilgrim missing from the bishop's palace – one who had come petitioning the bishop. He, too, disappeared at the time you found your pilgrim.'

That cheered Dafydd. 'So he is truly a pilgrim.'

'Perhaps.' Brother Dyfrig's tone was doubtful. 'Petitioners to the bishop often seek things other than indulgences and absolution – such as justice, patronage . . .'

Dafydd did not like Dyfrig's manner. He abandoned his contemplation of the rain and turned, regarding the monk with a stern expression. 'Who is the source of your information?'

'Everyone and no one.' The monk's smile was enigmatic. He enjoyed the role of sleuth. There was no dulling his spirit. 'There is much activity in Castel Cydweli at the moment,' Dyfrig continued. 'Two of Lancaster's men have journeyed from England to oversee the strengthening of the garrison. One of them is a one-eyed Welshman, formerly captain of archers to the old Duke, who has risen high in the present Duke's favour – he is recruiting archers for King Edward's next attempt at the crown of France.'

'Had these men anything to do with the death of the steward's son?'

'It is difficult to say how the presence of such authority might affect an uneasy truce.'

Dafydd tired of the monk's riddling. 'Speak plainly.'

The monk's mouth twitched, fighting a smile. 'This incident at Whitesands has the taste of Owain of the Red Hand about it, Master Dafydd.'

'By the Trinity, you mean the Frenchman who thinks he is the rightful Prince of all Wales? Rhodri ap Gruffudd's spawn?'

'His grandson, yes. There are many who find hope in his claim.'

'In every age there are many fools, Dyfrig.' But

Dafydd considered the monk's suggestion. If the death of John de Reine had anything to do with Owain Lawgoch, the pilgrim was in grave danger, not simply from the ineffectual Cydweli warriors, but from either Lawgoch's supporters or those loyal to King Edward. And it did not matter whether the pilgrim was innocent of the man's death – he was suspected, and that was enough to bring him trouble. And bring trouble to any who offered him sanctuary.

But God had put the pilgrim in his path – surely He had intended Dafydd to help the injured man.

Dyfrig took the opportunity to finish the cheese and the cider.

'You do not want for an appetite,' Dafydd remarked.

'As you said, I endured a long, wet journey to bring you my news,' Dyfrig said.

'Indeed. So you suggest that the pilgrim is one of Lawgoch's supporters?'

Dyfrig nodded slowly, as if still considering the possibilities. 'Or John de Reine might have been. His natural father did marry the daughter of Gruffydd ap Goronwy, who has been accused of supporting Lawgoch.'

The monk enjoyed imparting bad news. 'And these men sent by the constable of Cydweli?' Dafydd asked. 'Do you believe they are after a traitor to their King, not a thief?'

'They may believe they seek both in the same man. It takes some wealth to mount an invasion. Lawgoch might well have thieves working for him.'

'If you are right, my granting the pilgrim sanctuary might be misinterpreted.'

'But he is no longer here, is he?'

'No. But the Cydweli men returned – I do not think they would have bothered had they not been tolerably certain he had been here. My name is now linked with him. Even though I know not who he is.'

Dyfrig picked up his bowl, found it empty. 'I would welcome a brief rest,' he said.

And Dafydd would welcome time to think. He rose. 'If you encounter any of the Cydweli men, claim another house than yours, Dyfrig. I would not have them finding your presence a key to the pilgrim's whereabouts.'

'So he is on his way to Strata Florida with Brother Samson?'

'He may be.'

Dyfrig was almost out the door when he turned, head tilted, and said softly, 'All nature conforms to patterns, and so does man mimic nature in his activities. Mark you – John de Reine was the natural son of John Lascelles, who married the daughter of Gruffydd ap Goronwy, accused of giving shelter to a Fleming working for Lawgoch. And this daughter's name is the one name we know is somehow connected with the pilgrim – Tangwystl.' Dyfrig touched fingertips together, forming a circle with his hands. With a slight smile and a nod, he withdrew.

Dafydd put his head in his hands and prayed God that Dyfrig was wrong, that the pilgrim had no connection with Owain ap Thomas ap Rhodri ap Gruffudd.

Dafydd did not welcome death. Not yet. And not as the result of a charitable gesture. Sweet Heaven, what was God about, to visit this danger upon him?

Of all Welshmen, why was he drawn into Lawgoch's trouble? He had no faith in the man's honour. Rhodri ap Llywelyn, brother of Llywelyn the Last, had been the weakest of the brothers. How could one believe anything noble of his grandson?

Owen reined in his horse as he caught sight of a substantial farmhouse tucked in a cluster of oaks and willows. He wished to catch his breath and gather his wits about him. Through an opening in the trees he could see that the house was set safely back from a bluff that must dramatically drop off to the marshland below. Lascelles had been generous with his father-in-law; this was no common farmhouse.

A pretty young woman with Gruffydd's dark hair and handsome features opened the door, peered at Owen with curiosity.

He introduced himself.

Her eyes brightening, she bobbed a hurried curtsey and exclaimed in Welsh, 'They say you have journeyed to the edge of the world, Captain Archer.'

Owen laughed. 'Tales have a way of growing with the telling. I have sailed across the sea to France, but no farther.'

'They say that an Amazon took your eye.'

'And died for it,' Gruffydd said, joining the girl. 'My youngest daughter, Awena.' She bobbed again, ducked beneath her father's extended arm and scurried into the house. 'I am honoured, Captain, but I assure you that Tangwystl is not here, nor was she here yesterday.' The words were courteous but firm, the tone slightly strained. Gruffydd wore a simpler garb than he favoured at Cydweli, and his hair was not so carefully combed.

'I am here on my own business, not the steward's,' Owen said. 'I wished to thank you for reuniting me with my brother Morgan.'

Gruffydd closed his eyes, nodded. 'Forgive me. The earlier messenger from Cydweli alarmed my wife. But I should have guessed your purpose might be a different one. Come in, come in.'

As Owen had guessed from without Gruffydd ap Goronwy's house, this was the residence of a wealthy farmer, with a comfortable hall, a tiled fire circle, and above the far end, a solar. A boy in rougher garb than Awena's, a servant, Owen guessed, helped her ease a board on to trestles. A tall, exceedingly thin woman with the pale brows of a redhead carried a tray of bowls and a pitcher to the table. She wore a simple gown and the starched head-dress of a Welsh farmwife. She was barefoot.

Gruffydd led Owen to the table, sat him nearest the fire from which came a welcome heat after the long, damp ride.

'My wife, Eleri,' Gruffydd said, gesturing to the slender woman. Owen wondered at the marked difference in garb between Eleri and her husband and children. 'My love, this is Owain ap Rhodri, the former captain of archers about whom we have heard so much.'

Eleri stood at one end of the table, fussing with the bowls, spreading them all out, then stacking them, then spreading them out again. She seemed not to hear him.

Gruffydd put his hand on one of hers. 'Eleri.'

His knuckles were swollen and raw. He must do more work on the farm than Owen would have guessed.

Eleri wiped her hands on her apron, lifted her chin, then her eyes, as if someone had forced the motion. Her eyes lit on Owen for the briefest time, then dropped to the bowls once more. 'There is wine,' she said in Welsh, and began to turn away.

Hands on her bony shoulders, Gruffydd turned her back to the table. 'Sit down and enjoy our guest, Eleri.'

Awena moved to her mother's side, began to pour the wine.

'Come,' Gruffydd guided Eleri to a bench.

She sat down, then at once began to fuss with her gown, shaking out the wrinkles, smoothing her skirt. She patted her head-dress. When she had completed what seemed a ritual, she met Owen's gaze with momentary clarity. 'Are you from the castle?'

'I am staying there at the moment.'

'Why are you not out searching for my daughter?'

'Eleri, he is a guest at the castle, not one of the garrison.'

Eleri touched her shoulder, frowned at the hand that lay there, lifted it to her face, studied it. 'They said she brought a priest to visit me because of my illness. But I am not ill.'

'They were mistaken, my love,' Gruffydd said.

Dropping her hand, Eleri looked up at Owen with a twinkle of conspiracy in her sunken eyes. 'She never came. Nor the priest.' She leaned towards Owen and whispered, 'Is it true that Father Edern has come?'

'Eleri!' Gruffydd thundered.

Startled, the woman reared back and drew in her breath sharply, bowed her head. Awena put her arm round her mother, whispered something.

Gruffydd shook his head sadly. 'My wife is easily confused, Captain.' He raked a hand through his thick dark hair. Owen noticed an angry-looking, partially healed scar on the palm of the hand, remembered that the hand had been bandaged when they first met. 'She hears a name once and then believes it is familiar. How did you find your brother?'

Was it the abrupt change of subject or did Owen simply find it implausible that Eleri would ask after a priest she had never met? 'My brother looks prosperous and fortunate in his wife and children. I am happy for him.' How might he take Eleri aside and speak with her? Her husband and daughter kept such close guard.

Eleri suddenly rose with a jolt that shook the table, and gathering her skirts about her she went quickly across the hall and up the steps to the solar. Neither of her guards hurried after.

Gruffydd simply looked after his wife, his face sad, and said, 'You must forgive her. She is beset by demons.'

Awena seemed more appropriately concerned. 'Shall I go to her?' she asked her father.

Gruffydd shook his head, lifted his bowl. 'You must take your ma's place with our guests. Pour us more wine.'

'Forgive me,' Owen said. 'My coming here was ill advised on such a day.'

Gruffydd pressed his fingers to his temples as if

weary. 'You are not to blame. It takes little to trouble my wife.'

From the solar came a child's laughter, low and throaty. Owen raised his head in the direction of the sound, thinking how like his daughter Gwenllian it sounded. Eleri appeared once more, called to Awena to assist her.

Gruffydd rose with Awena, put a hand on her shoulder. 'Keep the child up above, Awena,' he said quietly.

But Eleri had already begun to descend the narrow steps with a child in her arms. When she set him on his feet in the hall, the plump boy ran directly to the table to stare up at Gruffydd.

He was fair haired and blue eyed, a child to make a father's heart swell with pride. Owen glanced from the lad to Gruffydd, who made an apologetic face.

Eleri now took the boy's hand and guided him round the table to Owen. 'His name is Hedyn,' Eleri said. 'Do you not think Father Edern would be proud of him?'

'Eleri,' Gruffydd said sharply.

But she ignored him. 'Can you believe that my daughter's English husband rejected this angel? Tangwystl should be reunited with her true husband.'

God's blood, Owen thought, was that it? The child was Edern's? No wonder the vicar's name was denied in the house.

Gruffydd ran his hand through his hair. 'She does not know what she says. She would shame Tangwystl with such a tale.'

Eleri crouched beside the boy on the rushes. Hedyn clutched her hand tightly and stared up at Owen.

Owen reached out to the child, missing his own. His fingers were firmly grasped. 'He has a grasp like my daughter Gwenllian's. How old is this fine lad?'

Eleri turned on Owen a radiant smile. 'Two in early summer. He is the image of his father.'

Gruffydd rose. 'It is best that you go now, Captain. I cannot quiet her when she behaves like this.'

Pale hair, full lips, Owen supposed one could see a resemblance to Edern, but no more so than to any fair man. Owen knelt to the boy, met his eye, was pleased when the child let go Eleri and grabbed for Owen's eye-patch with a gleeful shout. Some children feared his appearance. 'God go with you, Hedyn, and may your father have a chance to see what a fine lad you are.'

'Come,' Gruffydd said, 'I shall walk out with you.'

Awena wished Owen a safe journey and bent to take the child. Eleri rose and stood clutching her elbows and rocking slightly from side to side.

Poor woman. What had brought her to such a state? One thing was certain, Owen no longer wondered why Gruffydd came alone to the castle.

Out in the yard, Gruffydd stopped beneath a tree that provided shelter from the drizzle. He apologised for his wife's behaviour, for the tales she spun out of air.

'The boy is yours, not Mistress Lascelles's?'

Gruffydd wagged his head back and forth, not denying it, but suggesting that things were not so simple to explain. 'It is true that my daughter had a child before she was betrothed to John Lascelles. But I assure you the vicar Edern is not Hedyn's father. You see how my Eleri takes some truth and then weaves lies through it.'

'She seems devoted to the boy.'

'Devoted. Yes.' Emotion shone in Gruffydd's blue eyes. 'Out of adversity came some joy. It was Eleri who offered to take the child when my son-in-law said he must be fostered up.'

'Forgive me, but is she—'

'Trustworthy?' Gruffydd shook his head. 'Not so much as she was. Awena watches over the boy.'

'Then your wife has not long been so afflicted?'

Gruffydd turned away, walked out from beneath the tree. 'Ah. The rain has ceased.' Still he kept his back to Owen. His voice was less steady as he said, 'My dear wife was brought low by our troubles in Tenby. Taking her from her home – it is as if she was robbed of her soul.'

'You must count yourself and your family ill used,' Owen said quietly. A tragedy indeed if the accusation were unjustified.

The lad who had helped Awena in the hall now brought Owen's horse to him.

Gruffydd turned round. If he had been hiding emotion, he was now composed, though as he spoke he looked aside and spoke in a halting manner. 'It has been difficult for all of us, Tangwystl perhaps most of all. She believes she sacrificed her son for our welfare and fears he will grow to resent her. She expected Sir John to accept Hedyn as if he were his own, in the Welsh way. It is hard for her to hear the boy called a bastard. But she is now the wife of an Englishman and she must accept his ways. I have assured her that Sir John will do well by Hedyn, as he did by John de

Reine. And meanwhile the boy is at least with his kin, if not his mother.'

And thus were two good people made miserable by their union. Was it any wonder Tangwystl sought an escape from her marriage? As Owen mounted, he looked down on Gruffydd and asked, 'Why did she not marry Hedyn's father?'

With a dark look, Gruffydd lifted a hand as if about to slap Owen's horse into a canter, but he checked the motion and instead rubbed his forehead. 'Of course you would ask. Forgive my temper. He abandoned her when Lady Pembroke accused me of treason. Suddenly my daughter had no dowry, a tarnished name. There could be no official marriage because I could no longer pay.'

Owen well remembered that a traditional Welsh marriage was costly, with the marriage portion, a wedding feast for the witnesses, a fee for the parson, and an amobr for the lord. The Marcher lords encouraged the traditions because they pocketed the fees. But would a man with such a son as Hedyn, such a wife in deed, abandon such happiness for her father's lack of money? 'Surely to our people such an accusation would not necessarily tarnish her name? I should think many support Owain ap Thomas ap Rhodri in their hearts, if not openly.'

Gruffydd said only, 'In the end she found a better man in John Lascelles.'

One of more use to the family. 'Where do you think your daughter has gone?'

'Tangwystl is a passionate young woman. No doubt she and Sir John quarrelled and she means to teach him a lesson. I am confident all will be well.' So seemingly passionate about all else concerning his family, Gruffydd's indifference about his daughter's disappearance came as a surprise.

'Did the earlier messenger from the castle tell you about Father Francis?'

Gruffydd bowed his head and crossed himself. 'May God grant him peace.'

'Does it not worry you that your daughter disappeared on the day of such a violent attack?'

The dark eyes widened in surprise. 'Do you think the priest died defending her?'

Owen had not thought of that. 'I mean that it is believed she left with Father Edern.'

'Why would she be with him?'

'Your wife—'

'My wife is as you saw her, Captain, confused. I am confident that Sir John will find my daughter.'

'I pray you are right.'

'I am glad I was able to find your brother for you, Captain. And now, forgive my haste, but I must return to my wife.'

With that, Gruffydd turned back towards the house, dismissing Owen, who sat astride his horse staring at the man's retreating back until the groom asked whether anything was wrong. The young man watched Owen ride away, poised as if ready to sound an alarm if Owen turned back.

Owen saw little of the countryside as he rode back to Cydweli. The image of the pale, gaunt Eleri haunted him, as did her husband. He thought much of the poor woman. God's purpose in robbing the woman of her wits eluded Owen. Might it be a punishment? Because she had encouraged Tangwystl in the liaison that had produced Hedyn? She had spoken of Hedyn's father as Tangwystl's true husband – did God not recognise the oath between a couple? Many a Welsh marriage had been based on merely that. But if her state were truly the result of Pembroke's accusation, how might a God-fearing man understand it? He would add her to his prayers. She seemed a gentle woman.

A movement up ahead, beneath a tree beside the track, caught Owen's attention and drew him from his thoughts. A young boy had risen abruptly from a crouch and spun round. Now he greeted Owen with a cheerful blessing, one hand behind his back.

Poaching, Owen thought. And fearful lest Owen saw his catch and would comment, so he thought to disarm him with his bold greeting. 'You are welcome to whatever it is you hide behind your back, lad. I shall not be informing on you.'

'God bless you, sir, and all your children, and your children's children.'

'You wear your guilt on your face, lad. Learn to disappear into the shadows.'

A bit of Gruffydd ap Goronwy in the lad, Owen thought as he rode on. Sweet heaven, that was it. He was a gift from God, that lad by the roadside. For that was indeed what Owen had sensed but could not put his finger on – Gruffydd behaved as if he were indifferent, but he was not. He would have done better to have torn his hair and beat his breast than to feign indifference. What was he hiding? Was he involved in Tangwystl's disappearance?

Was it possible? Was Tangwystl there at the farm, even now? Had she gone there not to be with an ailing mother, but with her son? Was that why Awena and Gruffydd watched Eleri so closely? Fearful she might reveal the secret?

But then what had become of the vicar? It seemed unlikely the man would just depart, not without the bishop's retainers. For surely Edern would go nowhere but back to St David's – he had undertaken this mission to please the bishop. Yet he was gone, and the two retainers remained.

Owen wished Lucie were here. He needed someone to talk to, someone who would listen and ask the right questions to help him see what he knew, what he needed to know, and to whom he ought to talk. Geoffrey seemed unable to perform the role for him; he saw everything that was happening in terms of how it affected him and their mission. There was no sense returning to confront Gruffydd. Owen had no way to motivate the man to confide in him.

Where had it all begun? With the accusation against Gruffydd? With Lascelles's first sight of Tangwystl? With Tangwystl and the father of her son?

Or were those events merely ripples that had led up to the death of John de Reine? Why had Burley's men gone to St David's? Who knew the truth about the theft of the exchequer?

His heart pounding, his mind racing, Owen urged his horse to a gallop. He had much to do, and, God help him, that filled him with joy.

τhe duke's
receiver

A fresh wind cooled Owen as he rode towards Cydweli. Below him on his left the marshes shimmered in the afternoon sun, the winter-browned grasses shivering in the wind. In a few months it would be a green sea of grasses loud with birdsong.

Near the mill outside the town, Owen dismounted, ran his fingers through his tangled hair, and tucked his weapons into the pack on his saddle, remembering the gatekeeper's concern about armed strangers in the town. He felt guilty to have ridden his horse so hard and then to have left him standing in the cold shadow by the south gate, but Owen wished to stop in the tavern before he returned to the castle. And if fortune smiled on him and he won the taverner's confidence, he would tarry even longer in the town. He hoped to be directed to the house of Roger Aylward, the Duke's receiver who had been injured defending the exchequer. He wished to hear the man's own account of the incident that had sent four armed men off to St David's, John de Reine's destination. Though it was possible that Aylward, too, would tell a tale to hide the truth, Owen hoped that would not be so.

But first he wished to learn all he could about the receiver. At home, when Owen needed information about townspeople, he slipped next door to the York Tavern. Bess and Tom Merchet heard much while pouring ales and feeding wayfarers. The midwife Magda Digby was also a dependable source of information, as, too, was Owen's wife Lucie, who heard much – and intuited more – in her apothecary shop. He sorely felt the lack of the four of them at present.

The inn looked much like any other, far less imposing than the York Tavern, but the stone threshold had been polished by the feet of many patrons. Owen ducked through the open doorway, and then beneath beams blackened by years of smoky fires, one of which now burned dully under a rancid-smelling stew. The fare in this tavern was not up to Bess Merchet's standards, that was certain.

Barefoot, skirt tucked up into her girdle, a young woman knelt on the floor scrubbing a long board that likely served as the top of a trestle table. She glanced up at Owen's greeting, then scurried up and disappeared into another doorway.

A thin, sour-faced man appeared soon enough, eyeing Owen with cautious curiosity as he set down a tray full of drinking bowls. His sleeves were stained with food and drink.

'Would you be the taverner?' Owen asked in Welsh.

'From the castle, are you?' the man said in English.

Owen was disappointed. He thought a Welsh taverner might be more co-operative. But perhaps this one would be more impressed by his being one of the Duke's emissaries. 'Aye. I am recruiting archers for the Duke.'

The man screwed up his face, nodded. 'I remember now. Captain of the old Duke's archers, they say, and from these parts.' He tilted his head, looked Owen up and down. 'I should think they have made you welcome at the castle. What would you be wanting in my humble tavern?'

'I want some of your best ale, and a bit of conversation that has nothing to do with archers or France.'

'Or the disappearance of the steward's lady?'

So the news had spread to the town. 'None of that, either.'

'Good. He is better off without her, her father a traitor and her mother witless.'

The taverner did indeed seem knowledgeable. 'Will you drink with me?'

The man turned round, shouted for a pitcher of ale and two bowls, then led Owen to a small table in the thick of the smoke, scratching himself as he walked.

Owen did not like a smoky place – he did not like losing the sharp sight in his good eye when it watered, but this was not the time to argue. He did wonder whether the taverner had chosen the table to put him at a disadvantage.

'Beeker's the name,' the taverner said as he settled himself. He grunted at the young woman who set a pitcher and two bowls before him and hurried away. 'They tell me you are Black Rhodri's son.'

'I am Owain ap Rhodri ap Maredudd.'

'Aye, Rhodri ap Maredudd – that was Black Rhodri.'

'I never heard him called that.'

'Well, you were gone when the lightning struck, eh?' Beeker's nasty grin revealed teeth blackened by rot.

Owen poured himself a bowl of the ale and swallowed it down. It was thick and surprisingly tasty, though way below Tom Merchet's standards. 'Is it your custom to insult the man who buys you ale?' He held the taverner's unwilling gaze.

'I meant no offence,' Beeker muttered, 'thought you would know.'

In the end Owen bullied the man into telling him what he wanted, and threatened that part of his anatomy he was so fond of scratching if he informed Burley of his visit.

The receiver's town house stood two storeys and boasted glazing in the window of the jettied second storey, a fine oak door, a stone path leading down the side to a walled garden and a stone stairway leading up to the side door opening on to the second storey. According to Beeker, Roger Aylward had another, larger house in the country. Made his money importing wine. A prosperous merchant. He would think twice before accepting the 'honour' of the receivership again no doubt. What need had he of such trouble?

A barefoot serving girl opened the street-level door to Owen, then made him wait without while she hurried up the stairway to 'ask whether her master was at home'. Amusingly clumsy – for surely Roger Aylward must be at home, bedridden as he was said to be since the incident. Owen had a long wait – long enough to become well acquainted with a ginger cat who thought him likely to be hiding milk or meat on his person. His thoughts went once again to York: Jasper had a cat much like this; Crowder would sit on a sill watching the lad work in the apothecary, drowsing in the sun. At night he was one of the best mousers in York – he had the belly to prove it.

'Master Aylward will see you now,' the young woman called from halfway up the stairs, waking Owen from his homely reverie. As he reached her level she bowed her head and said softly, 'I am sorry you had to wait without.'

'It is no fors. I had a quiet moment with the cat.'

The master lay in state in a great oak bed, wearing a linen shift with voluminous pleated sleeves and a tidy linen cap tied beneath his chin. Lamplight revealed a fleshy man of sanguine complexion looking delighted to have a visitor.

'Forgive me for not rising to welcome you,' he said in Welsh, 'but my head still feels as if it is being ground to flour when I stand. I hope you understood why I did not invite you to our house when you arrived – that you had heard of the theft, my attack . . . ?' The gap in his teeth was evident when he spoke – in truth, the only visible evidence of his having been assaulted.

Why should the man apologise for neglecting what had never been expected? 'I had heard about your misfortune, Master Aylward.'

'But I am glad you came. I love to think about your

father, my old friend Rhodri ap Maredudd. Please, sit. The girl will bring cider as soon as she has time.'

Old friend? The unexpected connection was Owen's second gift this day. And why not speak of his family – it would make the rest all the easier. He took a seat on a comfortably cushioned bench at his host's bedside. 'I did hope to hear of him, and my mother.'

'You have been to Morgan's house?'

'Aye.'

'Then you know that they are both with God.'

'My brother saw no need to delay the telling,' Owen said. If the man knew his family, he knew Morgan's character.

'Indeed. My wife thought perhaps we should do the telling, but I thought it best coming from your kin. Of course your ma's going was a peaceful one, went to bed and did not wake. But Rhodri's—' Roger bowed his head and crossed himself. 'I confess I did not wish to be the one to describe it to you.' He clapped his hands as the serving girl backed into the room with a tray. 'Now I shall show you some hospitality and we can talk of your father's joys.'

Owen's heart lightened to hear of his father's pride in his being chosen one of Lancaster's archers, and how the family were at last accepted into the community, largely because of his mother's skill with herbs and his father's with ailing livestock. 'They were generous with the talents God gave them,' Roger said, 'and your friend Master Chaucer told me of your talents – how you have become indispensable to both the Archbishop of York and our Duke.'

'Chaucer? You have met?' Aylward seemed a master of surprise.

Aylward gestured to the serving girl, who sat quietly with some needlework in the light from the window, to pour him more cider.

'Yes, yes,' Aylward said as he held up his cup to be filled, 'it has been a day of pleasant meetings, good for the spirits of one so confined. And a day of sorrow. I have great sympathy for John Lascelles. He did a good deed, granted a heroic kindness to a beleaguered family to my mind, and he has had nothing but sorrow from it. Such a beauty she is, but so unfit to be the wife of one of Lancaster's stewards. Even so, you will not find me linking her with the beating of Father Francis. It will be the churchman, mark my words. Though I do not like to think it of Father Edern. I was fond of him when he was chaplain at the castle.'

His mind reeling with the effort to follow the track of Aylward's easy tongue, Owen remained quiet for a moment, though he nodded solemnly now and then to encourage his host. Had Geoffrey told him all this? To what purpose?

'I confess I was disappointed that you had sent your comrade to me,' Aylward continued. 'So I am glad that you had additional questions, though I swear by St David I can think of no reason Mistress Lascelles would take up with Father Edern.'

'Master Chaucer told you he was assisting me in an investigation?'

'He was wrong to admit that? But why should a man confide if he does not know to what purpose—' Aylward stopped as Owen waved aside the argument.

'I am glad that he was open,' Owen said. He was thinking fast. 'Did he tell you that we believe the steward's recent troubles – the theft, the deaths of John de Reine and the chaplain, and Mistress Lascelles's disappearance – have some common source?'

The ruddy face registered puzzlement, then amusement. Aylward tried to hide the smile by lifting the cup to his mouth, but Owen had seen it.

'You find that unlikely?' Owen asked.

Aylward took his time setting his cup on the table beside him, dabbing his lips with a cloth. 'Forgive me. I know nothing of these things. I merely— My good wife, you see, would like your theory. She is fond of blaming all her troubles on one source. And when you said— Well, in truth, it reminded me of her.'

If Roger Aylward was not telling the truth, he was a clever liar with a quick wit, for his explanation was credible in its singularity.

'I hope that you are not considered the source of all her problems,' Owen said with a smile.

Aylward chuckled. 'No, we are content in one another. And I do sincerely hope that you do not consider me the source of John Lascelles's troubles.'

'I should be a fool to sit here partaking of your hospitality if that were so,' Owen said, lifting his cup. 'But I do ask a favour, that you tell me in your own words all you remember about the night of the theft.'

The receiver closed his eyes, leaned his head back on the bounteous pile of pillows. 'Such a cursed night, and you wish to hear of it over and over again.'

So this, too, Geoffrey had requested. What was the man up to? 'One last time, Master Aylward. I should be grateful. I might then rest assured that I know all that can be known of it.'

Aylward opened one eye. 'You do not trust Master

Chaucer's memory? But you should, you know. He recited a long and most excellent tale of Seys and Alcyone that he is using in a poem of his own making, in honour of our Duke's fair Duchess so sadly gone from us.'

So that was how Geoffrey had won the man's friendship – by playing the bard. Owen would admire his ingenuity if he were not so angry. What was Geoffrey thinking, to come here and question the Duke's receiver? What did he know of the cunning necessary for such things? Well, he knew something, Owen could not deny it. 'I worry that he might not heed the finer details.'

Aylward sighed and began a recitation – for that was precisely how it sounded, a rehearsed description of the event. Aylward had sat alone at a table in the castle treasury having a cup of wine after a long session with his secretary, dictating letters to Lancaster and his Receiver General. During the past autumn Aylward had arranged shipping for the Duke's coming expedition, travelling to various ports in south Wales to do so, and he owed an accounting of his activities, results, expenses. Whilst he sat at the table, his back to the door, a stranger entered the room, grabbed him from behind, dragging him from his chair – which toppled backward and crashed with such a noise he had hoped to see guards at the door at once. But fortune was not with him that evening. With a knife to Aylward's throat the intruder made him open a chest, then flung the receiver from him with such force Aylward was thrown forward over the toppled chair – which is when he lost his tooth. When he stood up to throw himself upon the thief he was flung to the wall. And that is all he remembered.

Considering the heft of the man, at least what Owen could guess from the parts visible beneath the bed-clothes, the thief must have been a man of some considerable strength. And yet Aylward's vague description of the intruder made him of average weight and height.

'He had no accomplice?' Owen asked, frowning.

'No.'

'You called him a stranger. You saw his face?'

Aylward shook his head. 'He wore a mask and no livery.' He shook his head again, then moaned and called for the serving girl. 'My head,' he said in a hoarse whisper, as if weakened by the gesture.

'A cold compress, soaked in lavender water if you have it,' Owen said, 'and some feverfew in his cider. That should soothe him.'

The maid looked puzzled. Even Aylward opened his eyes.

'My wife is a master apothecary. I have learned much from her. It is the least I can offer, having been the cause of your present discomfort. God go with you, Master Aylward. You have been more than kind.'

Owen shook his head as he descended to the street. Aylward's account and his behaviour stank of deceit. But who would benefit?

'You look disappointed, Captain.' A man stepped from the shadows, leading Owen's horse. One of Burley's men, crook nosed and sinewy with large hands and a bald pate. Duncan.

'It is good of you to bring my horse to me, Duncan,' Owen said.

A gap-toothed grin. 'Did you learn what you wished from Master Aylward?' Duncan patted Owen's horse.

'Aye, that I did. He knew my parents well. But surely you did not come down from the castle to ask about my family?'

'Sir John rode out this morning and has not returned. The town porter said your horse was in a froth when you came to the gate. We hoped you might have news of the steward.'

Owen groaned. 'Another worry to distract the garrison? I shall never complete my mission.' His complaint rang hollow in his ears.

'Whence did you ride in such haste?'

Owen grabbed a partial lie from the air, one that might not be discovered too soon. 'From Gruffydd ap Goronwy's. I rode out to escort Mistress Lascelles and the priest back to Cydweli. But I found they had never been at the farm. I thought the steward should know as soon as possible.'

'Sir John sent you?'

'He had suggested it last night.'

'Odd.' Duncan handed Owen the reins. 'He sent someone else this morning.'

'Then I have spent my steed for nothing.'

'Aye. That you have.' Duncan motioned for Owen to go first.

Folk moved out of their way as they walked along Castle Street to the south gate of the castle. The townsfolk feared Burley's men, that was plain. Owen wondered why Burley's man had awaited him outside Aylward's house. Had Burley been warned of

Owen's visit? Was that the cause of Owen's long wait without?

Had Owen been trailed by Burley, perhaps since he left the castle this morning with Gladys? Duncan's boots and leggings were not travel stained, but that told Owen nothing.

What nagged at him more was the theft of the exchequer. As he walked, he thought back over Aylward's story. Nothing rang true about it – the receiver's rehearsed tale, his pretence of being bed-ridden, the implausible trail on which Burley had dispatched his men without a clear description of the attacker. And now Burley's man awaiting Owen outside the receiver's house – why?

'The constable wants to see you,' Duncan said.

'I thought he might.' And Owen wished to see him once he had more time to think all this through. An idea was slowly forming. And if he did not come to some understanding with the constable he would be tripping over him whenever he took a backward step. It was not a time for accidents. It was time to talk. 'Tell him I shall be with him by and by, once I have seen to my horse and my muddy boots.'

On a long bench in the practice yard, Burley sat with feet propped on a barrel. His fair hair was dark with sweat, his tunic muddy. Duncan leaned down to speak quietly, no doubt reporting his brief conversation with Owen. Burley nodded, waved Duncan away, smiled at Owen. 'I am glad to see you, Captain Archer. I feared that you, too, had deserted us.'

'It is good to see a constable who keeps himself ever ready for battle,' Owen said. 'But surely you might have asked the Duke for the funds needed for the garrison instead of feigning a theft from the exchequer?'

Showing no emotion, Burley ordered the waiting servant to disappear. 'Leave the ale,' he barked. The servant set a pitcher and bowl down on the bench beside Burley and hurried off. Burley poured, drank, belched. 'Better.' He turned back to Owen. 'It had nothing to do with the garrison.'

'I thought not.'

'What do you intend to do with your discovery?'

'Nothing. It does not concern me or my mission here.'

'What about Master Chaucer?'

'I cannot swear for him, but I would say that you would do better to worry about his impression of Cydweli's defences. Convince him that the garrison is fit and ready to defend the Duke's interests against the French or the Welsh pretender, and you will enjoy a long and profitable constableship.'

'And you? What do I have to fear from you?'

'If the theft is the worst sin on your conscience, nothing. But I am curious why you and the wealthy receiver found it necessary to steal from the treasury.'

'An unfortunate investment. A foolhardy venture . . .' Burley looked at his muddy boots. 'Never trust a merchant. He swore the risk was slight when he coaxed me into investing, and after the ship sank he swore it was as much a shock and disaster for him as it was for me. I had my revenge, though.' Burley's eyes crinkled with pleasure.

'The tooth?'

Burley glanced up and burst into laughter. 'And he cannot say a word about it, vain, pompous, stupid man.' He picked up a cloth and proceeded to dry his hair. The sky had once more clouded over, bringing a chill to the air.

Owen pitied Roger Aylward. He seemed a man who had taken few bad risks. And this one might have been easily dismissed if he had not brought Burley into it. 'Had John de Reine anything to do with it?'

'Nothing. And I had no idea he was off to St David's when I sent my men out – that was your next question, eh?'

Owen laughed. 'Aye.'

'He was on his way to Carreg Cennen, that is what we all thought. My men must have picked up his trail by accident. God's blood but I wish I knew where they were now.'

'I should think you might commend their enterprise.'

Burley snorted. 'Bumbling asses, they are.'

Owen was disappointed, but there it was. He had solved one mystery only to discover it had nothing to do with the important one. 'John Lascelles. Is it possible he supports Owain Lawgoch?'

Burley snorted. 'You Welshmen are obsessed with the French King's puppet. Do you know how many of your countrymen are over there fighting for the ugly Du Guesclin? As many as could fit in the ship.'

'It is one way to escape the stench of the English invaders.'

'So that is it,' Burley said quietly. 'I thought it odd, a Welshman recruiting archers. You are really here to meet with Gruffydd ap Goronwy. That was your purpose in riding to his farm.'

'I would be a fool if that were true. I know the Duke of Lancaster well enough to fear what he would do to a traitor in his household. Or a thief.'

Burley's expression was most gratifying. But he was not one to take a hit on the jaw without striking back. 'Your championing of a certain woman surprised me, Captain. I misjudged you at first. I thought you were of the steward's persuasion – ambition does not stumble on charity.'

So he had followed him. Owen straddled the bench, forcing Burley to abandon the barrel so that he might look him in the eye. 'And what woman was that?'

'Gladys, the castle whore.'

'I cannot take all the credit. She sought me out. Then I found it difficult to deny her.'

'Oh, aye. Many do.'

'Her sanctuary will not be disturbed?'

Burley shook his head. 'Only Duncan and I know of it. And of course Harold and Simwnt. I shall send those two for her when the chaplain's murderer is found.'

'Any luck with that?'

'You dined in the steward's rooms last night, you and Master Chaucer. What was his temper?'

'Melancholy. Not a mood that often turns to murder.'

'To my mind, it was him, his lady, or the Welsh vicar who beat the chaplain. Or in the lady's case, *had* him beaten.'

'What if I told you I know where all three have gone?'

Burley poured himself more ale, looked at Owen through half-closed eyes as he drank down the bowl. 'Of course. This is the sort of thing you do, smoke out murderers. But you came to recruit archers. What are those three to you?'

'Perhaps nothing.'

Burley nodded, as if he had made a discovery. 'The Duke has heard of Sir John's questionable marriage. You are here to observe him. But he is not a Welshman. Why would he support Lawgoch?'

Owen did not intend to speculate with Burley. 'I am going after the three of them. I do not ask for your men. Mine will suffice. Nor do I need a shadow.'

'Duncan would make an excellent guide.'

Duncan must be an excellent assassin. 'He would crowd me.'

'He will be ordered to keep his distance. You need not take all of your men, surely.'

'No.'

'What of Master Chaucer?'

Indeed. What of Geoffrey? 'No doubt he will do what he pleases.'

Owen's entrance made Geoffrey start and drop his pen. He cursed as a spot of ink trembled on the parchment, then slowly spread flat. 'Devil's own is what you are,' Geoffrey muttered, blotting the stain with frantic energy. 'Where have you been? Where is Gladys?'

'Safe.' Owen considered an apology, thought better of it. Geoffrey had much to answer for. 'So you are assisting me in an investigation, eh? And what did you learn on your rounds?'

Geoffrey wiped his nose, smudging it with ink, faced Owen with a comically stern face. 'I learned,' he said quietly, 'that Aylward gave a vague description which was then connected to someone who had been boasting in the tavern.'

'A vague description. Aye. And one that does not fit the tale.' Owen shook his head. 'The man has the story by heart, did you note that? And he looks far too hale and hardy to be still abed from an attack eighteen days ago.'

Geoffrey dabbed at the stain on his nose with jerky anger. 'What about the tooth?'

Owen hid a smile. 'What do you know of Sir John's disappearance?'

'That Burley thinks it coincided too closely with yours. And that he rode out with only his squire.'

'Roger Aylward thinks you are a bard.'

Geoffrey blushed. 'I made no claim—'

'Clever, that was.' Owen rose to answer a knock at the door.

Iolo stood without. 'You sent for me, Captain?'

'You, Jared and the bishop's men – prepare to ride out with me in the morning.'

'But the others? And the archers?'

'We shall return for them. We go to St David's on an errand for the Duke. Burley's man Duncan will accompany us.'

Geoffrey was right behind Owen when he turned from the door. 'What intrigue is this?'

'Burley has agreed that I am the best man to pursue Sir John and his lady. And Edern.'

'To St David's?'

'It is the logical place for them to go.'

'I am coming with you.'

'What of your mission?'

'It was my understanding that we shared the same mission. Has that changed?'

Sixteen

ḣE IS NAMED

Unsettled by Brother Dyfrig's information, Dafydd had spent the time since his conversation with the monk studying a growing patch of damp on the whitewashed wall above the garden window. The darkening patch seemed at first a simple matter, something about which to instruct the servants. But as the shape shifted, sending out tendrils of damp along unseen cracks in the plaster, he saw how insidious was this leak, how easily it might bring the wall down and the roof with it. How did such a disaster begin? Had a small animal nested in the thatch and worn away a portion by the wall? Had a cross-beam begun to rot? Was it merely God's will that the wall should fall?

So too with the pilgrim. Had there been a moment in which Dafydd might have seen the danger in shielding him? Had he been arrogant in granting sanctuary in his house? Was God angry that he had not taken the pilgrim to a proper sanctuary? Back to St David's, to the church of St David and St Andrew? Did God test Dafydd?

And all the while, darkness slowly spread over the wall before him like a plague of ants.

While Dafydd was thus absorbed, Mair appeared at his side, her lovely face darkened with worry. 'Forgive me, Master, but you did not hear my knock. You have taken no food, no drink since this morning. Are you unwell?'

'Unwell?' He considered his pounding heart, the dampness at the nape of his neck. 'My soul aches. Bring me a cup of cider.' As Mair hastened to obey, Dafydd called after her, 'God has answered me in your concern. Bless you.'

After Dafydd had refreshed himself, a wan late afternoon sun at last lured him into the garden. He breathed deeply, enjoying the sensation of a spreading calm.

And then Brother Dyfrig stepped out into the garden. Though the cowl shadowed Dyfrig's face, Dafydd sensed the monk's eyes on him. The author of his earlier anxieties, Dyfrig was the last person with whom Dafydd wished to speak, but he could think of no courteous escape. So he spread out his arms and bowed to the monk. '*Benedicte*, Brother Dyfrig.'

Dyfrig bowed, uncovered his head. '*Benedicte*, Master Dafydd.'

The hooded eyes considered Dafydd closely. It was not Dyfrig's way, this direct gaze. Dafydd dreaded more distressing revelations. 'You are now rested?'

'Dry and rested. God bless you for your generous hospitality.' Brother Dyfrig made the sign of the cross over Dafydd and the garden.

Perhaps it was the time to voice his concern. 'I have thought long on what you suggested,' Dafydd said, 'the connections – Tangwystl, my pilgrim, Lawgoch . . .'

Dyfrig nodded brusquely. 'You see the pattern.' He then glanced away, and in a quieter voice began, 'Master—'

'Worse!' Dafydd interrupted, not wanting to lose his train of thought. 'I see the danger. My intention was to offer the pilgrim sanctuary until he healed. I believed God put him in my path for that purpose. I did not intend to offer my life for him – by the Trinity, I do not even know his name. His family.'

'But I—'

'His politics is the only thing I do know.'

Dyfrig looked surprised. 'Do you?'

'You implied he supported that red-handed fool, Lawgoch.'

'No. I suggested a connection, not precisely what it was. Is the pilgrim a supporter of Lawgoch? Or did he murder Lawgoch's supporter? Was he the companion of the dead man, and if so, were they supporters of Lawgoch or King Edward?' Dyfrig shook his head. 'You still know nothing of the man. But—'

'But that he has brought me much danger. What of my honourable name?' Dafydd raised his voice when Dyfrig would speak. 'Knowing now how dangerous is the pilgrim's company, I am concerned for Brother Samson and his party. I would hasten to join them, provide an armed escort, but how can I leave my servants with these Cydweli men?' There. He had followed his thought to the conclusion.

Brother Dyfrig was shaking his head. 'You sent no armed escort with Brother Samson?'

Now the criticism began. 'I thought an armed escort would draw attention to them. A monk, his servant, and an ailing pilgrim – no one would make note of them.'

'No one but thieves. They think all men of the Church carry bags full of gold chalices and pilgrims' offerings.' Dyfrig dropped his gaze, softened his voice. 'But it is not of that I wish to speak. My conscience will not let me rest, Master Dafydd. I have kept something from you.'

Here it was, the dreaded revelation.

'The name of the man Cydweli men seek – it is Rhys ap Llywelyn, is it not?'

'It is.'

'That is the man you sheltered. Your pilgrim.'

Did Dyfrig think Dafydd would not have guessed that? 'I suspected it was so. He was too cleverly confused when we called him by that name. And for the Cydweli men to return in such a way, they must have been very certain of his identity.'

Dyfrig did not look up, showed no sign of relief at Dafydd's lack of surprise.

It set Dafydd to thinking. 'But what are you saying? You know him?'

'I know his kinsman.'

Dafydd felt his dread warming to anger. 'How do you know his kinsman?'

'He once did a favour for my family.'

A favour? By the rood, he knew him well. 'And Rhys's politics? Do you know them?'

'I do not. I believe that his difficulties are of a personal nature, not political. But of course if he did murder John de Reine . . .'

To become flustered with emotion was not the behaviour of a bard. Dafydd kept his voice calm by moving the anger downward. He rocked on his feet. 'How long have you known his name?'

'From the beginning.'

'Why did you not tell me?' Dafydd rocked a little faster.

'At first it did not seem important. I have never heard ill of Rhys. As far as I knew his greatest sin was that of loving a woman against her father's wishes. Such a sin did not alarm me.'

'Tangwystl is his beloved?'

Dyfrig said nothing.

'Of course she is – it was by her name that you knew him.'

'I imagined Rhys had been wounded in a fight over a cow, or defending a woman. But the death of John de Reine – that changed the game.'

'Indeed it should.'

'All the way from St David's I intended to confess my omission and tell you to whom you had given sanctuary. But when I learned the Cydweli men had returned, I thought it best you did not know. They would read only innocence in your eyes, your voice.'

'You fool. If they had believed my professed ignorance of the man the first time they would not have returned.'

'So it has turned out. They are shrewder than I had thought.'

'So why tell me now?'

'I cannot live with the deceit.'

'You cannot?' Dafydd heard his voice echo off the house, lowered it. 'You managed it well enough before.'

Now, at last, Dyfrig raised his head. He looked –

Dafydd could not believe it. He stopped his rocking. The monk's face was yet blank. Was there some flicker of contrition in those hooded eyes? He thought not.

'Forgive me,' Dyfrig said softly.

'What does it matter whether I forgive you? You have no soul. What are you that you can confess such a thing to me and show no emotion?'

Dyfrig began to drop his head.

'Look at me, not the soil at your marble feet.'

Dyfrig complied. Was it better to be regarded by those cold, hooded eyes?

'I now understand the danger involved,' said Dafydd. 'What must I do?'

'We must go after Brother Samson, protect him. We do not know whether the Cydweli men have comrades who knew their destination. Even now they might be on their way to this house.'

Dafydd had not thought of that. 'But my servants.' Mair had just stepped into the garden. Dafydd motioned for her to stay where she was.

'Your servants will be safe,' Dyfrig said quietly. 'What cause do the men have to harm them? Until they are recovered they depend on your servants for care and comfort.'

'We shall talk more of this over the evening meal.' Dafydd motioned for Mair to come forward. He was sorry for the shadows beneath her eyes, the frown that creased her high forehead. When would his household be at peace again?

'Maelgwn's youngest son has come with a message for you, Master Dafydd.'

Maelgwn farmed the land adjacent to Dafydd's property. He was an odd little man, fancied himself a vessel of prophecy. 'He wishes to tell my future, does he?'

'Not this time, Master. The boy says there are murderers in the wood.'

The barefoot lad bowed to Dafydd, stretched out his arms and bowed his head to Brother Dyfrig. 'May I have your blessing, Father?'

Dyfrig made the sign of the cross over the boy.

'What is this about murderers, lad?' Dafydd asked.

'My da says you are to come.' He was staring at Dyfrig. 'It is one of your kind we found.'

'You found a monk?' Dafydd asked.

The boy nodded.

'Tell me, for pity's sake, lad, in what condition did you find him?'

'Left for dead. His servant wept over him.'

'Was there another? A young man, a pilgrim?'

The lad shook his head.

'Do you know the monk's name?'

'His man calls him Brother Samson.'

Heartsick, Dafydd turned to Dyfrig. 'You knew no ill of him?'

'It was you sent them without armed escort,' Dyfrig hissed. To the boy he said, 'We shall come after sunset, lad. Tell your father we shall come.'

When the boy was gone, Dafydd turned on Dyfrig. 'We must find Rhys ap Llywelyn.'

'We must see to Brother Samson. You sent him off with your pilgrim.'

'The kinsman of your friend.'

'We must go to him.'

'Of course we must.' Make sure of Maelgwn's

221

care, then go in search of the pilgrim. 'We shall take Cadwal and Madog with us. And food and drink.'

'You should bind the captives so they cannot follow us.'

'They are injured. I shall leave enough men to guard them. And the dogs.'

'They are soldiers.'

'We have twice bested them.'

'Listen to me, Master Dafydd. I find it passing strange the Cydweli men lie so quietly in your hall. They are watching, waiting. You may be angry with me, but it was your refusal to behave as others would that has brought this trouble on your house and on Brother Samson. Another would have taken the wounded man back to St David's. That is an appropriate sanctuary. Not the house of a bard.'

'God put him in my path.'

'Perhaps you misinterpreted His purpose.'

Owen stood atop Cydweli's chapel tower and let the mist cool his head. The day had moved along too quickly, forcing him to make what might prove to be a rash decision. He prayed that he had not made a mistake, that he had not lost his knack for judging fighting men, that for all Burley's 'flawed soul' he could be trusted in his loyalty to Lancaster and Cydweli. In faith it was Father Edern who had referred to Burley's soul – it seemed he was hardly one whose judgement was to be trusted.

Someone came through the tower door. Owen drew his knife and glanced round, ready to defend himself.

'It is Iolo.'

Owen slid the knife back in its sheath. 'You are certain you were not followed?'

'I am,' Iolo said with confidence.

Owen was reassured, for he knew Iolo could steal through a place like a cat, from shadow to shadow, seemingly not even disturbing the air round him.

'Is this about Duncan?' Iolo asked.

'Aye. You are to watch him closely. Any move to attack any of us, or those we pursue, you know what to do.'

'I do, Captain.' Iolo also attacked like a cat – in a flash of movement and with deadly precision.

Dafydd, Brother Dyfrig, Madog and Cadwal led their horses from the stable under cover of darkness. All but Dyfrig knew well the trackway to Maelgwn's farmhouse, a muddy path worn low in the tall grasses and gorse that crowned the headland, then dipped down into willowy woods along a stream. The weather had turned yet again and a soft rain fell. The low clouds veiled the moon. The wood was quiet, and thinking on the wounded Samson, the four crept along on cat feet. Dafydd drew his hood over his hair to quiet the soft music of his ornaments – it was not the time to bell the cat. But the whisper of their horses' breath could not be stilled. When at last a soft lantern light welcomed them from the doorway of the farmhouse, Dafydd said a prayer of thanksgiving.

But Maelgwn's wife received Dafydd and Dyfrig with such a solemn countenance that they asked if Samson yet lived. She bowed her white-veiled head as she spread her arms and asked for Brother Dyfrig's blessing. He quickly gave it, then repeated his question.

'He lives, Father,' she said. 'But he burns with fever and his leg is broken. His man, you will notice, is unharmed.' She spoke the last as she stood over Samson's servant, who sat with head bowed beside his master's pallet.

Oil-lamps flickered on shelves by either end of the pallet. As Dafydd and Dyfrig approached, Brother Samson waked, blinking as if opening his eyes brought a shock of light. He lifted a trembling hand to his eyes to shield them. His breathing was uneven and painful to hear. His bald head was wrapped round with a clean bandage.

Aled, the servant, held a spoon of wine to his master's cracked lips. Samson opened his mouth, let the wine trickle in.

'Was it the pilgrim?' Dafydd asked. Aled nodded. Dafydd dropped to his knees beside the bed and bowed his head. 'Forgive me, Brother Samson.'

'This man was the attacker?' Maelgwn's wife hissed. She took a step towards the bed as if to protect her patient.

'No,' said Brother Dyfrig, staying her with a hand. 'But it was he who asked Brother Samson to escort the pilgrim to Strata Florida.'

'Brother Samson, can you hear me?' Dafydd whispered.

The monk moaned.

'It is Master Dafydd and Brother Dyfrig.'

Samson opened his eyes wide, looked at one, the other, then let his lids fall.

'Look at his servant, will you? Not a mark on him,' Maelgwn's wife said with a sniff.

Aled looked up, and spoke in a voice shrill with indignation. 'Brother Samson took off after the pilgrim.' Now that he showed his face, Dafydd could see the signs of much weeping.

'Tell us, Aled,' Dyfrig said sternly. 'We cannot know the truth of it unless you help us see it.'

Farmer Maelgwn had been sitting in the deep shadows in the corner of the room. Now he shifted, moved a stool close. His bushy brows knit together as he frowned down at the young man.

Aled wiped his nose on his sleeve and eyed his audience warily, but as Dyfrig opened his mouth to command him he nodded and began, 'We had not come far. The oak wood that is just beyond this farm. The pilgrim began to moan and fall forward over his horse. I dismounted and rushed to help him. He kicked me in the head –' the young man turned his head towards the light so all could see the bruise on his left temple '– and whipped my horse so he bolted, then rode off like the wind. Brother Samson spurred his horse and went after him. What was I to do with no horse?' Aled sniffed and searched the faces of his audience.

'Continue your tale,' Dyfrig said.

'I know not how long I searched, nor how far I walked before I discovered my horse at a stream. When I had calmed him I sat and wondered what to do . . .' Aled droned on and on, through indecisions, muddy accidents, a torn habit and a rumbling stomach until at last he came to his discovery of Brother Samson the following morning, soaked and shivering

225

beside the stream, his horse grazing nearby. 'From the gash in his head and his broken leg, I think he rode beneath a low branch and fell from his horse. He said he rolled into the stream to cool the pain of his leg, but then he rolled too far.'

'The chill is in his bones,' Maelgwn said. 'And the pilgrim has gone south.'

'Is this one of your prophecies?' Dafydd asked.

Maelgwn raised his eyes upward, lifted his arms and declaimed in a deep voice, 'The well filled with light, and then rising from the water came Carn Llidi, then Penmaen Dewi.'

St David's Head and the burial chamber above it. And where else would Rhys head but back to his unfinished business? Dafydd glanced over at Dyfrig. 'We must pursue him.'

'I shall sit with Brother Samson tonight.'

'And in the morning—'

'We shall decide what we must do.'

Seventeen

ST NON'S BENEFICENCE

Brother Michaelo sat up with a cry. 'Wulfstan!' He stared wildly at the far wall. Sir Robert was by his side at once, soothing him, reassuring him that he had only seen Brother Wulfstan in a dream. There was no ghostly monk in the room. It was the third time Michaelo had had such a nightmare. Sir Robert feared it was his own incessant coughing that disturbed the monk's sleep and brought on bad dreams.

Michaelo's eyes focused on Sir Robert, then the lamp beside his bed. Still he trembled and would not look out into the room. 'I saw him again, putting the cup to his lips.' Michaelo crossed himself. 'By all that is holy, how could I have done such a thing to that good man?' Seven years past he had served Brother Wulfstan a poisoned drink, hoping by the infirmarian's death to protect a friend.

'He did not die by your hand, Michaelo. God was

not ready for him.' The poison had made Wulfstan very ill, but had not killed him. It was the pestilence the summer past that had stilled Wulfstan's great heart. Sir Robert put a cup of wine in Brother Michaelo's trembling hands. 'Drink this.' He turned away to cough.

'My nightmares are making you worse. You should do to me what I meant to do to him.'

Sir Robert managed a smile as he fought another cough. 'It is a tempting proposition, I assure you,' he wheezed, 'but I would not let you escape your pain so easily.' He allowed another coughing fit. 'Nor do I wish to risk my immortal soul with your blood on my hands.'

' "*Evil shall slay the wicked: and they that hate the righteous shall be desolate*," ' Michaelo whispered.

Sir Robert thought it a fitting psalm, but the monk had stopped too soon. 'Then David said, "*The Lord redeemeth the soul of His servants: and none of them that trust in Him shall be desolate*." '

'I am not worth your concern,' Brother Michaelo said.

'Come. Drink the wine.'

Pliable in his need, Brother Michaelo gulped down the wine, shivered, then lay back down.

'God forgave you long ago, as did Wulfstan,' said Sir Robert. ' "*Blessed is he whose transgression is forgiven, whose sin is covered*." ' He paused, realised that the monk already drifted back to sleep. Sir Robert took away the cup, poured himself some of the physick Owen had left for his cough, and took it to his own bed, where he burrowed beneath several blankets and a skin.

Warmth eluded him, but as Sir Robert sipped the physick he felt his throat relax. At least he might now lie quietly for a while. He closed his eyes and thought of his long dead wife, Amélie. He saw her as she had looked the day he presented himself at her father's manor in Normandy and told Amélie's mother that she might have her husband back, uninjured and in good temper, for a ransom. She had withdrawn with her elderly father-in-law, returned leading the bewitching young Amélie before her. The young woman, eyes modestly trained on her slippers, curtseyed before him, then stood silently with hands entwined in rosary beads. She was offered in exchange for her father. 'A wife is of more use to you than a proud man who eats your food and drinks your wine while waiting for a chance to slit your throat, *n'est-ce pas?*'

Robert had loved Amélie, sweet *Jesu* how he had loved her. But he had not known how to show his love. As was his custom, he imagined a different ending to their tale, that she had not fallen in love with another, that she had awaited him and not Montaigne in the maze at Freythorpe Hadden on his return. How many times since Amélie's death had Robert walked that maze, imagining what it must have been like to be the one awaited, to have her fly into his arms when he found her in the centre. Hot tears slid out the sides of his eyes and coursed along his temples. He was an old fool, to yearn so for another chance with her. God had for His own mysterious reasons chosen to delay Sir Robert's happiness, to give it to him in the form of a loving daughter and two perfect grandchildren.

* * *

The unsettled weather of the day before gave way to a haze that promised sunshine later in the morning. Geoffrey took it as a sign that they had God's blessing. They departed by the north gate of Cydweli Castle to avoid most of the town. Though it was early, the sound of horses would bring folk to their doors, and Owen did not wish to call attention to his party. For all he knew the chaplain's murderer yet hid in the town. Let Burley deal with him.

Duncan and Iolo led the group, followed by Owen and Geoffrey, then the bishop's men, and Jared brought up the rear. Owen had misgivings about the size of the company. After all, they pursued only an older man and his squire. Speed would stand them in better stead than numbers. But fussing now would only cause delay.

Sir Robert opened his eyes to behold a new day, and Brother Michaelo already dressing.

'I was glad to see you sleeping peacefully,' Michaelo said.

Sir Robert sat up slowly, expecting to feel drowsy – he feared he had taken too much of the physick. But he felt quite well. So well that he proposed they return to St Non's.

'I wish to pray once more for my family, and I thought perhaps you might pray for Wulfstan's soul and a reprieve from your nightmares.'

Brother Michaelo agreed to the journey, though he made it plain that his own prayers would be for Sir Robert. 'I keep you wakeful with my nightmares and because of that your cough has worsened.'

'We are being too kind to one another,' Sir Robert protested. 'We become dull, frightened old men.'

'Old?'

Sir Robert was pleased to see Brother Michaelo flare his nostrils and tuck in his chin in horror. He preferred the monk's usual, self-centred self to the hovering companion.

The soft muzzle of a dog against Dafydd's face brought a cheerful awakening in Maelgwn's quiet farmhouse. It had a white coat so well brushed it almost shimmered and long ears so delicate the flush of blood showed through the white fur. Now it nuzzled beneath Dafydd's arm – for warmth, a good rubbing, or in search of some treasure Dafydd could not guess. He chuckled and praised the beast as he rubbed its head.

But Cadwal, sleeping next to Dafydd on a large pallet near the fire, was not so pleased with the visitor. 'Cwn Annwn!' he hissed. 'We face death on this journey.' The Cwn Annwn were hounds belonging to Arawn, a king of the Otherworld, who tracked those who were to die within the year.

The other men sought to calm him. The dog's ears might be called red, but that was because the dog's fur was so pale. His eyes were not fire, he did not drip blood; he was gentle and quite real, and his name was Cant.

'Had he approached you by night, and only you,' Madog said, 'ah, then we might cross ourselves and pray for your soul.'

Dafydd hissed at Madog to be quiet – his loose tongue would not help them calm Cadwal.

The farmer had entered the house as they spoke and stood shaking his head at Cadwal. 'Such a giant and a coward?'

'You would call me a coward?' Cadwal roared. Within a breath he was afoot, towering over the smirking farmer. Madog tried to grab his fellow's arms and pin them behind him, but he was no match for Cadwal's strength.

It was Cant's low growl that stayed Cadwal's hands.

'With a temper like that you may well be dead within the year,' Maelgwn said. 'Is this how you reward my assistance?'

Cadwal fell to his knees before the farmer and bowed his head. 'I pray you, tell me that you have not seen a vision of my death.'

Dafydd should have known better than to bring Cadwal to the house of a seer. The giant man feared nothing material and all things spiritual.

'I have not seen a vision of your death,' Maelgwn said. 'But we should all live in grace, for we never know when God will choose to call us.'

Still Cadwal knelt, his large hands clasped above his head in submission and prayer.

Dafydd touched the giant's shoulder. 'Be comforted. Maelgwn meant only to quiet your anger.'

In the end it was Maelgwn's wife who calmed the giant with a skin of wine and some bread and cheese.

The sun rose behind Sir Robert and Michaelo as they left the shelter of the trees. It reached down to light the sea and dazzle their eyes. Sir Robert tipped his pilgrim's hat lower over his eyes. Wind caught at their cloaks as they made their way with a host of other pilgrims down the path to the holy well. Sir Robert felt God's breath in the wind, the light of faith in the sun-dappled sea. His own breath caught in his throat, tears ran down his face. God had granted him a most precious gift in permitting him the strength to make this journey.

For once Brother Michaelo was a silent companion. Though they waited long for their turn at the well, the monk said nothing, standing with head bowed, his lips moving in silent prayer.

When his turn came at last, Sir Robert removed his hat and eased himself down beside the stone-roofed well. The water was clear but dark in the roof's shadow. A few early spring blossoms dressed the surface, offerings from pilgrims. A breeze shivered the water and moved the flowers to the edge. As the pool calmed, Sir Robert gasped and crossed himself, for his dead wife Amélie, her face pale and solemn, stared up at him, her dark hair a cloud that spread out to the edges of the pool.

'Amélie my love,' he whispered. 'Forgive me.' She closed her eyes, opened them, and as the vision began to dissolve he saw for one brief breath her sweet mouth turn up into a smile. 'My love!' He touched the water with his fingertips, but he felt as if his whole body dipped beneath the calm surface. Had she drawn him in with her? He smiled as the water closed over him.

He awoke in the field beside St Non's Chapel gazing up at the blue sky. Blinking rapidly against the brightness, he covered his eyes and fought the despair that had welled up within when he realised Amélie had not come for him. What gratitude was this, when he had been blessed with such a vision? When he withdrew his hand to welcome the light, a dark-eyed face filled the sky, a face vaguely familiar, though seen at an odd angle. Sir Robert must be lying with his head on the lap of the man who bent over him. The man's lips were moving, but Sir Robert could not hear him over the roaring in his ears. He closed his eyes again, tried to breathe evenly and quiet his pounding heart. Gradually the roaring faded to the steady drumming of the waves on the rocks below. Sir Robert opened his eyes again. The face reappeared. The man was very like Owen. But not like.

'Can you hear me now?' the man asked. French. The man spoke Parisian French – though his accent was not that of a Frenchman. Sir Robert could not place it. But he was delighted to be thinking so clearly.

'He may not understand.' Brother Michaelo's voice. He must be kneeling beside the stranger.

'I can hear you,' Sir Robert said in his best French. 'I had a vision.'

'A vision!' Brother Michaelo whispered.

'Ah. That explains the faint,' the stranger said.

'He has not been well,' Michaelo explained.

The effort to speak had made Sir Robert cough. He struggled to sit up. A strong hand supported him as a wave of dizziness made the field spin round. 'God bless you,' Sir Robert said rather breathlessly.

'God has blessed *you*, Sir Robert,' the man said, 'to see a vision at the holy well.'

Sir Robert could now see the man right side up, and

more than his face. With the narrow beard, dark hair and earring one might mistake him for Owen – before the terrible scarring of his left eye had forced him to wear the patch. But on closer examination Sir Robert realised that the stranger's hair was straighter and slightly lighter than Owen's. He wore simple clothes, a dark tunic, cloak and leather leggings. It was the clothes that jogged Sir Robert's memory. 'I have seen you before. Here. At the well.'

The stranger tilted his head to one side. 'There is nothing wrong with your memory. I have seen you here also.'

Brother Michaelo chose that moment to fuss, kneeling beside Sir Robert, feeling his forehead, his cheeks. 'You are chilled.' He took a flask from his scrip, handed it to Sir Robert. 'Drink this.'

Sir Robert sniffed. 'You carry wine in your pilgrim scrip?'

The stranger laughed. Judging from the network of lines at the corners of his eyes, he enjoyed merriment. 'You talk to each other as old friends. You are the secretary of the Archbishop of York, is that not so?'

Michaelo beamed, always ready to acknowledge his importance. 'I am indeed His Grace's secretary. He kindly sacrificed his convenience to allow me this pilgrimage. Are you acquainted with His Grace?'

The stranger's eyes lost some of their humour as he said, 'We have met.'

Sir Robert wondered at the sudden chill in the stranger's voice, obvious after such warmth.

Apparently Michaelo made note of it also. He did not sound so friendly as before when he asked, 'How did you know who I was?'

'When one travels alone, one enjoys gossip,' said the stranger, the warmth once more in his voice. He rose, adjusted his clothing, then crouched and extended his left hand to Sir Robert. 'And now, Brother Michaelo, I shall help you escort Sir Robert back to the palace. I am told that one is exhausted after a vision.'

As Sir Robert used the stranger's hand and Michaelo's shoulder to rise, he noticed that the former kept his right hand hidden in the folds of his cloak, even when it might assist him in balancing.

'You are here to heal your hand?' Sir Robert asked.

The stranger looked down at the hidden hand, back up at Sir Robert. 'I am not worthy of such a miracle.'

As they walked slowly away from the sea and the crowd of pilgrims, the stranger kept his left hand on Sir Robert's elbow. Brother Michaelo hovered on the other side.

'I am better now,' Sir Robert assured them. But they did not move away. 'Are you always so attentive to ailing strangers?' he asked, curious about the man.

'Long ago I had the pleasure of befriending your daughter and her husband, Sir Robert,' the stranger said.

'You did?' Sir Robert was amazed.

'You are acquainted with quite a few people in York,' said Michaelo, frowning.

'I had business in your fair city for a time. Captain Archer and Mistress Wilton were kind to me. And to a lad of whom I was fond – Jasper de Melton. What has become of the boy?'

Although he could sense Michaelo's unease, Sir Robert saw nothing threatening in the stranger's knowing his family. Indeed, it made him far more comfortable about the man's attentions. 'Jasper is my daughter's apprentice in the apothecary.'

The man was quiet a moment. Sir Robert glanced over, saw a tender expression on the man's face.

'Jasper was a great help to Lucie when the pestilence returned to York,' said Sir Robert.

'I am glad he has found his place in the world,' said the stranger, his voice thick with emotion.

Something nudged at Sir Robert's memory. But it was Michaelo who said quickly, 'I know who you are. The Fleming Martin Wirthir.'

'Ah!' Sir Robert nodded eagerly, recognising the name. Though if the man had not asked after Jasper he would have spent hours, perhaps days trying to remember where he had heard it. He had never met the man who had saved the boy's life, but he had heard much about him. Not all of it good.

'His Grace would be interested to know you are here,' said Michaelo, no friendlier than before. 'Is the musician with you?'

'You remember me so well. I am honoured,' said Wirthir. 'No, the musician is not with me. Ambrose now resides in Paris and often performs for King Charles.'

'When I next see my daughter and her husband, I shall tell them of your kindness to me,' said Sir Robert. He found Michaelo's hostility embarrassing.

'Forgive my boldness, Sir Robert,' said Wirthir, 'but I would ask whether you have the means to send a messenger to Captain Archer.'

'A messenger? Why?'

'I have an urgent letter for the Captain. Do you have someone you might send to Cydweli?'

'How did you know where he is?'

'Gossips took interest in his escorting the body of John de Reine back to Cydweli.'

'Ah.' Of course they would have talked of it. Sir Robert could see no point in pretending Owen was elsewhere. 'You mentioned a letter?'

Wirthir drew a roll of parchment from his purse. Once again he suffered awkwardness in using only his left hand. 'I believe that Captain Archer will wish to ride to St David's at once when he reads this.' He held it out to Sir Robert, who noted that it was wrapped in a string and sealed.

'Why would you wish to draw Captain Archer here?' Brother Michaelo asked.

Sir Robert shook his head. 'Peace, Michaelo.'

But Martin Wirthir bowed to Brother Michaelo. 'You deserve what little explanation I can give, to be sure. I know something about the death of John de Reine. And there are two nearby, arrived today, with whom the Captain would wish to speak.'

'But this is not the business on which the Captain has come,' said Sir Robert.

'It has to do with the other business. A question of treason. A dangerous liaison.'

'How do you know of this?' Brother Michaelo asked. 'Were you the Fleming involved in the troubles in Pembroke?'

Wirthir grinned. 'Pembroke is full of Flemings, Brother Michaelo, planted there by your wise King.'

'But—'

'I said peace, Michaelo!' Sir Robert snapped. If

for no other reason than to alert Owen to Wirthir's knowledge of his interest in Gruffydd ap Goronwy's trouble, he must now send the messenger. To add a letter could do no harm – provided Sir Robert read it first. He bowed to Wirthir. 'I do have a man I might send. He is trustworthy. But you have not explained. The two who arrived – why is that important to Owen? Who are they?'

'The wife of the steward of Cydweli. And the priest who travelled to Cydweli with the Captain. It is best that I say no more. One of them may be in danger. But I would ask you to tell no one of our meeting save the messenger and Captain Archer.'

'Presumptuous—' Brother Michaelo clamped his mouth shut as Sir Robert gave him a dark look.

'You can trust us,' Sir Robert said.

Wirthir handed him the letter. 'God bless you.'

Sir Robert tucked the letter into his scrip. 'May God watch over the messenger.'

They were now at Patrick's Gate. Martin Wirthir bowed, wished them Godspeed, and withdrew into the crowd.

'I wonder what is wrong with his right hand?' Sir Robert said.

'He has none,' Michaelo said. 'Do you not remember? Beware that one, Sir Robert.'

Eighteen

THE PIRATE'S
WARNING

As he walked down the slope towards the cathedral, Sir Robert felt sweat trickling down his back. High up on the cliff over St Non's Bay the breeze had been chilly despite the bright sun; but here in the valley there was no breeze. He pushed back his hat, plucked at his pilgrim's gown, its rough cloth beginning to itch as the sweat made it stick to his skin. And such a weakness in his legs. He was embarrassed how he leaned on Brother Michaelo's shoulder for support.

'You do not need to suffer in that coarse gown,' Michaelo said, putting an arm round Sir Robert. Michaelo's habit was of a very fine, soft wool cloth from Flanders, sewn by a tailor in Paris. 'You are wretched enough with the cough.'

'Your parents did no favour to the Church when they gave you to God,' Sir Robert muttered as he wriggled in his clothing, 'you who devote yourself to the delicate art of balancing just on the edge of your vows.' Perhaps it was good they walked so close together, for Sir Robert's voice was so weak his companion might not hear him if he stood upright and at a normal distance.

Rather than returning the insult, Brother Michaelo asked, 'You do intend to read the letter?'

Sir Robert felt it a risk to send the messenger without knowing the contents of the letter – what if he was being used to lure Owen into a trap? But would Owen trust a letter with a broken seal? 'It is sealed.'

'A seal can be eased open and resealed if one has the skill.'

'And you do?'

Michaelo bowed slightly. 'Some failings are useful.'

God bless him. 'What was it that he did, Michaelo? To lose the hand?'

'It was a madman who did it. It has nothing to do with us.'

'What did Archbishop Thoresby want with him?'

'He needed a witness. Martin Wirthir did not wish to oblige.'

'Come,' Michaelo urged. 'The porter will surely remember whether the wife of Lancaster's steward arrived with the vicar.'

But the porter did not recall seeing Father Edern with a woman, though several women had arrived at the palace that morning.

'It is no fors,' Sir Robert said as they passed through the second doorway and into the great hall. 'The letter will tell us whether to trust him.'

They went to their chamber, where Michaelo expressed delight to find the brazier still alight despite the warm afternoon. 'We are fortunate they consider you old and infirm,' Michaelo said as he set a pot of water over the fire. 'We need the steam for the seal as well as for your lungs.'

Precisely. Because I *am* old and infirm, Sir Robert thought as he eased down on the bed. His head pounded and his limbs trembled. He had not coughed in a while, but his chest felt heavy and he experienced an unpleasant rumble with each breath. It seemed no time at all before Michaelo joined him, presenting the scroll without seal.

'Shall I read it aloud?' Michaelo asked.

'My eyes are not so bad as that,' Sir Robert said. But in truth he found the writing small and crabbed. 'Perhaps so. I have a headache.' He lay back on the pillows. Brother Michaelo tucked a few more behind him, slipped off his shoes.

A servant knocked, entered with a tray of wine, water and fruit. Michaelo took the tray and sent the servant away.

'It would not do to give them bad example,' Michaelo said. He was obviously enjoying the intrigue. He began to read aloud:

'Right well beloved friend,
I recommend me to you and pray you take
heed of my tidings. I have in my custody a
man who may give good account of a certain
incident on Whitesands. He is hunted by many,
but his gravest danger is from one who seeks
to silence him and whose treasonous act begat

all this trouble. I have no doubt the traitor will
follow hard upon two who arrive today. Come
to me in the place at which you rose from the
valley with your burden.
Godspeed.
Pirate.'

'At least he does not hide his profession,' Michaelo
said. He looked up from the document. 'I do not
like this.'

'Nor do I. But Owen must at least be warned that
Martin Wirthir is here and knows of his interest in
traitors to the King. We must send it.' A messenger normally took three days from here to Cydweli,
though it was said that a fast rider with fresh horses
each day might make it in two. If the messenger left
this afternoon he might be there by Sunday. And yet it
was now mid-afternoon. 'Summon Edmund. He will
ride at first light.'

'Not at once?'

'What is the use? He would not get far by nightfall.
Better he be fresh at the beginning.'

'But time is of—'

'—the essence. I know. And yet I have always found
it wise to sleep on something as important as this
missive. When I served the King I was respected for
my thoroughness, which comes only by taking one's
time.' Sir Robert smiled. 'Besides, my friend, it will
give you time to reseal this letter.'

Michaelo chuckled. 'True enough. It takes a steady
hand, and I am much excited.'

'Does His Grace know of your skill with seals?'
Surely the Archbishop of York received documents

meant for his eyes alone. He was sometime advisor to the King.

'If His Grace guesses it, he keeps his own counsel. Will you tell the Captain of Brother Dyfrig's prying questions about the missing pilgrim and the Captain's purpose in Wales?'

'God bless you for assisting my memory. Edmund shall tell Owen of the monk's interest and who arrived today. Wirthir takes care to mention no one and no place by name.'

After Edmund had been informed of his journey and had been given the information to memorise and instructions to come at first light for the letter, Brother Michaelo urged Sir Robert to drink some soothing herbs in honey water and lie down to rest until the evening meal. Sir Robert refused to rest – he must go to the chapel and give thanks for the vision with which God had blessed him. Few men were granted such a gift, to be assured through such a vision that his prayers had been answered, that Amélie forgave him. He had delayed his thanks too long already, though surely God would see that it was important to read the letter and prepare Edmund. But to delay his thanks any longer would be unforgivable. Brother Michaelo acquiesced, but insisted on accompanying Sir Robert in case he felt faint and needed help. As the Fleming had said, to receive a vision was exhausting to a mortal man. And Sir Robert was already weak.

Weak, yes, Sir Robert thought. But with the messenger instructed and Amélie's forgiveness assured, he felt at peace. He no longer feared death, nor did he wish to delay it. He did not confide these thoughts to Brother

Michaelo for fear the monk would misinterpret his intentions and put a guard on him. Already he hovered too much.

'I must give thanks for St Non's beneficence, Michaelo. Not only for my vision, but for Martin Wirthir's assistance.'

'We shall see whether we ought to be grateful about his assistance.'

'Why do you distrust him?'

'Honesty is not his trade, Sir Robert. At best he has been a pirate, at worst a spy for the enemies of our King. Why should we trust him?'

'Because he has been known to step out of his role – remember what he did for Jasper. But be that as it may, I wish to go to the chapel. Come.'

'What was it that you saw in the waters of the well?' Michaelo asked as they stepped out into the corridor.

Sir Robert described Amélie's face, her fleeting smile. 'It is the healing for which I prayed.'

Brother Michaelo crossed himself. 'Truly you have been blessed, Sir Robert.'

'I pray that you have been likewise blessed, that you will dream no more of Brother Wulfstan.'

'Perhaps my bad dreams are a substitute for my conscience.'

At the door to the chapel Sir Robert stayed Brother Michaelo. 'I know you mean well, my friend, but I would be alone in my devotions.'

'What if you fall into a swoon? Who will find you?'

'Come for me in a little while.'

*   *   *

The chapel was dim, though a jewelled light came through the stained-glass windows behind the altar and illuminated a slender woman who knelt on the floor. Candles burned on the altar and in a niche before a statue of St David. As the draught from the door made the flames flicker, the woman turned round. Sir Robert closed the door as gently as possible and, steadying himself with a hand on the wall, lowered himself to his knees by the statue of St David. The woman turned back to her devotions.

Sir Robert thought the psalms most appropriate, songs of praise for a beneficent God.

> *I will bless the Lord at all times: His praise shall continually be in my mouth.*
> *. . . O magnify the Lord with me, and let us exalt His name together.*
> *I sought the Lord, and He heard me, and delivered me from all my fears.*
> *. . . This poor man cried, and the Lord heard him, and saved him out of all his troubles . . .*

But his mind wandered from his devotions. How difficult it was not to think of Amélie, to study the face so recently before him. He had never thought to see that face again, had feared that even after death they would be apart.

> *The righteous cry, and the Lord heareth, and delivereth them out of all their troubles.*

Sir Robert did not know that he was weeping until a woman's voice asked with tender concern, 'Are you unwell, sir?'

She smelled of exotic oils. He glanced up, puzzled.

'Forgive me for disturbing you in your devotions. But I heard you weeping . . .' Her veil shimmered in the candlelight. Silk? Cloth of gold? Sir Robert could not tell, but she seemed a vision, not a mortal woman.

He lifted his hands to his cheeks, felt the tears, shook his head. 'An old man overcome by memories. It is I who must beg your forgiveness.'

'I hope they are happy memories.'

'As of today, yes,' he said. 'By the grace of St Non. I went to the well to pray for my family, but I was blessed instead.'

'Then I should leave you to your happy memories. You will be all right here?'

'God bless you, yes, my lady.' For surely she was a lady, though her accent was Welsh.

'God go with you, my lord,' she said, and rose with the rustle of silk.

Her scent lingered long in the chapel.

Dafydd and Dyfrig agreed that the pilgrim would likely return to St David's. But they did not agree about their own destination. Brother Dyfrig felt duty bound to remain with Brother Samson and escort him to Strata Florida as soon as he might comfortably make the journey; Samson's servant was not sufficient escort. His first impulse was to carry Samson back to Dafydd's house and nurse him to health; then Dafydd and his men must escort the two monks to the abbey. 'You have unleashed a violent criminal and must protect us from him.'

Dafydd was outraged. It was God who had set Rhys

in Dafydd's path. He must follow Rhys and help the pilgrim face his own duty – to give account in the bishop's court of the incident on Whitesands. Who was Dyfrig to question God's purpose in this? And Brother Dyfrig, who knew Rhys's kinsman, should accompany Dafydd to St David's. Brother Samson could await them here. Maelgwn believed he had already gained God's grace from the monk's presence in his household – he had been blessed with several visions since Samson's arrival. And to return to Dafydd's house was too much of a risk – the Cydweli men could not be fooled indefinitely. When Dafydd and Dyfrig returned from St David's they would all provide a proper escort back to the abbey, to which Dafydd would repair to meditate on God's purpose in testing him in such a manner.

It took little coaxing to engage Brother Dyfrig in Dafydd's pursuit of Rhys. In private, away from the others, Brother Dyfrig agreed with Dafydd that Aled's account of the attack and the monk's wounds suggested that Samson was not injured intentionally, that he had foolishly pursued Rhys and suffered an accident. It might in faith be good for Samson to lie abed among these simple people and learn some humility.

Then Maelgwn insisted on a round of bargaining. In the end he agreed to a goat from Dafydd's farm upon their return in exchange for Samson's care.

And thus Dafydd, Brother Dyfrig, Madog and Cadwal departed in the early afternoon. They were almost a merry company, with food, water and a bit of wine to comfort them and a mission to fill them with purpose. The day had begun overcast but now the sun beat down and warmed their muscles, a soft wind cooled them as they rode. To join the road south it was necessary to circle back near Dafydd's house, but they kept to the far side of the hill and joined the road when they were safely past. Madog advised a hard ride through the afternoon with no pause until sunset; they would all rest easier with a good distance between them and the four armed men from Cydweli, who being wounded would ride more slowly if they attempted to follow.

A warm, sunny day is a joy for a short distance, but soon the sun and the wind dried their eyes and parched their mouths, the dust from the road crept into every fold of their skin and clothing, clung to their hair.

On the first evening of their journey towards St David's, Owen's company had paused at St Clears Abbey. The abbot had not had the honour of playing host to John Lascelles, nor had he had word of the steward and his squire, but he did provide a valuable piece of news.

'A tinker came by telling of a great procession moving from St David's to Llawhaden. You know that Bishop Houghton is fond of the castle. So fond that he is building a new south wing – they say he lives in comfort there, watching the road between Carmarthen and Haverfordwest.'

Bishop Adam de Houghton was in Llawhaden. It was a climb from the main road and might cost them half a day, but Owen thought that if it was the bishop Lascelles was wanting – and he thought it was – the steward might alter his course to see whether Houghton was in residence at the castle.

Owen's party rode hard, but a pause to assist a merchant with a crippled wagon delayed them, and they did not approach Llawhaden Castle until late afternoon on the second day of their journey.

They found the bishop in the yard by the stables surrounded by four fine, sleek hounds, their tails wagging as they competed for their master's attention. Houghton himself was in leggings and a tunic that reached only to his knees, high boots and a short cape. His colour was high and the crown of his soft hat wet with sweat. 'Gentlemen, gentlemen, you have caught me in sin, riding out to hunt in the Lenten season. But I tell you I did it to clear my mind. There is nothing like a swift chase to bring a man to his senses.'

Geoffrey's eyes were merry as he bowed to the bishop. He had told Owen earlier that he welcomed another chance to observe the pilgrims at St David's and the bishop himself, who seemed a singular character, far more interesting than the political churchmen who surrounded the King. Geoffrey hoped that on this visit they might dine in the great hall at St David's bishop's palace with the other well-born pilgrims rather than in the bishop's hall. 'I want to study the pilgrims so I might describe them in all their variety.' But what he now found so amusing about Houghton, Owen could not guess.

Nor did he long think on it. For as the bishop tugged at his gloves he stepped between Owen and Geoffrey and said under his breath, 'While your men take some refreshment, we must talk. And you will spend the night, of course.'

Adam de Houghton led Owen and Geoffrey round the

new wing of Llawhaden Castle under construction. The dust of the stonework stung Owen's eye – the brisk wind carried it even out of the lodge in which the apprentice masons worked at their benches. A chapel and chapel tower, far advanced in construction, were the first phase of the plan. Houghton intended the south range to extend round the yard and enclose it, so that the existing hall and kitchens would be protected by a gatehouse and a range with additional towers. The range would include suites of lodgings for his retinue and guests.

'It shall be a sign to those who pass along the road between Carmarthen and Haverfordwest that the lord of this March, though he be a man of God, is yet a lord indeed.'

But Owen was restive. 'My lord Bishop, I am but a plain soldier and know little of such works. You had news for us?'

'Forgive me. I waste time when I have much to tell you. Come.' He led them to a garden that used the rear wall of the kitchen, the west side of the hall, and the steep bank of the ditch as its enclosure. They settled on benches beneath a pair of apple trees, seemingly stunted by their confined home and yet pregnant with tight buds.

'Now we need not fear someone will overhear,' Houghton said.

They were indeed well situated away from the kitchen doorway and windows, away from any hedge or wall behind which someone might hide. But what was the need?

'You have a spy in your household?' Owen asked.

'These are uneasy times, Captain. With King Charles

of France eyeing our shores I prefer to be overcautious and thus ever ready.'

'Is it of this you wished to speak?'

Houghton shook his head. 'No, no. It is of another matter, one that has weighed on my mind all the day. And once again you arrive just as I have need of you. I need not have risked my soul in the hunt, for here you are, and God's intention is clear to me. He has sent you to resolve the troubles in John Lascelles's household, I am sure of it. Though I am surprised to see you. I should not have thought the Duke's men had time to pursue runaway wives.'

Geoffrey drew in his breath. A man so conscious of his status did not like to be perceived as pursuing something trivial. 'We are here on a far more serious matter.'

But Owen noted what had escaped Geoffrey. 'We said nothing of runaway wives. Do you speak of Mistress Lascelles?'

Houghton nodded in response to Owen, 'I do.' But his eyes were on Geoffrey. 'What is this matter you speak of?'

'Father Francis, chaplain of Cydweli, has been murdered,' said Geoffrey. 'I should say beaten – the attacker may not have known the result of his work. The chaplain was found wearing the cloak of your vicar, Father Edern. On that same day, Mistress Lascelles and Father Edern fled the castle. We are perhaps in pursuit of accomplices in murder.'

'Holy Mother of God.'

'What do you know of Sir John's troubles?' Owen asked.

Houghton took off his embroidered cap, ran a hand

through his damp hair. The pale strands caught the setting sun. 'What do I know? Certes we all know about the death of John de Reine, and now the flight of Mistress Lascelles.' He set the cap lightly on his head. 'And that Sir John pursues his wife.'

'And we pursue him,' Owen said. 'But how has the news reached you here?'

'By the man himself.'

'Sweet Jesus, he is here?' Owen sprang up.

The bishop raised a hand to halt him. 'He arrived early this morning and departed before midday.'

Owen yet stood. 'We might have caught him had we stayed on the road.'

'You might have indeed. But what you gain from stopping here the night will be of value to you. Both parties have had much to say of their troubles.'

'You have news of Mistress Lascelles as well?' Geoffrey asked as Owen eased himself down, most unwillingly.

The bishop gazed at Geoffrey for a moment, his eyes friendly but remote, as if choosing his words. 'More than that,' he said at last. 'I know precisely where she is, for I sent her there. With that cunning vicar.' A twig dropped in the bishop's lap. He picked it up, twirled it between his beringed fingers, studying it. 'I knew when Brother Dyfrig and the Archdeacon of Cardigan recommended Edern for a vicar choral that I should have made inquiries. But my mind was on other matters. How we come to regret such sluggishness.' He shook his head. 'Edern is a sly one. Too sly for me.'

Sluggishness indeed. Owen wished the bishop's tongue were more sluggish. 'What has Father Edern done?'

Houghton tossed the twig, shook his head at Owen as if chiding him. 'But you know. He has assisted Mistress Lascelles in escaping from her husband. Though why she trusted such a rogue as Edern I cannot imagine. Such a beauty! One can see why Sir John is so desperate to win her back. He will not. I do not see it happening. He will not win her heart.'

'Because of the child?' Geoffrey asked. Owen had told him about Hedyn and the misunderstanding between Tangwystl and Sir John regarding the boy's status.

'Certes the child is a tragedy, but more so are her feelings for the lad's father. I blame that schemer, Gruffydd ap Goronwy. Sir John swears he had no idea that the young woman apparently considered herself married to the young man, and I accept his word on that – he is not the sort of fool to pursue a woman who cannot possibly pledge her heart to him. He believed she had been abandoned by the young man. And surely Gruffydd had cause to let him think so.' Houghton paused, dropped his head, seemed to withdraw into his thoughts for a moment. 'And yet when I said to Sir John that he was better off without his Welsh wife, that considering the rumours surrounding her father it had been a most unsuitable marriage for him, and that now he might remedy it by acknowledging that they had wed when she was already bound to another, he refused to hear of it. Foolish, stubborn man. "I will have her!" he shouted.'

'What is to be done?' Geoffrey asked. 'If Sir John is determined to keep her, who is to dissuade him?'

'In truth, when our friend the Duke informed me

of your coming, I was surprised that you were not carrying letters to Sir John and myself ordering that the marriage be annulled. It was a dangerous choice, the daughter of a traitor, for such a key man in the Duke's Marches. I do not understand Lancaster's hesitation.'

Owen did. 'Until now the Duke had no cause to question Sir John's loyalty. He thought to wait until he had our report.'

'I fear neither Sir John nor his lady will wait for that,' Geoffrey said.

Houghton slapped his thighs. 'It is in the hands of the Church now. It must be.'

Owen asked what he proposed.

'If we find that Mistress Tangwystl (for that is how she wishes to be known) was bound to the father of her son by law – any law – we shall dissolve Sir John's marriage. And then there is the letter Father Francis signed.'

'And Gladys was called to witness,' Geoffrey whispered to Owen.

Houghton frowned. 'Gladys?'

'It is nothing,' Owen said. 'Can you tell us what the letter said?'

'You may read it if you like.' Houghton drew a rolled document from his sleeve. 'Mistress Tangwystl carries the copy I had my secretary make. I planned to send this original with my own comments to William Baldwin, Archdeacon of Carmarthen.'

It was as Owen had guessed, Tangwystl claimed the right to separate from her husband after finding him thrice bedding Gladys, and Father Francis had signed as a witness. Shortly before he died, if Gladys's story was true, and so far Owen had found no cause to doubt her.

Geoffrey, reading over Owen's shoulder, asked, 'What of Mistress Tangwystl's family? Was not the purpose of the marriage to save her family? Did she not win them a home through it?'

Houghton took back the document, rolled it up and stuck it back up his sleeve. 'Sir John has been a fool all round, it seems.'

'My lord,' Geoffrey began, 'the maid Gladys—'

'—is a woman of considerable charms,' Owen said. He smiled at Geoffrey's irritated look. It was not the time to distract the bishop with details of Tangwystl's scheme.

'Mistress Tangwystl is also a woman of considerable charms,' Houghton said. 'And Sir John's wife. He should have looked to home.' He clasped his hands together and rested his chin on them for a moment, frowning down at the ground, which was now dark beneath the trees that caught the twilight in their branches. 'God will be the judge of Gruffydd ap Goronwy. Perhaps we already see God's hand in this trouble.'

Owen thought of Eleri and Awena. What would become of them?

'I do not expect Sir John's family to be troubled by an annulment,' Houghton said. 'I should think they are far more troubled by the marriage itself. He has not taken his wife to England to meet any of his kin – did you know? Yes, I can see that you did.'

'You said that you sent Mistress Tangwystl somewhere,' Owen said.

'To St David's. By now I should think she is safely quartered in the palace.'

'Why is Father Edern helping her in this?' Geoffrey asked.

Houghton glanced up as the light disappeared, creating a sudden chill. 'Father Edern, Edern ap Llywelyn, is the uncle of Mistress Tangwystl's child.'

Sly creature, dissembling fox. Owen must clutch the bench to stay there and listen to the bishop's meandering tale. He wanted action. He wanted Edern.

But why had the vicar chosen this moment to take Tangwystl from Cydweli? What had the letter and her flight to do with the chaplain's beating?

'As they have all come to me I mean to settle this matter,' Houghton was saying. 'The Archdeacon of Carmarthen shall hear their stories, their pleas, and judge the case, Cydweli being in the archdeaconry of Carmarthen. And yet there is a problem – the father of Tangwystl's child must also attend to this matter, but he is missing. He was there, you know, at St David's, had come with a petition to see me, and then he vanished.'

'The young man who left his belongings at the palace,' Owen said. 'Does Edern know where to find him?'

'No.'

A scenario came to Owen. What else might have distracted John de Reine from his meeting with Owen and Geoffrey but a greater challenge to his father's honour? A motive so personal it had confounded Owen, who had looked for political causes.

'Perhaps we know why he disappeared,' said Owen. 'Suppose this young man, Rhys ap Llywelyn, and John de Reine met on Whitesands to test the honour of their two households – in combat.'

The bishop's eyes were sad. 'If you are right, I fear we have a tragedy on our hands. Rhys ap Llywelyn is the victor, but in law he is a murderer. He must answer for that at the tourn of his lordship, which would be Pembroke, unless Hastings' chief steward agreed to allow him to be tried by Lancaster's great court – at which John Lascelles resides. Either way, I do not see the possibility of his buying a *redemptio vitae*.' Houghton had folded his hands in his lap as he spoke, and now dropped his head, as if praying.

His summation was met with silence. Geoffrey closed his eyes and shook his head slowly, side to side, as if disbelieving. Owen marvelled at the bishop's clarity of mind.

As the sun set, a breeze fluttered across the lately tilled garden beds and whispered in the branches, dimly lit by torchlight spilling over the garden wall from the courtyard. It was a chilly breeze. Bishop Houghton rubbed his hands together. Geoffrey rose and asked for the nearest privy.

While Geoffrey disappeared round the corner of the kitchen, Owen and the bishop moved to the courtyard, which was more protected from the evening air.

'How much of this does Sir John know?' Owen asked.

'Only that his wife was here and now is safe in the palace of St David's, and that my archdeacon shall consider their case. I also promised a Welsh judge in attendance to explain her arguments, which are based on the law of Hywel Dda.'

'And Mistress Tangwystl? Does she know you believe Rhys to be a murderer?'

Houghton snorted. 'Do you think that a man of the cloth does not understand how the heart rules in love?'

'You took a risk, trusting both to obey you.'

'I saw no reason for Mistress Tangwystl to do otherwise. But Sir John – all day my mind misgave me. But was I to lock him up in my dungeon? He is too high in the Duke's service to treat him thus. In the morning you must hurry, catch him, guide him to a safe harbour.'

And keep him away from his wife and the vicar? For it now seemed to Owen that Lascelles was the one most likely to have attacked the chaplain, though he had timed it ill. Still, what did it mean that Tangwystl and Edern had not talked of the chaplain's beating? Gladys's story would have it they were likely aware of it. Was it not a sign of guilt to say nothing of this to the bishop?

Nineteen

an ambush

At sunset Dafydd's company paused by a stream to water their horses and to wash some of the dust from their faces before presenting themselves at a large farmhouse they had sighted down the road.

A rustling in the underbrush alerted them to intruders. Cadwal and Madog grabbed their knives and swords, Dyfrig ducked beneath his horse and pulled out a dagger, Dafydd grabbed a good stout branch in one hand, his own dagger in another, and prayed that it was but a wild animal come to drink at the stream. The noise stopped. Whatever it was, it knew it was discovered, just as they knew it of themselves. Wretched uncertainty. Should they run or stand their ground, demand it show itself or stay silent, hoping it would pass? A branch cracked behind Dafydd. He spun round, saw nothing. Sweat caught a lock of his hair as he moved his head, blinded him for a moment. As he reached up with the stick-burdened hand to brush away his hair, something huge rushed up and caught him. The attacker cursed as Dafydd jabbed blindly with his dagger. He fought down Dafydd's hand and pressed it to his side.

It was one of the Cydweli men. Behind him, Dafydd now heard shouts, cries, grunts, and felt the ground tremble as the horses fled in terror. He prayed God his harp survived. Dafydd tried to pry himself loose from his captor but was held tight. He tried another tactic, standing still, almost limp, and then suddenly pushing out his elbows with all his strength. For a few heartbeats Dafydd was free, free to wheel round and view the disaster. Cadwal and Madog thrashed and cursed and stabbed at a fishing net that had caught them. Dyfrig sat on the ground nursing what looked to be a broken arm. As his captor's arms reached for Dafydd, he pushed away.

'There is no need. We are defeated.'

Brother Michaelo deemed it prudent to have a meal sent to their room that evening, but Sir Robert rose from his nap refreshed and insisted on dining in the great hall.

'Mistress Lascelles may be there,' Sir Robert argued. 'I may learn something of value to add to Edmund's message.'

As Sir Robert reached for his sandals, Michaelo clucked his tongue and held up soft leather shoes. Reluctantly, Sir Robert put on the warmer shoes. He doubted a chill would worsen the rumble in his chest, but he understood that Michaelo meant well.

'You should rest.' Brother Michaelo tugged at Sir Robert's plain pilgrim's gown. 'But if you insist on this, might I suggest you wear a gown that befits your station? Men – and women – are more likely to confide in equals or those of higher degree.'

Michaelo had a talent for this intrigue. Sir Robert opened the chest at the foot of his bed and shook out a silk gown. The monk nodded his approval.

As Sir Robert dressed, Michaelo stared up at the painting of King Henry crossing Llechllafar. 'I tell you what I do not like. That Wirthir would not tell us the significance of the vicar's escorting the steward's wife to St David's.'

'What do you fear from him?'

'That he will lure Owen to St David's through us. Suppose he is *the* Fleming? Surely you remember that Gruffydd ap Goronwy was accused of offering hospitality to a Fleming who was a spy for the fool who calls himself the redeemer of the Welsh – the French King's puppet . . .' Michaelo turned to Sir Robert, who had sat down heavily on the bed, breathing in painful gasps. 'My friend, you must rest.'

Sir Robert shook his head. Soon there would be time enough for rest. An eternity.

Michaelo helped him sip some warm honey-and-sage water. 'I had not meant to upset you. I pray that I am wrong and he means to help the Captain.'

Sir Robert coughed after the first gulp, but then the drink soothed him and steadied his breathing.

'You see?' Michaelo said. 'This is what you need. A quiet evening.'

'You have given me even more reason to find out all I can for Owen.' Sir Robert rose with care, was pleased to feel steady on his feet – as steady as he ever felt these days. 'Come. While we walk to the hall I shall tell you about the lady in the chapel.'

When Cadwal, Madog, Dafydd and Dyfrig were bound and quiet and the horses rounded up, the Duke's men built a fire and shared round their captives' food. One of the men tried not to use his right arm, not completely mended from the ambush at Dafydd's house; one limped and his blood still stained a bandage round his forehead; and another held his arm pressed to a bandage round his middle.

'You are all injured,' Dafydd said. 'How did you get past my dogs?'

'Poppy juice,' said the limper. 'Your servants were so generous with it, I shared my bounty with your hounds. Soaked into a trencher they thought it a treat.'

His heart pounding, Dafydd said, 'By St Roch, if you have harmed Nest and Cadwy . . .'

'Rest easy, old man. They merely slept.'

'And my servants?'

'They fared no worse than we did.'

'How did you overtake us?' Madog asked.

The one with no visible injuries except for the cut on his arm where Dafydd's dagger had grazed him, settled back against his saddle and grinned. 'We discovered you on the road behind us.'

'How is that possible? We rode like the wind.'

'Be quiet!' Dyfrig hissed. 'Tell them nothing.'

'There is nothing to tell,' Dafydd said. They had tarried too long at Maelgwn's house, that was plain.

'Where is Rhys ap Llywelyn?' demanded the spokesman.

Dafydd frowned, shook his head. 'I have told you before, I do not know this man of whom you speak.'

'You ride south. To St David's?'

'To complain of your attack and ask the Arch-deacon of Cardigan to intercede for us, demand of your lord reparation for the damage. Now we have even more to complain of.'

Dyfrig glared at Dafydd.

Dafydd ignored him. As if his words made any difference in their plight. What could be worse than being tired, hungry, aching from the attack, and trussed up like slaughtered pigs? But at least his harp had survived the wild ride through the underbrush unscathed.

Liveried servants greeted Sir Robert and Michaelo at the door of the great hall and escorted them to the high table. The servants poured wine and hurried away to greet more guests.

At the next table Brother Michaelo noticed several Benedictines. 'Perhaps I might assist you in your inquiries by gathering the gossip of the clergy,' he said, rising. He eased his way round to the monks' table.

Sir Robert glanced round, irritated with Brother Michaelo for leaving him. Without the benefit of the monk's eyesight he could not make out much of the crowd. But a rustle of silk and an exotic scent made Sir Robert turn.

'My lady.' He bowed to the woman who had hesitated behind him.

'My lord,' she said, inclining her head. A warm smile in a beautiful young face. 'Are you recovered from your memories?'

'I have managed to escape them for the evening.'

She told the servant that she would sit where she had paused. 'Am I intruding?'

'Not at all. Forgive me for not rising, but it has been a tiring day.'

She slipped in beside him. The servant poured wine.

'Tangwystl ferch Gruffydd,' she said.

Holy Mother of God, could this be? Could the object of their discussion be this lovely lady? 'Sir Robert D'Arby,' he said with a little bow, 'of Freythorpe Hadden in Yorkshire. And my companion, when he returns, is Brother Michaelo, secretary to His Grace John Thoresby, Archbishop of York.'

'I am honoured,' she said quietly. 'You and Brother Michaelo are pilgrims?'

'We are. Though dining in such a hall, with such company, is not the behaviour of a pilgrim.'

'You have travelled far. In the chapel – I heard how you struggle to breathe. You are brave to come on such a journey. Forgive me, but I wondered how your wife could bear to let you go when your health is so delicate.'

He bowed his head. 'My wife died many years ago.'

'The happy memories you spoke of – were they of her?'

Sir Robert stared into Tangwystl's green eyes, pale, like emeralds, and he felt he could confide in her. He told her of his vision. While he spoke, he saw her colour deepen, her eyes grow moist. He apologised for upsetting her. 'I should not speak of such things.'

She touched his hand. 'God bless you, Sir Robert. I would hear more of her, your Amélie.'

They were interrupted for a time by Brother Michaelo's return and the arrival of the first course. And the second. Though meat was not served in the palace during Lent the variety of fish and pastries seemed decadent to Sir Robert. He ate little, in truth just picked at his food, and Brother Michaelo fussed.

'He is a good friend to you,' said Tangwystl.

'He would lose me all the indulgences I hoped to gain by this pilgrimage,' Sir Robert said.

'Your Amélie forgave you. Was that not the purpose of your pilgrimage?'

'I had not dared to hope for that.' He told her of Lucie and her family, the miracle of their all surviving the pestilence, how he had feared for her, being an apothecary. 'I came to give thanks. God allowed me to live long enough to witness my daughter's happiness.'

'Your daughter is an apothecary in York?' Tangwystl glanced over at Brother Michaelo, who sat quietly, leaning slightly in their direction, obviously trying to eavesdrop. 'And he is the secretary to the archbishop. I remember now. Captain Archer and Master Chaucer escorted pilgrims to St David's. That is how they came to be here when John de Reine was found.'

Sir Robert hoped he had not now silenced her. 'It gives me joy to hear they made it safely to Cydweli. Did you meet Captain Archer?'

'Your daughter is fortunate. He seems a good and gentle man.'

'I am content for her.'

Mistress Tangwystl grew quiet. So now she did not trust him. Sir Robert was sorry for that. But in a little while she turned to him again and asked him about his grandchildren.

'I have a son,' she said in such a sad tone Sir Robert thought she might be about to correct herself and say 'had'. But she did not. She described a fair, chubby boy with a laugh so rich that all who heard must laugh with him.

'Sir John must be proud,' said Sir Robert.

'No. He is not. For Hedyn is not his son.' She changed the subject to the bleak, treeless character of this westernmost part of Wales.

Brother Michaelo paced impatiently as he waited for Sir Robert, who was taking his time saying good-night to the fair Tangwystl. He had walked her to her chamber and was rewarded with an invitation to accompany her on the morrow to St David's Well at Porth Clais. Sir Robert could feel the monk's eyes boring into his back but he did not care. He had found a way to help Owen and he felt rejuvenated.

'You are playing the fool with her. She is beautiful, I grant you – but she is your enemy.' His hands tucked up his sleeves, Michaelo leaned slightly forward as he walked, head bowed. He walked too fast for Sir Robert, who paused and waited for Brother Michaelo to realise he was alone.

When the monk turned back with an impatient sigh, Sir Robert said, 'I would empty my bladder before retiring.' They headed for the privy in silence. But as soon as they had done their business and were back on course, Sir Robert took up the argument. 'You are being the fool. How is she my enemy?'

'Her father is a traitor to the King. Have you forgotten?'

'We do not know that he was. John Lascelles did not think so. Surely he would not have taken her to wife if he had.'

'Lascelles.' Brother Michaelo nodded vigorously. 'Did you note? She is not using his name.'

'By all that is holy, why do you persist in this? Many women choose what name they will.'

'And of all men, who would be the one to follow her here, but her husband? Can it be he is the traitor of whom the Fleming speaks?' Brother Michaelo tilted his head, awaiting a reply.

Could it be so? 'Would Sir John be so blatant in his treachery? Marrying the daughter of one of his accomplices? One who had been caught in his treachery?'

'It might explain the woman's flight, had she discovered it,' said Michaelo. To escape a father who was traitor only to discover she had married another.'

'She is Welsh. She may not count it treason.' Sir Robert was tired and confused. 'She told me something passing strange. She has a son, but Sir John is not the father.'

'You see? A Godless family.'

Sir Robert did not wish to pursue that. 'You looked disappointed when you returned to the table. The Benedictines knew nothing?'

'I wonder whether I should tell you what I learned. Will my words be repeated to Mistress Tangwystl?'

They had reached their chamber. Sir Robert opened the door. 'You tire me, Michaelo. Keep your news to yourself.'

As Michaelo was about to shut the door, a young man in the bishop's livery slipped from the shadows in the corridor. 'I come from the Pirate,' he said softly. 'With urgent news.'

Michaelo pulled him into the room, shut the door. The young man was dishevelled and breathless.

'How did the Pirate get a message to you?' Sir Robert asked.

'He has his ways. I cannot say, my lord. He tells me to say only this. Father Edern has left the palace. The traitor follows him. The Captain must hasten to his aid.' The young man dropped his head.

'That is it?'

A nod.

Sir Robert dug in his purse, gave the young man a groat. 'Go swiftly to my man Edmund, summon him here.' He told him where he might find him.

Sir Robert and Brother Michaelo awaited Edmund in sombre silence, except for a begrudging 'Thank God you insisted on delaying his departure' from Michaelo.

It was not until Edmund had gone and they lay quietly side by side that Sir Robert remembered their argument in the corridor.

'What did you learn from your brethren?'

The monk lay on his side. 'We would not share a room, much less a bed, you know, but that I am to help you should you weaken. It is my duty to be quiet now, allow you your rest.'

How was the monk to be borne? 'I cannot rest but you tell me.'

'You threaten like a child. And now we go on so, you think I have much to tell you. I do not. They

269

knew of Dyfrig, that his house is Strata Florida, a nest of Welsh rebels, they say. Though they have not heard Brother Dyfrig himself mentioned in that way. They say the monk used his influence to get Father Edern his position as vicar. But the most interesting part is no longer news: that Father Edern is already gone from the city.'

At dawn Owen's party gathered in the courtyard to receive Bishop Houghton's blessing, then mounted and rode from Llawhaden.

They now carried Tangwystl's letter requesting annulment and a letter from the bishop, to be delivered to the Archdeacon of Carmarthen in St David's. 'I shall follow you to St David's anon, but in such a circumstance it is comforting to know these documents are in a company of seven armed men,' Houghton had said. He had also asked that Owen ensure no more blood was shed over the matter. 'I would not have St David's in turmoil during Passiontide.'

'God forgive me, but to that I cannot swear,' Owen had said. 'We can but pray that we find a peaceful resolution.'

Geoffrey had taken exception to Owen's reply, though he waited until they were alone to voice his disapproval. As Owen set his boots by the brazier to dry overnight and shook out his clothes, beat off some of the dirt, Geoffrey had paced with hands behind his back. 'Why could you not swear that you would do all you could to prevent further violence?'

'Why should I lie to the bishop? Peace or violence may not be in my keeping.'

Geoffrey stopped at the bench where Owen sat,

looked down on him with an impatient shake of the head. 'You have no tact. He will remember what you said.'

'And blame me if anyone is wounded? You speak nonsense. Houghton is a reasonable man.'

'He is a powerful man. A friend to the Duke. You would do well to impress him.' The last point was emphasised by a wagging finger.

Owen pushed the finger away and bent down to his pack. 'I am not looking for a bishop to serve. I have had enough of Thoresby. You would do well to undress and rest for tomorrow's hard ride.'

Geoffrey sighed loudly and sat down to remove his boots.

Owen sank down on the bed. 'With all this, Sir John sounds more and more like the murderer.'

'If he is, he is a clever player,' Geoffrey said. 'And we were his unwitting audience.'

'But why did Edern and Tangwystl say nothing of the chaplain's injuries?'

Geoffrey had slumped down on to the bed with a groan. 'I do not like to think it of them. But it is troublesome. Mistress Tangwystl had called Gladys to the chaplain's room to witness his letter. Gladys heard them calling her. Surely they would have returned to that room seeking her.'

'That is what I am thinking.'

Geoffrey suddenly pounded the bed with his fist. 'But Gladys said nothing of them looking into the room. Therefore—'

'They did not. Why not?'

'Oh. I see.'

'Aye.'

Owen thought of that now as they rode off in pursuit of the three. Was Sir John a clever player? Or were Edern and the fair Tangwystl the dangerous ones?

a tender heart

In the middle of the night, a knee to his back woke Brother Michaelo. Sir Robert tossed and thrashed in bed, gasping for air. Michaelo sat up, mounded the pillows that had been thrown round the bed, and pulled Sir Robert up to a seated position against them. A hand dug into Michaelo's shoulder.

'Blow out, Sir Robert,' Michaelo coaxed, as Owen had taught him. 'Blow out and you will remember how to breathe in.' He demonstrated with a hearty, puffy exhale.

Sir Robert's face creased up, and with a gasp he began to laugh. The laughter led to coughing, and breathing.

'I am glad to be so amusing,' Brother Michaelo said. The cloth Sir Robert held to his mouth was flecked with blood. 'Rest here a moment while I bring the steam.' On the brazier sat a pot of water in which sage leaves simmered all the night. Michaelo tiptoed over the cool tiles, pulled down the sleeves of his linen shift to pad his hands, lifted the pot and carried it to the bed. Sitting it on Sir Robert's blanket-covered lap, he told him to bend over it and breathe deep. Sir Robert obeyed. At first his breath creaked and wheezed, but gradually it quieted. When the cough began, Michaelo moved the pot to the floor and brought a pan for the flux. So much blood. The blood-speckled flux of the past few nights was now heavily streaked with crimson, though still watery. Or was that the weakness of Sir Robert's blood? Brother Michaelo held Sir Robert's head while he coughed. A physick of herbs and poppy juice in honey water to quiet him and allow his sleep, a compress over his hot cheeks and forehead of soothing lavender water, and soon Sir Robert closed his eyes, breathing evenly.

Michaelo returned the sage water to the brazier, shoved the pan beneath the bed, and washed his own face and hands with lavender water, then sat up in bed with a cup of wine. He did not expect it to calm him enough. He knew that he would sleep no more. His heart was too heavy. When he had finished the wine, he drew out his rosary beads and began to pray.

At last dawn turned the sky to a dull grey in the high window above the bed, and Michaelo rose, dressed as quietly as he could, and took up a post in the doorway to wait for Edmund. Though he thought he had given Sir Robert enough of his physick to allow him to sleep for a few more hours, he feared that the expected knock on the door might wake him.

Edmund soon appeared, garbed for a journey and flushed with anticipation. Michaelo put his finger to his mouth as he stepped out into the corridor and closed the door to the room behind him.

'You are ready?'

'The groom is even now leading my horse to the North-west Gate.'

'You remember all we told you?'

Edmund opened his mouth to recite. Michaelo motioned for him to whisper it in his ear. The corridor appeared empty, but a clever spy could make it seem so. Edmund duly whispered his messages. Michaelo was impressed how thoroughly the young man had them by heart. He was quicker than he looked.

'You have a safe place for the letter?' Michaelo asked as he drew it from his sleeve.

Edmund pulled a bag from beneath his tunic. It hung from his neck on a strong leather thong. Deeming it sufficient, Michaelo handed him the precious letter. Edmund placed it in the bag, pushed it back down his tunic.

'And there it shall remain until I hand it to Captain Archer, I swear that to you on my life,' Edmund whispered with a pounding of his chest.

Brother Michaelo smiled at the young man's dramatic flair. Better to be so excited than frightened. 'God watch over you on your journey, Edmund, and lend you wings. *In nomine Patris* . . .'

Edmund bowed his head to receive Brother Michaelo's blessing.

The monk prayed that God still accepted him as a vessel of His blessing. His task accomplished, Michaelo returned to the chamber to sit beside the bed and recite his office. He would be there to reassure Sir Robert that Edmund was on his way.

Waking from a dreamless slumber, Sir Robert found

Brother Michaelo, head bowed, praying at his bedside. The aroma of fresh baked bread drew his eyes to a table beside the bed. A flagon, bread, apples and cheese. His stomach fluttered. He had awakened anxious. Slowly he remembered. The letter. Edmund was to come at dawn for the letter. Sir Robert looked up at the window. It was clearly past dawn.

'Holy Mary Mother of God,' he said as he pushed back the covers.

Brother Michaelo looked up from his prayers, smiled. 'You awake with energy. You must have slept well.'

'Edmund. The letter.'

'All is well. I saw him off at dawn. He has the message by heart and the letter tucked beneath his tunic.'

Feeling his heart begin to pound, his face grow hot, Sir Robert leaned back on the pillows and took a deep breath. 'What right had you to do it for me?'

'You had a difficult night. You need your rest.'

'I needed to do this for Owen!'

'You have. I was merely your go-between.'

Sir Robert closed his eyes, fighting tears of rage. An old man's tears. An old, feeble man. When had Brother Michaelo become his nurse?

'Forgive me, Sir Robert,' Brother Michaelo was saying. 'I have not meant to offend you.'

When Sir Robert trusted himself to move without the tremors brought on by anger, he sat up and began to help himself to some honey water. When Brother Michaelo leaned forward to assist him, Sir Robert slapped his hand.

'And you will not accompany me on my excursion

with Mistress Tangwystl. I have not missed the end of Mass in the cathedral?' That was when Tangwystl was to come to the porch to meet him.

'No, you have not. But do you think you have the strength?'

'If you allow me to break my fast in peace, I shall.'

By mid-morning a mist hid the sun and the painted stones of the palace beaded with the damp. Sir Robert stood in the porch of the great hall, one hand on the wall beside him, looking out at the courtyard, hoping that it was merely the air in the hall that had brought on the dizziness. But still his head pounded and he felt as if he pulled each breath from the hands of a demon set on suffocating him. The porter hovered solicitously.

'How terrible you sound, Sir Robert. Ask for a pitcher of hot, spiced wine and a good fire in your chamber. Do not go abroad on such a day. You are not well. The damp will worsen your chest. Let me send for Master Thomas, the physician who attends the bishop when he is in residence. He will attend you. He is from Cardiff.'

'Do not trouble yourself,' Sir Robert said, fighting the demon for each word. 'I await a friend.' But how would he manage the long walk to St David's Well, and especially the long upward climb back?

The porter summoned a servant. 'Help Sir Robert to his room. Find his companion, Brother Michaelo, if he is not in their chamber. And bring Sir Robert hot, spiced wine. Make sure his fire is kept burning all the day.'

Sir Robert tried to refuse, but he managed merely to shake his head and say, 'I must await her.'

'You were not nearly so bad as this when Captain Archer departed,' said the porter. 'He will blame us, he will. To whom should I make your apologies?'

'Mistress Lascelles of Cydweli.'

'Aye, Sir Robert. I shall tell her you have been taken ill.'

'No, I pray you.' But what could the porter say instead? Sir Robert gave in and nodded. 'Of course you must.'

He burned with humiliation as he was led away. How awful was old age, to be too weak to defend one's right. But where was Mistress Lascelles? Surely the bells had long since rung? Had she left without him? Or was his mind as crabbed and useless as his body? Had he imagined she had invited him to accompany her to St David's Well?

Satisfied that the physician seemed sufficiently attentive to Sir Robert, Brother Michaelo took a break from the stifling atmosphere in his chamber and the terrible sounds of Sir Robert's laboured breathing. He kept trying to breathe for his friend, and the effort had left him light-headed.

Though the great hall was not empty, folk inhabited it in clusters, ignoring all but their own companions. In such a crowd Michaelo felt sufficiently invisible. He paced about, muttering not prayers but complaints. 'Strike me down, Lord, for I am the sinner, not Sir Robert. What is the use of holy wells and pilgrimages if the good are not rewarded? For he is a good man, Lord. Did he not devote years of his life to performing penance – and for what terrible sin? That he treated his wife as most other men do theirs? With indifference born from ignorance? Was this such a sin that he cannot be forgiven? What of the pride of kings? Archbishops? Bishops? What of these Welsh clerics who openly break their vow of chastity? When shall they suffer?' As Michaelo elaborated on his complaint, his pacing grew more energetic until one of the Benedictines from the previous evening approached with concern.

'Is it your friend, Brother? Has God called him?'

Michaelo crossed himself. 'No, God be praised. I am worried for him, that is all.'

'He is in God's hands, Brother. Be at peace.'

Chastened, Michaelo retired to a corner, keeping an eye on the door through which the physician would come. He wished to speak with him away from Sir Robert, find out the truth, how ill he was.

Perhaps that was why he did not notice Mistress Lascelles until he heard the rustle of her silk gown as she settled on the bench beside him.

'*Benedicte*, Mistress Lascelles.' Shimmering silk and a gossamer veil – was this her garb for a walk to Porth Clais? Even Brother Michaelo felt shabby beside her. 'Sir Robert wished very much to accompany you to St David's Well.'

'There will be another day.'

Would there? Brother Michaelo prayed that she was right.

'Forgive me for intruding on your thoughts,' she said. In her voice, Michaelo heard sympathy. 'I saw you here and I thought you might wish for a companion. Sir Robert is very ill?'

'I fear that he is, Mistress Lascelles.'

'I pray you, my name is Tangwystl ferch Gruffydd. Would you call me Tangwystl?'

Brother Michaelo bowed his head. 'Mistress Tangwystl. It is pleasing on the tongue.'

'Such shadows beneath your eyes. You have watched the night with him?'

'He woke in the middle of the night in great distress. After that I could not quiet my thoughts. I shall wear out my rosary beads before he strengthens.'

'I had such a time, not long ago. My family was forced to seek sanctuary in St Mary's Church in Tenby. You know the story, of course.'

'I do.'

'Would you prefer to pray?'

'No. No, please, distract me from my fears.'

'It was my mother for whom I prayed. My son Hedyn was an infant, he knew nothing of our troubles, and my sister Awena found it an adventure, to sleep in the house of God, to take her walks in the churchyard. But my mother grieved so for our house, our old life, she fretted and fussed over Hedyn, and daily her eyes sank further and further into her face, the flesh fell off her bones, her voice grew shrill, her words confused. I kept the rosary with me at all times, praying myself to sleep, praying as I suckled my child.'

'And did God listen?'

Tangwystl looked away. 'You should see my son.' Her voice trembled. 'He is as beautiful as the angels.'

Michaelo bowed his head and crossed himself. 'Sometimes it is difficult to forgive God for His absences.'

'I know,' Tangwystl whispered.

'Your mother is alive?'

'Oh, yes. But she is not the woman she was.'

The physician's gown of red and grey caught Michaelo's eye.

'Forgive me,' Michaelo said as he stood up abruptly. 'I must see Master Thomas.'

Already the physician and his servant were near the door to the porch. Michaelo pushed his way through servants and pilgrims without apology. Some shouted after him, which caught the physician's attention. He paused, eyebrows raised as Michaelo panted a *Benedicte*.

'*Benedicte*, Brother Michaelo. I wondered where you had gone.'

'I thought Sir Robert would prefer to be alone with you, Master Thomas. But I must know the truth – is he – will he be strong enough for the journey back to York?'

Thomas's long, bloodless face betrayed no emotion. 'Does he speak of returning?'

The question chilled Michaelo. 'What do you mean? What has he— Sweet Jesu, he is to die in this distant land?'

Thomas placed a hand on Michaelo's shoulder. 'Come. Let us sit and talk.' He led Michaelo to a bench beneath a high window, out of the bustle of servants and guests. 'How did you come to make this journey with him?'

'His daughter's husband is on a mission to Wales for the Duke of Lancaster. Both Sir Robert and I thought to join their company for the journey out here. After Easter we should be able to find a party of pilgrims returning to England.'

'His son-in-law. Is he here in St David's?'

'No. In Cydweli.'

Master Thomas's eyes followed a small group of pilgrims. 'So many souls praying for grace, hoping to win Heaven by this journey. And yet Sir Robert came here to pray for his family. To offer up his life for their continued health and happiness.'

Michaelo tucked his hands up his sleeves, then withdrew them as they spread the chill to his arms. He rubbed them. 'Perhaps I might send for Captain Archer.'

'His son-in-law?'

Michaelo nodded.

'It would be best to ask Sir Robert what he wishes.'

Michaelo forced the question that wished to stick in his throat. 'He knows that he is dying?' His heart raced with the effort.

'Oh yes. He says he made his farewells in York, that his daughter understood. But you do not seem prepared for this. He did not tell you of his intention?'

What need was there to shake his head? The physician could see his distress and sighed.

'Perhaps he did not wish to see the sympathy in your eyes until it was unavoidable.'

'Why here? In a country that is so strange to him?'

'He told me that he has gone on pilgrimage to places far stranger than this,' Thomas said. 'It is difficult for the healthy to understand how weary the sick become. Every breath is a struggle for Sir Robert. Death seems a release. A gift from God.'

Sir Robert had made his farewells to Lucie Wilton. And Owen? Why had no one told Michaelo? 'But he was not so ill as this when we departed York. He did not labour to breathe, his colour was far better than it is now. How could he have known?'

'Perhaps God told him.'

Brother Michaelo looked up, fearing the physician made light of Sir Robert. But he saw no lifting of the corners of the mouth, nor other sign in his demeanour. 'What can I do for him?'

'He accepted a stronger physick to ease the pain, allow him to sleep, though he says he will not take as much as I recommended. He says he must have his wits about him, he has much to do. There is of course no reason to insist he keep to his bed. But do not let him venture forth alone. He is weak, and the physick might confuse him.'

'His suffering is terrible to watch.' Michaelo pressed his jaw beneath his ears where he felt an odd tension. 'I wish I could breathe for him.'

'You are a good friend to him.'

'I should pay you.'

Master Thomas shook his head. 'Not now. I shall return in a few days to see him. Sometimes a man changes his mind as the pain worsens. He may need more of the physick.'

Michaelo sat on the bench long after the physician departed. He did not trust himself to go to Sir Robert, not yet. The depth of his feelings perplexed him. Whence came this sorrow? What was Sir Robert to him? In faith, Michaelo's concern should be his journey home. He should make inquiries about the other pilgrims, discover who was from the north. What of the Benedictines with whom he had spoken the previous evening? He could not remember their house. What a fool he was. Losing his memory over an old man who never had a kind word for him, who criticised him incessantly, who contradicted his every word. He put his head in his hands, clenched his jaw to fight the tears that threatened.

'May I sit?'

Michaelo recognised Tangwystl's exotic scent. He raised his head.

'I should go to him.'

'Come, then. I shall accompany you.'

Twenty-one

A FIERCE AND TERRIBLE LOVE

Sweat pooled beneath the leather patch on Owen's eye. The late morning sun shone through a low cloud layer and the air felt heavy. The weather was strangely warm for the end of March. Owen felt he stank as much as his horse.

They had ridden with little pause since early morning. Owen was pleased with all in the company. His six companions neither complained nor lagged behind. And for their efforts they now approached Haverfordwest. They should arrive in St David's by sunset.

From behind a slow-moving caravan a rider suddenly appeared, approaching at a pace equal to that of Owen's company. He was upon them before Duncan cried out, 'The Duke's livery!'

Owen felt a shiver of dread when he recognised Edmund. He dismounted and met the messenger, who was grinning from ear to ear.

'I thought to ride clear to Cydweli to find you, Captain. God has been good.'

And if they had entered Haverfordwest a moment earlier, they might have missed him.

'God meant us to find one another,' Owen said. He drew Edmund away from the group to a spot across the road beneath a venerable oak. It provided little shade with no leaves, but too much shade and they would be chilled. Owen called to Geoffrey to join them. The latter brought a wineskin to pass round, which drew fervent thanks from the messenger.

Owen leaned against a low branch. 'Do you come from Sir Robert?'

'I do, Captain.'

'How fares he?'

'Poorly. But well enough last night to give me messages to learn. And I have a letter.' Edmund drew a sweat-darkened pouch from beneath his tunic, handed Owen a sealed roll.

'Tell me what you have by heart,' Owen said. As Edmund repeated his news, Owen was encouraged to hear that Edern and Tangwystl had arrived safely in St David's – he was glad the vicar had obeyed the bishop. The priest's hurried departure, however, and with trouble on his heels, was disturbing.

But most potentially troublesome was the source of most of Sir Robert's information, Martin Wirthir, a Fleming who often worked with the French. Geoffrey would not like that. Owen wondered about Geoffrey. Could he trust him to co-operate with Martin if necessary? And what of the bishop's men? If they accompanied him to meet Martin, would they be keen to tell of the Fleming in St David's? Sweet Jesu, the more he worked at this knot the worse it grew.

And how many others may have noted the Fleming in the area, or overheard his conversation with Sir Robert? Owen examined the seal on the letter. It looked undisturbed, but there was a slight stain on the paper to one side of the seal that gave Owen pause. 'Who handed you the letter?' he asked.

'Brother Michaelo,' Edmund said. 'I have touched nothing.'

Owen nodded. 'Can you tell me anything else? This Brother Dyfrig who asked so many questions. Is he in St David's?'

Edmund slapped his leg. 'I feared I had forgot somewhat in the middle. He departed the city a week hence. And Sir Robert knows not where he went.'

'Excellent, Edmund. You have proved yourself a worthy messenger,' Owen said. 'Go join the others. You will ride back with us. And Edmund—'

He stood to attention. 'I shall say nothing to them of my messages, Captain.'

'I know that you will not, Edmund. But more than that, try not to flinch if we tell a different tale than what you know to be true.'

Edmund grinned. 'Aye, Captain.'

'Who is this Martin Wirthir?' Geoffrey asked as he settled down on a root beneath the tree.

Owen eased himself down on to a rock, stretched his legs, tapped the letter absently against his leg while he considered how to handle Geoffrey. He resolved to tell him as little as possible about Martin. 'One who has helped me in the past. Saved the life of my wife's apprentice. I have not seen him in a long while.' When had Martin learned Owen was in Wales?

'He works for King Charles?'

'He has also worked for members of King Edward's court. It means nothing about Martin's personal allegiance.' The seal on the letter gave no clue to Martin's current politics – it bore the impression of the letter M or W, depending on how one held it. Owen broke the seal, smoothed the parchment on his lap, read slowly. The words themselves, and the signature, felt true to him. But how had Martin known that the death of John de Reine and the movements of Tangwystl and Edern were of interest to Owen? He handed Geoffrey the letter.

Geoffrey's face creased with worry as he read. 'Such caution to name neither man nor place. "A man who might give good account". The murderer, do you think?'

'Or a witness.' Owen rose, began to pace as he thought what to do. Whoever the man was, he must be shielded. But what of Edern and the traitor who pursued him?

Geoffrey turned over the parchment, studied the seal. 'You think someone tampered with this?'

How he studied every gesture. 'Sir Robert is an old campaigner. He would not send a messenger without knowing the content of the missive.'

'Your wife's father is a man of many skills.'

'His hands are no longer steady enough for such work. But Brother Michaelo . . .'

'Um. He does seem a slippery one. I do not doubt it.'

'We must hasten to St David's.'

'You will meet with this Martin Wirthir?'

'Do you think we dare ignore this?'

Geoffrey squinted up at Owen. 'You are plotting something that I will not like.'

'There are three in our company who must be handled with care.'

'The bishop's men and Burley's man?'

'Aye.'

'I heard what you said to Edmund.'

Owen called to Iolo, who appeared to be telling an amusing tale to the other men. Edmund jostled him when he did not respond. He glanced up, caught Owen's eye, and hurried over. His companions watched with apprehension.

'This the others must not hear,' Owen began.

'They will not.'

'Is there a way to reach Clegyr Boia from the road we ride?' Martin's letter had requested they meet where Owen's company had exited the tunnel from the bishop's palace.

'Round the far side of St David's and out beyond the North-west Gate,' said Iolo.

'I cannot ride there without passing the city?'

Iolo dropped his head, considered. 'From here there is no easy way over the River Alun.'

'Impassable?'

'No, but ill advised in spring. Better to cross it to the north of the city.'

'Why do you wish to avoid the city?' Geoffrey asked.

'We know at present whence trouble might come,' Owen said. 'But if we pass near the gates of St David's, who knows who might see us and follow us to Clegyr Boia? It is a risk.'

Iolo shook his head. 'A risk it is, Captain, but we might call more attention to ourselves picking our way where horses never go.'

Geoffrey looked pleased.

'Come, then.' Owen rose, dusted off his tunic. 'We ride hard to St David's.'

From his bed Sir Robert gazed on the wall painting of King Henry crossing Llechllafar. Sometimes, as Sir Robert fought for breath and the room spun round him, it seemed the King stepped not upon a bridge but on to a ship that rode a whirlpool.

To give in to the demon clutching his breath – at times he saw that as a blessed release. But that was sinful. It was for God to choose his time. He hoped that it was not sinful to take Master Thomas's physick – he feared that it soothed him too well. He feared, too, that he would lose track of how often he asked for it, but Brother Michaelo assured him he would watch that neither he nor Mistress Tangwystl dispensed so much it would muddle his wits. Mistress Tangwystl – another sinful pleasure. She had returned with Brother Michaelo and asked whether she might sit with Sir Robert, said that she wished for occupation that might quiet her mind.

Sir Robert welcomed her with joy, for in Brother Michaelo's face he saw the physician's sentence. The monk's mourning eyes and unnaturally gentle behaviour reminded Sir Robert too much of his approaching end.

'Go and walk about,' Sir Robert urged Michaelo. 'You grow too pale.'

Michaelo refused. Sir Robert turned to face

Tangwystl. 'I grew weary of tossing on the sea with King Henry.'

'King Henry?' she whispered as she leaned down to Sir Robert, blotted his brow with a damp, scented cloth. The movement loosened her wide sleeves. Pale, shimmering silk, it gave her wings.

'The fresco,' said Brother Michaelo, nodding towards the wall.

Tangwystl sat back, studied the painting. Sir Robert thought her a vision of beauty as she sat beside his bed, hands resting on her silken lap, eyes reflecting the glow of the fire in the brazier.

'The red-handed man in Myrddin's prophecy – some say that is Owain Lawgoch, he who my father is accused of assisting. But as I heard the legend, the red-handed man was to wound the king while he was yet in Ireland.'

'Let us pray that King Edward does not cross the Irish Sea,' Brother Michaelo said.

A servant brought a cup of hot honey water, added a few pillows behind Sir Robert to raise him high enough to drink.

'You are well attended,' Tangwystl said when the servant withdrew. In the light from the brazier her hair beneath the gossamer veil seemed a vibrant red. 'I wish to do something,' she was saying, 'but I cannot see what you might need. I must make amends for being late for our walk this morning.'

'As you can see, I would have disappointed you had you still wished for my company on your way to St David's Well.' Sir Robert was pleased that his breathing seemed easier. He did not wish to frighten Tangwystl with his struggles. 'If you have no hopes of someone else to accompany you to the well, you might tell me of yourself. In what part of this fair country did you dwell before you took your place as lady of Cydweli?'

Tangwystl bowed her head, and for a moment Sir Robert worried that in some way his request had offended her.

'Do you know the tale of Rhiannon?' she asked.

'No. Please tell me.'

'It is a sad story. Do you mind a sad story?'

'The best ballads are sad ones, I think.'

Tangwystl frowned and smoothed her skirt, shook out her sleeves, as if composing her thoughts. And then she began. 'She was Pwyll's lady, lord of Dyfed. Theirs was not an easy courtship, for when he declared his love for her she was already betrothed. But with patience and trickery they disposed of Pwyll's rival. Rhiannon proved a generous lady and at first all Pwyll's people loved her. But when after three years she had not borne a son, Pwyll's men turned against her and urged their lord to cast her aside. Pwyll refused, and it seemed the gods rewarded his loyalty, for Rhiannon at last bore him a son. But on the night of the birth, Rhiannon's handmaids failed to keep watch. In the morning, the child was gone. Fearing that they would be punished, the women killed a chicken and smeared its blood over Rhiannon's mouth while she slept, then ran from her chamber shrieking that the unnatural mother had eaten her son.' For a moment, Tangwystl sat silently, her hands folded, her head bowed. When she began again to speak, her voice was unsteady. 'Seven years Rhiannon suffered humiliation as a punishment for this sin she did not commit. Seven years she wept for her son alone, with no one to comfort her. Seven—' Tangwystl's voice broke and she covered her face with her hands.

'Do you weep so to tell the tale?' Sir Robert said. 'You must speak of something happier – I would not have you suffer pain for me.'

Though Tangwystl dropped her hands, she kept her head bowed. 'I share Rhiannon's suffering,' she said, her voice yet hoarse with tears, 'for my son has been taken from me. I suffer my loss as she did, with none to comfort me. And my suffering shall stretch beyond seven years.'

How tragic she looked, and how lovely. A mother's grief for her lost child was becoming to a woman. 'If God took him from you, there is nothing to be done but take joy in those yet to come. But does your husband not grieve with you?'

Tangwystl took a deep, shuddering breath. 'It is because of John Lascelles that my son is lost to me.' She shook her head, as if trying to rid herself of the thought. 'Such a tale is not for you, good Sir Robert. I do not come here to burden your heart with my sorrow.'

'I would be honoured to be so burdened, my lady.'

'It is not good for your humours.'

'According to the worthy physician, there is little can be done for my humours. In faith, it does me good to hear your story. It is a debt paid, mayhap. Once I caused great unhappiness by being blind to a woman's sorrow – my wife's. I was a fool. I might have found joy with her, and she with me, if when I saw her tears I had asked for what she wept. Instead I called her ungrateful and left her alone in a strange place that

I had given her no reason to love while I went back to soldiering. Please, gentle lady, speak to me of your sorrow. Amélie will smile on me if I listen.'

Tangwystl had lifted her face to Sir Robert, and though her eyes still shone with tears, a smile trembled on her lips. 'I shall gladly help you with that.'

'Come now. Tell me your tale.'

She nodded, but was silent a while, her eyes on the fire. When at last she began, her voice was stronger. 'A long while ago it seems, though it is not more than four winters past, I met a man who looked to me to be the best of all that is mankind. He was sharp of wit, honey tongued, and skilled in anything to which he turned his hands, whether it be casting nets in the sea or ploughing the land, carpentry or smithying. And withal he was blessed with a countenance that made a maiden blush to look on him. He favoured me with his attentions. I gave him my heart. But my father, having no son and therefore knowing his land would go to my uncles and their sons, wished to marry me to someone with sufficient wealth that if my sister did not wed she would yet have a comfortable life in my household.

'But I would have Rhys. Rhys ap Llywelyn was his name. *Is* his name, God grant that he yet lives. I knew that my father would not wish to risk the anger of a well-born husband if I were no longer a virgin, and so I lay with Rhys. And we conceived a child. Hedyn, my son. When I told my father of my joy, he cursed Rhys and banished me from his house. Rhys and I did not care – we lived happily as husband and wife in the cottage of a cousin who took pity on us. But when our son was born, my father repented his anger and prepared for our wedding. And then the Lord of Pembroke accused my father of treason. To be sure, you must have knowledge of that.'

'There was no wedding then?'

Tangwystl bowed her head. 'No. Though we claimed sanctuary in St Mary's Church and lived there a long while, our vows were never sanctified by a priest, nor did my father acknowledge our marriage in the law. But I had no time to think on my troubles. I had to look to my mother, who seemed to wither in spirit with each day. Hedyn was the only joy she knew.

'And then my father, who had escaped to seek help, returned in the company of John Lascelles. He was not yet steward of Lancaster's Marcher lordships. It was not the first time he had come to us. He had been our guest once a few years earlier when my father had arranged a ship for him, and when it foundered, my father saved his life. Sir John offered us sanctuary in the March of Cydweli and even a farm he had it in his grace to dispose of. All he asked in return was my hand in marriage.

'I took Hedyn and went in search of Rhys, who also sought help for us, but he was not at the cottage. His cousin knew not where he had gone. Our thirty days of sanctuary had run out and my Lord of Pembroke's men were coming for father. We could not stay while I searched for Rhys. And everyone said that without land, without a name, how was my father to see us wed?

'Still I waited. My parents were two days gone when the earl's men came. When I fled to Rhys's cousin's house he shunned me, fearful lest Pembroke should call him traitor also. Weak and frightened for my son – he was but an infant – I followed after my parents. I did not go far before I met Sir John on the road, hastening back to save me. In my despair he comforted me.

'But never did I think that for my comfort and that of my family I must hear my son Hedyn branded a bastard. Father had told me that Sir John knew of the baby and welcomed it. I did not know English ways. I did not know how you chastise the child for the parents' sin, which was not even sin among my people. Rhys and I loved, we lived together as man and wife, and had my father not met misfortune we would have been wed.

'Where am I to find the strength to tell my son he is a bastard? That when Sir John returns to England I must accompany him, but Hedyn will stay in Cydweli? My son weeps when I leave him now, but how long will he remember me?'

'Sweet lady.'

'So you see, I am alone in my sorrow, as was Rhiannon, and punished for what I did not do.'

Sir Robert wished to agree with her, but she had lain with a man against her father's wishes, and without the blessing of the Church. An extreme punishment, but not an unusual one. 'What of Rhys? What happened to him?'

'He had gone looking for work. He knew nothing of what had happened until I was gone. His brother tells me he suffered much, and that at last he had come to St David's to ask the bishop to intervene, to declare my marriage to Sir John invalid.'

'Is that what you want?'

'That is why I am here.'

'And Rhys?'

'I do not know. He left here without a word to anyone.'

But Sir Robert thought he saw something in her eyes that belied her denial.

Twenty-two

A QUESTION OF TRUST

At Newgale, where the road dipped to the ocean, a brisk wind cheered Owen's company, cooling them after their long, hot ride. It promised a chilly night, and though the men thought it would be spent in comfort at the bishop's palace, Owen knew that might not be true.

The closer they drew to St David's, the slower their pace, for there were many pilgrims on the road, and all on foot. At last by Nine Wells they dismounted and walked their horses. It was late afternoon, but Owen was confident they would reach St David's before sunset. Still, time was against them. In a few days the bishop would return to the city for Passiontide, and all must put aside their worldly pursuits for Holy Week. Who might slip through Owen's fingers while he knelt in the cathedral?

A pointless worry. He would do all he could, then

use the time to pray God saw fit to show him how he must continue.

Sir Robert's breathing quieted and slowed.

'He sleeps,' Brother Michaelo whispered.

'Would you like to walk out in the courtyard with me?' Tangwystl asked. 'Sir Robert is right. You are very pale. And you have more vigils ahead of you.'

'I should watch with him.'

'Watch him sleep? The servant will come for us if there is need.'

Michaelo leaned close to Sir Robert, listened to his chest. There was a damp, insidious rumbling now. He made the sign of the cross over Sir Robert.

'What is it?' Tangwystl asked.

'I am not certain, but I do not like the sound. It is as if his lungs have turned to liquid.'

Tangwystl put her head to Sir Robert's chest. It seemed to Michaelo a long time she stayed there, and when she raised her head, she did not meet his eyes, but sat silently with head down for a moment. Then she rose, told the servant to make sure to keep Sir Robert's head propped up on the pillows, that he must not be permitted to lie flat.

'It is the end?' Michaelo asked.

'My little brother lived for some time after his chest made such a sound,' Tangwystl said. 'But my mother knew when she heard it that he would not recover. Come. Let us walk a while.'

The light from the high windows and the bustle of the pilgrims stunned Brother Michaelo when he stepped from the corridor into the great hall, so long had he been in the dark, quiet sickroom. He had forgotten it was yet day. Mistress Tangwystl gasped beside him. She, too, must find the change a shock.

'My lady, what a pleasure to find you here.' A tall man in travel garb bowed to Michaelo's companion. He was dusty and stank of horses, but his clothing was fine.

'My lord,' Tangwystl said softly, her eyes on the man's muddy boots as she curtseyed.

'And now yet another churchman escorts you. Are you a friend of Father Edern?' the man asked with a sneer.

Brother Michaelo liked neither the man's tone nor his expression. 'I am Brother Michaelo, secretary to the Archbishop of York, and not acquainted with the priest you named. Mistress Tangwystl has assisted me in the sickroom of a friend all the day. And you, sir, if you deserve to be so called, speak your name.'

'John Lascelles.'

Dear God in Heaven.

'I see my name is familiar to you. And has your lovely companion told you that she is my wife?'

As they approached Bonning's Gate to the north of the city, Owen dismounted and called to Duncan and Geoffrey to step aside.

To Duncan he gave the orders to take all the horses save Owen's and Iolo's to the palace stables. The two were off to meet someone who might help them.

'Why Iolo?' Duncan asked.

'He was born in Porth Clais. I need him as a guide. Go, Duncan. Rest. We might ride out again soon, so take rest when you can.'

Tight jawed, Duncan took the rein of Geoffrey's

mount in hand with his own and joined the others, gave them the orders. Iolo moved aside with his mount, giving the two men privacy.

Geoffrey had occupied himself smoothing out his clothing and beating off some of the dust while Owen gave Duncan his orders. Now he faced Owen, his eyes hard with suspicion, and said, 'You and Iolo?'

Owen drew out the leather pouch that held the letters from Tangwystl and Bishop Houghton. He slipped the thong over his head, held out the pouch to Geoffrey.

Geoffrey hesitated, then took the proffered pouch. 'What are you doing?'

'One of us must see that these documents are safe with the Archdeacon of Carmarthen.'

'You mean to leave me here while you meet with Martin Wirthir?'

'There is no need for both of us to confer with Wirthir.'

Geoffrey dropped his head, but Owen saw how his hands clutched the pouch. 'I am not one of your men, to lead round at your will.'

'I would not trust these papers with one of them. There is much to explain to the archdeacon, and they could not do that.'

'You will join me after talking to the Fleming?'

'I shall do whatever will resolve these troubles. If I must ride to protect Father Edern and his brother, so be it.'

'What if Martin Wirthir is a spy for Owain Lawgoch?'

'It does not matter. What does matter is that it suits him at the moment to assist us.'

'What do you think of Owain Lawgoch?'

'He is King Charles's puppet.'

With his eyes on the pouch rather than Owen, Geoffrey asked, 'Is that what you really think?'

'So this is what we have come to, a matter of trust. Do you trust me?'

Geoffrey raised his head, studied Owen's face. After what seemed to Owen an eternity in which he wondered about his next move, Geoffrey shifted, sighed, and slipped the leather thong over his head. 'What else must I do?'

Owen told him the rest of his plan.

Hallelujah, God is merciful, Michaelo thought as he looked over Sir John's shoulder and saw Geoffrey Chaucer enter the great hall. Sir Robert will be overjoyed to see his son-in-law. But Chaucer appeared to be alone. He caught Michaelo's eye, shook his head. Michaelo searched his mind quickly for something to say that might keep his companions sparring.

'You have come chasing after your wife, Sir John? She is not permitted to go on pilgrimage in this holy season?'

'I have come seeking a man of God, monk, to take back with me to the garrison of Cydweli. Some wretch attacked our chaplain. He was so brutally beaten he died of his injuries.'

'Father Francis?' Tangwystl said in a voice so small Michaelo turned to her in concern. Her complexion had lost all its glow and colour, and as he watched she put a trembling hand up to her cheek and crumpled in a faint. Sir John caught her up as she fell. 'Where is her chamber?' he demanded, his face ashen. 'Dear God, I did not mean to frighten her so.'

The hall was suddenly alive with people offering assistance. A bench was dragged over, a servant came running with wine. Sir John lowered himself on to the bench with Tangwystl still firmly in his arms. He bent over her, whispering her name, trying to get her to take some of the wine.

Brother Michaelo sat down beside Sir John, weak with relief. His ploy had almost been his undoing.

A fog was rolling in off the sea, dulling the late afternoon sun to a twilight dimness and evening out the shadows. Owen and Iolo met the fog as they climbed up out of the valley. As it thickened they dismounted to lead their horses along the uneven ground. The countryside was quiet except for the gulls riding inland on the fog and a lone dog who barked a warning as they passed close to a rocky outcrop, then disappeared behind it. Owen listened for the sound of its herd, but only the gulls called.

How unused to such quiet he was. York was never silent. Even when he lay awake at night he heard children calling out, babies crying, cats fighting in the street, boatmen calling to one another, the crier making his rounds. And even on the journey from York their company had been large and noisy, with Sir Robert and Brother Michaelo bickering all along the way. Owen had grown unaccustomed to silence. It made him uneasy.

They circled the base of Clegyr Boia, walking slowly, watching the ground, seeking signs of recent encampments or riders.

'I would guess he has camped up top,' said Iolo.

'Where he would be so easily seen?' Owen said.

'If you saw a fire atop this mound, what would be your first thought? That a mortal man camped here?'

'No.'

'They also say there are cellars where one might hide. Though I never found one.'

And so they led their horses up a well-worn path to the top of the mound. It was bare of trees, but thick with gorse and treacherous with half-buried stones and timbers, and to one side the crumbled walls of an ancient fortress.

'If I were hiding atop, I would stay in the shadow of those walls,' said Iolo.

As they picked their way through the tangled underbrush, Owen suddenly straightened, sensing more than seeing someone approaching.

'So I was right. You did follow fast behind the fleeing lady.' A figure materialised from the fog.

'Is this Wirthir?' Iolo whispered.

'Aye.' Owen raised his voice. 'I cannot think how you know me so well, Martin. I like to think I am cunning and subtle. But you were right, we followed the lady and her lord.'

'And the hapless priest,' said Martin. He was now at arm's length.

'You two might be taken for brothers,' Iolo said, looking from one to the other.

Martin gave him a little bow. 'I take that as a compliment.'

Owen introduced Iolo. 'He knows Dyfed well. I thought he might be of use. Have you sent someone after Father Edern, to shield him from his shadow?'

'I travel alone, as you know, Owen. The choice was

the priest's life, or that of a man who has a tale to tell that many will be keen to hear.'

Martin's manner of speaking was the same as Owen remembered it, gently mocking.

'An amusing tale?' Iolo asked.

'No, not amusing. Before I take you to him, there are things I would tell you, Owen. Do you wish Iolo to hear this?'

'I do.'

'His name is Rhys ap Llywelyn, the brother of the priest Edern.'

Tangwystl's missing lover. 'He had disappeared from St David's,' said Owen. 'How does he come to be here, in your care?'

'I played Samaritan. Not as well as another who spirited him away from Whitesands, but I flatter myself that he lives because of my care.'

'Whitesands.'

'I hope that someone you trust will take him into the bishop's close and see that he is delivered up to those who will hear his story and mete out justice.'

'He is the murderer of John de Reine?'

'If to be the one who thrust the knife into the man's gut is to be the murderer, yes. But he defended himself against two men, one who had met him on the beach intending to kill him, and Reine, who came upon them and thought to defend the other against Rhys.'

'Who was this third man?'

'The one who now follows Father Edern, thinking he will thus find Rhys and finish his interrupted work.'

'Then Edern is in no danger?'

'From this man? I do not trust what he will do.'

'Why did you not deliver Rhys up to the bishop's council?'

'He was in no condition to walk in alone and state his case, and I do not wish to call attention to myself. Nor could I warn Father Edern, because with the other near I had to keep Rhys by my side—' Martin had begun leading them towards the ruined fortress. 'You need this one witness, and by my count he is innocent. I would save him from the Devil if I can.'

'Rhys does not know of his brother's danger?'

'He must not. He would insist on going after, and he would not survive. You will see how weak he is. If I were he, I, too, would desire to win this battle. The cunning fox has robbed him of his wife, his son—'

'John Lascelles? But I thought . . .' Owen paused as Martin shook his head. 'Gruffydd ap Goronwy?'

'The very man.'

'What is your interest in this business?'

'Can a man not be merely a Samaritan?'

'Not you.'

Martin laughed, but did not answer the question.

Brother Michaelo wished that he might accompany Mistress Tangwystl to her chamber and stand guard. Sir John might clutch her and worry over her now, but his behaviour had been far less loving before the lady fainted. Michaelo was relieved when a high-born woman shooed the spectators aside and took over, rubbing Tangwystl's hands and holding a strongly scented cloth to her nose until she coughed and opened her eyes.

'Come now,' said the woman to Sir John, 'you must allow me to make her comfortable whilst you make yourself presentable.' She looked pointedly at Sir John's muddy boots. One of the bishop's clerks joined her.

Tangwystl struggled to sit up. Sir John clung to her, but two determined sets of hands pulled her away and assisted her in standing.

'Milady is better off walking to her chamber,' said the gentlewoman. 'And then she shall rest undisturbed until I see some colour back in her cheeks.' She called to a servant to see to Sir John's comfort. 'You look like a man in need of a drink.'

As the woman and the clerk whisked Tangwystl away, Michaelo prayed that the sanctity of the valley and the proximity of St David's bones would inspire Sir John to peace. But in truth, the man did not now look threatening as he let a servant guide him out of the crowd.

Michaelo was glad of the quick and peaceful resolution. He hurried away, eager to discover how Master Chaucer had arrived so soon.

He was not disappointed. Master Chaucer awaited him at Sir Robert's bedside and quickly rose to join Michaelo by the door.

'*Benedicte*, Brother Michaelo,' said Geoffrey. 'God bless you for your quick wit in the hall. I would not have Sir John discover my presence tonight. I have work to do. *We* have work to do. I had thought to bring Sir Robert with me, but . . .'

'He should not be disturbed.' Brother Michaelo

glanced over at the bed. The servant assured him that Sir Robert had slept soundly since he departed.

'He is much worse than when we left for Cydweli,' Geoffrey said.

Brother Michaelo flushed, hearing criticism in the man's voice. What could he know of the care Michaelo had lavished on Sir Robert? But perhaps it was a comment innocently meant. 'Master Thomas, the bishop's physician, has been here. His physick has quieted the cough and allowed Sir Robert to rest. But he can do little else.'

Geoffrey crossed himself. 'I hope that the Captain can join him soon.'

Michaelo was disappointed. 'He is not here, then?'

'Yes, but not in the city. He is meeting Martin Wirthir at Clegyr Boia.'

'I hope we did the right thing, summoning you. But how did you come so quickly? It is a miracle.'

'No miracle. We were approaching Haverfordwest when we met Edmund. We had followed on the heels of John Lascelles, who I see has found his wife. How long has he been in St David's?'

'He is just arrived.' Michaelo told Geoffrey what had happened.

'Oh, sweet lady, I am sorry she is unwell.'

'She was well until Sir John appeared. What is this about an attack upon the chaplain?'

'I shall tell you all while we wait here. But first, do you know the tunnel in the undercroft?'

'I do.'

'We are to go down there after the rest of the guests have retired for the night. The Captain may have someone to hand over to our care.'

'Why the tunnel?'

'It may be someone who must be kept hidden until the proper time.'

Michaelo thrilled to the prospect of more intrigue. He was developing quite a taste for it. Perhaps he had spent too long in a sickroom.

Martin, Owen and Iolo were picking their way among the ruined walls when they all froze at the sound of someone stumbling on loose rock behind them. They held still, listening. But their shadow also paused. Not likely a dog or lost sheep then.

'Duncan,' Iolo said. 'I can smell him.' He drew his knife. 'He is mine.'

'Bring him to us,' Owen said as he took the rein from Iolo's hand. 'Alive.'

Iolo slipped away from them.

'This Iolo has the blood-lust?' Martin asked.

'If Duncan is here, one of Iolo's comrades lies somewhere wounded or dead.'

'Who is this Duncan?'

'He was sent by the Constable of Cydweli to spy on my activities.'

'A peculiar use of a spy, to place him openly in your company. This constable did not care whether his man survived?'

'We are both at present working for Lancaster. It is an uneasy truce. But you are right, it is also a fragile one.'

They heard a shout, a curse, then all was silent except for a lone gull circling overhead.

In a little while Iolo appeared, supporting Duncan, who limped badly. Owen was surprised by the latter's silence until he saw the gag round his mouth. His hands were also bound behind him.

'Your man is efficient,' Martin said. 'I could use such a man.'

For what, Owen wondered.

'Come then.' Martin led them to what seemed a pile of stone that had fallen from a crumbling corner wall of Boia's fortification. He crouched down, felt along the ground, grabbed the edge of something in his hand. 'Are you still strong, Captain?' he asked.

Owen had forgotten Martin had but one hand, so adept had the man become at hiding the fact. Crouching beside Martin, Owen let him guide his hands. The two lifted, and revealed a trapdoor. Light glimmered from a lantern within. Martin knelt at the opening, pulled up a post with cross-beams fashioned into a ladder, and climbed down. The others followed, with Iolo the last, as Duncan needed steadying hands to lower him. Martin pulled the trapdoor closed above them. For one uneasy moment Owen felt as if he were being entombed, but then noticed moonlight above. A smoke hole. What was this place, he wondered as he looked round, a den for smugglers?

It was a low-ceilinged, stone-walled chamber, perhaps once a dungeon or a storage area. In one corner was a raised platform piled with rags, in the middle of the room a bench and a milking stool that held the lantern. In another corner was a chest, atop it two saddles.

'Where are your horses?' Owen asked.

'In a shelter nearby,' said Martin. He lit an oil-lamp from the lantern.

The rags on the platform moved.

'Rhys,' said Martin, 'I have brought Captain Owen Archer. Owain ap Rhodri to your people. You remember I told you he would help you.'

The man sat up. He was young, with what looked to be fair hair beneath a dirty bandage that encircled his head.

Owen crouched down beside Rhys, saw where the blood oozed. 'Your ear?'

'Yes,' Rhys whispered. His hand hovered over the bandage, but he did not touch it.

Owen saw the pain in the man's eyes, the lines on his face. And he noted something else, beneath the grime and suffering. 'I see now what Eleri meant. Your son was made in your image.'

'You have seen him?'

'And your lady.'

'She is well?'

'Well enough. She is here, in St David's. Did Martin tell you?'

Rhys glanced at Martin, confused. 'You did not tell me Tangwystl was here.'

'I did not wish to tease you with the knowledge until there was someone who might take you inside.' Martin joined them. 'His ear was almost severed. A monk stitched it up with care, though Rhys departed before it could heal properly.'

Rhys put a hand on Owen's. 'You will take me to her?'

'I will. And your wounds will be tended.'

'They will throw me in the dungeon.'

'By and by, perhaps. But I hope that my father-in-law will be able to keep you hidden for a few days, allow you to regain your strength.'

'You will take him tonight?' Martin asked.

'Aye. We must wait a while, until the palace quiets. Then I shall take him through the tunnel. Sir Robert awaits us on the other side.'

A shuffling sound reminded Owen of Duncan. He had thought to take him back, also, but now he knew too much.

Twenty-three

FOG

While the Cydweli men buoyed their courage with their last skin of wine and watched the swirling shadows beyond the fire's reach, particularly round the standing stone at the edge of their encampment, Dafydd rested his head against the rough bark of the tree to which he and his companions were tied. He gazed up through the bare, twisted branches, watching the fog twirl and dance around the stars. He was remembering a morning mist that once kept him from the arms of a beauty with slender brows, a promised tryst in a greenwood. How the mist had cloaked the land with a blanket of darkness, stilled the birds, chilled his heart. A fog at evening was not so hopeless. The white, sharp light of the stars and the moon might penetrate it. Such a night was meant for dreaming.

And yet these English cursed it. What had they hoped for? To ride all through the night? Had they mistresses in St David's?

'It is the stone,' said Madog. 'They do not like the stone.'

'Nor have they liked the crosses along the way,' said Brother Dyfrig, 'though they call themselves Christians.'

'I do not like the standing stones at nightfall,' said Cadwal. 'We are near a burial chamber, did you know? On the hill above us. I feel them up there, watching us. This stone by our camp is a part of their burial honour. They do not like us to be here.'

Dafydd pitied Cadwal. He paid for his strength and size with a fear of the Otherworld that could be as crippling as a physical weakness. 'What do you fear? That the dead will rise and smite you for camping near their grave? Why should they care about you? And on such a night? Why would they leave the Otherworld to shiver in such dampness? To trip over their gossamer garments?'

'Are you making a poem?' Dyfrig growled.

'Perhaps. Have you an entertainment to propose? But of course you will spend this time in prayer.' Though Dafydd had seen precious little prayerful behaviour in the monk.

'It is a pity you did not think to recruit help from Newcastle Emlyn. It was not far from Maelgwn's farm,' said Dyfrig. 'We would not be dragged through the countryside starving had you planned better.'

Dafydd laughed. 'My uncle, Llywelyn ap Gwilym, *was* constable of the castle, but he is long dead. And his son tolerates me only so long as he hears no tales of mischief. He would chase me from the house if he knew of my offering sanctuary to the wretched boy. He would not understand. Besides, the castle is not so close to Maelgwn's farm. You clutch at the air with your complaint.'

'Would that I could clutch at something,' Dyfrig said. 'I can feel nothing in either arm.'

'Be grateful,' said Madog. 'Last night you could not bear the pain.'

Brother Dyfrig truly suffered more than the others. His broken arm was splinted and bound close to his body, but even so he endured much pain from the jostling ride, and today he had fallen on his arm as he dismounted. Their captors had merely laughed.

'I would rather feel the pain than nothing,' Dyfrig said.

Cadwal hushed them.

'What is it?' Dafydd asked.

The giant sat with head cocked, listening to the darkness behind them. 'Horses. Back beyond the light,' he whispered.

'Dyfrig,' a voice called softly. It might almost be mistaken for the wind in the brush. Still, Dafydd held his breath, fearful that their captors had heard. But their own loud talk and the crackling fire must have masked the sound, for no shouts challenged the darkness.

'It is Father Edern. And a friend. We shall cut your bonds when the fire dies down.'

Dafydd, overjoyed to be saved, strained to see the priest, but the fog still blurred the brush.

All four captives grew quiet, listening to the darkness.

'They notice your silence,' Edern whispered.

'Aye, they look this way,' Cadwal hissed. He and

315

Dyfrig were bound to the side of the tree facing into the clearing.

'Chatter among yourselves as before,' Edern whispered. 'But not so loud they understand you.'

Cadwal was the first to start muttering. He worried about their horses. How were they to escape their captors without horses?

Madog joined in. He saw no problem. While their captors slept, they would take all of the horses.

'But we cannot ride tonight,' whispered Dafydd. 'We would lose ourselves in the fog and risk the horses.'

'We take shelter nearby till morning,' Madog murmured. 'Perhaps the burial chamber.'

Cadwal groaned.

'What if they find us before morning?' Dafydd wondered.

'We should fall on them and bind them up,' Cadwal hissed. 'Then we wait here until dawn. We are now six against four and three of them are already wounded.'

'So am I,' Dyfrig muttered.

Dafydd warmed to the new adventure. 'We shall attack them while they sleep.'

'They will not sleep,' Dyfrig whispered. 'Surely one skin of wine passed among four soldiers would not put them to sleep.'

'But look at them,' said Cadwal, 'they rub their eyes, sink lower on to their blankets.'

Dafydd could not see them, being tied to the tree facing away, with Madog. 'Perhaps they have at last found the wine with poppy juice,' Dafydd whispered. 'I meant it for Brother Samson, but Maelgwn did not seem to need it. I thought it might ease the pilgrim when we find him, for surely his wound has opened with his flight.'

'I was sorely in need of it yesterday,' muttered Dyfrig.

'I did not think our captors would give it you,' Dafydd whispered. God watched over them, to let their captors find that wine tonight. But Dafydd prayed that they had not dug deeper into his saddle-bag.

'Drop your heads now,' Edern whispered from the darkness. 'Make them think you sleep.'

The floor of the tunnel was slippery. Owen shone the lantern over the walls and ceiling and saw how the stones seeped. At the edges of the floor lay piles of debris and crumbled stone. When Owen had passed this way with Father Edern he had not allowed his eye to wander round, anxious to reassure his men, not add his unease to their fears. For he did not like being beneath the earth, in a stone vault. And seeing how stone had been hollowed for this purpose, he thought now this must be the work of the Old Ones, those who had cut the great stones for the burial cairns, who had lifted them into the air to rest on the upright stones. He must have a care not to step into the Otherworld.

Rhys was unsteady on his feet and walked with an odd, rocking motion from side to side, catching himself on alternating sides of the wall with outstretched hands. Owen imagined his hand slipping through the wall to the Otherworld. His hand, arm, head, body would disappear . . .

'I do not like this place,' Rhys whispered.

'Nor do I. And I must return alone. While you are being tended, given wine, a pallet on which to sleep, I shall be crawling back to Clegyr Boia. Think on that and thank God you are not me.' As for Owen, he might be relieved to move more quickly when not encumbered with his weak companion, but he thought he much preferred having human company to share the darkness.

'What is that?' Rhys hissed. 'A darkness up ahead.'

Owen shone the lantern. 'The door. We are at the palace undercroft.' He pushed on the door gently, not wishing to alert the wrong person to their presence. It did not move. 'Now we must await our deliverers.' Owen shuttered the lantern to allow only a faint light, eased down on to the stone floor. At least this close to the palace it was dry. But uneven. It was difficult to find a comfortable seat.

Rhys crouched down beside him. 'This is a hellish spot.' His voice trembled, with weariness, Owen guessed, not fear. His breathing was laboured though it had not been a difficult journey.

Owen shone the thin line of light up the tunnel. 'There. We should see anything that cares to approach.'

'What if no one comes to unbar the door?'

'Then we return to Clegyr Boia. But let us not be hasty. They must await a quiet moment, when no servants are about. Sit down. Your legs will cramp if you crouch like that for long. Tell me about that day on Whitesands.'

Rhys eased himself down against the opposite wall so he faced Owen. 'I do not like to think on that day.'

'The Archdeacon of Carmarthen will have the same request. It will go easier if you have rehearsed it. Come. You owe me something, do you not think so?'

Rhys bowed his head. Again he held his hand over the bleeding ear, though he did not touch it. 'I have no need to rehearse it. I cannot forget it. His eyes. I have seen the eyes of the Devil, burning with hate.' Rhys's words echoed as he fell silent a while, if not speaking but breathing quickly in pain might be called silent.

Owen did not like Rhys talking of the Devil in this dark place.

In a while, Rhys raised his head. 'You have seen my son, and Tangwystl. You see what I have lost.'

'I do.'

'All for the greed of Gruffydd ap Goronwy. I cannot believe that my love carries any of his blood in her veins.'

'He betrayed you to save his family.'

'That is what he says. He was entrusted with money for Owain Lawgoch collected by his supporters. One of Owain's men was to land in Tenby and come to his house for it. But when he came, Gruffydd said he had it not. Others knew that he did. What had he done with it? That is what robbed his family of their home, their name. Owain's man disappeared, but before long it was heard that someone had denounced Gruffydd to my Lady Pembroke.'

'Did Gruffydd not need money for your marriage to Tangwystl?'

'Did he plan to use Owain's money for our wedding? Perhaps. But I do not believe it. Still. When I received the message that he had come to St David's to talk to me, I hoped—' Rhys put his hand to his ear. 'It burns.'

'Aye. I do not doubt it. How did you come to meet him at Whitesands?'

'I was here, in the bishop's palace, waiting to present my petition to the bishop. I hoped Bishop Adam would annul Tangwystl's marriage to Sir John, seeing that we were already pledged to one another. One day a pilgrim just arrived sought me out, said a man with a silver wing over his temple awaited me at Whitesands. That I would learn something that would help my petition.'

'And so you went to Gruffydd, hoping he wished to put things right.'

'I do not think I had such hope. But news of Tangwystl and my son, I wished to know they were safe and thought of me. He did have news, told me Tangwystl believed I had abandoned her fearing I might bring my family down with hers. But I should be comforted to know that she loved John Lascelles, and that Sir John told all that Hedyn was his son. I had not seen Gruffydd's greed in all my troubles until that day on the beach. In my anger I said too much. I told him that I meant to tell the bishop the truth of Pembroke's accusation. He fell on me. I saw in his eyes that he meant to kill me. He is a strong man, and larger than me. And he was well armed. But suddenly he fell away and cried, "Murderer! Help me!" And another man now fell on me, sliced at my throat, but caught my ear. I thrust with my knife. Dear God, I shall never forget the feeling, as if my arm went through him, so deep went the knife. And my ear. Sweet Jesus, I thought I was burning in Hell, the pain was so hot. I pressed my head to the cool sand. I think I must have been screaming and screaming with the pain. But no one heard. And I remember nothing else until a tall, white-haired man lifted me to his horse.'

'This Samaritan. Why did he help you and not Reine? And where was Gruffydd?'

'I do not know.' Rhys took a deep, shuddering breath. 'But they told me later that someone had murdered Sir John's son at Whitesands. I do not understand why Gruffydd did not help the man who came to his aid. I cannot see how I could have fought off both of them. I cannot think but that Gruffydd let the man die.'

It was strange. Owen had begun to think Gruffydd and John de Reine had acted together, to silence the one who threatened Sir John's marriage. He remembered Gruffydd's bandaged hand, the scar. 'Gruffydd's hand was badly cut – perhaps trying to grab your knife. But it was his left hand only. He might still have helped John de Reine.'

'I will be hanged, I know,' said Rhys. 'But first I would see Tangwystl. Tell her I did not abandon her, but had gone seeking help. Will they let me see her?'

'Tell Sir Robert your story, and I am certain he will bring her to you.'

'And my son? Is he with her?'

'No.'

'At least to see her. Tell her.'

*   *   *

Father Edern shook Dafydd awake. 'Your hands are loosed. Move slowly out of the firelight.'

Still confused from sleep, Dafydd massaged his wrists, wriggled his legs, his arms, then rose to a crouch. He was glad to move. And the first thing he wished was to relieve himself. He headed for the brush, with the priest hurrying after him.

When they were well into the brush, Edern asked, 'Where is Rhys ap Llywelyn?'

'Would that we knew,' said Dafydd. 'We might be safely home in bed, dreaming pleasant dreams. And pissing in private.' The priest ignored the hint and stood behind Dafydd while he lifted his gown. So be it. Nature would not wait. His urine steamed in the cool, damp air. When he turned round, the priest was ready with the next question.

'But these men were after him, were they not?'

'They were indeed. Barbarians. They broke into my house to find him. And he, the ungrateful wretch—'

'He is my brother.'

Dafydd raised his eyebrows at Madog, who had just joined them. 'This priest is the pilgrim's brother.' He turned back to Edern. 'That makes him no less ungrateful. I saved his life, granted him sanctuary in my home, and he murders the monk who nursed him and runs away.'

'You exaggerate, Master Dafydd. Brother Samson is not dead, nor was he attacked – he was injured in a fall,' Madog said. 'Come. We must move quickly.'

'What about Cadwal and Brother Dyfrig?' Dafydd asked.

'I have cut their bonds,' said a dark-haired stranger. 'But they must remain by the tree, so that if your captors look over, they suspect nothing.'

'This is Gruffydd,' said Edern. 'He, too, seeks my brother.' He told Gruffydd about Rhys's escape.

The man stood there a moment, flexing his left hand and breathing hard.

'Are you injured?' Dafydd asked.

'Do you know where Rhys was headed?' Gruffydd asked, his manner brusque.

'So much for offering sympathy.' Dafydd shook his head. 'How would I guess where the young man went? His grave, in the end.'

'We believe he returned to St David's, to finish his business there,' Madog said.

Dafydd grabbed Madog by the sleeve and moved him away from the others. 'You fool,' he said under his breath, 'you give these men too much information.'

'We owe them our lives,' said Madog. 'And we now have no reason to head south. They will see to the young man. We are finished.'

Dafydd shook his head. 'We are not.' He noticed Gruffydd and Edern moving closer and said in a louder whisper, 'I wish to complain to Bishop Houghton and the Archdeacon of Carmarthen about the treatment we have received from the hands of the Cydweli men. We demand recompense!'

'We shall get none,' Madog muttered.

'We shall see.' Dafydd nodded to Father Edern.

'You two. Come help us plan our ambush,' Edern said.

But Dafydd went his own way, towards the saddles

and packs of his party, which had been piled near their tethered horses. He knelt to his pack, rummaged inside. '*Deo gratias*,' he whispered. His torch heads had not been removed.

'What did you draw from your pack?' Gruffydd asked.

Dafydd did not like the man's tone. 'Why do you watch me?'

'They are torch heads,' said Madog. 'Brimstone, salt-petre, Jew's pitch, camphor, oil of Peter, terebentyne, and a goodly amount of duck's grease.'

'You would light torches and call attention to us?' Gruffydd said.

Dafydd was not about to answer such a ridiculous question.

'We shall create confusion so that we seem an army falling upon our captors,' said Madog.

'Slitting their throats would be quicker and quieter,' Gruffydd said.

'Can we trust him,' Dafydd asked Edern, 'this rude southerner who takes life so easily?'

'Be at peace,' said Edern. 'We shall of course do your bidding, Master Dafydd.'

Rhys had grown quiet and Owen fought sleep when at last he heard the bolt being drawn on the other side. He shuttered the lantern, held his breath. Something might still have gone wrong. The door swung wide with a creaking that woke Rhys. He gripped Owen's forearm.

Geoffrey's form was a reassuring sight.

'Dear God, I am thankful you found your way safely here,' Geoffrey said. 'When Edmund found

Jared unconscious and Duncan gone we feared the worst.'

'You feared rightly, but Duncan was no match for Iolo. How is Jared?'

'He will recover, but he is in no condition to ride in the morning.'

'Then Edmund must bring our horses and gear.'

'I shall accompany him,' Geoffrey said.

'But you—'

'The letters are delivered. Brother Michaelo is able to see to the rest.'

Owen had risen. He peered out into the corridor, saw only Brother Michaelo behind Geoffrey. 'I thought to see Sir Robert here.'

Brother Michaelo cast his eyes downward. 'He is confined to his bed, Captain.'

'He is worse?'

'He is very weak,' said Michaelo. 'The bishop's physician can do nothing more than ease the pain and the coughing.'

Owen crossed himself. 'Tell Sir Robert I am near, and that his message may save a life. Several lives. I will come to him as soon as I can.'

Rhys joined them. 'You are not staying here?' he said to Owen.

'I must see to some things outside the city. But I will return soon.'

'This is the man?' Geoffrey said.

'This is Rhys ap Llywelyn, brother to Father Edern, father of Mistress Tangwystl's son.' Owen explained to them Rhys's injury, and his request to see his wife.

'What things outside the city?' Rhys asked.

'They do not concern you,' said Owen. He turned to Geoffrey. 'You might do more good interceding for him while I am gone.'

'Brother Michaelo will do just as well.'

To argue too much would merely make Geoffrey more wary. 'So be it. Be waiting below Clegyr Boia after first light.'

'What of Duncan?'

'It would do him good to play hermit for a few days.'

Twenty-four

MYRDDIN AND THE ONE WHO SLEEPS

How peacefully the captors slept, heads on their saddles, feet close to the fire. All but one, who had just awakened, and now sat with arms wrapped round his knees, a blanket round his shoulders, staring up at the fading wisps of fog.

Dafydd stood a moment behind the standing stone, weighing one of the torch heads in his hands, considering his aim. But first, some drama for the wakeful one.

Inhaling deeply, Dafydd stalked out from behind the stone, arms outstretched, his eyes wide and staring. This was the signal for Cadwal and Dyfrig to leave the tree. Cadwal scurried to join Madog, Edern and Gruffydd; Dyfrig took up a post opposite Dafydd. In his most bardic voice Dafydd now shouted, 'Who trespasses in my sacred place!'

The wakeful one started, looked on Dafydd and cried, 'What apparition is this?'

Now Dafydd raised his right hand yet higher, and, roaring, threw the torch head at the fire. A ball of light glowed within the fire, expanding with a loud crack. The flames roared towards the heavens, then fell in a fiery fountain. Burning cinders were stars in the night, landing on the surrounding grass, and the blankets of the Cydweli men, who, waking now, shrieked and scrambled along the ground like panicked crabs. A pity, Dafydd thought, for the fire was magnificent.

Now Cadwal, Gruffydd, Edern and Madog came striding out of the dark towards the frightened men, who were thrown into confusion. The fire, Dafydd and the standing stone, or the four attackers – which terrified them least? Two turned towards the fire. Dyfrig now stepped forth. Raising his good arm, he tossed in the second torch head.

This explosion was louder and more violent than the first. The four who descended on the captors hesitated, shielding their eyes, but quickly saw the advantage and pushed forward. The waking one had more of his wits about him and, getting to his feet, pushed past Gruffydd and seemed to be getting away.

Dafydd rushed towards him. Too late he saw the firebrand hurtling his way. He stepped aside, but tripped on the uneven ground. As he fell he felt a terrible heat near his head, smelled burning hair and duck grease. Had he mistaken God's purpose? And was he thus struck down for his presumption?

Dyfrig was at Dafydd's side at once. One handed, he rolled Dafydd through the damp grass, then told him that he should lie still a moment, the others had the battle in hand.

Dafydd gladly lay there, listening to the sounds of

the fray across the clearing, thanking God for his life. At last he mustered the courage to feel his cheek. He rejoiced to feel skin, whole and unblistered.

With his good arm Dyfrig helped Dafydd sit up. 'God watches over you. The brand caught only your hair.'

Dafydd touched the singed, brittle mass. A clump turned to powder in his hand. He began to laugh.

'I thought you would howl over your loss, and you laugh.' Dyfrig tried to smooth Dafydd's damaged hair. 'It might have been so much worse.'

'But it was not. I shall from now on listen to Madog. He warned me I used too much duck grease. But I do love a great blaze.'

Madog joined them, shook his head at the sight of Dafydd's hair. 'We must cut the other side. A bard must not look like the King's jester.'

'The English might disagree,' said Dafydd, 'but shorn I shall be. I accept my penance without complaint.'

'You have bound them all?' Dyfrig asked Madog.

'Bound them all together.'

Dafydd grinned at the thought of the wriggling, angry mass of limbs and foul breath.

But Madog was not laughing. 'What do you know of these men who came to our aid, Brother Dyfrig? The Cydweli men know both of them.'

'Do you now regret telling them so much?' Dafydd asked.

'Perhaps,' said Madog.

'You may trust them, for pity's sake, they have saved us,' said Brother Dyfrig. 'They are known because Father Edern was chaplain to the Cydweli garrison not so long ago. The other is the new father-in-law of Lancaster's steward.'

'Is he not the one who took Rhys's love and gave her to the Englishman?' Dafydd said. 'Why does Father Edern trust him?'

'I do not trust him,' said Madog. 'And if they are all from Cydweli, why are either of them helping us?'

'We have cause to trust Edern,' said Dafydd, 'he is our pilgrim's brother. But Gruffydd – he is dangerous. And now he knows what we know. Clever, Madog.'

Owen gulped in the cool night air, said a prayer of thanks for a safe journey. The tunnel had seemed endless and had echoed with phantom footsteps that stopped when he stopped, whispering voices that hushed when he held his breath. It was far worse traversed alone. He did not think he had experienced such terror since childhood. The tunnel was haunted, he had no doubt of it.

Martin Wirthir sat on the boulder that had been rolled away from the entrance. 'The fog has lifted.'

'Where is Iolo?' Owen asked, pleased that his voice did not betray his recent experience.

'Guarding his catch. God forbid I should ever find him my enemy.'

'Iolo has hungered for action. Escorting pilgrims was not to his liking.'

'You know him well.'

'He reminds me of my younger self.' Owen leaned against the rock, lifted his head to the stars. 'I thank God I am not a miner.'

'I was glad you did not ask me to come with you. I have watched how the shepherds round here cross themselves as they pass this place. Though I have felt no terror out here, I would not like to have the darkness close behind me.'

'I felt them there, all round me, the carvers of the ancient stones. I have never feared them before.'

'Yours is an ancient country, full of mysteries, like Brittany.'

'Rhys was glad to leave the tunnel.'

'He is safe?'

'He is. He told me his tale of that day at Whitesands.'

'A strange, ugly tale, is it not?'

'John de Reine's part in it puzzles me. I begin to think he shadowed Gruffydd.'

'And Gruffydd took the opportunity to eliminate him – with Rhys the unwitting executioner.' Martin nodded. 'This Gruffydd has no conscience.'

'And was it he who brought the corpse to St David's? To brand Rhys a murderer?' Owen was quiet awhile, considering this new idea. Was it possible Gruffydd ap Goronwy was so cold blooded?

Martin broke through his thoughts to ask whether they would be joined by any more of Owen's men in the morning.

'One of my men, and Geoffrey Chaucer.'

Martin shifted on the stone. 'King Edward's man, Master Chaucer. I should not have chosen him to accompany us.'

'I did not. He insisted. I am not pleased. I had thought Geoffrey would take care of Rhys and allow Brother Michaelo to tend to my father-in-law, who is very ill.'

'Sir Robert is a brave man, to make such a journey at his age.'

'I do not think he will leave this place.'

'St David's. It is a sacred place, is it not? It seems a good place to die. Sir Robert had a vision at St Non's Well, did you know?'

'A vision that gave him cheer?'

'So it seemed to me.'

'God is with him, then.' But what of Lucie? Owen must write a letter to her, entrust it to the first person he met going east. Not that a journey was possible for her, but Lucie would wish to know how it went with Sir Robert and be with him in prayer.

'I have been so long away from my people,' Martin said. 'As you had been. Has it brought you joy, returning to your people?'

'I do not know how to answer that. But I think – were Lucie and my children not waiting for me in York, I would stay here a while.' Owen sensed much behind Martin's question. 'Why are you here, Martin? Are you the Fleming for whom Gruffydd ap Goronwy's family has suffered so much?'

'They have suffered because of Gruffydd, not me,' said Martin. 'Your people have a tale about one who sleeps – is it in a cave? – and one day will wake from his slumber to save your people.'

'Arthur.'

'Sometimes he is called Owain.'

'Owain Lawgoch? Tell me about him.'

'We call him Yvain de Galles. His men believe he is the redeemer of your people. He has the courage, I do not doubt it. And he is like Bertrand du Guesclin in inspiring loyalty in his men.'

'Why is he in France?'

'His family sent him there to keep him safe while he grew and learned.'

'Do you follow him because he will redeem my people?'

'I am not a follower. He hired me because I was recommended. Do I disappoint you?'

'Had you sworn allegiance to this man I would have called you a liar,' said Owen.

'A man can change.'

'But you have not.'

Martin laughed. 'Nor have you.'

Some would disagree. 'Tell me this. When Gruffydd ap Goronwy decided to keep Lawgoch's money, was it you betrayed him to Pembroke?'

'Not to Pembroke, to his mother. In the past I have worked for the Mortimers. I expected Gruffydd to repent, come to me begging for help. Which would come at a price. But I underestimated Gruffydd's greed, and John Lascelles's passion for his daughter. The money vanished into Cydweli.'

'Do you ride after him to retrieve the money?'

'No, my friend. That is gone. I would not risk riding into Cydweli – the constable there is too challenging.'

'He is a good soldier.'

'Aye.' Martin sighed. 'But it is not such a loss. Already more pours in from your wealthier countrymen.'

'So why do you pursue Gruffydd?'

'King Edward will think well of the Mortimers – and Pembroke – if they deliver up one of Yvain's men. And so I shall keep the Mortimers in my debt by presenting their scapegoat. Though I cannot appear with him, they will know how he comes to be in their hands.'

'But what he did – he is not truly one of Owain Lawgoch's men.'

'No.'

'Would not King Edward be doubly grateful if the Mortimers delivered you to him?'

'Perhaps, my friend, but they still have need of me. I am very good at what I do.'

'You say Gruffydd has no conscience. I might say the same of you.'

'Ambrose would agree. But perhaps it is merely that I have no country, no allegiance. Now your Master Chaucer. He is my opposite.'

'He is indeed. Be ware of him, Martin. It suits him well to play the fool, but he is not.'

'I thank you for warning me.'

Owen dreaded their meeting, Geoffrey and Martin. 'Do you know the route Father Edern would have taken?'

'Yes. The road through Croes-goch and Fishguard to Cardigan. Rhys was taken to a house that overlooks Cardigan Bay.'

'How can you be so certain he would travel that road and no other?'

'Because it is the way Yvain's men go when headed north.'

'Father Edern.'

Martin chuckled. 'You do not sound surprised.'

'He is more than he seems, of that I have been certain since I met him.'

Martin rose. 'Shall we close off the tunnel and see whether Duncan yet lives?'

His touch was light. He might not have wakened Dafydd had he been careful of the rings. But how many men wore such hair ornaments? Dafydd opened his eyes slightly, glad of his long lashes. Gruffydd crouched beside him, easing one item at a time out of the saddle-bag Dafydd had tucked beneath his saddle, which he used as a pillow. Searching for more torch heads, Dafydd guessed. Well, he might search Dafydd's pack and never find them – Cadwal carried what was left. Dafydd grinned and made dreaming noises that startled Gruffydd and sent him creeping away.

The man must be watched.

At dawn, Michaelo was wakened by Master Chaucer's noisy ablutions in a bowl of scented water. Chaucer had shared the extra bed with Rhys ap Llywelyn.

'How did the young man sleep?' Michaelo asked, tiptoeing across the cold floor to check the fresh bandage.

'Fitfully, with much muttering and moaning. He feels on fire. I rose twice to give him wine. You will be busy, with both of them.'

'You did not concern yourself with my difficulties when you declared yourself Jared's substitute,' Michaelo said. He sensed an unspoken purpose in Chaucer's determination to ride with the Captain.

'The sooner we find Father Edern, the sooner Captain Archer may sit at Sir Robert's bedside and make his peace with him.'

'Will you watch my charges a little while?' Michaelo asked. 'I have an errand.'

'Be quick about it.'

Brother Michaelo wished him Godspeed and hastened off, glad to escape and half-hoping Chaucer
would be gone when he returned. He found him
insufferable, smugly self-important, and imagined the
man wooing new acquaintances at court with tales in
which all the world came off as fools but himself.

Michaelo also thought Chaucer would disapprove
of his present mission. He hastened through the great
hall and through the corridor that led to the guest
rooms in the east wing of the palace, leaning against
the wall as a servant hurried past with a pot of night
soil sloshing dangerously. There were privies in the
palace, but in the middle of the night most pilgrims
preferred to stay in their chambers.

At the door of the chamber shared by Tangwystl
and several other noble ladies, Michaelo knocked.
He asked a servant to tell Mistress Tangwystl that
she was needed in Sir Robert D'Arby's chamber.

With that, Michaelo turned to retrace his steps,
expecting Mistress Tangwystl would be long in dressing herself. But he had just stepped into the great hall
when he heard the whisper of silk behind him.

'God be with you, Brother Michaelo.' Tangwystl
caught up with him, her colour high. 'Sir Robert
is worse?' she asked breathlessly. 'He had a difficult night?'

'Bless you for your haste, Mistress Tangwystl. I
did not mean to alarm you with my summons.' For
in addition to her breathlessness she looked about
to burst into tears. He had not intended that. 'The
patient did toss and turn, and I thought he might find
comfort in your gentle company.'

'I shall gladly sit with him,' she said.

Michaelo slowed his pace as he escorted her through the hall and into the short corridor that led to his chamber. At the door, Michaelo reached up to tidy Tangwystl's veil, loosing a corner that had been caught up in the circlet round her head. She looked puzzled by the gesture.

'Forgive me, Mistress Tangwystl. I do penance every day for my fussing. Come now.' He opened the door, led her into the room, and when she would cross to Sir Robert's bed, Michaelo called softly, 'Mistress Tangwystl, would you be so kind as to look at this young man, tell me whether we ought to send for Master Thomas?'

'My lady,' Rhys said, 'you outshine the sun.'

Tangwystl stood a moment, poised as if about to flee, then sat gingerly on the bed, reaching with trembling hand towards the soiled bandage. 'My love, what has happened?'

Rhys took her hand, pressed it to his lips, and with a sob she bent to kiss him.

Smiling to himself, Brother Michaelo slipped over to take up his prayers at Sir Robert's bedside. Chaucer had departed. All was going according to plan. God be praised.

Twenty-five

MARTIN'S REVENGE

When next Dafydd woke it was Brother Dyfrig who disturbed his rest. Dafydd sat up, confused by the dawn light filling the clearing. But the sight of the four men tied together in a grim bundle and laid at the foot of the standing stone brought back the night.

'Are we agreed we leave them here until such time as it pleases us to inform someone of their hermitage?' Dafydd asked.

'They are hardly hermits, with so much companionship,' said Dyfrig.

'Their what? Their barracks? Monastery?'

'We must ride out while your men still keep their knives in their sheaths. We shall stop at a church, tell the priest we outfoxed a band of robbers – that he should send the sheriff to collect them.'

'The sheriff. They will not like that.'

'I would not think so.'

Dafydd noticed Gruffydd searching the packs of the vanquished. For food, he wondered, or for trouble? 'Speaking of thieves, Gruffydd has busy fingers.'

'That he has,' said Dyfrig.

Shifting to show Dyfrig the scattered items, Dafydd was confused to find the ground clean. He pulled the pack from beneath his saddle, found the items tucked away. 'Did I dream?' he wondered aloud.

'No,' said Dyfrig. 'He crept back and returned it all to the pack. I was glad of that. It is best if he does not know we watch.'

As Dafydd pulled on his riding boots he experimented with phrases extolling the virtues of this monk, with his hooded eyes and devious mind. He was considering to what heroic ancestor he might compare Dyfrig when his subject drew a sharp knife from the sheath on his girdle. Dafydd had always admired the tooling on the leather, thought it a most unmonkly accessory.

'You contemplate some violence against Gruffydd after all?'

'I thought I might trim your hair. I shall need Madog's assistance, since I have but one arm.' Dyfrig laughed. 'Do not look so worried! I have much practice in cutting hair, though scissors are my usual tool.'

Dafydd reared back in mock horror. 'I want no tonsure!'

Owen watched Martin going about his morning business. He managed well with but one hand, using the stub of his wrist when fingers or flexibility were not important. Owen thought it not as great a loss as that of his eye, but he guessed Martin would not agree. What we have lost we most cherish.

Geoffrey and Edmund awaited them at the foot of the path from the mound. Geoffrey addressed Martin in excellent French and commended him on his *élan* – 'To call to yourself the very men from whom you would be wise to hide.'

Martin laughed. 'I have no wish to live so long that I must suck my food and be carried round in a chair. But in truth I do not deserve your admiration. It is my Lord of Pembroke I serve in this. I would bring Gruffydd ap Goronwy to answer for his treachery.'

'Gruffydd? Can it be true?' said Geoffrey. 'Has Sir John been such a fool to believe in him?'

Owen tried not to exhibit surprise at Martin's half-truth.

Owen felt haunted by the ancient stoneworkers as the company rode north, past burial chambers and standing stones. And the crosses – were they the work of the same people, converted to Christianity? As a child in the mountains of Llŷn he had been accustomed to the stone monuments, had listened to tales of ancient priests, mythic giants, and believed them all to be true. It was long since he had thought of those legends. Had the stoneworkers disappeared into the Otherworld, leaving their artwork? Why? Had he truly heard their voices in the tunnel? Had they been calling to him?

Geoffrey rode up beside Owen. 'Martin says we go to the home of a bard. What do you know of him?' He leaned across his saddle, peering at Owen.

'Jesu, but you look grim. Are you thinking of Sir Robert?'

Owen did not think it wise to tell Geoffrey his thoughts. Too Welsh, he would say. 'Aye. You spent the night in the room. He is much worse?'

'He is. I am sorry, Owen. But you have been good to him. You should have no regrets.'

Only the regret of losing Sir Robert. 'You asked about the bard. Dafydd ap Gwilym is one of the greatest bards of our day, so they say, and an ardent lover. Are you eager to meet a fellow poet?'

'I am not certain.'

As the sun rose higher in the sky, the company paused at a stream to let their horses drink and to wet their own dusty throats.

Iolo and Edmund commenced bragging about their love conquests, their skill with knives. Owen found himself envying them. Well he could remember taking part in such contests. And often considering himself the victor. He busied himself stringing his bow while he listened. Though he doubted they would encounter Gruffydd today, he meant to be ready.

Martin joined the men and turned the talk to Gruffydd's skill in escaping. Geoffrey, who was still digesting the news of Gruffydd's treachery, asked how Pembroke's men had managed to corner him.

'We did not,' said Martin, cleverly continuing the lie. 'He tucked his family in a church and fled to Cydweli, where he knew of an obsession he could bend to his will. We must be ready to surround him. And if you are tempted to slay him, remember that we might need him to tell us how he has disposed of Father Edern.'

'Why are you here alone?' Geoffrey asked.

Owen realised Geoffrey sought to make Martin trip over his lie.

But Martin was too clever. 'When I discovered him here, I had two choices – to wait until I might get word to Pembroke Castle, or to enlist the aid of my old friend, who had good reason to wish to help me.' He smiled at Geoffrey, then returned to discussions of strategy.

Geoffrey rose, moved over to Owen. 'The bard's house near Cardigan is still a few days' ride. Will you keep that strung all the while?'

'I do not mean to lose Gruffydd. While the day is fair, my bow will be at hand.'

The company paused on a hilltop overlooking Fishguard harbour, a cluster of houses in an elbow of land, fishing boats upturned on the sand, bobbing in the water. Owen advised against riding down into the town. They would be noticed; Gruffydd would charm the information out of someone there and know to hide. They had begun the descent on the inland side of the outcropping when Iolo, who was now riding vanguard, motioned for them to halt.

Ahead, down on the road, were six horsemen riding south. Two were in white robes. 'Cistercians,' Edmund guessed. 'But what of the others?'

They used the shelter of a stand of trees to move down closer to the road.

'Only one monk,' said Martin. 'The other has no tonsure.'

'Would Gruffydd ride in such company?' Owen had imagined him alone. The four in darker robes all wore hats that shaded their faces. But one of the men was Gruffydd's size.

'One becomes far less noticeable in a company of travellers,' Geoffrey suggested. 'And if I am not mistaken, that is Father Edern riding beside the monk.'

Martin turned in his saddle, asked Owen and Geoffrey, 'Shall we surprise them?'

Owen dismounted with bow and quiver of arrows, slid down to the edge of the clearing. 'Go.' He pulled out an arrow, fitted notch to string, pulled back and sited on Gruffydd. He might kill him, rather than maim him. Was he certain Martin spoke the truth? For if he was not . . . 'God guide my hand,' Owen prayed.

Heads turned to see what descended upon them. The white-haired, white-robed man flung his arms up and shouted something. Father Edern seemed to recognise some of the men and called to the monk, who had put spurs to horse. Two of the men, one a giant, rode off in pursuit of Gruffydd.

For Gruffydd, oh, he had not even turned to see who or what pursued him, but had taken off at a gallop angling cleverly up the hill whence the riders had come.

Owen let go the arrow, and as he put another to the string he watched his first hit Gruffydd's shoulder. The man slid sideways in the saddle, but his stirrups held. Owen aimed, let fly the second arrow. Now Gruffydd jerked forward and down, clutching his thigh. When the giant grabbed his reins, Gruffydd slumped forward, his head resting on his mount's neck.

*   *   *

Dafydd watched the arrows arch towards Gruffydd and envied the archer. Last night's firestorm had been a wondrous show, but this – this was far more frightening. That a man, a mortal man, had trained his body to become such a weapon – for what were the bows or the arrows without the man strong enough and with the skill to use them? Dafydd rode towards the stand of trees. He must meet the archer, be the first to praise him. He dismounted.

And what was this? The archer covered one eye to improve his aim? But surely it was the wrong eye. To challenge himself then? Oh, what a man was this, who stood so calmly, his back against the tree, unwinding the string from the bow and watching Dafydd's approach with head turned so that the uncovered right eye might see him plain. The Norman beard seemed out of place on his Welsh face, but it suited the archer. As did the scar that Dafydd could now see plainly.

'I am Dafydd ap Gwilym Gam ap Gwilym ab Einion Fawr, Chief of Song and Master of the Flowing Verse. My praise lasts longer than a horse; my love songs would lead a nun astray; my satire kills. I come to praise the Archer,' he shouted.

The man bowed his head, 'I am honoured, Master Dafydd,' he said in a northern accent. 'I am Owen ap Rhodri ap Maredudd, once captain of archers for the great Henry of Grosmont.'

Fortunate Henry. Dafydd tilted his head, considered the archer's accent. 'Llŷn?'

Martin and Owen sat apart from the others, sharing a skin of wine under the trees.

344

'You have not lost your skill, my friend,' said Martin.

'I did not hit precisely where I intended. The one in the shoulder – it is close to the bone, difficult to remove.' He and Dyfrig had removed the arrow from Gruffydd's thigh, but left the one in the shoulder for a barber or physician. Gruffydd had growled when Owen lifted his left hand and asked whose knife had so wounded him, Rhys's or John de Reine's. 'He will be in much pain as the flesh swells round the arrow.'

'And do you not think he deserves to suffer?'

Geoffrey glanced over towards them with an enigmatic expression. 'You are watched,' Owen said to Martin. 'Gruffydd has denounced you to all as a spy for King Charles of France. And he has told Edern and Dyfrig that the money he keeps is for Owain Lawgoch – that you meant to steal it for the French King.'

'Brother Dyfrig and Father Edern know me,' said Martin. 'They know that Gruffydd lies to save himself.' Edern had quickly realised how foolish he had been to trust Gruffydd.

'But Geoffrey . . .'

'He watches me, I know, though he is much distracted by Dafydd.' The bard had honoured them by bringing out his harp and singing several of his songs.

'I was curious to watch Geoffrey and Master Dafydd together,' said Owen. 'But so far Geoffrey keeps his distance.'

'Ah, but he listens.'

'Geoffrey is ever listening.'

'Ambrose should be here. He would enjoy Master Dafydd's songs.'

'He understands Welsh?'

'No, but I can hear the meaning of the bard's words in his voice and the harp.'

Dafydd's love songs took Owen back to his courtship of Lucie. Though the words were beautiful, they echoed how awkward Owen had felt in the presence of Lucie's beauty and gentilesse. How he missed her.

And he realised he would miss Martin. 'When do you leave us?'

'Soon, my friend. My work is finished, much thanks to your skill. I was right to send for you.' Martin sat back, looked Owen in the eye. 'And what of you? Will you stay with Sir Robert until the end? Or will you go off to finish your work at Cydweli?'

'Sir Robert may live a long while.'

'Do you believe that?'

Owen looked away, unwilling to answer.

The company were welcomed that night by a farmer and his family who inhabited a large farmhouse. They considered Dafydd's presence a great honour, and offered up their beds to the company. But first the men feasted on plain but abundant food and drink. All sat in threes on the rush floor. Except Gruffydd, who lay on a pallet by the fire moaning and begging the farmer and his family to have pity on him.

Edern marked the effort. 'He is exhausted from loss of blood, and yet he manages a remarkable performance.'

'And what of Martin Wirthir?' said Geoffrey. 'Slipping off in the midst of such a company. And no one made note of it.'

Owen saw Father Edern and Brother Dyfrig exchange glances.

'We should search for him,' Geoffrey said. 'You have heard what Gruffydd says of him.'

'We shall continue south,' Owen said. 'We have a murderer to deliver to justice.'

'But tomorrow we must rest,' said Brother Dyfrig. 'It is *Passio Domini*, the beginning of Passiontide.'

'Is it wise to give Gruffydd another day to work on the sympathies of our hosts?' asked Owen.

'I propose that we observe the day as pilgrims,' Dafydd said, 'walking rather than riding, and fasting all the day. Would that satisfy our men of God?'

'The greatest sinner of us all must ride,' Edern said, nodding towards Gruffydd.

'Would you prefer to bear him on a litter?' Geoffrey asked.

Twenty-six

ELERI'S COURAGE

On Monday, in the early afternoon, the weary company dismounted at Bonning's Gate – even Gruffydd, who all felt had been pampered enough. They led their horses slowly past the houses of the bishop's archdeacons and the Treasurer of St David's. At the gate to the bishop's palace, they were given a message from Brother Michaelo urging Geoffrey and Owen to come at once to the house of William Baldwin, the Archdeacon of Carmarthen.

Owen yearned for refreshment and a chance to cool his feet in some scented water. He was envious of the others, surprised when Father Edern and Brother Dyfrig declared that they, too, would attend the archdeacon.

'And what of the injured man?' asked the porter. 'Do you need assistance with him?'

'No,' said Geoffrey, 'the archdeacon will wish to see him.'

Dafydd, however, felt no need to attend the meting

out of justice. 'I shall speak with the archdeacon anon, concerning the Cydweli men and their affront to me.' He strode regally through the gate with his men and Owen's.

Geoffrey stood beside Owen, watching Dafydd. 'I wish you had not praised his poetry. I should like to think he is all show and no substance.'

'Perhaps you shall look back on him when you are his age and think him not so strange.'

'For that I would need to be Welsh.'

Laughing, Owen turned to follow the others. Geoffrey hurried to join him. Father Edern and Brother Dyfrig walked on either side of Gruffydd, steadying him when he stumbled. Their halting procession was watched by many as they crossed Llechllafar.

The Archdeacon of Carmarthen's was a grand house, set off from the other archdeaconries in a meadow across the river from the palace, towards Patrick's Gate. Their unexpected numbers flustered the archdeacon's clerk, who left them standing at the door while he hurried off to consult with his master. But he soon returned, leading them into the archdeacon's hall and seating them in the rear.

A group of petitioners were apparently there before them. Brother Michaelo stood to one side, listening. But as Owen's eyes adjusted to the dimness, he was astonished. That Rhys ap Llywelyn, John Lascelles and Tangwystl ferch Gruffydd stood before the Archdeacon of Carmarthen did not surprise him. But they were accompanied by Eleri ferch Hywel, the maid Gladys and Richard de Burley.

It was Burley who spoke. '. . . Gladys had come forth, fearing God's wrath over the murderer's, and told me she had heard loud voices, ran to Father Francis's room. Gruffydd shouted, "You shall pay for this," as he shook Father Francis. The chaplain shouted a curse. Gruffydd hit him, then threw him to the floor.'

'Who tells such lies of me?' Gruffydd cried out, rising from his seat at the rear of the hall. 'Who tells such lies?'

At the sound of his voice, Eleri had stiffened. She now turned, walked slowly towards the voice.

'Eleri?' Gruffydd sank back down. 'What have they done to you? Who brought you here?'

'Who?' She cocked her head. Her gait was slow and halting, like that of a sleepwalker. 'Who brought me here?' she asked in calm voice. 'But my husband, you did. You tore us from our home, tore our daughter from her husband and her child. But that was nothing. Nothing compared to what I have heard today, husband.' She stood over him. 'You killed the son of the man who tried to help us.'

'I did not kill him, Eleri.' Gruffydd's voice was suddenly gentle, caressing. 'It was Rhys. And you would have him marry our daughter?'

'What did *I* marry?' she cried, clenching her fists. '*Who* did I marry?'

Gruffydd looked round at the others. 'In God's name, she should not be here.'

Father Edern moved towards Eleri. 'Come. I will—'

'No.' The word came from deep in Eleri's throat. 'No,' she moaned, and threw herself upon her husband, tipping him to the ground. She grabbed his hair, lifted his head, and brought it down hard on the stone floor.

'Mother!' Tangwystl cried, running to her.

Eleri pounded Gruffydd's face with her fists.

Owen pulled Eleri away. Dyfrig knelt to Gruffydd, who breathed raggedly.

'Hang him! Hang him for all to see!' Eleri shrieked as Owen picked her up and carried her from the room.

Owen lay on a bench staring unseeing at the sky. His thoughts were with the Archdeacon of Carmarthen. If it were Owen's to rule on Gruffydd, would he send him to Pembroke? Or hang him at the crossroads, as Eleri wished?

'They tell me that your wife is a beauty and a Master Apothecary.' Dafydd's face displaced the sky.

Owen sat up.

Dafydd joined him on the bench with a sigh. 'It is a pity she did not accompany you.'

'I feel her absence keenly.'

'You left the deliberations. You are displeased with the archdeacon's judgement?'

'He had not as yet come to any decisions. In truth I withdrew because Master Chaucer clearly needs no assistance. He understands the law and has the honeyed tongue of a poet.'

'Geoffrey Chaucer a poet? He looks like a cleric and behaves like the King's fool. Surely he is no poet.'

Should Owen tell him that Geoffrey thought Dafydd a proper fool? He thought not. 'It is true Geoffrey does not play the bard. But he is cunning. And his jesting distracts folk so they do not notice how closely he studies them. We shall all be in his poems some day, mark me.'

351

'You describe a lawyer, not a poet.'

'What do I know of such things?' Owen motioned towards the archdeacon's door. 'It opens.'

First came Father Edern and Brother Dyfrig, then Gladys.

'Sweet angel,' Dafydd said.

Rhys and Tangwystl came forth, followed by a servant carrying Hedyn. Rhys leaned heavily on Tangwystl. Sir John followed, his eyes on Tangwystl. Burley accompanied him, talking with great animation.

'I think we can judge from this that Tangwystl has prevailed,' said Owen.

'It is a good law, that a woman may denounce her husband for being such a fool as to be caught by her thrice with another wench,' said Dafydd.

'I would not have thought you a supporter of such a law.'

'He is a fool, who is caught once. But thrice, and with the same maid,' Dafydd shook his head. 'He deserves no woman.'

'Sir John thought he did her bidding.'

'Doubly a fool. Look at her – so proud. And beautiful. What need had he of another?'

They grew quiet as Sir John approached. His age sat heavily on his features, gouging lines of sorrow. Owen pitied him.

'God's blessing on you, Captain Archer, for bringing the Devil to justice,' said Sir John.

Owen could not think what to say to him.

Burley had come up behind. 'I would talk with you, Captain.'

'By and by,' Owen said. He rose, led Lascelles towards the river, away from Dafydd and Burley. 'I do not feel I have earned your blessing, Sir John. But I am glad I have cleared both your name and that of your son.'

They stood by the bank. The sound of water was soothing.

'The archdeacon has declared your marriage null?' Owen asked, for it was in the air between them.

'I did not give him the opportunity. When I saw them together, and he with the child—' Lascelles closed his eyes, took a deep breath, faced Owen. 'She was never mine.'

'No. She was not.'

'But I had a son. A son who loved me, who braved my anger to warn me against Gruffydd. He urged me to leave him to the Mortimers. And I would not. Could not, God help me, for I loved her so.' Lascelles was silent a moment. 'John must have come after Gruffydd, hoping to find proof.' He pulled a cloth from his scrip as he turned away, blotting tears.

Rhys and Tangwystl were crossing Llechllafar. Owen and Lascelles silently watched them passing. After a while, Lascelles nodded to Owen and walked on.

The serving maid Rhonwen curtseyed to Owen and withdrew to the corner. He sat, took Sir Robert's hand. It was dry and cold, his skin felt thin as a flower petal.

'God granted me a vision,' said Sir Robert.

'Tell me, Father.' Owen bent close, Sir Robert's voice was so weak.

'Amélie. She forgives.'

Owen squeezed Sir Robert's hand. 'I am glad of it.'

'And you? Did you find your family?'

'My youngest brother, Morgan.'

'No others?'

'All gone but for Morgan and my sister Gwen, who is at the convent in Usk.'

'You must go there, see her. Lucie would think it fitting.'

'I shall try.'

'Tell me about your brother.'

So Owen told him of Morgan, and of Elen. How it was Morgan who convinced Gladys to tell Constable Burley that she had seen Gruffydd ap Goronwy shake Father Francis and throw him to the floor, Morgan who had escorted her to the castle. He described Elen. 'Lucie would like her.' Owen stopped, thinking Sir Robert had drifted off to sleep smiling. But when he began to rise, Sir Robert clutched his hand.

'Brother Michaelo has been good to me, Owen. Remember that.'

The house reeked of onions and beer. A child and a puppy rolled in the rushes. Owen had taken off his boots and propped his feet on the edge of the table. Geoffrey sat on the table, back against the wall, legs stretched out before him. Burley and the alewife shared a bench – they seemed unable to keep their hands off each other. All held large bowls of good thick beer. Father Edern had brought them to this place, in the midst of the vicars' houses, after Burley had sent Edmund and Iolo off to retrieve Duncan.

'The alewife will be chased out when the bishop arrives tomorrow for the remainder of Passiontide,' Edern had told them, 'best drink all you can tonight.'

Owen intended to, though he hoped he might keep his wits clear enough to find out more about how it was that Burley had escorted Eleri and the boy to the city.

'Your brother had been at Gladys, you see, not in the usual way—' Burley kissed the round breasts pushing up from the alewife's bodice, '—but preaching at her about mending her ways. It wakened her conscience, she says. You were too gentle with her, you see. A bit of preaching, a bit of threatening was what she needed.'

'Threatening?'

'I would wager your brother threatened to throw her out if she did not accompany him to the castle and tell me what she knew.'

'But what of Eleri?'

'I took Gladys with me when I went to Gruffydd's house, demanding to see him. And while I talked to Eleri, Gladys was in the kitchen with the servants, spilling all she knew and weeping and saying she was for the nunnery. The daughter Awena heard it all, came running in to her mother. The lady went quiet, watching her hands in her lap, and then she looked up, looked me square in the eye and said Gruffydd had gone to St David's, he knew what Tangwystl was about, and we must go after him. She meant her and the boy. She said she feared what lengths Gruffydd would go to in order to keep Sir John content – as if murdering Rhys and Tangwystl would ever bring contentment. She withdrew for a while, returned with a pack. Coins, gold, a treasure. Owain Lawgoch's treasure. Gave it to me. For safe keeping, she said.'

'You will restore your debt to the exchequer?'

'Sweet Jesus, it was more than enough for that. I gave the rest of it to Sir John, to use as he saw fit. I believe he has given it to Mistress Tangwystl. I pray she gives none of it to that mad, self-important bard who attacked my men and left them for dead.'

'They had twice attacked him,' said Geoffrey, 'once in his home. Certes they are safely in the sheriff's gaol, not lying on the road.'

'A sheriff's gaol, God's blood—' Burley was stilled by a consoling kiss.

Twenty-seven

'. . . A VERRAY, PARFIT GENTIL KNYGHT'

L eaving Burley and the alewife to their lust, Owen and Geoffrey walked out among the vicars' houses. Light from lamps and hearth fires showed through the chinks round the doors and shutters. From one house came such a snoring that the two laughed. The night was clear, with bright stars. Tonight, the cemetery seemed to Owen a peaceful place, the rich scent of the earth comforting. A willow beckoned them towards the river, where the stars shimmered and danced.

'Will Sir Robert lie here?' Geoffrey asked, leaning against the willow.

'He asks to be buried in the cathedral.'

'You will commission a monument?'

'Aye. Martin told me of a stonecutter who does fine work.'

357

'Martin. You should be more careful about your loyalties.'

'He is a good man.'

'He is an enemy of our King.'

'Now and then, and sometimes his ally. Did you mention Martin to the archdeacon?' For all Owen knew, Baldwin, too, might be a Lawgoch supporter.

'No.' Geoffrey glanced over at Owen. 'I could not think how I might do so without betraying you. I was vague about who had befriended Rhys.'

'Martin served us well.'

'Have a care you do not return the favour.' Geoffrey straightened. 'After Easter I shall leave with Brother Michaelo.'

'You are satisfied with the garrisons?'

'They will hold against the French. You will stay with Sir Robert, then return to Cydweli?'

'Do you doubt me?'

'I think that in this country you have found that which you had lost, a sense of your own honour. Mayhap it is enough to have it rekindled. I pray that is so.'

Is that what Owen had found here?

'What of this monument?' Geoffrey said in a heartier tone. 'Will Sir Robert be a knight or a pilgrim?'

'A knight. But with a pilgrim's hat at his feet.'

'A truly perfect, courteous knight. It is fitting. You are sending Brother Michaelo away with a letter for Lucie, telling her all that has come to pass here?'

'Several letters. I have carried her with me.'

'You are fortunate in your marriage. Come. It has been a long day.'

In the morning, Sir Robert rallied a little, and used the

time to talk to Owen of the things that had worried him as he lay there.

'What of my sister Phillippa?' As a widow she had returned to Sir Robert's household years before. 'She will be lonesome at Freythorpe.' The manor was within a day's ride of York, but the road was often impassable in winter storms.

'We shall bring her to live with us. She will enjoy the children, and they her.'

'What of Freythorpe Hadden? Lucie will not give up her work to live there. Who will live there and keep it for your son Hugh?'

'I shall find a steward I trust to live there. And Lucie will insist on a good accounting.'

Sir Robert was satisfied. 'Then I can rest.'

Shortly after the angelus bells, Sir Robert fell into a pleasant dream of Lucie and Amélie in the garden at Freythorpe. He was awakened by an unfamiliar sound, a delicate jingling. He found a white-haired man at his bedside, sipping wine in an elegant mazer. A most amazing man, with rings and combs in his white hair. He wore a white gown embroidered in silver and gold thread. Was this St Peter?

'Ah, you waken, Sir Robert.'

'Am I at Heaven's gate?'

'St David would be gratified to hear his church called that.'

'You are not St Peter?'

The man tilted his face to the ceiling and laughed like a madman. When he was quiet, wiping the tears from his eyes, he said, 'I have been called many things, Sir Robert, but never a saint.'

'Who are you?' Sir Robert asked.

'Dafydd ap Gwilym Gam ap Gwilym ab Einion Fawr, Chief of Song and Master of the Flowing Verse.'

And a delightful braggart, Sir Robert thought. 'It was you who took Rhys off to sanctuary?'

'It was. But I came to honour you, not boast of my goodness. It is said that God granted you a vision at St Non's Well. I pray you, tell me all.'

Sir Robert talked of Amélie until he was exhausted. The bard was a most attentive audience. As was Geoffrey Chaucer, who joined them halfway through the tale.

When Brother Michaelo discovered Sir Robert hoarse from talking, he asked the two poets to leave. Geoffrey and Dafydd departed the chamber together.

'A God-fearing, gentle knight,' said Geoffrey.

'God-fearing? Gentle? He was a soldier,' said Dafydd. 'I lost many a sweet mistress to a soldier's arms. And each time I mourned them, knowing how ungentle their new lover would be. You heard his tale. By the Trinity, how I would have loved the fair Amélie.'

'But Sir Robert did love her. I wept to hear his tale. What he lost! It is no wonder he spent so much of his life thereafter on pilgrimage.'

Dafydd considered the short-legged man walking beside him. His eyes did show traces of tears. He had a heart then, but had he the soul of a poet? 'Are you married, Master Chaucer?'

'I am. To one of our late Queen's ladies of the chamber.'

Death to a poet, marriage. The match had helped

the man's career, no doubt. 'What does she think of your poetry?'

'She despairs of the ink stains.'

In the late afternoon, Owen returned from his audience with Bishop Houghton, just arrived in the city for the remainder of Passiontide, to find Brother Michaelo kneeling at the foot of Sir Robert's bed, praying the rosary. The maid Rhonwen knelt there, hands folded, head bowed.

Dear God, was Sir Robert already gone? Owen hurried to the side of the bed, said a prayer of thanks as he heard the dying man's uneven breaths.

Noticing Owen standing there, Michaelo and Rhonwen rose.

'God prepares to take him,' Michaelo said. His eyes were red with weeping. 'He has not complained, not once in all—' The monk's voice broke. He ducked his head and turned away to blot his eyes.

'Does he know we are here?' Owen asked.

'I do not think so.' Tucking his beads and his cloth up a sleeve, Michaelo turned back to Owen. 'You must have some time alone with him.' He made the sign of the cross over Sir Robert, then withdrew.

Rhonwen had already slipped away.

Owen knelt down, took Sir Robert's cool, dry hands in his, and bowed his head over them. He thought of his daughter Gwenllian, who was so fond of her grandfather, so captivated by his tales of soldiering. He must tell her how even in his last illness Sir Robert had courageously spied for the Duke of Lancaster.

Suddenly Sir Robert moved his hands in Owen's.

Lifting his head, Owen caught a faint smile on the old soldier's face. Sir Robert opened his eyes wide, parted his lips as if about to speak. But no sound escaped, not even the laboured breaths that had marked his last moments. His hands went limp.

Owen felt for a pulse. When he found none, he took a silvered glass, held it to Sir Robert's lips. No breath fogged it.

'May Amélie be waiting for you with open arms,' Owen whispered.

He placed coins on Sir Robert's eyes, then bowed his head to pray.

But first he wept.

EPILOGUE

April's rains relented for a day and Dafydd, Brother Dyfrig, Cadwal and Madog at last prepared to depart St David's.

In the courtyard of the bishop's palace, Father Edern blessed their journey and Tangwystl held a stirrup cup to Dafydd.

'My husband's saviour. You shall ever be in my prayers, Master Dafydd.' Her smile lit the heavens.

'Be joyous in your lovemaking, my lady,' Dafydd said, wishing she might nestle in his bed. But alas, he must be satisfied with the kiss with which she had thanked him for Rhys's life. And was that not sufficient to give him happy dreams for many a night?

'You look far too gladsome,' Brother Dyfrig noted as they led their horses through Bonning's Gate. 'I grant you suffered only singed hair. But what of my arm? And poor Brother Samson – will he ever be clear in his wits?'

'Was he ever?' Dafydd laughed. 'It was worth all the suffering, my friend. I feel alive, refreshed, blessed and fulfilled.'

'Rhys might have found his way to St David's had you left him on the sands.'

'He would have been dragged to Cydweli by those barbarians. I do not doubt I saved his life.'

'Tangwystl speaks true, I think. She will keep you in her prayers.'

'And I shall keep the memory of her sweet lips, her wondrous scent.'

'Will you write a poem about her?'

'I wrote one long ago, though I did not know it.'

And as they rode off, Dafydd sang:

'I love her, source of all bliss.
Ah men, neither Taliesin
Nor free-flattering Merlin
Ever loved a lovelier:
Strife-stirring copper-framed face,
Proud beauty, far too proper.

Gull, if you glimpse the fairest
Maiden's cheek in Christendom,
Should I win no sweet greeting,
Ah God, the girl dooms me dead.'

AUThOR'S NOTE

In *The Apothecary Rose*, the first book in this series, Lucie Wilton chided Owen Archer for his neglect of his family in Wales. He had left his country as a young archer more than fifteen years earlier, and since then he had neither returned to Wales nor had he communicated with his family. While journeys across such distances were not rare, they were not undertaken lightly, for the dangers involved, the time and the costs made wayfaring serious business in the late middle ages. Thieves made use of the woodland and isolated roadways to prey on travellers. Weather washed out bridges, flooded fords. Maps were few and inaccurate. Accommodations were uncertain. Merchants, soldiers, tinkers, members of a lord's household who followed from castle to castle, these people had little choice in the matter. Pilgrims embraced the difficulties as the very road to salvation. But most people embarked on a journey only if necessary. Lucie herself has never travelled farther from York than her father's manor.

Communication was also difficult: humble farmers such as Owen's family would neither read nor write nor was Owen, as an archer, likely to have been literate. It was only in his later career as a spy that he learned to read and write, in order to send and receive reports.

Hence, Lucie's strictures are harsh, because even had Owen written a letter to his family they would have had to find someone to read it to them. Their local parish priest might very well be illiterate, or might read only Welsh. And Owen, having been educated for his role as Lancaster's spy, would have had no cause to learn to write Welsh.

In short, like many soldiers, Owen would have no way of knowing the fate of his family, though he would be well aware how negative the news might be: life was difficult for the common man in Wales as elsewhere, and the Black Death had ravaged the British Isles several times since his departure. I think he would be quite ambivalent about a journey into Wales, though more so regarding Cydweli, where he might have news of his family, than St David's.

St David's was and remains a major pilgrimage site. William the Conqueror, Henry II, and Edward I and Queen Eleanor all journeyed to St David's. The peninsula in which the city nestles has been a sacred place throughout human occupation, at least from the neolithic period. High up on Carn Llidi are small burial chambers, and Coetan Arthur, a larger cromlech, is in St David's parish. The peninsula is dotted with sacred wells, chapels, standing stones. In St David's day (sixth century) the sea routes to the peninsula were often more reliable than land routes, and trade was brisk with Ireland, and also with Brittany; the mixing of the Celtic cultures is apparent in the area's artefacts and legends.

The Bishop of St David's was an important churchman. Adam de Houghton, the bishop at the time this book is set, was to become Lord Chancellor of England in 1377, through the influence of John of Gaunt, Duke of Lancaster. His relationship with Lancaster was complex – for Adam was a lord in the Marches, and thus a peer of Lancaster's in that role. Yet as the third son of the King of England Lancaster was clearly Adam's superior overall, and the bishop courted his patronage to further his career.

To explain the government of Wales at the time is complicated, for Wales was not a single political entity. It was a collection of lordships, some ruled by the English (the March of Wales) and some by the Welsh. The English and the Welsh lived side by side in an uneasy peace. King Edward III's grandfather had fortified the Welsh Marches with formidable castles, not only to protect the English rulers from the Welsh, but also to keep the Welsh from inviting into the country unwanted allies – such as the French. Many English town charters banned the Welsh from living and trading within the walls, even those who took a Welsh partner in marriage; but being inconvenient for trade, such bans were eventually ignored.

The corner of Wales in which this book takes place is heavily English. To simplify matters I have referred only to the four most prominent Marcher lords in the area: John of Gaunt, who controlled Cydweli (Cydweli Castle) and Iscennen (Carreg Cennen); John Hastings, 2nd Earl of Pembroke (Pembroke Castle and Tenby); Adam de Houghton, Bishop of St David's (Llawhaden Castle, the bishop's palace at St David's); and Edward Plantagenet, the Black Prince (Cardigan Castle). Each Marcher lord had his own administrators and observed his own unique combination of Welsh law and English common law. When his people travelled through other lordships it was customary for the lord (or more likely his steward) to provide them with letters of the March, which identified them as being under the lord's protection.

Tangwystl invokes one of Hywel Dda's laws known as a group as 'The Law of Women' in order to annul her marriage with John Lascelles: 'Should a woman discover that she is dissatisfied with the legal persona that has been imposed upon her by marriage, or simply wishes to be separated from her husband, she can do so legitimately under Welsh law by proving that he has been discovered with another woman not less than three times, has leprosy or bad breath, or is impotent. In Welsh law . . . a man's wife can injure or even kill her husband's cywyres, "mistress", with her two hands, and remain free from having to make any compensatory payments.'* Although it is unlikely that this law was widely invoked by the late fourteenth century, and even less likely that an Englishman of Lascelles's status would be expected to abide by it, Tangwystl hopes that Bishop Houghton will sympathise with her situation.

Owain Lawgoch, or Owain ap Thomas ap Rhodri ap Gruffudd, was the great-nephew of Llywelyn the Last, who briefly united the Welsh lordships against the English in the thirteenth century. Lawgoch had been brought up in France and had proved to be an excellent military leader. King Charles of France encouraged Lawgoch's claim to be the heir to Llywelyn the Last – Owain would no doubt be an invaluable ally, with excellent harbours from which the French might stage an invasion of England.

For me, one of the greatest pleasures in writing this book was my daily contact with Dafydd ap Gwilym and Geoffrey Chaucer. Dafydd was gliding towards the end of his career in 1370 (I use Rachel Bromwich's estimation of his life spanning 1320–1380), and Geoffrey was embarking on his first great poem, 'The Book of the Duchess'. But age aside, they were quite different individuals in their lives as well as their work. A Welsh bard travelled the country, playing his harp and singing his songs in the houses of his patrons. Dafydd lived as a bard, though in his earlier years he also served as a tutor to his patrons' children. Geoffrey was a civil servant, climbing through the ranks. He did not live by his poetry. Dafydd dressed in a manner befitting a bard; Geoffrey dressed in a manner befitting an agent of the Duke or the King. Reading Dafydd's poetry is like looking over his shoulder as he reminisces about his triumphs and his disappointments.

---

* Christopher McAll, 'The Normal Paradigms of a Woman's Life in the Irish and Welsh Law Texts', in *The Welsh Law of Women*, Dafydd Jenkins and Morfydd E. Owen, editors, University of Wales, 1980, pp. 20–21.

He celebrates love, both physical and sacred, nature, God and his patrons, from a deeply and often amusingly personal point of view. Geoffrey places himself at a distance in his poems, though readers are often tempted to see his bumbling narrators as self-portraits. He is a consummate observer of human nature. Dafydd laughs at himself; Geoffrey laughs at mankind. If I were to describe their differences in a nutshell, I would say that Dafydd would today most likely be a songwriter/performer with a flamboyant style all his own. Geoffrey would be a novelist with a poetic flair, but in his writing, not his appearance, a novelist who might be mistaken for the manager of the bookshop in which he is giving a reading. But as soon as he began to read, the drab illusion would be shattered.

Also available from Candace Robb

The
Riddle of
St. Leonard's

Read on for an exciting extract from the fifth Owen Archer Mystery . . .

The two laboured through the high grass along the riverbank, sweating in the hazy sunshine. There was no breeze to ease them once they left the river. They were chided by frogs and bees disturbed by their passage and that of the boat they pulled up on to the bank behind them. When they had tethered the boat to a sapling, they set off across the fallow field leading to the cottage. Nettles caught at his leggings, her skirt, as if urging a retreat. Gnats and flies hovered close, tasting their sweat, then followed along in a noisy cloud. Crickets warned of their approach. Close by a horse whinnied and stomped.

Owen Archer and Magda Digby exchanged uneasy looks; they found the farm too silent. Absent were the sounds they strained to hear: those of a family going about its daily work – a scythe whistling through the tall grass, a bucket clanking against the side of the well as the groaning rope lifted it, children squealing in play. Though Owen and Magda had been told that they would be greeted with silence, they had hoped to find

Duncan Ffulford and his family hard at work, proving the fisherman's tale to have been fermented in a bottle.

Owen paused at the edge of the field, swatting flies from his face as he swept his head from side to side to study the yard; he had the use of only his right eye, his left scarred, blind, and patched, and thus he must compensate for half the range of vision with which he had once been blessed. His sweep took in a thatch-roofed cottage, its door yawning wide, no smoke drifting from the hole in the roof's centre; a dusty yard with a horseless cart sitting as if being prepared for use; a barn and other outbuildings behind the cottage, quiet but for the impatient horse, likely in the barn.

Owen turned to his companion. 'Where's the child gone to, I wonder?' The fisherman had claimed a girl crouched on the riverbank, calling to him as he drifted by that her mother and the babies were dead, and her father too sick to help her bury them.

Magda shaded her eyes with a gnarled, sun-browned hand. She faced the barn. 'Thou hearest the beast, Bird-eye?'

'Aye. 'Tis little noise to mask it.'

'Likely the child keeps it company.'

'Should we first go to her, then?'

'Nay. 'Tis best Magda and thee know the worst. Into the house with thee. But first attend thy protection. There is no wind to carry off the vapours.' From a pouch at her waist Magda drew two cloth bags filled with scent, handed one to Owen, held the other over her mouth and nose. These would protect them from the noxious vapours that spread disease.

Owen looked down at the bag with doubt. 'And who holds these to our faces whilst we bury the dead?'

Magda met his argument with a sniff. 'Cover thy face, thou contentious Welshman. Provident care when thou canst take it is better than none at all.' Without more ado, the tiny midwife strode across the dusty yard and stepped into the cottage.

Owen lifted the bag to his face and followed, having found it wise in the past to take Magda's advice. He ducked through the low doorway.

Within, the cot was dark, the only light coming from chinks in the thatch and walls, illuminating the dust that swirled with their every movement and the flies that swarmed round the four bodies, two children lovingly tucked in the wooden-framed bed beside a woman, and a man lying on the floor near the remnants of a fire. Magda crouched down by the bed, lifted the covers with a stick to examine the bodies. Even through the scented bag Owen smelled the putrefaction, gagged, retreated to the yard to catch his breath.

Magda joined him. ''Tis the manqualm, Bird-eye.'

Owen crossed himself. 'Let us find the child. She might tell us where to find a priest.'

Magda, hands on hips, squinted up into Owen's good eye. 'Thou thinkst to find a priest will say the proper prayers? Thou wouldst take such time with this?'

'They died unshriven, I've no doubt. And they should be buried in consecrated ground. 'Tis my duty as a Christian man to do what I may to help them to Heaven. I know it is not your way, Magda, but it is mine. And theirs. I must try.'

Magda did not argue, perhaps in thanks for his agreeing to accompany her on this mission. Heading towards the barn, she paused at the cart. 'Duncan thought to load his family into the cart and bury them? Take them to the priest? Or had he thought to flee it with them?' Magda grasped the side of the cart, touched her forehead to it, as if suddenly weary. 'And the worst of it still to come, Bird-eye. Thy Lucie will work from dawn to dusk, as will Magda, and what availeth it?'

'Come, Magda. Let us find the child.' Owen walked past the cart, across the rutted yard to the barn. The horse began once more to whinny and stomp. One ear to the door, Owen sought the sound of another living thing within. He heard the rustle of straw. Perhaps the horse, perhaps the child.

The barn door was warped by the river damp. Owen used his strength to lift it and swing it wide. Peering in, he saw an old nag in a stall. He approached it slowly, calming the uneasy creature with murmured reassurances. As Owen reached the nag, he picked up a cloth, rubbed the horse gently until it quieted.

Magda had followed him.

Owen patted the nag. 'Duncan Ffulford was better off than I had thought, to own a horse.'

'Aye, and he was proud of her. She carries her years lightly thanks to their tender care. Now, be quiet, Bird-eye.' Magda stood in the middle of the barn, listening. Her multicoloured gown seemed to flicker in the pied light. 'She is above.' Magda motioned for Owen to precede her. 'Her name is Alisoun.'

As Owen stepped away from the horse, it nipped him gently on the arm, calling him back. Even the beast feared the unnatural quiet of the farm. Owen crept up the ladder to the hayloft, tucking his head down to avoid a pitchfork or knife. In times like this, a child on her own would do well to protect herself. As Owen was about to clear the ladder with his head, he said softly, 'Peace, Alisoun. I come in peace.' He held his hands up to show the child he had no weapon. 'A fisherman told us you needed help.' He prayed God it was indeed Alisoun up there.

'Who are you?' a child's voice demanded.

Much comforted by the high timbre, Owen said, 'Owen Archer, captain of the archbishop's retainers and husband of Mistress Wilton, master apothecary in York.' He was not sure which might prove more reassuring.

'Climb up slowly.'

'May I use my hands on the ladder?'

'Slowly.'

Owen obeyed, easing his head up, then moving up one rung, two, and stopping there, at eye level with the girl, who stood sideways, skirt hitched up into her girdle, bare, dirty feet planted firmly apart, her upper body expertly poised with a small bow and arrow read to shoot. 'Turn so I can see the left side of your face.'

Owen turned towards the light coming from a hole in the thatch, giving the girl a full view of his scarred left cheek and eye, the leather patch.

With no relaxation of her stance, the child demanded, 'Who accompanies you?'

'Magda Digby, the Riverwoman.'

Alisoun stepped to the edge of the loft, glanced down. 'What do you want here?'

Owen was about to chide the child for her disrespectful tone, but Magda spoke before he could.

'Magda comes to bury thy family and take thee back where she will find a home for thee.'

'This is my home.'

'Aye, that it is. But thou must have a mother's care, eh? Thou art but eleven years.'

'I would not have you for a mother, you old hag.'

'You should watch your tongue,' Owen warned.

Magda again did not react to the discourtesy. 'Thou blamest Magda for thy mother's poor state after Tom's birth, aye. Thou needst not worry. Magda does not yearn to play thy mother.'

Alisoun let the bow slacken. She stared down at the straw. 'My father is dead then?'

'Aye, God grant him grace,' Owen said. 'So we're needing to take them to consecrated ground and find a priest. Can you show me the way?'

The child shrugged her bony shoulders. 'The priest wouldn't come when Father tried to fetch him.'

Owen was not surprised; it was a common tale in times of pestilence. 'If you take me to him, I will persuade him to do his duty.'

'I would not have your wife for a mother, either.'

Tempted to give the unpleasant, dun-coloured child a lashing with his tongue, Owen controlled himself. He must do his duty and be done with her. 'We shall discuss your future once we've buried your family. Now take us to the priest.' He descended the ladder.

After a few minutes, Alisoun followed. At the bottom of the ladder she let down her skirt and shook out the hay and dust, smoothed back her braided hair, then fixed Owen with a steely glare. 'My future is my own concern.'

A matter to be discussed later. 'Come, child, we have much work to do.'

Alisoun rolled her eyes and sullenly headed for the door. As Owen watched her depart, he noted how thin she was, realised she might be hungry. 'Shall we try to feed her first?' he asked Magda.

'Do not waste thy time fretting about that child, Bird-eye. She will not hesitate to demand what she wants.'

'She is always so wayward, then?'

'Oh aye. Watch thy back with that one.'

Owen made for the nag. 'I shall hitch her to the cart.'

'Magda will prepare the bodies.'

When Owen led the nag from the barn, Alisoun stood halfway across the yard, waiting with an impatient look. Owen noted how the child averted her eyes from the abandoned cart and from the house. She had tender feelings, then, though she hid them well. As he worked with the cart, he tried to talk to her. 'I would wager you not only hold the bow as a trained archer does, but shoot it well, too?'

'I can fell coneys and squirrels. Why do you want to know?'

Owen decided to echo her lack of courtesy. 'Who taught you?'

'I asked you a question.'

'I choose not to answer.'

Silence. Then, without preamble, Alisoun said, 'My father taught me.'

'For protection?'

'What else?'

'There had been trouble?'

Hands on hips, Alisoun squinted up at Owen. 'You're nosy.'

'You are rude. We are quite a pair.'

The child ducked her head, turned, sat down in the dirt. Owen found her silence refreshing. He led the nag closer to the house, so he might more easily shift the bodies.

At first Owen thought the stone church empty, but as he moved to the centre he discovered a prostrate form before the altar. He turned to Alisoun. 'What is his name?'

'Father John.'

Owen approached the priest. 'Father John?' The figure stirred, but did not rise or respond. Owen knelt beside him, whispered into his fleshy neck, 'I pray you forgive me for intruding on your prayers, but I've come to fetch you to say prayers at the gravesides of four of your parishioners.'

The head turned, an eye peered at Owen, then the priest began to push himself up, but he was lifted to his feet instead. Owen grinned down at the short, corpulent man, filthy and stinking of onions and ale. 'Gather what you need. We must waste no time.'

Father John glanced at Alisoun. 'They are dead?'

'You know they are.'

'May God have mercy on them.' Father John crossed himself. 'How long ago did they perish, my child?'

'I am not your child.'

'She says you refused to go to them when her father requested your presence, Father John. Why was that?' Owen asked.

The fleshy face crinkled round the eyes and mouth as the priest raised his folded hands to his breast and cringed. 'Whence come you to this place?'

'York.'

'Ah. Then surely you noted the portents? The wind that came up from the south. The days the sky was dark, but the rain did not come. And the great multitude of flies. I have felt it my duty to pray. When Duncan Ffulford came, stinking of the pestilence, bringing it into this sacred place, I prayed for his soul and those of his family. But I could not touch them or I might be struck down, unable to pray for the other souls in my care.'

Owen gathered the fabric on the priest's chest and lifted him off his feet. 'You have found a convenient way to satisfy your conscience, priest. You do not deserve to wear this gown. But as you are all we have to hand, we must make do.'

Father John's face was purple. His eyes bulged out. 'It is a sin to attack a priest,' he gasped.

Owen let him go.

The priest began to crumple, then caught the pillar beside him and raised himself upright, breathing hard.

'What you have experienced so far is hardly an attack,' Owen said. 'But you might wish to avoid learning the difference. 'Tis a small thing we ask, that you perform your priestly duties.'

Later, as Owen dug, he wondered what had come over him. He was not wont to treat a priest so. Had the child so irritated him? Or was it the madness that came with the pestilence? Might he be infected with it already? He prayed God that if so he died before he carried it to his family. As the priest stepped forward to say his prayers over the graves, Owen found himself praying as much for his own family as for the Ffulfords. Magda stood quietly, eyes closed, one gnarled hand clutching the opposite wrist. She did not pray, so she always said, and yet her stillness suggested a state, if not of devotion, then of concentration. On what?

And what of the child? Owen felt a twinge of guilt about his lack of concern for her. Her obstinacy was no reason to forget she was a child who had just lost her entire family. He glanced over to the foot of the graves where Alisoun had stood. Gone. He looked round, did not see her.

Soon all three were hurrying about, calling the child's name.

But she had vanished. And the sun was the gold of late afternoon.

'The river calls,' Magda said. 'Has the child any kin nearby?'

Father John frowned down at his feet. 'There are many Ffulfords in the parish.'

Owen could see no point to another search. The child had expressed her desire to choose her own accommodations. 'I shall trust you to go among her kin and let them know the child's situation, Father John.'

The priest frowned at the task, but nodded. 'It is my duty, of course.' He glanced at the horse and cart. 'I can see to them.'

Owen could well imagine. 'Tell her kin the horse and cart are at the farm, priest.' He began to move away, turned back for a final warning. 'I will return to check on the child's safety. And her horse.'

'You'll find naught to anger you, Captain.'

In the boat, Magda seemed to nod in slumber. Owen rowed downriver silently, squinting against the afternoon sun that glinted on the brown water of the Ouse. He was thinking about the Ffulfords. So far most of the half a hundred deaths in York had been among the aged or the very young. But today he had seen a couple struck down who looked his wife's age. They had been very thin, a result of last summer's failed harvest, perhaps.

'Winds from the south. Flies. The priest named them harbingers of the pestilence. But what of the bad harvest?' Owen wondered aloud. 'Might hunger so weaken the people that they succumb to the pestilence?'

Magda opened one eye. 'The girl shows no sign of illness.' She drew a small bottle from the wallet at her waist, opened it, handed it to Owen, who paused in his rowing long enough to take one drink. Then Magda drank. 'Was a time thou wouldst accept naught from Magda, Bird-eye.'

And not so long ago at that. Owen grinned. 'Perhaps I was not so thirsty then.'

The Riverwoman gave one of her barking laughs. 'Aye. Mayhap.' She took another drink, put the bottle away. 'Magda would give much to know what calls back the manqualm from time to time, Bird-eye. A bad harvest?' She tilted her head, thinking. 'Each time it has followed one, 'tis a fact. But not every bad harvest summons it. Thy priests say 'tis the scourge of thy god, punishing thee for thy unholy ways. Mayhap 'tis why Magda survives. She is invisible to thy god.' She grinned, showing her teeth, white against her tanned leather skin.

So ancient and still she had all her teeth but one, and that one she had lost as a child. No one knew how long ago that had been. Magda was not inclined to say. But folk round York spoke of her as having lived on her rock in the mud flats of the Ouse just north of the city since the time of King Canute, hence the Viking ship turned upside-down that served as her roof. Owen knew Magda was too mortal for such a life span, but there was no doubt she was old. And rich with the wisdom of a life spent healing the sick and bringing children into the world. And thinking for herself: though she lived as saintly a life as a good Christian, she was not a Christian and found the Church's teachings poor, superstitious excuses for common sense. A dangerous opinion, but strongly held. Owen valued in her friendship her clear mind, common sense and a fresh perspective, free of fear.

'But how do thy priests explain the deaths of infants, Bird-eye?' Magda no longer smiled.

'To my mind it is the parents who are punished by such a death, Magda, not the child. I have heard it said that such a child was too good to live; God chooses to take such children directly to Heaven so that the world might not taint their souls.'

A snort. 'So thy god leaves only the unworthy on earth? Bah!'

Owen felt uneasily like agreeing with Magda. But was that not blasphemy? 'We cannot always know the Lord's purpose.'

Magda wagged her head. 'Thou art not taken in by such nonsense. Thou wast wise to send thy children off to Freythorpe Hadden.'

'Was I?' Since the first rumours of pestilence,

Owen's wife, Lucie, had wished to get their children out of the city. Eight years earlier she had lost her first child to the plague – Martin, her only child with Nicholas Wilton, her first husband. So Lucie had conceived a plan to send Hugh and Gwenllian to her father's manor in the countryside, where his efficient sister Phillippa was also in residence. But there was one problem: Lucie had still nursed their son Hugh, born the past winter, and as master apothecary she could not leave the city at such a time. How was one to find a reliable wet nurse in the midst of pestilence.

And then Magda's granddaughter Tola had come down from the moors with her infant, Emma, and her two-year-old, Nym, grieving for her husband, who had been savaged by a wild boar. Lucie had befriended the young widow and asked her to be Hugh's wet nurse.

Owen had not been easily persuaded that Tola should take his only son out of the city. It was true that when Death stalked a city, people changed, grew wild in their despair, unpredictable in their deeds. Perhaps the children would be safer in all respects in the country. But . . . 'The country did not save the Ffulfords,' he thought aloud.

Magda, who had let her chin drop to her chest again, opened one eye, squinted up at Owen and grunted in sympathy. 'Tola and her young ones are best away from Magda's house, where the sick are wont to come. 'Tis not so different at an apothecary.'

'The sick are not brought to the apothecary.'

'Nay. But those who care for them . . . Oft they succumb. Why dost thou debate thy decision? 'Tis done.'

It was difficult for any parent, this pestilence that seemed most fatal to children. But for Lucie it was doubly hard because of the loss of her first to the plague. The hope that her family was protected by God's grace could not buoy her.

How much worse would it ever be for Alisoun Ffulford, having lost both parents and siblings?

'Are there any more in Alisoun's family, Magda?'

The Riverwoman jerked awake. 'Eh?' She shaded her sleepy eyes with a hand.

Owen repeated the question.

'Nay. Parents, three children, 'tis all.' Magda shifted, began to lay her head back down.

'So what does she guard in the barn?'

Magda grumbled and rubbed her eyes. 'Herself. Her valuable horse.'

'Why did she run from us?'

'Why should she trust strangers, eh? Be patient, Bird-eye. The child will come to Magda or thee in her own time.'

'How do you know?'

Magda lay down her head, closed her eyes. 'Some things cannot be otherwise, Bird-eye.'

As Owen rowed towards home, the fly-ridden farmhouse haunted his thoughts.

The boat rocked dangerously as Magda suddenly sat forward, eyes scouring the sky downstream. 'Fire in the city. Dost thou smell it on the wind, Bird-eye?'

Owen was breathing deeply with the effort of rowing. But he smelled no more smoke than usual. 'Even in summer folk tend their fires, Magda.'

The Riverwoman frowned up at the air. 'Nay. 'Tis more than that, Bird-eye.'